The Day She Disappeared

THE DAY SHE DISAPPEARED

Winner of the Joffe Books Prize 2022

SAM GENEVER

Revised edition 2025
Joffe Books, London
www.joffebooks.com

First published as *Savage Territory* in 2022

Cover art by Imogen Buchanan

ISBN: 978-1-80405-983-1

There were only two times when men confessed to me.
They accepted themselves whether the rest of us could accept them or not.

– Segert Berger

PROLOGUE

Just before dawn, Keano Botes lay awake in his small bed. His curtain was half-drawn and he could see the darkness receding, being pulled slowly back. He twitched his toes under the light summer sheet and listened to his parents talking in their bedroom. It was summer holidays, and Christmas was just around the corner. The only time of the year he woke up without some fight and compulsion by his mother.

He turned around and sucked his thumb, touching the gap in his mouth where his front tooth was sprouting out slowly like the expanding tree he'd been climbing in his dream.

The night lamp in his sister's room was shining dimly, across the hall from him. The door was wide open and her bed was empty. She'd woken up, sweaty from hopping with a rabbit in her dreams, her hair stuck to her plump cheek, and had dreamwalked to her parents' bed.

Keano, hearing his father's footsteps approaching, instinctively pulled his thumb from his mouth and lay like a statue, the way he made his sister, Elani, play when he was tired of her.

But his father didn't slow down to check up on him, and walked past his room. A few moments later, he heard his father walk back down the dark narrow corridor toward the master bedroom. Two shots rang out.

Keano ran to his parents' bedroom and saw his sister sitting up straight in their parents' bed, in her favourite pink and purple nightie. One tear on each fat cheek.

Their father was standing in the corner, between the curtain and the old oak cupboard. He was bare-chested, wearing only his favourite red shorts with the white trim. He used to wear them to go jogging when he was younger, before Keano was born. His 9mm revolver was in his right hand by his side.

Keano looked at his father, standing there, his chest moving up and down slowly. And his eyes travelled to the body on the floor. Their mother's chest open and dark-coloured like the parquet tiles on the floor. Her mouth half-open like a guppy.

Then Elani started crying. The nightmare that had moved her running to her parents' bed was a quaint memory compared to the horror she could see reflected in the mirror of the wardrobe.

Their father was still standing surveying the damage coldly when Elani's sobs roused him. She took another breath, to reach inside her guts and let out the demon of a cry that was inside her. Her father took one step towards the bed, raising the gun in his hand.

'Elani, wake up!' Keano shouted at her. He used the same voice his father used when a pedestrian crossed into traffic without looking, his foot heavy on the accelerator. Move or get run over.

She widened her eyes like a lightning bolt had hit her, and ran to her brother at the door.

They ran toward the corridor, a bullet missing them narrowly and hitting the bedroom door. Their father walked after them. Neither could hear him, only the sound of their own breathing. But they could feel him, casting a powerful shadow in the doorway.

They ran past their bedrooms through the living room to the front door. In the twilight, Keano could make out the still heaviness of the wooden-back sofa and the two soft over-stuffed chairs. Elani's colouring-book lay open on the round dining table, the crayons strewn across the image of a smiling locomotive.

The front door was locked. Keano only tried it twice, then changed direction. He needed to protect his younger sister and the thought cleared his mind. Her hand was warm and soft in his, but was shaking as she cried.

He turned and pulled her into the kitchen. When the two of them played hide-and-seek he always hid in the broom cupboard, and Elani never found him, because she couldn't reach the handle. Even on her tiptoes.

He put his hand on her mouth as he closed the cupboard door. The smell of furniture polish enveloped him.

'Shush, you have to be quiet for me.' Keano blinked back tears as he put his stubby fingers on his sister's mouth.

She shook with fear, her tears rolling fast and warm on his hand. He tried not to think of his mother lying in her room, dead. And he didn't think about why. There was no universe where the father who kissed them goodnight on their foreheads and prayed in church every Sunday would be aiming his gun at them. He shut his eyes and tried to bale out of this dream.

Before Keano was shot, his only feeling was sadness. Because his sister would have no one to protect her now. And because for ever she'd have seen two people shot in front of her, and he only one.

After Elani was shot, they lay together in the broom cupboard, the eggshell-coloured vinyl splattered with their brains.

Jacques put the gun down on the kitchen island. In the blue-green light, he saw the order of Sunette. The aluminium sink was wiped down, and the dishes packed away. The dishcloths were folded into thirds — he'd always wondered how she'd done that — and were hung on the oven rail. He touched the yellow-printed daisy flowers, held it to his face, inhaled the smell of it and cried, because he loved his wife so much. Keeping one dishcloth in his hand, he walked through to the garage, and rifled through his equipment. He could hear one of his neighbours trying to quiet their dogs. It wouldn't be long now. He didn't bother returning the lock to the garage door, and just left it on the driveway.

He and Sunette had always been house-proud. They were proud of everything they'd done. She was always arranging and cleaning the house, and Jacques was a keen gardener. He bought a top-of-the-line lawn mower when he got the horses right. Then it became a reminder of the money he was losing. And then he lost his stupid job for nothing. And the hotel wouldn't take him back. What was he supposed to do? Beg?

The spare petrol he'd kept for the mower came in handy now, as he poured it on the curtains in his bedroom, his marital bed and down the corridor and through the kitchen. He didn't want anyone to see his children's faces like that.

He wanted to say sorry to his mother-in-law, Janette. She'd given them the deposit for the house as a wedding present. He was sorry to let her down, but he wouldn't have to think of her again.

Jacques stuffed the daisy dishcloth in the petrol can and left it in the broom cupboard. And walked to his bedroom. The orange and blue flame travelled past him, quicker than he could've imagined. When he got to the room, the bottom of the bed was already on fire.

The last shot was to his temple, as his wife's head lay in his lap.

CHAPTER 1

24 July 1983

Augustine didn't know where they were going to sleep tonight. She couldn't go back home with Justice. His father not knowing their whereabouts was the only advantage she had. The late morning was bright but unusually cool. The sky was a lazy powder-blue, and the streets she was walking were calm after Saturday night's mischief. She stuffed her handbag with nappies and a bottle. She threw a few things into a small backpack, picked her baby up in a hurry and ran from her boyfriend's house, while he was at the grocery store getting a roast. There wasn't enough time to search his house for money. They had to get out.

Sweat trickled down her back. Carrying Justice was like carrying a sack of hot sweet potatoes. She'd made it across town to Greenside, but now what? She'd gone into shops and offices looking for work. But with the baby, no one wanted her. Churchgoers waved *No* when they saw her. Now wasn't the time to have an ego. Getting a job as a maid was the easiest way out.

When she was at high school, she'd stash her cigarettes or outside clothes in the maintenance cupboard, and — she

5

remembered — it was close to the toilets. The public toilets would be inside a park or sports ground. She could stash her backpack there. She walked quickly to the Botanical Gardens, following the signposts for the toilet. She changed Justice first, then relieved herself. When the coast was clear she pushed against the maintenance door and it opened with a gentle creak. As she covered the bag with reams of handtowels, she hoped someone wouldn't steal their last two pairs of freedom clothes as a prank. It looked like nothing, but right now it was almost her entire world.

* * *

She walked down Greenway, across the dying stream, and headed towards the park. The houses there were bigger; perhaps they needed household help. She knew enough about these neighbourhoods to knock on the door and then stand far back.

'Oh.' A woman answered the door, her hair frothy from blow-drying a curl into her fringe. 'Who are you?'

'Missus,' Augustine said.

The house was set back from the road; large evergreen trees were clipped into hedges. Augustine had missed the intercom at the driveway and opened the gate that led up a path to the front door. 'I'm looking for a job.'

The woman looked at her. A film of perspiration glistened on her upper lip. 'I thought my husband had left his keys,' she said.

'Sorry, Madam. I am very good with housework, Missus.'

The woman looked over Augustine's head, as if expecting her husband to run up the path. Since the baby, his jogs had become so long she thought he was training for the Two Oceans marathon. 'We already have help.'

'My son won't be any trouble. He is a very quiet child.' Augustine hated begging, but hammed up the servitude angle. She stood a little hunched over, as if her body was burdened with decades of hard work.

'What is his name?' the woman asked, leaning to look at the baby Augustine was carrying on her back.

'His name is Justice.' Augustine flattened her accent more.

'A beautiful name for a beautiful boy.' The missus smiled, and Justice gurgled a baby-laugh at her. This pair appeared to her as a fresh conjuring. 'I can't pay you a lot of money. There is not a lot to do around here. There are only four of us in this house.'

'OK, Missus. As long as I can have a place to stay.'

'You can't bring trouble here. I don't like a commotion,' she said firmly.

'Yes, Missus. It's only me and Justice now. No commotion. I can start today.' Augustine took in the broad shoulder pads in the bright yellow dress, the tight yellow belt and white high heels, and wondered what this woman did after getting dressed like this. She definitely wasn't doing any cooking. 'I cook a really good supper, good rice and gravy,' she lied.

The woman wiped her right hand nervously on her dress and stood closer to the door. 'Well, that's always good. Better you start tomorrow. Come anytime between eight and nine o' clock in the morning. Your job will be to help my newborn.' Her smile as she closed the door was tight, and made Augustine slightly nervous. She heard the hastened sound of keys and the lock snap, but waved gratefully as she walked down the long driveway to the road. She was sure the missus was watching her from the window.

Augustine spent the first part of the afternoon walking down the Braids, looking over the low fences at the lawns and houses. Sweat trickled down her back.

Eventually, she huffed back through the gates of the Botanical Gardens as if she had crossed a finishing line. Evergreens bordered the road and provided shade as she walked up the brick lane. She worked hard to maintain an upright posture. Her chest and shoulders hurt. She felt a strain in her neck, a thick extension cord pulled beyond its reach.

Men and women jogged downhill with purpose, their shoes crackling leaves and startling squirrels and small lizards. The runners breathed low, sweat flying off their forearms. Civilians ambled to the left in case they were tackled by a grinning amateur marathoner, or a random sweat speck landed on an ice cream. Augustine weaved through lovesick couples and picnic groups to the female toilets to retrieve her bag. This time she didn't care if the toilet was empty; she needed to get her things. Then she looked for an empty seat across from the lake where she could relax her muscles and her mind for the first time that day.

There was hardly a cloud in the sky, and a low breeze from the lake rustled through the trees. The red soil was exposed in patches, and the air smelled of both dry grass and rotting roots. Justice burst into hysterics at the ducks coming out of the water. She imagined that every Sunday could be like this, walks in the park with her son. Not like this morning, when she'd gathered her things quickly from the broken drawers at Teddy's house and come across town, knocking on doors for work.

The lake became a dirty dark grey, and the ducks swam off in disinterested groups. The chill of evening started to creep through the trees as the light slanted through the tangled branches. A panic trickled into her consciousness that she didn't have a place to stay. There was no place to go. Her life would always be divided in two parts. Before and after today. She woke up this morning in her boyfriend's bed. Justice slept in till almost seven, and the moon was still visible through Teddy's window. She went to make some coffee and enjoy the silence from the men in her life. Teddy got up early for a run. He liked the cold morning air.

'I'll go get some shopping, too,' he'd said, 'and walk back.'

While he was out, she opened the box in the TV console and realised her life was just a dream.

Augustine sat at the bus stop outside the park, a dark trembling thud in her chest. She didn't want Justice to feel it. She wanted him to always know that everything would be OK. He could only ever learn that from her; otherwise, he'd spend his life never knowing it. She'd been sitting there for forty minutes, feeding Justice fluffy barbecue-flavoured chips. Doing an inventory of her money in her purse, talking herself into going home, and then talking herself out of it. She'd have to go back home, or to her best friend Rosalind. She could've pulled that off, no problem. Back in the day before Justice. But not now.

A green double-decker Metro bus wound slowly up the hill, spewing black clouds of exhaust smoke. Its low headlights the simple eyes of a caterpillar. Augustine put her hand out, and thought her only bet was to ask the driver for some help and direction. Then, if he couldn't help, she'd go to her parents' home, act as if everything was fine, and steal out at six in the morning.

But Teddy might show up. No way he won't.

Augustine walked up the dusty black steps of the bus, the skinny driver blinking impatiently at her. He had his radio on, and turned it down abruptly when she started talking.

'Sorry, Baba. I am looking for a place, you know.' She looked back at her baby. 'Where can I go?'

The engine was still running loudly, and she shouted her situation louder than her pride would usually permit.

'What?' He blinked at her rapidly. 'Where do you want to go?'

The bus lurched slightly as he released the brake, and she felt for a second like she was in that moment between sleep and consciousness. When you feel like you're falling, and you kick the sheets and blankets and your shoulders shake. Augustine's mouth went dry. She hadn't had anything to drink, she realised, since the morning.

An old woman was sitting in the front seat, knitting a blue-and-white scarf in cable stitches.

'Where do you want to go, man?' he hissed impatiently, over the cranking engine noise. His skin was sleek with an alcoholic fever. Augustine swallowed hard and turned to get off the bus.

'You should come with me to church tonight,' the old lady said. She put her knitting down and patted the seat next to her. 'Come to the church; there is always place for one more. And someone can help you from there.'

Augustine moved to put her hand in her old blue purse to get some coins.

'Don't bother paying him.'

'What? She must pay, *wena*,' the driver shouted through his plastic grate.

'Here, clip my pass one more time.'

'She must pay.'

'Hey.' The old lady raised her voice. 'I said, clip my pass one more time. And stop holding everyone up here.'

He clipped the ticket and drove off quickly, forcing Augustine to clutch the diagonal railing opposite the stairs to stop herself from falling.

'He only wants you to pay so he can drink your money. He never gives anyone a ticket. Come sit.'

Augustine understood this, but wasn't sure what it implied for the bus fare. Was she supposed to pay the fare to the old lady instead?

'How much do I owe you?'

'Nothing, my child. Keep your money and feed your child.'

'Thank you.'

'It's a rough world out there; even a little bit can help.' The old woman pointed her head to the window. The world out there.

The bus lurched forward, leaving the gardens and evening joggers in the distance.

Augustine felt waves of relief and shame. She didn't want to be this person. She wanted better things for herself. Better things for her son. A loving home, and a human for a father. Now he had neither. She was close to tears when the old lady picked up her knitting.

'Now, now, my child,' she said, not looking directly at Augustine. 'You cry in a pillow when it's dark and nobody is watching.'

That was the best maternal advice Augustine had ever received. Her own mother was a broken woman, not up to the job of parenting, but this old lady with a straight back and sharp knitting fingers had given her some sort of armour to carry with her.

'You're right, Ma. You are right.' She raised her head.

The old lady returned to her knitting, humming to herself.

'Just call me Zula.'

* * *

The church Zula took her to was in a room in a neglected printing works just outside the city centre. One window was broken and covered carefully with the cardboard from a toilet paper box. The walls were bright green, with patches faded from sunlight and rain.

Zula stood with her eyes closed, her arms slowly opening in a quiet dance of receiving the Holy Spirit. She was calm, and Augustine thought that in the big room of the old lady's body there wasn't a place that she didn't control. The Holy Spirit only went in where it was invited. Augustine didn't understand the hymns they were singing, whether it was in Xhosa or Zulu or a mixture of both.

When they'd climbed off the bus, the old lady had cursed the bus driver for stopping in front of an overspilling litter box.

'You want a fat woman to walk through there?' she said, appraising the gap she didn't want to squeeze through. She was standing at the top of the stairs. He moved the bus forward, a short distance, but fast enough to make her lose her balance.

'*Mampara*,' she spat matter-of-factly. As Augustine looked at the other passengers, they stared blankly back at her, their faces registering no emotion. She realised it was a universal fact. He was a *mampara*. She wasn't sure if it meant he was a frog or an idiot, but she knew it wasn't a compliment.

The street was thick with busy movement. The furniture and clothing shopfronts were closed and darkened. The only colours now were of neglect and poverty. The worn-out blue of overalls straining over bony shoulders and patched cars affectionately termed *skorro-skorros*. The cracked black of shoes with holes in them. Bright grocery bags filled with potatoes, chicken feet, a cow's head, spinach. The dark grey coolness of empty store fronts.

Augustine never came to this part of town anymore. It was getting dark. She walked behind the old lady, weaving through the long taxi queues going to the townships. Alexandra, Soweto, and other names she didn't know. The only noises came from the taxis' blaring loud music or loud hooting. The sounds of doors sliding open or shut and the two-tap of a hand on a bonnet that it was time to go.

The sun would've set, and the coldness of winter would've crept in, by the time they got home. If they were lucky, there would be streetlights where this lady lived. They walked a few blocks away from the main street. Justice was neatly tucked on his mother's back. The blanket up to his neck, keeping him warm. The quietness made Augustine nervous. The old lady walked with little effort in her step. She was fit from years of negotiating traffic.

When Augustine had first walked into the broken-down church, she noticed the broadening eyes shining in surprise. And she adjusted the expression on her face. She was the curiosity in this place. She knew those looks; she'd given them herself throughout her life. When a stranger came in the midst of her friends. She appraised the health of their skin, the texture and care of their hair. Her old dumb stares came to visit her on new faces.

There were about two dozen or so men and women inside the room. The men stood alongside the wall in conspiratorial conversation that stopped when the three of them walked by. The women greeted Zula from afar.

'Come this way,' Zula said softly. She placed her hand on Augustine's forearm and guided her through the room.

Zula walked to a scattering of women sitting on old and patched-up office furniture, drinking tea and eating yellow sponge cake. They wore an assortment of berets and scarves, and two of them crossed and uncrossed their feet as Zula approached.

'Have some tea and take some milk for him,' Zula said, pointing to a kettle.

Zula's friends didn't get up from their seats, but shouted with delight when she was close enough to hug. The noise excited Justice, and he kicked his legs and smiled at the women. The women looked at Augustine, not saying anything. Augustine was relieved that they didn't see her, but the two of them — her and her baby as one entity.

'Thank you.' Augustine walked to the meagre refreshment station. Two fresh pints of milk, an old white kettle, misshapen spoons and mismatched floral mugs. She put the kettle on to boil.

'Would anybody like a cup of tea?' she offered, using the high English she only used at the principal's office or at job interviews. Even Justice gurgled, not knowing who that voice belonged to. She smiled to herself when she heard him.

A short woman with a crooked tooth jumped up. 'Show me the Mister on your back.' She untied him from Augustine. 'He's a cute little Mister.'

'Whoa, his ears are cold.'

'Put some milk and hot water on for him,' they all chimed.

'Can I have a cup of Rooibos? The bags in the black tin. There.'

'I have a scarf to put on his head.'

'Aay, a scarf is no good. Knit him a woollen hat, man,' Zula quipped.

So the conversation had started around tea and her son. Augustine couldn't match the voices to the faces, and it didn't matter. The old lady took the biggest mug of tea from her, rocking Justice on her lap. Augustine wasn't sure he was old enough for that, but she didn't say anything. She crouched down to Justice's level and stayed beside Zula, not taking her eyes off his tender neck. He reached his long body for the bottle and Augustine smiled, feeding him as she patted his short fine hair.

She felt safer now, for the very least. Although she wondered where she and her son would survive the night, Justice at least had some food in his belly. She had three disposable nappies with her, and she didn't have money to buy any more. She hoped that he would be able to keep in his motions until after the service, at the very least.

When the evening service finished, the pastor came straight to the old lady. He kissed her on the cheek and gave her a long embrace. Perhaps she was always bringing in strays, but he seemed nonchalant about the stranger and her son in their midst. He nodded his head in universal thanks for what must have been the old lady's praise.

'This is my son, Pastor Moloi.'

He wore a perfect wide smile. Broad lips rimmed his bright white teeth. He was — if she hadn't been convinced by his sermon — a quietly charismatic man. Justice responded to his smile with a small gurgle.

Pastor Moloi laughed. 'And now I see how you are connected. The mothers of very handsome sons.' He held his head back as he laughed. His shoulders shaking lightly.

Augustine laughed at his mock arrogance, and the compliment and the grace that he had shown her by not asking her any questions. It was clear that she was here for help. Out of the corner of her eye, she tried to register Zula's age.

'Please join me for dinner, will you three?' He waved to some of the departing congregation at the door. They nodded and left. 'My wife is in Polokwane and I hate to eat alone.'

'Yes, of course. We mustn't let you eat alone after a sermon like that,' his mother said.

Augustine crinkled up her nose at this, having no idea what the sermon was about. Zula noticed.

'I'm glad you agree, Augustine. Come, come, my son has a car,' she said.

So, this was where Augustine and Justice were to spend the cold Highveld night. In the home of a son of the Lord.

Augustine excused herself to go to the toilet, taking her bag with her.

'Take your time. The little man is safe. I'll change his nappy.' Zula said, smelling Justice's bottom.

The bathroom was at the end of the dusty printing factory. The cistern was running slowly when she entered the toilet. For a moment, she worried that it was leaking and the back of the tank would be wet. She took Teddy's photographs out of her bag. On the back of the envelope, she wrote *Teddy Beukes, Teacher at Kliptown Catholic Secondary School, 1983,* in black ink. Then sealed it in a plastic sleeve, wrapped it in a white Pick-n-Pay plastic bag and taped it with masking tape that she'd taken from the same drawer as the photos. She looked at the skinny brown roll of tape now, curling her lips up in disgust. She'd thought she knew Teddy. He'd been her maths teacher at high school. He'd asked her out for a meal when she was a cashier at Khan's grocery store. They'd fallen in love. She had his baby. But he was a liar, a snake, a criminal of the dirtiest kind. She spat in the toilet, then washed her hands in the grimy sink.

* * *

At the end of the night, when the old woman was leaving her son's house to go home, Augustine thanked her. Her son, the tall very reverend pastor, was standing at his front door ready to walk his mother to safety. The light from the streetlamp festooning his face in an orange glow.

'If you don't find what you want tomorrow, you know where you can find us,' Zula said to Augustine, as she put a white woollen scarf around her neck. Her face shone in the dark. A thin film of oil from the mutton fat still covered her lips.

Augustine wasn't sure what she meant. Find her on the bus, or find her in the church?

She recognised Augustine's confusion. 'There.' She pointed to a small house at the end of the road. 'That is my house.' She said each syllable distinctly to eradicate any confusion.

'Come, child,' she said to her son, 'walk me home.' The pastor nodded, and they turned towards the night slowly.

'There are some blankets in a box behind the sofa. Please.' He closed the plywood front door gently.

Augustine could hear their footsteps on the cement tiles and the slow metallic sound of the rusty little gate opening. Their voices in a deep slow symphony. She hoped Justice would be a man like that one day. She got the blankets out and made a bed for herself on the sofa.

Then she took one of the last two photographs she had of Teddy, which she'd stolen this morning from the drawer in the TV console. Again, she wrote *Theodore Beukes, Kliptown Catholic Secondary School*, on the back of the photograph. Before she sealed the envelope, she wrote her tomorrow address. Thinking about it now, she should've done that earlier, too. *Augustine Pillay, 68 Belgravia Road, Greenside.*

She taped the white envelope to the bottom of the plaster-wood dinner table. *You can't buy this type of insurance.* Tomorrow they'd be OK. She'd start her new job as a live-in domestic worker at a beautiful estate close to the park. And she could take Justice for walks on a Sunday and save for a car, then a deposit for a flat or a small house. Get Justice into a cheap daycare. He didn't need much at this age. Six months. That's all she needed.

Under her blanket, she held the sharpest knife she could find from the pastor's kitchen drawer. This was no time to be naive, or believe in angels. People you love turn out to be monsters. You can't trust the son of a kind stranger. Not when you're alone in a tiny house, and an enemy to everyone in this neighbourhood.

She wasn't one for believing one side of the story. The scandals of kiss-and-tell didn't fascinate her. The women in the neighbourhood would come over when her mother had a day off. They'd spend it in the living room. Talking and complaining. Complaining and gossiping. Drinking tea and commiserating with soap opera characters. Augustine didn't bother with those broken women, who were shameless in their bad choices, and who kept Augustine's mother from cooking dinner.

And now Augustine and her child lay in a stranger's home. Hoping he was who he said he was.

* * *

When the gate opened and closed again, Augustine shut her eyes tight, then turned her back to the front door. The pastor said goodnight softly, as he walked to the bathroom to brush his perfectly shaped teeth. Thinking about his wife in Polokwane, and what she would say this time about his mother, who only came to visit when she was saving a soul, and how she lived alone just down the road. He left the front door unlocked. *The girl can leave any time she pleases.*

CHAPTER 2

It was almost 2 p.m. when Teddy Beukes drove the free-way to Augustine's neighbourhood. The roads were set in a grid. All of them were almost exactly the same width, and all the matchbox houses were the same size. Rows and rows of two-tone cartoon-sized houses with sharp angular roofs. He remembered asking Augustine about this one night when he dropped her off after a movie. She laughed a bit, and tilted her head down to him the way she did when she was stating the obvious.

'Because they belong to different people. This side of the house belongs to one family, and the other side to someone else. See, they have two gates.'

'That doesn't make sense.'

'That's the way it is, sense or no sense.' She shrugged her shoulders, and moved the side of her mouth. She looked cute when she did that.

'Your whole house belongs to you, though.'

It belonged to her father, but she knew what he meant. 'Yeah. Look, we're rich.' She giggled, with a wide smile.

Now he was driving the dusty road to find Augustine. When he came back from grocery shopping, he thought it was just one of her little games. He'd said the wrong thing before he left, and she'd taken Justice and gone home to teach him a lesson and cool off. But something was wrong. Usually when they had a fight, she took everything just to make a point. But she'd left her favourite jacket hanging on the back of the kitchen table. The atmosphere in his house felt different. He dropped the roast and ran from the kitchen to the lounge. When he opened the drawer, everything looked fine. Old *YOU* magazines stacked up with *Autotrader* and his mother's old *Reader's Digest* — but when he lifted the back of the false bottom, it came off too easily. And he could tell, immediately, that some of his trophies had been taken. She was going to ruin his life, and he had to find a way to stop her.

He put his arm through the steel grille and knocked on the door. Nobody answered. He kept on knocking. Still no answer. Old man Johnny, the neighbourhood watchman, was sitting on his crate at the corner, listening to the radio and staring right at him, picking his teeth with a small twig. Teddy walked towards him, and then Johnny found the sand at his shoes very interesting.

'Are they home?' Teddy asked.

'Even the police say, "good day".' Johnny raised his eyelids slowly.

'Good day, Johnny. Are they in?'

'Who?' Johnny decided he liked testing this boy's patience. He didn't have power over anyone, otherwise. His wife was dead and his dogs terrorised his tenants, growling at them and jumping the fence at night. Sometimes, even with four new C batteries, his radio didn't work.

'You know who,' Teddy persisted, staring down at him.

'They're in. Why do you think they aren't answering the door?' he added innocently, as Teddy walked back to the front door.

There was a twitch at the front curtains down the road. The children in the street stared as they walked past the house. Little skinny boys and girls with legs ashy with play.

He knocked again, this time a bit harder. He waited a few moments, then walked back to his car. The front door opened, just enough for Augustine's mother to get her voice through.

'What do you want, Theodore?' The question an arrow, and his name a poisonous tip.

'Why didn't you answer the door?' His voice was deep with anger.

She refused to answer him.

The atmosphere in the street was charged with electricity from the twitching curtains. Women came out of their houses and stood on their little *stoeps* or at their fences. Mrs Pillay opened the door, and stood protected behind the burglar bars. Johnny turned the radio down.

'Where is my son?' He was mad. 'I want my son.' He started back towards the house.

'Get off my property. Don't come any closer,' she warned, her eyes large as a dragon's.

'Where is my son?'

'I don't know.' She folded her arms across her chest.

There was silence. Women were standing at their fences, and those who couldn't leave their kitchen posts opened the curtains and stared out the windows, not even trying to be inconspicuous. There were no secrets on this street. Teddy didn't know how deeply she could lie. He felt the bile rising in this throat.

'Stop lying to me. Do you want me to call the police?'

The cops were always there when you didn't want them. The children were scared to play in big groups, and the teenagers instinctively knew to keep their numbers small.

'Call the police and tell them what?' She opened the door wider, since she had an audience now. 'Do you think I must be scared because the white man is going to call the white cops?' She let the question hang in the air.

Teddy turned to the side and saw the women standing around, looking at him. He turned around to face them, ready to give them a speech. The sight of Johnny standing in his old blue jeans and torn-up old white T-shirt stopped him. His hair looked whiter and his wrinkles seemed deeper. He stood with his legs far apart and strong. Connected to the earth. Teddy and Johnny looked at each other, and for the first time Teddy saw the old pool hall brawler, the lady-killer, the deep schemer.

'I'll be back,' he said to Mrs Pillay. He turned around.

'I'll be here.' Her voice was deeper now, with the powerful energy of a dormant majestic volcano. Teddy got in his car and drove off, his tyres screeching and creating a little wave of dust behind him. She stood in the doorway to watch him go, to display her strength to the neighbourhood. She was the last man standing. She greeted everyone in a sweet voice, pleased with the outcome of her little drama.

And Johnny sat back down on his plastic crate and turned up his radio. He nodded in her direction and, in his silence, contemplated his next beer.

* * *

The next day, Teddy sat outside the Home Affairs office, leaning against the poorly painted black banister of the disabled ramp. He squinted in the sunlight at the green-yellow certificate, uncertain what to do next. He knew the police were out of the question. No wonder Mrs Pillay was so sure of herself. Until he established paternity, there was nothing he could do. He needed a lawyer, and that wouldn't be cheap. He needed to think.

He felt sick.

He picked a random lawyer's name from the Yellow Pages, Wesley Petersen, and arranged to meet him.

Mr Petersen was a middle-aged man who wore a curly ponytail and had a wide smile. He gave off that slippery vibration that cheap lawyers involuntarily radiate.

'Mr Beukes, how can I help you?'

'I need help locating my son.'

'OK, where did you lose him?' Petersen laughed at his own joke. He sat upright and cleared his throat. 'Sorry, bad taste.'

'His mother won't let me see him. In fact, I haven't seen her since the day after she gave birth,' Teddy lied. Petersen wasn't writing anything down, so Teddy spoke slowly, to give some gravity to his situation.

'OK, you find him, and then what?' Petersen looked at Teddy, expecting an answer.

'I never thought that far. I have rights, and I want to claim them.'

'That's all good and well, but what do you want?' Petersen asked him matter-of-factly.

Teddy was confused. 'What do you mean, what do I want?'

Petersen changed tack, realising Teddy was taking this as a personal attack.

'Tell me about your relationship with your son's mother. Why would she not put your name on the birth certificate? Domestic abuse, arguments, what? Be honest. I'm not judging.'

They talked for a few minutes. At the end of it, Petersen had better advice than Teddy had expected. He didn't like it. But he listened.

'So, you dated a student. OK, a previous student, whatever. It doesn't matter. In any case, you didn't introduce her to your family or your friends, even when she was pregnant. You understand the Immorality Act and all, you can't marry outside your race. You want your son to have your name now, but he'll have no claim to anything else.'

'Laws change. It's not going to be like this forever,' Teddy said.

Petersen kept his thoughts on this to himself. He didn't want to judge the sources of his paycheques, but he did have a daughter at high school, and the thought of one of her teachers grooming her gave him the chills.

Teddy continued talking through his emotions. He knew this was all shakier than he'd thought. 'My son is my family, and nothing can change that.'

'Legally, he isn't. You want to establish paternity, you need to do a paternity test. That costs money. And you need access to him to get it. The ball is firmly in her court. You will have to play nice.'

'What the hell?'

'You don't want to piss her off.' Petersen took a card from his small wooden box on his table. He sighed as he got up and passed it over to Teddy.

'This is a private investigator, Segert Berger. He specialises in these types of things. Call him. He can track her movements.'

A cleft was deepening between Teddy's eyebrows. Petersen knew that look: this man-child had no idea what he had got himself into. And he didn't know what he wanted, either. He stood up and buttoned his brown jacket to conclude the meeting.

'Helen will help you with the bill and invoices.' Petersen opened the door and smiled his broad, snake-oil smile. 'When you are ready, we can come up with a plan together. In the meantime, call Segert.'

Helen was a bleach blonde with long legs and a look of teenage nonchalance that was too young for her. Teddy figured she must've been about twenty-three or four.

'That's two hundred and fifty rand, sir.' She didn't make eye contact with him, but got the invoice book and pen ready.

'Mr Beukes. You can make the invoice out to Mr Beukes.' He stood close to the end of her desk, so she'd have to move her legs. She didn't pay him any attention, and wrote his name in bold cursive on the invoice.

'Do you need to make another appointment?' She looked at him now. She had light green eyes, which, it seemed to him, never held a smile.

'No, not yet. Thank you.' He left her there, stretching out and crossing her legs under the reconditioned desk. She didn't register his departure, and called the next client. Teddy wondered for a second if he was losing his slickness. She was just a bimbo anyway, he decided. He waited for the lift, but decided to take the stairs.

He fingered the business card. 'Segert Berger. What kind of name is that?' he asked himself, in the bright sunshine of downtown Johannesburg.

* * *

'Teddy, right? Welcome to my office.' Segert Berger waved Teddy towards him. He was sitting in the passenger seat of a white van, a camera on his lap. He had a severe permanent tan. His black eyes shone through his olive skin like two bullets. Teddy suddenly understood he was on a case, and didn't know whether to stay mute or carry on with his play.

'Sit.' Segert nodded towards the driver's seat. 'What is your situation?'

Teddy didn't know how to answer the question. He felt suddenly more unprepared than ever to be in this situation. 'I need to find my son, and his mother.' He raised a manila envelope he'd been carrying.

Berger picked up his camera absentmindedly. 'Runaway or ransom?'

'Runaway.'

Teddy looked back at the man beside him. Berger had broad shoulders and strong tan arms. Teddy decided he must be ex-military.

'Could be easier; could be harder. Do you know her family and friends?'

'Her family, yes. But they are telling me she's not with them. Their information is in here.'

'So, it's my job to find out if they are telling the truth.'

'Basically.'

Berger had his back to the passenger window, but something in his peripheral vision made him turn around. Maybe it was one of those instinct things.

'I have your number. I'll call you. Seven fifty a week for the first two weeks. After that, we can renegotiate.' He changed his voice into a deep, almost guttural drill voice that was designed to make sure no one would try to renegotiate.

'OK.' Teddy got out of the van, as Berger jumped into the driver's seat.

'Get walking, man.' Berger's voice was low, his eyes wide in mischief. Teddy could see him murmur something to himself, and heard the movement of a heavy object in the back of the van as Segert manoeuvred out from the parking spot. Segert enjoyed what he was doing for a living.

Teddy was regretting how much Augustine was costing him, and the fool she was making of him.

CHAPTER 3

Tuesday morning was dark with clouds. Segert drove across town to the South Rand mortuary. It was closer than driving all the way down to Augustine's old neighbourhood. If she and the baby were dead, he'd still charge Mr Beukes for the full week and save money on petrol.

The registrar was an old white woman of pension age, with brightly dyed orange-red hair and thin lips that were smeared with a dark red lipstick. She looked as if she'd allowed an amateur cosmetologist to enjoy her hobby without restraint. Her mug was rimmed with faded red kisses where she hadn't washed it properly. Her eyes were enlarged by her cat-eye glasses, and she wore a dark beaded necklace that resembled a rosary, but finished as a daisy in the middle of her bosom.

The reception area was empty except for two well-maintained, middle-aged coloured women who were sitting alongside each other on a short wooden bench on the far wall. They were immaculately put together: expensive flats, hair combed in style and wearing all-weather macs, one in navy blue, the other in tan. He wondered if they were American. One of them had been crying and was rocking backwards and forwards on the seat, shaking her head. Her friend or sister was holding her bag, passing her tissues.

The registrar put her magazine away and took off her glasses as he approached her.

'Get many tourists here?' Segert said, and nodded towards the women.

'Not tourists. Can I help?' She cleared her throat.

'Maybe. I'm looking for a young woman, and I'm wondering if you have any unclaimed bodies, Jane Does.'

'This is the morgue for the blacks and coloureds. The white girls, even the Does, are at the hospital.'

'Yes, I'm looking for a coloured girl. Her family is looking for her. No one's heard anything. And they can't face coming to the morgue,' he lied.

If she was surprised, she didn't show it. 'How old is she?'

'She's twenty years old; here's a recent photo. She's got long, curly black hair, but it could've been cut short.'

'I'm the wrong person to show that to. There's a coroner you can talk to.'

'OK. Can you call him?'

'She's busy dealing with something at the moment, but her attendant can help you.'

The attendant turned out to be a man so young he still had pimples on his cheeks. He looked like he was trying unsuccessfully to grow a moustache. He glanced quickly at the women against the wall and invited Segert to a small side room. In the centre stood a round table with a box of tissues on it.

'Guess this is where they tell you the bad news,' Segert said.

'This is where Beverly in reception brings people to sign paperwork. The tissues and the photos of the crashing waves are her touch. I'm Willem Du Plessis. You're looking for a missing woman?'

Segert handed him the photos of Augustine and Justice.

'Oh man, two of them, hey. We see a lot of unclaimed babies, mostly girls. Any distinguishing marks, on either of them?'

'Not really.'

'There's plenty of girls been here, around her age, especially in the last few months. Have one here now, about the same age. Her skin is slightly lighter, but it could be that in death her skin became a bit paler. Unfortunately, I don't have a face to compare, really.'

Segert grimaced. 'Well, I don't have access to her dental records or even her fingerprints.'

'The one I have now does have fingers. If you can get those prints, that would help.'

'She hasn't been in any trouble, so there isn't a record of her fingerprints. She doesn't drive, either.' Somehow Segert didn't think Teddy would have anything they could use to lift a sample.

'Why so many dead girls recently?' he asked, suddenly curious.

'Strangled and beaten prostitutes have been turning up for the past two years. I would say it's one guy. How tall is she?'

'She's one hundred and seventy centimetres, about forty-eight, fifty kilograms.' Segert thought about the two women in the reception. Were they so upset because they had found the answers they wanted, or because they were still looking? 'What happens to the ones you can't identify?'

'If we can't notify any next of kin, then we keep the body for as long as we can — the most is about a month. But that's only for exceptional cases. Babies, old people who seemed otherwise well looked after. Children who've been in a hit-and-run. Young men and women her age, we tend to move on quickly.'

'Move on where?'

'For burial at the municipal cemetery. There's so many of them, and, unless it looks like they were involved in a serious violent crime, we just pack it all in, so to speak.'

'Do you take any notes, compile a list?

'We, me and Annette Valencia — the senior coroner — have a docket book with some notes and photos. Do you want to have a look?'

28

Ja, am I allowed?'

'I'm not sure, but you're trying to locate someone and I've seen enough of these bodies. It would be nice to see a body reunited with her loved ones. How long has she been missing? We tried cataloguing by type of death, but that was pointless.'

'Let's start six months ago, to be safe. Starting with the babies. You said there were only a few baby boys left unclaimed. Let's start there.'

Willem took Segert into a small room and left him there with the docket book. It was gruesome. Babies that had been found alongside rivers, abandoned in bins and in bus stations. Segert had witnessed death before. He'd seen people killed in war. Lidless eyes in the dark as bodies lay strewn on a thicket. You didn't stop to think. Just concentrated on the thick raindrops falling on your shoulders and beating on your head. Moved on your belly in the storm, in a firefight, until the sound of mud droplets on your boots sounded like piano music.

You can tell on the face of an abandoned baby what loneliness is, Segert thought. In the army, he had friends; he wasn't alone. And no one died alone. He didn't even remember the training. What he remembered was the time he was out in the bush, listening to a black tracker tell them how old the enemies' tracks were, which way to go.

The nights were peaceful and beautiful. The sky was always orange and pink at dusk, and the soldiers lay talking on the dried grass. Talking about women, and the first drink they'd have when they got home. Very few of his buddies died in combat. They overwhelmed the enemy. And it was worth it: they were keeping the Commies out, and if Cuba hadn't got involved, everything would've been OK. He didn't care so much about the politics, but there was no way he was going to live in a world where he didn't win. He knew it was a proxy war, and his guts weren't in it, but he would've fought for anything to keep winning.

The rain beating lightly on the window shook him out of his thoughts. In the distance, lightning cracked sharply. It was unusual for this time of day, and Segert wondered if his dogs, a pair of saddle-coloured Alsatians, were OK. The dry food he'd left out for them would get soggy in the rain. He always fed them at night, but this morning he'd left them a snack in case he got back late.

Segert looked back at the book before him. Willem was right. There were only five boys. They ranged in ages from a few months old to almost walking size. There were two who resembled Justice, but were too old. They had been cleaned, naked with their genitals covered. Someone had taken the photos with the bruises exposed. The photos had been taken frankly, and with meticulous detail, but without care.

The women were a different story. The folder was thick, and, after the first dozen or so dockets, he gave up. The women had been in various stages of neglect or abuse when they were brought in. They'd been found at random places, some of them overdosed or hit by a car, but the vast majority had been murdered. Segert looked at the strangled victims, and their deaths seemed so unreal that they couldn't be final. Perhaps they would be resurrected to their old lives, to heal the purple marks around their necks, grow new fingernails, and then die again peacefully.

Willem, who had left, came back with a cup of coffee. 'I assumed you had it black with three sugars.'

'I'll take it,' Segert said, happy for the distraction, even though he loathed sweet coffee. 'You shouldn't be showing me this.'

'Are you squeamish?'

'Nee, I just think this is police business.'

'What? Like you just go to the police station and say, "I have a missing girl," and they look through this file for you?' Willem laughed lightly. 'You want to find a missing coloured girl, and I'm trying to help you out.' He closed the docket book. 'But the police aren't going to spend resources on this. These are prostitutes and druggies, maybe a runaway here and there. Money is going to securing the suburbs and patrolling the townships. There's a lot going on now, and no one cares about prostitutes, not even white ones.'

Segert wanted to disagree. White prostitutes would've made the tabloids. But then, who wanted to admit there were white prostitutes, and what would be the point of dragging their families through the mud?

'You said you thought this was all the work of one man. Is it only coloured women? Has anyone contacted the white mortuary?' Segert asked him.

'Everything is perfect over there. Just a stopover before heaven,' Willem said dryly.

Segert laughed in spite of himself.

'They only contact us. We can't really contact them.'

'What do they contact you about?'

'Don't worry about it. We've been collecting bodies, day after day, week after week. And the visions of those bodies, they stay in my memory. The police force is weaponised now. They don't have the detective expertise, anymore.'

Ja, for sure. How long has this been going on?'

'About two years now, but it could be longer. These are the bodies the police picked up, because the killer leaves them out for us to find. It reminds me of a cat I had when I was a boy, who used to bring me birds and lizards he'd killed. He wasn't hungry; he just liked to hunt and wanted to show off his skills.'

'He? You think it's one guy? Where does he leave the bodies?'

'Leaves them at mine dumps, freight train stations, behind a mall.'

Segert felt that one day the killer would just leave a body in front of the morgue.

'These are the one I have now, and the last few strangulations.' Willem leafed through the book and pointed them out to Segert.

'The girl you have now, that's beat up. Was she strangled?'

'Her head's missing. Been decapitated. Not enough neck left to tell for sure.'

31

Segert took a big gulp of his coffee and stuck his tongue out.

'It has that effect on me, too,' Willem said.

'It's not that, man. I don't take sugar, that's all. I'll just have a look at the rest of the dockets and take some notes.'

'Suit yourself. When you're done, leave it with Beverly. But we will be needing this room.'

Segert spent an hour in the back room, reading through Willem Du Plessis and Annette Valencia's notes. Photocopying pictures of dead women. After a while, they became indistinguishable, and any sympathy he'd felt had dissipated. He kept the picture of Augustine clipped on his notebook. Eventually he just made himself believe she was alive and got out of there.

'I hope you don't have to come back here,' Beverly said, walking to the kitchen to make a cup of tea.

'Me too.'

* * *

The rainwater in the parking lot was evaporating in steam trails. The sunlight leapt across his bonnet and hit him straight in his eyes. He threw his notebook in the back. He was relieved to be back in his van. He needed to shower and brush his teeth and exercise and then shower again. Get the mortuary out of his skin. The day wasn't a bust. Girls like Augustine were invisible, until someone had a need for them or they were in the wrong place.

If she'd dumped the baby and was now hooking, there were plenty of places to search. But Augustine had a taste for the familiar. She'd been with Teddy, her schoolteacher. Before she was pregnant, she worked at Khan's supermarket, a few blocks from where she grew up. That suggested she'd stay either close to Jo'burg train station, or around the coloured areas.

Segert rolled his van through the South Rand suburbs and townships, the Jo'burg sun glowing on his arm through his rain-streaked window. He loved driving in this city. The highways were long and broad, well-lit to drive through at night or race on with your brah. Few enough cars so that you could drive home drunk and not mess up your insurance. The suburbs and settlements were set far back. This city was planned for drivers. The highways, at least.

His foot hovered over the clutch as he entered the city. Segert turned down Newtown towards Old Park Station, which used to serve as the main station in the days of the Gold Rush. The barrel-vaulted roof was unmistakable as the home for a steam locomotive. The canopy had been moved about thirty years ago, having survived the city's industrial explosion. It had been the departure point for men and munitions during the World Wars, and the relocation point for British refugees during the Boer war. The roof and its parts were about two hundred metres long, supported by an elevated podium strengthened by archways. It wore the history of these parts. Now it stood over the old goods yard. The ground flattened for loading trucks and cars, the archways heavy with the smell of urine and petrol. The sand was red and clay-like in patches. Broken pieces of beer bottles and cans were strewn in the corners.

Across the road were two cheap hotels and a small grocery store. Three working girls were standing there. One was wearing a tight yellow mini-dress with wide frills on the end and red pumps. She had short hair in black spirals, chestnut skin and slightly bucked teeth. By the tightness of the skin on her legs, she was around twenty-two, but her face accounted for nights lived in smoky bars. She walked around the tiled front of the shop quite proudly.

It was getting on for two in the afternoon, and Segert was hungry. He parked and walked to the shop to get something to eat.

The shop smelled of stale air and dust. There was a deli oven filled with thick red Vienna sausages and oily pies. Segert picked up a Coke and thought twice about a packet of barbecue chips on promotion at the counter.

The working girl was waiting just by the door. 'Well, hello, how can I help you today?' She trailed her index finger down his forearm as he passed. 'Do you want to go for a drink?'

'*Nee*, I mean, no, thank you,' he corrected himself quickly. 'I was wondering if you can help me.'

'Whatever you need. Some brown sugar?'

Segert stood against the wall, opening his can of Coke. He held out the photograph of Augustine. 'I'm looking for this girl, and I was wondering if you saw her around here.'

'Oh no, leave me alone. I'm busy.' She pricked her hands up as if she'd touched something hot, and walked away.

'She's missing.'

'Mister, I'm busy. Put that picture away. I'm not looking.'

'Wouldn't you want someone to help if your parents were looking for you?'

'My parents? Sure. They'd like a piece of this money I'm making.'

'She's got a child, and the father is looking for both of them.'

'Really? And where do you come in the picture?' She turned around, appraising him.

'I'll give you twenty rand if you look at the photo.'

She walked back towards him. 'OK, I'm ready.'

He handed her the photo.

'Let me see the twenty,' she said, then slouched against the wall where they'd just met. She scanned the parking lot, twirling the photograph lightly in her hand. The two other working girls were clocked onto a VW hatchback, intercepting the two men on the way to the hotel.

Segert took two tens out of his back pocket and waved them at her.

'Can't say I've seen either of them this side. And that's good, I don't need that type of competition. She's pretty, nice eyes. There's a few places like this. I can tell you where to look for another twenty. But it's going to cost you a lot more than a twenty to get a girl in that van, Mister. I'm just saying.'

'What's your name?' Segert asked.

'Brown Sugar, *Bruin Suiker*, whatever you want it to be.'

'I mean, your real name.'

'Doesn't matter; that girl's gone. Long time. Brown Sugar's just here for the sights. Give me the money; I'll show you the night. Maybe even my backlight. Toot toot.' She laughed.

'Maybe you're my brown angel in disguise.'

'Smooth, Mister Sugar Tongue, very smooth.' She wriggled her hand under his arm and he passed her the money. She walked him down the street and told him where to keep looking for a girl like Augustine.

CHAPTER 4

Augustine never had a Monday morning like this. Out of the small window she could make out the bare hint of dawn.

Figures had been on the street all night. The sounds of a car door slamming made her jump, and she'd watched the business of the street. Now, someone whistled a signal down the road, and a car blinked it headlights in reply. The lone man under the streetlight across the road went inside. She held the sharp knife in her hand. She hadn't closed her eyes that night. Justice was asleep. Augustine bundled him up and walked across the small living room to the bathroom. She had to be as quiet as a mouse and finish all her ablutions, then make her way out of Soweto back across town to start her new job. Nothing was on her mind. She was clear. The photographs were zipped in a plastic bag in the inner pocket of her bag. She had to figure out a plan of how to use them, but for now they were the insurance she needed against her ex-boyfriend and high school maths teacher.

She ate a piece of dry bread by the window, and when she saw the first school children appear on the road, she knew it was safe to be out in the street. The sun was lighting a mackerel sky of fleecy white clouds. The weather would break within a few hours. A winter storm was coming.

She opened the door and walked down the small path to the rusty gate that established the property line. Before she got there, she heard Pastor Moloi open the front door. He was in a sea-green jumper and his pyjamas.

'Where are you going?'

'I need to go now.' She looked up at the sky.

'Understand. Did you eat?'

She nodded.

Pastor Moloi eyed her bag, the strap close to Justice's sleeping head. 'Wait there, I will walk with you to the taxi, make sure you go the right way.'

He emerged a few minutes later, wearing black shoes and a pair of slacks.

'Looks like a nice day, better than yesterday,' Pastor Moloi said, not referring to the weather. He let them walk out first and closed the squeaky gate behind them. 'Having you here has reminded me to oil this gate and take care of my house. I should always be ready for guests.'

'Thank you so much for letting us stay.'

'It was only a few hours — it was nothing. My wife is in Polokwane.' He told her again. He was groggy so early in the morning. 'Do you know it? If she was here, you'd have been better looked after.'

'You've done so much already . . .' She trailed off, not sure what to say. She hadn't been counting on him waking up. She still had his sharpest kitchen knife in her bag, which was under her left arm.

Most of the school children and their mothers and grand-mothers greeted the pastor, glancing quickly at Augustine, then moving on fast to the end of the street. The taxi guard put his head out the sliding window and whistled a sharp tune as the minibus drove down the street. The taxi was empty, and they were keen to start business.

'This one is yours. Can I give you something for the little one?' He passed her two five-rand notes quickly. 'It's not safe to sit in the front here with the driver. Sit in the first row here in the back. You will go all the way to town, then change there. You know where to find my mother and me, if anything changes.'

The taxi filled up with school children and workers, then eased off into the street. Augustine put the two purple notes in her bag, and waved goodbye to the pastor.

* * *

At the hedge of trees in front of the boundary wall at 64 Belgravia Road, Augustine quickly checked the street, then scratched a shallow hole and threw the knife in, covering it lightly with the red sand. She wiped her hands and pushed the black intercom button. The breeze was blowing harder now, and the sky was becoming a bowl of clouds.

'Hello?' an old female voice answered.

'Hello, Madam. I am Augustine. I start today.' She moved her weight from one foot to the other.

'Wait a minute, please.'

There was a long silence, while the voice on the other end went to find out what was happening.

One thought kept racing through Augustine's mind: *I hope Mrs Diamond didn't change her mind*. She looked back at Justice, who had his hand in his mouth. Smiling happily at her. He was teething now. He was growing up so fast.

'Hello?' The voice again, from the house.

Augustine held in her breath now. 'Yes, Madam.'

'Please meet me at the side entrance past the front door.'

The electronic knock of the gates made Augustine exhale, and she smiled from the sides of her eyes, holding back a tear.

The voice on the intercom manifested itself as an older black woman with short black hair that was grey at the temples, wearing a black-and-white maid's uniform. She introduced herself as Maggie.

'Oh, you have a baby.' Maggie stood on the red-brick step leading to the servants' entrance, which was really a converted two-car garage.

'Yes, his name is Justice, I'm Augustine by the way.' She extended her hand. To which the old lady replied by wiping her hands on her apron, turning around and going indoors.

'Let me show you where everything is.' She walked through a small lobby with coat hooks on one side. 'I wasn't expecting anyone, so I'm afraid nothing is prepared for you two.'

She stopped in the doorway of a small room, bare but for a small three-quarter bed and a dilapidated wooden cupboard, which had its door ajar. A few dusty metal hangers were exposed lying abandoned at the bottom.

Augustine said nothing. She made no noise, no sigh or exclamation. That way, there was nothing for Maggie to object to.

'I guess you have no choice but to like it. This isn't the Holiday Inn, you know.' Maggie walked into the room.

'Thank you, Madam.' She remained respectful, even though it was tiring her.

'I will get some blankets for you later.'

'Yes, OK.'

This was met with a stern look.

'Yes, thank you very much.'

'Put your child down for a minute while I show you the bathroom and kitchen.'

Augustine felt like a fever was lifting. She would live modestly, probably doing the type of work she had once thought she was too good for. But this was her get-out-of-jail card.

Maggie showed her around the grand manor. A big upstairs-downstairs house that was out of a magazine. Through the large kitchen window, Augustine could see a gardener tending hydrangeas at the far end of the back lawn.

'Is Missus Diamond in?' She stopped walking, looking around the house for signs of the lady of the manor. 'Should I say hello?'

'She knows you are here. You must get cleaned up first. You will have a slow start today.'

'Oh, OK,' Augustine said, unsure of herself.

As they walked back past the living room, Augustine noticed a solitary red giraffe soft toy lying on the ground.

* * *

About thirty minutes later, Maggie knocked on Augustine's door, beckoning her to come.

'All right?' she asked.

As they walked past the living room, Augustine noticed that the red toy giraffe wasn't lying on the floor anymore.

They stopped at a door that was ajar, then moved into the small dining room close to the kitchen.

'This is the breakfast room,' Maggie whispered, before she knocked on the door. 'The Diamond family is expecting you. Just say good morning, to announce you are here.'

The Diamonds were eating breakfast at a long oval-shaped oak table. A light blue blanket was draped over a chair, and the lady she met yesterday at the front door was rocking an elevated Moses basket with her foot as she ate a fruit salad. Her husband was wearing a dark grey suit and white English shirt. His jacket hung on a butler rack, away from the table, as if it was another man occupying the room. Mr Diamond was reading a newspaper, his back to the door. When he turned around to greet Augustine, he wasn't happy to see her, but greeted her all the same. He was thin and athletic, with sharp blue eyes. Both he and his wife simply nodded at Augustine and waited for the door to close.

'I wish you'd told me about our new additions,' Martin said to his wife, without looking at her.

'New additions? You mean the maid? So formal. Are you hungry? You've only had coffee this morning.'

He snapped the newspaper.

Through a forkful of cantaloupe, Kimberly said, 'I need someone here to look after Nicholas.'

'When did this happen, and what about Maggie?'

'She can't do everything, and she goes home every December. I can't take that away.'

'I think you can manage without someone for a month. But when did this happen, Kim?' Martin insisted. He'd put his newspaper down.

'Yesterday.'

'Is this your hormones?' Martin asked.

'Hormones? You look after a baby all day and see how you fare.'

'I just went for a run yesterday; I told you. And isn't she a bit young?'

'Yesterday? It's not just yesterday. And usually the wife worries about young maids. This is the first time I've heard a husband object.'

'You know what I don't like, Kimberly? You asked me to start work late this morning, but you knew this woman was coming here.'

'You're a family man now, I don't like that you're always working late and staying out.'

'There's two of them, I doubt you've thought this through.'

'If it was me, would you want me to leave my baby? Besides, I feel like I'm catching the flu again. She can look after Nicholas.'

He could tell he was on the losing end of the argument. If they argued much longer, the baby might wake up. 'Very clever, the flu made me do it. I have to work; you don't understand.' He took a sip of his coffee, which was too cold and bitter now.

'I understand. I understand very clearly.'

He watched every twitch on her face. 'You've never had to work,' he said.

'If I was the type to work, would we even be married?'

'Don't talk to me that way.'

'What are you going to do, run away? If I asked you very nicely, would you come home after work? Or even just tell me everything you're doing?'

'Keep your maid.'

'I am.'

He leaned back in his chair. 'But don't make any more decisions without me. I mean it.'

***

The night was colder than usual. The afternoon thunderstorm had released the heat from the asphalt, and the humidity made the night feel cold and unbearable. Condensation was forming on the inside of Teddy's living room window.

He was sitting on his sofa, a beer in one hand and an empty chocolate box in the other. The TV cabinet that Augustine had rifled through was open. He'd been foolish to keep his Polaroids in there. And in a chocolate box. Doesn't matter that it was covered with car magazines and an old mathematics supplementary syllabus. For some reason, when he was out shopping for a roasted chicken and nappies, she'd rifled through his things. If she ever got back to his school, then his life was over. He'd have more than prison to worry about. He watched a small swarm of insects dance around a streetlight and opened another beer. He'd have to pay whatever price Segert Berger demanded to get to Augustine, and to get those Polaroids back, or silence her forever. He'd have to be patient, there was no rushing this. The worst thing would be to spook her and make her fear for Justice. He'd have to take it a little step at a time.

***

The low beams approaching up the driveway lit up Augustine's room. She watched her son, then turned to watch through the window without leaving her bed. It was late, past midnight, and the house was silent. Martin Diamond parked the car in front of the servants' quarters, slamming the door. He was wearing the same suit from this morning, with a fresh shirt that had packaging lines. He walked along the front of the car, moving his jaw without talking, denying himself an emotion that would make his lips turn into a smile, then opened the passenger seat and got out his briefcase. Augustine could hear the contents slide with a thump. He opened the front door and went straight to the study. She heard a wooden drawer shut and then him going to wash his hands.

When Augustine went to clean the study the following morning she found Pastor Moloi's steak knife displayed on a neat blue handkerchief on top of Martin's desk. She felt panic rising in her throat, but picked it up and took it to the kitchen. She was going to be fired just as she'd started. She'd have to go back home to Noon and Teddy would find them. Martin walked into the kitchen as she was stacking the knife in the kitchen drawer.

'Found that knife outside in the bushes, last night.'

'Oh,' Augustine said. 'Good morning, sir. What should I do with it?'

'I don't know, throw it away. You can't expect us to eat with it.'

He was already walking out of the kitchen when he said, 'You know, we never have to worry about danger in this area. Something must've changed.'

'Perhaps it was just some teenagers playing a prank.' Augustine's voice was nervous.

'Even children in this area are too sensible for stuff like that, I guess that's why you moved here.'

Augustine took a deep breath, trying to shake off the emotion that was building up inside her, then threw the knife in the rubbish bin. She was going to be skinned alive, one way or another. In any direction she looked, no one was looking out for her.

CHAPTER 5

Up until Augustine's arrival, Maggie had been the only permanent staff left in the large house in Belgravia Street, a hangover
from the days when Kimberly's parents, the Fullers, lived there
with their children. Maggie had been the nanny to Kimberly,
and to her brother Ryan, who was dead now.

Back in those days, you didn't call her *nanny*. She was a
domestic, helper, servant, keeper or cleaner. She was permanent but adjustable. She was furniture.

'Huh?' Augustine said, startled, as she turned around.

'"Excuse me,"' Maggie corrected. She moved to the kitchen
quickly, leaving Augustine standing there uncomprehending.

Augustine sprayed a plume of polish on the dirty rag and
walked over to the windowsills, carrying a bucket of hot soapy
water and old newspapers, still in a daydream. It had been
three weeks of polishing furniture, mopping floors and cleaning babies' backsides. Cleaning an extra baby's backside wasn't
so bad when it gave you a roof over your head.

Still, without any recourse available to herself or her child,
Augustine carried the light air of a lodger who would be there
for an indeterminate but finite amount of time. As if it was
up to her, somehow, how long she and her child would stay.

Maggie couldn't take it.

Maggie kept everything working like clockwork.

The floors were swept with an old plastic broom, the bristles soft and flexible. The small pile of dust was collected in a matching grey scoop, scrubbed and cleaned daily. They were left to dry outside the kitchen door, on the side of the *kopje* stone step, where it could catch the early afternoon sun. Next to the stiff broom for sweeping outside, round the patio and swimming pool.

Maggie was packing the breakfast dishes away into the corner cabinet. Through the window, she saw Paulus, the part-time gardener, a sinewy man a year or two older than herself. He was standing in among a collection of gardening tools, uncurling wire mesh and wooden poles he'd already cut down to size. The sharp edge of the cutters glared in the light. He'd been instructed to wrap a wire mesh around the hydrangeas in the back garden. They hadn't died to the ground; the azure blooms still shimmered against the spade-shaped leaves. But Martin Diamond, her ma'm's husband, had insisted this year that Paulus protect them.

'I've a premonition about a frost this winter,' Martin had told her, one day back in May. He'd walked indoors to pour a drink of water. 'My wife is smitten with those flowers.' He wiped his mouth with his hand and went out the kitchen. 'Great job, Paulus,' he shouted, as he walked round the back to his car.

Maggie turned the wireless onto her favourite station as soon as Martin was out of earshot.

This is Radio Bantu, and I'm Winnie Mahlangu with the news at 3 p.m. The decapitated body of a young woman was found at South Deep mine. The body was clad in a short dress and high heels and one hand clutched a fistful of dirt. The body is still unidentified, and no arrests have been made. Medical examiner Willem Du Plessis was unable to corroborate if the slaying was connected to the series of killings of young prostitutes over the past few months. Now, stay tuned for the weather.'

Winter afternoons in the Highveld were hot. Maggie could see big pools of sweat on Paulus's forehead as he hammered the tiny stakes into the ground. Martin didn't know what he was talking about. It was already August, the coldest was over. She'd been here for almost thirty years, and, as long as she could remember, the hydrangeas bloomed every summer.

CHAPTER 6

Kimberly got the winter sniffles and they just wouldn't go away. Augustine cemented her place when Kimberly's wet cough became a bark. She kept Nicholas fed and changed throughout the night. But no matter how much Kimberly rested at night and slept late in the day, that wet cough turned into a whoop.

The phone rattled with anxious calls from society friends when Kimberly was admitted to hospital for a respiratory infection. The first week they wanted to send flowers: 'Is it OK? When will she get out?'

The second week, they called for updates on her health, but mostly to update their social calendar.

Now, it was radio silence, but the Maggie the Commander still kept the daily maintenance and show-home routine.

'Even if no one's visiting,' Maggie would say from the kitchen, trying to inspire the cadet, Augustine. She was uncertain how to modulate her pitch. Paulus and his ilk she could just bark orders at, and send food to, but Maggie wasn't taught how to manage in this upwards-downwards way. Some days were better than others.

After breakfast, the floors were washed, the windows wiped. Maggie sprayed window cleaner on an old towel to

47

tackle the streaks. The absent smell of brewing coffee pinched her in the heart. Kimberly had normalised the house somehow; she was the last of the Fullers, who'd always owned the house and whom Maggie had always worked for. In her absence, Maggie kept busy.

'Where is Mr Diamond?' Augustine stood with Justice on her hip in the kitchen doorway.

'Staying with his sister in Pretoria,' Maggie replied. She was taking down a silver tray to polish and spied the pair from the corner of her eye.

'Still?'

'Yes,' she answered.

Even though Augustine was dressed in her uniform, she had taken the two weeks that Kimberly was in hospital as a semi-holiday. Loose, lightly greased tendrils escaped from her hair bun. She sank into her right hip as she held the child. The line of her posture, in Maggie's mind, resembled a flat tyre.

Maggie imagined that Augustine had stood in the same posture on her neighbourhood street corner. Under sharp sunlight as a dirty child, and under the orange glow of the streetlamps, witnessing the humdrum and the exciting — chewing gum and asking friends and neighbours intrusive questions. *The devil makes work for idle hands and mouths*, Maggie thought.

Augustine retreated to her bedroom, picked up a blanket and pillow, and carried them into the living room for Justice to lie on. Maggie's coldness didn't bite her, but she wanted to get away from the acrid sting of it.

'It's a good thing I don't need a letter of recommendation,' Augustine said to Justice, as she laid him down with the bottle of cool milk she'd just made, brushing his hair back from his forehead and kissing him on the nose. She burped him, then laid him to sleep in a corral of sofa cushions. She walked upstairs mumbling to herself, giving a sharp side-eye in the direction of the kitchen.

Late morning, the wind shifted and Augustine could smell the dewy wetness of the lawn, bougainvillea and flowers from the garden. Every day, she opened the windows in the Diamonds' bedroom to let fresh air in, patted any dust off the bed and yanked the duvet straight, then scrubbed and cleaned the en-suite bathroom. She sniffed the face creams and perfume. Touched Mr Diamond's shaving foam and their soap dispenser. Sampled some hand cream. The overhead lighting was soft and warm, a small cluster glass chandelier attached to the ceiling. She twirled, appraising herself in the mirror. Her breasts were bigger, and her stomach had a small curve to it. She was a woman now, a working mother.

She pulled up the shower grid to clean the strainer. Clumps of long blonde hair and human oil and skin were mixed in with God knows what. Augustine almost gagged. The mystery of white people had been solved. They took shits in soft light.

That day, before the smell of Handy Andy bathroom cleaner overpowered the smell of fresh-cut grass blowing in through the bathroom windows, Augustine had gingerly opened Mrs Diamond's wardrobe door. She'd sprayed furniture polish on the hinges to prevent any squeak. The interior, dark and cool, held four wooden shelves. The bottom kept an assortment of jerseys; merino and cashmere cardigans in a variety of colours and patterns she'd never seen in all one place, not even at the Truworth's ladieswear section in town.

She gazed at a pile of thigh-length cable knit navy cardigans with extravagant buttons. She touched them to check. No, the buttons weren't plastic. Thin hip-length button-down cardigans to wear on a summer's evening, to dinner with her friends, maybe. Augustine put her hands on them, knowing that Maggie had folded them with precision and placed them delicately on each shelf. A half-dozen colourful scarves hung on the inside of the wardrobe door. Augustine pulled the two-step ladder she'd brought in with her from the upstairs linen closet and stood on it, furniture polish-sprayed cloth in hand. She reached into the top shelf. Perfume and nail polish remover. She wiped the bottom of the shelf, picking up some dirt and dust. Pushing everything to one side, and then another. Augustine was momentarily transported back to her former life working in the supermarket. Doing a stocktake of what there was and how much everything cost.

The slight smell of dry iron dust signalled that it was lunchtime. The sun was baking the mud in the garden to powder. Tonight, the soil would be frosted, and then turned to clumps of mud again in the morning.

Augustine's stomach grumbled, shifting her out of her daydream. She bent to pack the two-step ladder in the bottom of the linen closet, and accidentally knocked down a small oriental mother-of-pearl box embedded between old-fashioned tablecloths in a dark corner of the closet. She reached in to pull it out, listening for Maggie to start calling her, or the sounds of Justice stirring. The box was about a ruler length across and ten centimetres wide. She thought back to Kimberly's bright yellow-gold necklace and assortment of gems. She suspected she'd find these treasures within. The motif of the box reminded her of the patterns she'd seen inside Indian jewellery shops. She sat on her haunches, not caring if she tore a hole in her stockings. Inside, the box was lined with red velvet, which cushioned three white plastic pill bottles. The ink on the labels were faded. She couldn't read the prescription, but it was for Leonie Meyer, and the earliest bottle had been dispensed by Dr Vorster two years ago.

Augustine was no genius. But she knew, whoever Leonie Meyer was, these were Kimberly's pills. She'd been sick for a long time. She was someone who had everything, blonde hair and expensive perfume, yet she hid something in the dark bottom of the linen closet. It was something that Maggie didn't know, because, if she had, Maggie would've hidden them in a far better place than this.

* * *

Maggie heard the clicking sound of the front gates opening. She was lying on her bed, watching *The Bold and the Beautiful* in her black-and-white uniform. She pulled the net curtain from the window behind her, and recognised Mr Diamond's white Mercedes-Benz gliding slowly up the driveway. She got up. Checked her reflection in the mirror. Sprayed some glycerine mist on her hair and put on her apron. She looked at herself in the long mirror on her cupboard and tried in vain to smooth the wrinkles from the back of her overall. She hoped Mr Diamond wouldn't mind that she wasn't wearing stockings, and slipped on her black shoes at the door. They were boys' school shoes, really.

Maggie closed the door, then, still hearing the loud jingle of a Coke commercial, turned back to her room to switch off the small TV. She hurried past Augustine's room and peeped at the pair sleeping. And caught Mr Diamond by the front door.

He was by himself. Maggie tried to remain hopeful, pushing the thought of the worst out of her head.

'Mr Diamond.' Maggie stood to the side of the front door. Her bottom against the back of the sofa. She must have startled him, because he let out a small gasp.

'God, Maggie, you gave me a fright.' He noticed her expression deflate. 'I hope you haven't been standing there since I left.' He laughed.

She didn't laugh back. 'No, Mr Diamond. Can I get you anything?'

'No, no, I don't need any help. I'll speak to you later. Relax.' Martin went up the stairs, not saying any more.

She wanted to ask after Mrs Diamond, but knew first-hand how annoying questions could be.

* * *

Mr Diamond hurried downstairs, looking for Maggie. He had a small suitcase packed at the front door. Maggie eyed it from the kitchen, saying nothing. Her hands were in the apron, bracing her thighs for bad news. He walked towards her and handed an envelope with a note inside.

'This is your wages, and expenses for the house for the next month.'

He left her a list of bills to settle and left the number of the accountant, in case of any issues.

'For both of us?' she asked.

'For you, the gardener and the new person.'

Maggie was none too pleased. This meant that Augustine was staying on. She was worried for Ms Kimberly of course, and Nicholas. Both of them needed support. But she was worried for herself. She didn't like managing someone, especially someone so young, who could work for so many years longer than her.

Martin saw her expression. 'You will have to be dedicated to Kimberly, as a nurse when she comes back. And she will come back soon.'

Maggie blinked with relief.

'The new one is here to help you. Besides, you go away for a month every December. We'll need the extra help.'

'I don't have to go back home this year, Mr Diamond,' Maggie said.

'You've earned that holiday after all these years. You should enjoy your homeland while you still can. We don't need to be looking after *you* if you don't have the rest you need.'

She swallowed the allusion to her age, and said, 'thank you, sir.'

'Paulus you can pay every Friday, he's only casual. It's the end of the month, so you can pay yourself and the new girl a whole month. Keep the money in a safe place.' He walked briskly to the front door. 'Everything will be fine.'

CHAPTER 7

Segert was sitting at a wooden bar counter of a restaurant that had too many wooden panels, sipping a pale Mexican lager and tending to a small bowl of tortilla chips. The restaurant was in Rivonia, a wealthy suburb of Jozi's second city, Sandton. The tables were packed with office workers and early evening dates. He was wearing a black pair of slacks, the leg crease stiff with sweat and dirt. They'd been wiped clean dozens of times with a damp towel and never sent to the dry cleaners. They were a gift from a woman who wanted to change him, his ex-wife. But they'd come in handy on more occasions than he could remember. Today, he was trying to pass as a salesman type, and had paired the trousers with black shoes, a tan belt and light blue pinstripe shirt. A black jacket, draped on the stool next to him, held a space for a companion who was never coming. Wes, his friend and contract employer, had lent it to him when he'd given Segert the Richard Reader file. It was a simple industrial espionage case. Follow the mark, who was a marketing executive at SASOL Chemicals, get the prices of paraffin and wax. The client wanted to remain anonymous. If it went well, there would be more work.

The bartender refilled his bowl with chips and asked him if he wanted another beer, even though Segert's drink wasn't half-finished.

'Give me a can of the best,' Segert said easily. He was spying his mark, Richard Reader, in the faded brewery mirror behind the bar.

'A Castle coming up.'

'Put a tequila on the side.'

'No problem. Are you waiting for someone?' the barman asked.

'Just killing time. I'm going for a leak.' Segert left R10 on the counter, readjusting his trousers as he walked. He didn't notice the pair of young women clocking him and smiling at each other.

He walked to the end of the bar, past the toilets and through the door to the parking lot. He spotted Richard Reader's white Nissan in the left corner of the parking lot. Two cars down from the exposed black wire fence and green transformer box. He walked to his car and took out the black nylon toolkit from the cubbyhole, then walked casually to the rear of the Nissan, scanning through the windows for Richard's brown leather case. It wasn't there. He pulled a small flathead from the bag and slid off the chrome covering from the lock, then worked the screwdriver into the lock and popped it. Within four seconds, he had opened the boot and the brown case. It wasn't locked. The inner sleeve had what he was looking for. Two sheets of A4 paper with the prices of wax and paraffin.

He took out his small Minox camera. Took photos from every angle of the two sheets, including the blank reverse sides. Placed them back the way he found them. Closed the boot and walked back to the restaurant. He sauntered back to his stool and downed the tequila shot, then filled his mouth with beer. He gobbled a few more chips, tipped the bartender and left Richard Reader none the wiser, talking to his date over a steaming hot plate of chicken enchiladas. She seemed engrossed as he was talking, leaning in slightly with a smile playing on her lips as she sipped from a glass of red wine.

It was a cool winter night. The windless air chilled his ears. He flicked the jacket onto the passenger seat of his blue BMW saloon. Out of habit, he turned up his sleeves after he started the car. He sat for a few minutes warming the engine, then reversed out of his spot. The Southern Cross glinted in the clear sky as he scanned the buildings round the car park. He waited a few beats for Reader, but knew he was still entangled with his date. The car park was three-quarters full, and it was a school night. Sandton was always busy with food and sex and commerce. The smell of hot cooking oil and cayenne pepper and meat from the restaurant chimneys filled the air.

The traffic was mostly all gone. Segert turned right on Wierda Road, back to his place. A few people were walking the roads, couples holding hands and drunken men walking in pairs or threes, stumbling and laughing at crude jokes. His mind ran back to the dockets he'd seen at the morgue. There was no news of the murders in the papers; they didn't exist. He'd had Augustine's case for just over a month. If her body hadn't turned up, he'd have to find her alive, no matter what hole she had crawled up in. He'd already renegotiated the fee with Teddy to five hundred a week. He hadn't taken on other cases to focus on the Richard Reader case. Besides, Teddy hadn't brought him many details about her. The photos of the mother and child, and her parents' address.

Segert drove down Louis Botha Avenue and followed the Southern Cross to Kliptown Road Station. It was a part of town he'd driven through, but he never had any business to stop. A corridor of large kitchen and furniture showrooms punctuated by spaces for mixed manufacturing. Ever since the construction of the highway close by, the area had fallen into decay. He parked under a light at the entrance of the station motel.

The dusty hotel bar smelled of wet cigarettes and mould. The smell of old urine wafted in from the train platforms and made its home inside here.

'What can I get you?' the bartender asked. He was in his mid-thirties with a mischievous look in his eye.

'A beer. Castle.' Segert sat down at the bar.

'Yes, boss.' The bartender delivered the bottle with a flourish. 'A glass for you?'

Segert shook his head, and turned around.

Brass miners' lamps were sconced on the walls between windows, giving the room bright tones of yellow and brown that hid the dust and cobwebs. The ceiling was incredibly high, harking back to the Gold Rush days. Maybe there had been a mezzanine at one point. Four large brass station lamps radiated from the central decorative plaster feature. The music was low, and people were talking and drinking at tables. A few prostitutes were sitting on men's laps, sipping wine.

'Howzit, china, haven't seen you before,' the short man sitting next to him at the bar said.

'Nah, I'm not a regular. You?'

'You can say so. I room upstairs.'

'Oh, really?' Segert turned to talk to him.

'It has its charms. Good for transport. What brings you?'

'I was looking for a girl, thought maybe she'd be here.'

'All the girls here are by the hour. I'll get you the best; I know you.'

'Nee, nee, not like that.'

'You need Dutch courage, my friend,' his new friend insisted. 'The name's Lee.' He clinked his beer bottle against Segert's.

Segert asked if Lee had heard of Augustine. He showed him the photo.

'Pretty face, I'd remember her. Put the picture away.'

The photo was already damaged and bent from living in his back pocket. He kept pristine photos of Augustine and Justice in his notepad.

Lee wasn't ashamed or shy about his proclivities. He took Segert to a table just past the centre of the room and introduced him to his friends. It occurred to Segert that it was the first time he'd spoken to a group of coloured men. Spoken to so many at once. They were relaxed with drink and the prospect of sex, and they invited him to sit down, teased him, made rude jokes. Perhaps in this place of easy sex, every man with a little money was equal. Over the two or three hours, they rotated through rounds of beers, and they shared a tucked-away tenderness that perhaps had drawn them together, to this place. Or maybe it was the sauce.

'That's a sweet picture. Someone would pay her, enough to go away and not see them in this place again,' Craig said. He was about thirty, was slender, and had a natural charisma. His head moved a lot when he spoke, so it gave him the effect of being a comedian. Everything he said was flippant and funny.

Somebody whistled from the far corner of the room when Brown Sugar walked through the door. She nodded and scanned the room as she made her way to her pimp. But nobody else noticed her. The room was smoky, and the atmosphere filled with lazy sex jokes and bets for the local soccer game on Saturday. She was late. She was just a dumb skirt who'd get cut if she tried to steal someone's spot. So, when she walked to Segert's table, the other prostitutes were confident on the laps of tonight's amour. Maybe she could relieve someone of some change or a drink at the bar. There were always old men in the cobwebs. The spoils had already been taken and divided.

When she headed straight for Segert, both prostitutes chuckled. Every professional should be able to tell, he was tight. Nobody was getting a red cent out of him. They could muscle her out easily tonight. Tomorrow and yesterday was a different game, but tonight she was on their turf.

Brown Sugar walked up to the table, chin up, accentuating her thin long neck. She was wearing makeup tonight, and her eyes were big and intelligent. Her lashes round and blackened with mascara, a golden shimmer across her eyelids. Her lips were smudged lightly with the remnants of a light mauve lipstick. Her long nails were coral orange. She was turned out.

She swung a small red bag behind her shoulder. She was tipsy or high, and walked as if on the edge of a cliff in her high heels.

'We meet again.' She smiled at Segert. 'You have a new look, though.'

He hadn't noticed her walking towards him, and wasn't prepared for the energy shift across the table.

'New job?' she asked.

'I've got business. Same as you.' Segert put a grin in his eyes. 'Can I get you a drink? Let's go to the bar.'

Ja, I have a minute for you.'

'I bet you do,' Segert said, so that everyone at the table could hear him. 'Maybe I'll catch you guys later.'

So far, the most satisfying thing about the night was the looks on their faces when he and Brown Sugar walked off.

'You can put a bottle on your expense account for me, Mister.' She winked, stroking his hand.

'You like taking things too far.'

'It's a crime to have fun now?'

'What you having?'

'Brandy and Coke.'

'You look nice. How's your night?' Segert asked.

'Thank you. Big date, let's leave it at that.'

'Let's.' Segert took a sip of his beer.

'Still looking for your girl?'

Segert thought for a second, then just went along with it. 'Yes.'

'Told you.'

'What was that? I don't recall.'

'She doesn't want to be found.'

'You're only talking about yourself.'

She was gulping her drink. 'Aren't we all, Mister.'

'Pro wisdom,' Segert said flatly.

'Did your friends over there help you?' She nodded in their direction.

'Where'd you go tonight, anyway?' Segert asked her, ignoring the question.

Her pupils were dilated and her body seemed looser than it should be. 'To heaven and back, then to this *blerrie* outpost.' She laughed.

'Do you stay here?'

She just chuckled. 'Don't worry about me, I'm fine. Especially now I'm talking to your poor white self. Imagine, who knew my night would end like this?'

Segert didn't mind her insults. She never pretended to be something she was not. He could deal with that. 'Have you seen my girl around?'

'No. And I'm not asking anyone else, either. You're not turning me into a search party.'

'I thought I'd get you into recruitment,' he joked. 'It's dangerous on the streets.'

'Not this again. Thanks for the drink. I have to go.'

She strutted off, spilling her drink as she went, to a back table and handed over the little red handbag to her young pimp sitting at a table with two other men. He opened it, took out the money and nodded, then handed her a key from his jacket pocket. Then he gave her a kiss, a kiss that a loving boyfriend would give. And then didn't seem to talk to her again.

Segert leaned his foot against the footrail underneath the bar, finishing his beer. '*Tot siens.*' *Until I see you again.* He nodded to the table he'd been sitting with as he walked out.

'*Saloot.*' They raised their glasses a fraction.

Before Segert started his car, he took a picture of the Outlier Bar. The washed-out grey exterior and chipped windowsills red with rust, the interior light shining through the dirty curtain net.

If only time was kinder, what a beauty she'd still be, he thought. In the distance, he could make out the orange flames from a steel drum heating the homeless under a highway.

He checked the parking lot, then got out of his car again quickly, and ran around the back of the hotel, towards the small alley by the railway fence. It smelled like a toilet. He put his camera in his belt and relieved himself quickly. He looked through the window for Brown Sugar, and took out his Pentax camera, taking a few quick shots of her and zooming in on her pimp. Then he started back to his car.

From inside, he heard someone shout, 'The Boers are here!' and the sound of glass smashing on the floor as a table was overturned or pushed aside. He slowed down at the edge of the alley and peered around the edge slowly into the parking lot. There was no one there. No police vans or oncoming sirens.

They mean me? he wondered.

Then came the sound of dozens of shoes running onto the train station platform. Four men jumped across the railway line onto the opposite platform and disappeared through a hole in the fence and up a spiral staircase into the darkness of the flour mill parking lot.

Brown Sugar was hurrying in stuttering haste along the outer edge of the platform, her hand gripping her pimp, who could've been gone already. A crowd was running past them, bumping her along. She wanted to shout at them, and her pimp wanted her to let go.

For Segert, it was the most honest display between man and woman he'd ever witnessed. They were both trying to get away; he was stronger and faster, and she was holding him back. Still, they tussled lightly and got away safely together. Both of them mad at each other.

Then, at the top of Kliptown Road, came the flash of lights driving like a bullet towards the Outlier Bar. The lights of an unmarked police car. No one inside the bar would be able to see the lights unless they could see right up to the highway.

The flash of his camera, and his pale face peering through the window, was the cause of tonight's drama. Walking back to his car would expose him as the culprit to the night turning sour. He slinked against the fence and headed towards the darkness underneath the ramp of the highway. He didn't want to answer any questions. He tore across the open field. The stones and gravel underfoot sounded like the stitches holding his life together were coming undone. He was running out of his skin. He ran towards the nearest concrete columns under the highway. He looked back and saw the siren had already passed the Outlier Bar and was heading straight down the road. It was a black undercover car with sirens on the dashboard. He turned to watch it pass, then looked back to the motel. The police car slowed around a corner and disappeared around the edge of a perpendicular road.

Segert ran towards the corner. At the next column, two men were standing by the side of a perforated steel drum fire, their eye sockets deep with hunger and violence. They appeared to be roasting a large rat on a skewer, and drinking a five-litre bottle of clear wine. They were the type of people who had lived with violence since they were children and preferred to live on the edge of society. Segert carried on walking towards the road. He'd walk back to his car under the streetlamps.

When he got to the curb, he noticed the police car parked further along the road. The industrial estate showed little sign of life, just the distant sound of a hammer clanging steel. No one was on the street. The undercover police car was empty. Across the road was a grey van with the South African National Police Force yellow-and-blue insignia printed across its double doors.

Segert walked round the corner, into a road where the buildings were all dark. A car drove along the road behind him, and the headlamps reflected the yellow eyes of a feral cat sitting on the brick wall of an ironmongers called ToolShed.

Segert checked the cab of the van, but it was empty. He peered into the buildings for any tell-tale signs: lights and voices. Three doors down, he saw the glow of a chlorine crime scene light shining dimly under the edge of a black steel side gate. Then came the squeaking wheels of a trolley towards him. It was Willem Du Plessis, pulling a body trolley. An older coroner was walking behind the trolley, not touching anything.

Segert jogged towards him. 'Hey, Willem, what's going on?'

Willem was surprised by the voice. 'Hey, what you doing here?'

'I just saw the sirens and came over. What happened?'

'Nothing. Looks like this guy had a heart attack and was lying here since the weekend. The sirens give them a hard-on.' He nodded to two plainclothes policemen coming out through the gate. 'They're just here to relieve the uniforms, so they can go back on patrol. Did you find your girl yet?'

'No.'

'That's why you're chasing sirens?'

'It's a long story. Can I tell it to you some other time?' Segert eyed the older man, who grunted deeply under his breath and opened the back of the van.

'Sure. You know where I am.'

'You working nights now?'

Willem opened the back doors of the coroner's van. 'Just helping out. I'm back to days on Wednesday.'

* * *

Segert walked back to his car along the road, avoiding the chaos under the highway.

His car was now the only one in the lot. Him taking a leak in the alley had cost the bar a good night and the girls some business. He laughed as he turned on the ignition and reversed out the parking lot. Everything that touched Augustine's case went a sharp left. He cruised the highway north, his window open. The cold air beating his shirt lightly. The cold air kept him planted in the present. The long open highway was the safest place to be, but sometimes it gave his mind too much space.

By the time Segert parked in his driveway, Orange Grove was quiet. His ears were ringing from the circus laughter and war stories of the bar, the sound of crashing glass and overturned tables. He smelled of smoke and beer and his stomach was still empty. The 7-Eleven was closed. He only had baked beans and wet dog food in the cupboard. Solomon's Saloon was still open, but that would start a spiral that would pull at him for weeks. So he fed his dogs and ate the beans out of the can.

He developed the pictures in his dark room and made plans to exercise with the dogs the following day. He still needed to wrap up another lightweight industrial espionage case. He'd only have to break into an office at night, copy faxes, some paperwork. It should be easy.

When he finally made it into bed, he lay there strumming the hairs on his flat stomach as he drifted to sleep, thinking about Richard Reader and his spreadsheets; about Brown Sugar and a skinny little pimp with sweet kisses and a gold tooth; about Augustine and little baby Justice in that life.

CHAPTER 8

It was 5.39. A happy yellow sun shone on the corner of the TV screen. Augustine left the TV on all night — she still wasn't used to the place and had trouble falling asleep. It was the first of September, the unofficial beginning of spring.

The house creaked in its own murmuring sleep. The low humming of the fridge and freezer in the kitchen down the hall was comforting: food was close. Her stomach rumbled. Outside, a red-winged starling squawked, defending his nest from a feral cat that crept up trees, destroying nests and tearing at little birds. Last Friday, Paulus had picked up a broken nest at the bottom of the cypress in the back garden. He'd thrown the little chick corpses in the black bag with the mowed kikuyu grass, twigs and dried leaves.

The right side of Augustine's head was sore, a strange trailing sensation that went across the right side of her face as if a tiny axe had hit her across the head. The call of the bird stung her inner ear.

Justice was lying next to her. On his back, with his arms stretched out. She couldn't imagine a baby girl lying like that. She herself was curled up like the capital letter C around him. His eyes flickered in a dream, and then, sensing her breath, opened as he woke up. He moved his crooked face close to her and made a high moan. She kissed him on the forehead and shooed him back to sleep. She looked at the room around her: the rust-coloured walls; the old pink floral curtains that she pegged to the pole on the wall to keep them from falling down; the tiny black-and-white TV that was her only source of adult conversation most days.

Maggie kept her shining the furniture so hard, one day she was sure to start a fire. Paulus only came on Mondays and Fridays, to water the lawn and trim the evergreen hedges that lined the allée to the front door. No one ever used that side of the house. The door at the side of the living room at the end of the driveway was the door all the guests used to enter the house. The front door was a relic from a time when neighbours used to visit each other, walking in the streets and popping over for a slice of milk tart.

Augustine's room was still bare. She'd wrangled her month's salary from Maggie, making excuses for nappies and formula. Maggie held back a week of wages. It was a good compromise. But it was long enough; she needed her own things, and Justice needed more toys and clothes. The only things she had were the clothes she'd come in and some things she'd bought at a charity shop in Rosebank. She touched the knob on the TV, turning the sound all the way down before switching it on.

Two presenters were sitting on a couch talking to someone, and she could tell from the guest's clothes and heavy spectacles that he was talking about something dry. Justice's breathing had become heavy and slow again. His finger wrapped around a lock of her hair. She opened his hand, one finger at a time, and got up out of bed, putting the pillow down on her side so he wouldn't fall out.

The floor creaked under her feet and she froze, listening for any movement from Maggie in the bedroom next door. Through the wall, all she could hear was a short sleepy snore as the older woman turned over. Augustine put on her socks and went to the bathroom. She ran a small hot bath, turning the taps open only slightly, so the water flowed noiselessly. Maggie would complain if the pipes started making that pulling noise. The coconut oil in the small plastic bottle on the windowsill was hardened from the overnight cold. She tossed it in the hot water to soften. It would be impossible to get her any of her fingers into the top, besides her pinkie, and all the oil would be at the bottom out of reach. Her nipples shrank slowly, but the cold strengthened her resolve. She had to get her things back. Today was the day she'd be heading back to Noon. She finished up, shivering in the cold of the small space. Making sure to put everything back carefully in its place.

Maggie's light was on now. Augustine would have to find the courage to ask a favour before she gained momentum for the day. The fear Maggie might refuse, and might enjoy refusing her, stung her skin like ants. She'd have to do it now.

* * *

Augustine'd wasted a few hours in the mall downtown, eating breakfast in the Wimpy diner, people-watching. She saw a man in the crowd ahead of her, up the escalator. The way he stood and the shape of his head pinched her in her breast, and dug deep until it touched the rawness of her heart. And though she'd never suffered from a fear of heights, sitting there drinking a hot chocolate in the Wimpy bar, she recognised this vertigo. Tucked behind hedges and walls and in the corner of a servants' quarters, she had thought about Teddy less and less. But now she was out in the open, and the same feeling slipped into the bottom of her belly. Not the nervous beat of butterflies. It slipped down thick and glutinous, cylindrical and heavy in the pit of her belly. The man could have turned around and reached into her stomach and taken that pulsing thing inside her.

When she bought the train ticket at the central station, she'd been worried someone might recognise her and she'd be caught on a forty-five-minute ride telling lies or making excuses to a nosy neighbour. She presented her ticket as soon as the platform was announced and walked to the newspaper stand. She bought a newspaper and tabloid magazine and walked to the last carriage.

Augustine's nose twitched the air outside Noon station. Then she crossed the intra-city road, and walked back into her old township. There weren't that many cars in the driveways; anyone who had a car was gone to work. The cars that were left behind were like hospital patients, waiting for an organ transplant. A headlight missing, a car up on bricks waiting for new tyres.

Augustine's house was further up Flamenco Circle, a road that went right around the neighbourhood. The street had one of the two only access routes into the township, and was located about ten kilometres from the closest police station. She lived in the musical section. The streets in the three-by-five-kilometre rectangle were called Pitch and Fiddle Streets, Saxophone Way, Harmonica Road. Truant teenagers wore their navy-blue school blazers and grey slacks as they sat in Rhapsody Park, smoking cigarettes on the swings and round-about. That used to be her; she used to sit there with her friends. Corkie, the scraggly mutt that belonged to Uncle Elvin in the first house on the corner, was still running down the street, smelling grass and fences. He smelled her shoes, and she paused to pet his head and say hello, but he barked at her. Startled, she struck out with her handbag, and he ran back down the road.

There was a fifty per cent chance her mother'd be home, but Augustine hoped she was still catching the day shifts at the local depot for the South African Brewery during the winter.

'Hey, you, what's-your-name?' Augustine called at a boy walking ahead of her on the pavement. He was short but strong, with thick skin and a strong backbone. He'd stopped in his tracks, and, when he turned to who was calling him, an angry look flashed in his almond-shaped cat eyes.

'What?' he asked, his nose flaring and his shoulders widening.

'Did you see my mother this morning?'

He looked her up and down. *Your* mother?' He spat out the words. He was that special type of independent child. He lurked the streets alone during the day, confronting feral dogs and begging for change. Then joining groups of kids after school for playtime before disappearing when the streetlights came on. 'I've got my own problems.'

She'd forgotten everyone's dramatic sensibilities in this section. Perhaps it was something in the drinking water.

'OK, OK. Sorry.' Mothers were a common problem. 'Did you see her?' she asked again, softening her tone.

'Do you have any sweets?' he asked her innocently. No trace of the angry quiver in his eyes.

'No.'

'Do you have money for a cool drink?'

'No.' She tutted and started walking up the road towards her house.

'What about money for some milk?' He walked behind her for a short while. 'Money for some chips? I'm hungry. I didn't even have breakfast.'

'I don't have money for you.'

'Why?' he asked.

She scoffed. She had things to do, and here he was asking for money. He walked towards a wind-beaten path of dried overgrown grass that went between two houses, then bent to pick something up.

'Ask Uncle Johnny,' he shouted, as he rubbed the sand off the discarded cigarette and disappeared up the path.

* * *

Augustine half-expected her mother to be home, pushing her flat feet around the living room in her old brown slippers. But the house was empty. The dishes from the last few nights lay in the sink. Pots filled with water over the gravy line to soak overnight, coffee cups and the cheap white plates caked hard with stew or curry. She tapped the plates with her finger and a cockroach scrambled under a bowl at the plughole. Its long antennae twitched quickly, giving her that itch she got when she looked at insects and rodents. The net curtain over the sink was thick with dust. It had never been washed, not for as long as she could remember. She'd never noticed before how dirty it was from the sand and the dust flying in with a low winter wind. It drooped from the effort of filtering the familiar sounds of the outside. The sound of a train in the distance, the faintest whirring of a helicopter. Someone was throwing stones or smashing shopfronts.

The bright-coloured plywood and aluminium kitchen chairs were chipped at the edges, revealing splinters in the back. Whoever was here last hadn't bothered to push them back under the table. There were white crumbs on the tabletop and black ants around the tiny sugar granules from a morning cup of coffee. She tripped on the corner of weathered vinyl flooring as she walked out of the kitchen, too uncomfortable with the dirt to make a cup of tea. It needed washing and straightening.

'I hate this house,' she mumbled to herself, before straightening up.

At the end of the narrow hall was a photo portrait of her as a toddler. The type of textured photography popular in the seventies that made photographs resemble paintings. The picture stopped her agitation for a second. She'd forgotten about it. The hall was narrow and dark, the floor crunching under her shoes with the debris of sand and pavement pebbles.

The door to her parents' bedroom was partly closed and she only glanced through the crack of the door out of habit. The room smelled of old cigarettes and damp. She held her breath and listened, then carried on to her bedroom. The door was closed. She pushed it open, half-expecting it to be a portal to her old life, full of remnants of adolescence mixed in with the early beginnings of Justice's life. But her bed was strewn with laundry. Her father's underpants, some with holes in the crotch; a half-dozen or so of her mother's bras hung carelessly from the bottom metal bedframe. The rest was a mix of winter clothes — polo necks, jeans and odd towelling socks. She scanned the room for the radio she'd got for her sixteenth birthday. The desk was dirty and had her mother's long wiry shed hair and round brush sitting abandoned in front of the small mirror.

The floor hadn't been swept; the furniture hadn't been polished. Her room hadn't been kept as a shrine. Her parents weren't waiting for her. If they had ever, it was a passing impulse. In her place was the detritus of her mother's habits. At least her father hadn't put his cases of empty Coke bottles in here yet. For now, they were still piling up in the kitchen.

'They didn't even leave space for Justice.' She looked at her face in the mirror. The disappointment vibrated on her skin.

From the chest of drawers under the window facing the small backyard, Augustine pulled out and packed the playsuits and small collection of bibs and booties that belonged to Justice. Pushing the crinkled laundry onto the dusty floor, she folded them expertly. Justice had outgrown most of them, but she was taking them anyway. Maggie would be proud of her folding now.

She took her jeans and her Sunday best shoes, which she never wore to church, because her father would never drive her. She wore them instead to some aunty's house for lunch or a family wedding.

She went through her drawers, folded her underwear and laughed at the tight little T-shirts and strappy vests she used to wear. She pulled together her jeans and Justice's things. She went into her jewellery box and retrieved her small green identity document and Justice's papers. Her whole life, now folded in four neat rows on her old bed. She used to dream of pop stars and schoolboys. Wondering who would kiss her next, did the boy she like notice her, what was the man she was going to marry doing, right now.

Augustine got down the two tattered vinyl box suitcases from the top of the old oak wardrobe. Then she said her good-byes to the cobwebs and dirt in the crevices of 108 Flamenco Way.

'I'm never coming back,' she said to herself. 'Not if someone is sick, or if someone is dying. Didn't even leave a place for their grandchild.'

She locked the black burglar gate protecting the front door and threw the key through the top of her parents' bedroom window. And she walked down the road with the two old suitcases holding the only things she wanted from her old life.

Old man Johnny was sitting at the end of the street listening to his radio, leaning against the streetlamp.

'Afternoon,' she said, as she passed.

A junkie lay in a heap under the drooping leaves of a small false olive tree on the pavement. Children would have to step over him on the way home from school.

'See you, aye,' Johnny said, waving at her as she walked down the street.

Augustine reflected that he must have seen all sorts on this street. People coming and going. Evictions, repossessions. The neighbourhood was in a divorce boom. There was a lot to witness from where he sat every day. He would greet her just the same if she came back, carrying those two suitcases and her baby on her back.

The wind smelled of newspapers and dirty car engines. The sun was baking the asphalt and burning into her fore-head. She turned the corner and stopped at the feeder road to the train station. The distance to Noon train station was too long to walk with suitcases, too short for a minibus taxi. If one came past this way to the station, it could already be full, no space for her.

She could walk it, badly. Sweating and looking more des-perate and broken than when she arrived. Augustine's eyes were riveted on the empty school ground in front of her, as she decided what lies to tell nosy taxi drivers if they asked about her luggage, or where she was going. She'd pay extra for the luggage of course; then say she was dropping it off for an aunty or granny.

'*Keep it light*,' she told herself, '*be fresh*.' She put the mask of her old self on her face.

An empty taxi was going into Noon but stopped dead when it saw her.

'Station?'

'Straight to town,' she answered.

They negotiated a price and she set off, leaving Noon in the rearview mirror.

The centre of Johannesburg was getting busier, but there was one more thing she had to do. She walked up the road to the big post office on Jeppe Street. She was out of place carrying the bags on her sides on a busy city street. Across the road, a man paced the pavement, appraising her. Her hair was tied up, and her neck muscles showed a little strain as she walked. He stopped at a lamppost to inspect his nails, and watched her walk past the gates for the post office vans then step into the old post office. He hadn't seen Augustine in years. She was a few years younger than him, but she'd grown into a fine young woman.

A grey armoured Transit van was parked close to the entrance, obscuring him. He crossed the road and waited at the side of the entrance to talk to her when she came outside.

He leered through the glass doors and saw her walking towards the bank of counters in the corner. She could use the help with her bags, he told himself. If she was withdrawing money, it would be a bonus. His father would be proud of him this time. They could offer her a lift to wherever she as going.

* * *

The building, like everything in this part of town, was part of a glorious moneyed era. The arched doorways could swallow her

72

and her two suitcases easily. The hands on the glass clock on the entryway told her it was almost three o'clock. She'd better get moving. Secrets were never her thing. Her best friend, Rosalind, would know what to do. She was the smart one. She'd be mad, give her a speech about how she hadn't been in touch for so long, but she'd come through. That much Augustine knew.

The Central Office was a large art deco building. She went to the closest public phone and called Rosalind. The answering machine picked up, and Augustine guessed Rosalind was still on her way back from campus.

'Hi Rosalind, guess who? Long time. I'm — we're fine. Wanted to say hi. I'm away for a while. I'll send you a letter soon.'

She had two of Teddy's Polaroids left. She didn't look at them — those ugly photos with the too-young girls — as she placed one in an envelope and wrote a short letter to Rosalind. Then she approached the counter, leaving her luggage at the stationery island. She bought stamps and enquired about renting a post box. Then she opened a savings book for Justice.

There was just one thing left to do before she went back to work.

She called Kliptown Catholic Secondary School and asked for Teddy. Teaching hours were over, and she figured he was in the teachers' office or the tiny school library.

She decided to try the office first, and leaned on the inside of the phone booth to steady her nerves.

'Hello, Teddy Beukes here. Hello?'

'It's me, and, before you ask, I'm not going to tell you where I am. Justice is fine.'

'Good. I was worried about you both.'

'Stop lying. Both of us know what I found. You're sick.'

'What do you want?' he whispered. There was the clink of china, as someone in the background got up to make a cup of tea.

'Get a pen. I need you put R500 a month in this account.' She gave him the account number. 'The account belongs to

Justice, and I registered it at the main post office. So . . .' She trailed off, unsure what to say next.

'For how long?'

'Until Justice is eighteen; what do you think?'

'You're not going to do anything with those pictures. If I go to jail, you won't get any money.'

She hadn't thought that far. For a second, she didn't know what to say. Then she said, 'You know what happens to guys like you in prison? The only person keeping you alive is Justice. If it wasn't for him, I would've gone to the police station a long time ago.' She hung up the phone. Two money guards walked across the lobby, and Augustine hung back, retreating into the telephone booth. She took Justice's savings book and the last Polaroid and popped them in the security box, leaving the key in her wallet. Better to be safe than sorry. If she was stopped by police she didn't want to have this with her anymore.

* * *

Two uniformed men exited the arched doorway. One carrying a gun and behind him another pushing a trolley filled with a case of money.

'Hey, move,' the man with the gun yelled at him.

The man with the cash stopped to look, then nodded and walked to the back of the van.

'I'm waiting for someone,' the man said.

'Go wait somewhere else.'

'Can't a man just wait in peace?'

'Go!' He waved his gun.

The pavement cleared of pedestrians and people coming out of the post office turned around and went back inside.

The man knotted his fist but walked away. 'Where am I supposed to wait then?'

'Go across the road, must I show you?'

He walked down further down the street away from the entrance and watched the cash transit men climb in the van.

He gave them the finger when they drove off. His father always told him he had to keep a low profile, but he never listened.

* * *

Augustine left the post office at the side entrance to Kruis Street. It was closer to the bus station. She felt lighter, without any dirty Polaroids stuck in her wallet.

'Hello, my child,' Zula said, climbing slowly up the bus stairs. 'I see you have your bags with you, hey? You are OK now.'

'Yes, Mama. Yes, you helped me a lot.' Zula was happy to see her and this meant that her Polaroids were still undiscovered.

'You must come out with us again. The church is organising a trip next Saturday.' She was careful not to apply any pressure. These young ones don't like people telling them what to do. Silently, she placed a small, typed pamphlet in Augustine's hand.

'Yes, yes. I must.' Augustine rearranged her suitcases in the aisle. 'I'm so happy to see you.'

'And your baby?' the old lady asked, pulling her wool.

'He's at home with the maid,' Augustine said. It wasn't strictly a lie, she convinced herself.

'Well, you landed on your feet.' The old lady didn't look up to catch the lie in Augustine's face.

'I have nine lives,' Augustine joked, hoping the old lady wouldn't question why she was still catching the bus.

Zula was searching in her bag for a piece of paper. 'Do you have a pen?'

Augustine nodded and handed her an old blue pen from her handbag.

'You can always call me at my son's place.'

'But he's married, I don't want to—'

Zula shushed her. 'He's a man of the cloth, his wife is used to it.'

They sat together in silence and Augustine didn't know when she'd sit next to a friend again, saying nothing.

When the old lady got off at her stop, she turned to Augustine.

'That other thing you left behind . . .' she bit her lips together. 'Give it up to God.' She nodded as she descended the stairs.

Give it up to the junkie, Johnny on the corner, or God.

CHAPTER 9

Segert Berger drove down the sandy streets in Noon. The tiny angular houses, once bright purples, lime green and pinks, were losing their powers. Like players in a hysterical showband that blew all night, then collapsed under the first charge of the sun. He passed Augustine's house and parked across the street, a few houses up, close to a local mechanic. His box-shaped BMW invisible among a collection of Volvos and Camrys in for a tune-up or oil change. He left the car on the curb and walked down the street, taking in the view. An old man sat on a black crate at the top curve of the street behind him, listening to a small transistor radio. Mixed teams of boys and girls were playing soccer in one half of a park between two parallel roads. Younger ones were playing on the swings and slides. Nothing out of the ordinary.

Segert crossed the street without looking for traffic and moved to talk to a skinny boy around nine or ten. He was sitting alone on a red merry-go-round, inspecting his soccer ball for a leak, his lips pursed as he whistled. He looked up at Segert's approach and continued caressing his ball, but he stopped whistling.

Segert made eye contact. Since the boy didn't move away, he thought he might strike up a conversation.

'You from here?' Segert asked, as he sat down on the next slice of the merry-go-round.

The boy put the ball down by his foot and looked at Segert, but said nothing.

The soccer match slowed down. There was less shouting, and the ball was passed gently from player to player. Both keepers had their eyes on Segert and the boy.

'Do you know a girl called Augustine? She lives down the road just past the end of the park, over there.' Segert pointed to her house, half-concealing an R10 note in his palm. The boy's eyes widened for a second, then he restrained himself.

Ja, I know Augustine.' The boy gave an imperceptible signal, and the game resumed its previous pace.

'When did you see her last?'

The boy stared off in the distance. Berger knew he was imagining what he could do with a ten rand he had not planned on getting.

'Eh?' Segert prodded him gently. Still no answer. Just another large-eyed look. He started to push the merry-go-round with his left foot.

He extended his arm, and the boy smartly opened his hand without looking at Berger. The kid had cool. He had to give it to him.

'I haven't seen her for a while,' he lied. She'd been here two weeks ago, she didn't give him any change even for a cool drink. But, no matter, he wouldn't tattle. If this man was looking for her it was trouble for her.

'How long is a while?'

'A good few months, Mister. Long.'

'Do you know where she went?'

The boy hopped off the merry-go-round and kicked his ball to the ground, moving closer to the other kids on the makeshift pitch.

'I don't bother with girl business,' he said matter-of-factly. He did a few tricks with his ball. Showing off for his friends and Segert. Both teams cheered for him, and Segert walked off, holding back how impressed he was by the wild-cat's skill. If he truly kept out of girls' business, he might have a future somewhere someday.

The old man on the crate looked on bemused. He'd been watching the exchange along with everyone else and, when Segert walked to his car, he felt the slow eyes following him. He turned around and walked up the street towards him.

'Hello, boss.' Segert was playing his cards. If he wound him up, something might fall out.

A loud commercial played on the radio as the two of them tried to outstare each other. Segert, standing up, felt he had the advantage, but the old man kept looking up at him.

This one has a lot of pluck, Segert thought. 'I'm looking for Augustine.'

'Another one.' The old man laughed a single laugh and looked towards Augustine's house.

'What do you mean, another one?'

'Another oppressor.'

'Who was the other one?'

'The one that sent you here.'

'What makes you think someone sent me here?'

'You look used to taking direction.'

But not you, thought Segert. *Nobody tells you what to do.*

'Can I buy you a Coke?' He tried breaking the ice.

'And a packet of cigarettes, Dunhill. And matches and a loaf of brown bread.'

'Must I throw in a small packet of polony?'

'Suit yourself.'

When Segert came back, he extracted that the man's name was Old Johnny, he had a dog and Augustine had returned home about a month ago and packed up her things in two old vinyl suitcases, one cream and a brown one with a thin navy border. She hadn't been seen since.

'She took her bags; she's living it up somewhere. But she'll be back.'

'A month?' Segert asked. If he said a month ago it was probably two weeks ago, maybe even one. Everybody told half-truths. Nobody around here was going to tell him the truth. But his story did fit with the little boy's. He turned to look at him playing soccer, but everyone had gone. 'Here's my card. Give me a call when she comes back, or you hear anything.'

Johnny took a long sip of his warm beer. 'Everyone thinks there's something out there, places to go. There's here, and that's it.' His foot tapped along to a radio commercial.

CHAPTER 10

The pink tube of processed meat reminded Segert of dog food. The garlic smell and pink colour had always made his stomach feel a little loose. Johnny had eaten chunks of the polony like it was an apple, followed by large gulps of beer. Berger couldn't get away from the smell of garlic and beer burps fast enough. He drove out from Noon, not registering anything around him: the dogs wrestling with laundry drying in the backyard, the people walking on the pavement or even the colours of the houses. Memories existed somewhere. And he had no use for a memory of this place. If he needed to come here again, he would rediscover it, and let the experience slip shapeless over him.

Segert stopped at a Checkers supermarket to buy two cans of Pedigree for Trigger and Simba. He called Teddy from a payphone while he waited for his take-away burger from a Steers quick-service restaurant. Teddy answered on the third ring.

'Look, man, I think she's really left her parents,' Segert said.

'What do you mean?'

'I spoke to some people here, and they haven't seen her for a while. Some people said she came one day when her parents were at work and took her stuff.' Segert side-stepped that his informant was Johnny, the defiant old man on the corner.

81

'So, what does this mean?' Teddy asked.

'One of two things. She is somewhere, I don't know where, but maybe a friend or relative knows. Or she is somewhere nobody knows, and that makes it a big net.'

'Well, you have to find her. I know she's still in Jo'burg.'

'Is there something you want to tell me?'

'It's just a feeling. I can't describe it.' Teddy was lying. He'd received an empty postcard just two days ago, postmarked from Johannesburg Post Office. The front was of a group of Swazi girls, dressed in their traditional skirts and elaborate white-and-green beaded necklaces, that skimmed their bare breasts. It was the type of postcard you could find at any souvenir shop, probably for sale at the local post office, and meant nothing on its own.

'I need names and numbers of close friends and relatives of hers. People her own age. Do you have any?'

'She used my landline a few times. I still have some bills; I can check.'

'I need all the information you've got, Teddy. Don't give it to me in dribs and drabs.'

'OK, OK. I'll call you when I've got it.'

If Teddy wanted to piss his money up the tree, Segert wasn't going to stop him. Single mothers were always looking for the fathers of their children. As far as he knew, this one skipped town with the baby and didn't want anything from him. The Lord really knows how to make different kinds of people, Segert thought. He licked his upper lip absentmindedly. He would've had a drink on the way home, but Teddy'd killed his mood and all his big regrets began with a drink in a dark mood.

* * *

Later that week, Teddy gave him a few numbers from his phone bill with a jumbled explanation of the people the numbers related to.

Teddy was a real slob, Segert realised, just no attention to detail. He hadn't thought about it before, but Teddy was from a different generation. A soft generation that couldn't tie their own shoelaces or find their own arses. Gone were the days when men were men. Strong and decisive. Segert wouldn't even leave Teddy in charge of his dogs. Sure, he was nice to have a chat with, even in his faded stovepipe jeans, but he was beginning to wonder if Augustine had maybe done the right thing. Still, that much was none his business. Finding the baby was really the deal, because that's what Teddy was paying for.

After making a few calls, he tried a woman called Rosalind, referred to in his notes as Augustine's cousin.

'Hi, I'm looking for Rosalind,' Segert asked in his most casual voice.

Rosalind became nervous when she heard the voice. This was the kind of voice she heard when she was behind on her accounts. 'Er, speaking,' she said.

Sensing her anxiety, Segert tried to soften the Afrikaaner thumpiness in his voice. 'Hello, I'm looking for your cousin Augustine. Have you seen her?'

'No, I haven't,' she answered quickly. 'I know she had a baby a short time back. I haven't even seen him.'

'Do you know if anyone has seen or heard from her?'

'What's this about? And who are you?' Her voice went down a defensive octave.

'I'm Segert Berger. I was hired to find her.'

'By her parents?'

'Yes,' Segert lied. 'Sort of.' He knew he had to lessen any deceptions, so he added, 'Well, if I find her, your aunt and uncle will know where she is, too.' That was in the neighbourhood of the truth, at least.

'I haven't seen her, and they're not really my aunt and uncle. Augustine and me sort of made ourselves cousins. But I know someone saw her a good few months ago. I can't remember where.'

'Really?'

'Yes, you know, really.'

Good God, she has a bite, Segert thought.

'It's one of my neighbours, down the road,' Rosalind finished.

'Does this neighbour have a phone number?'

'I'm not sure she'd like me giving her number to strangers. Give me yours; I'll pass it on.'

He gave her his full name and number. 'If I don't hear from her, I'll just keep calling your house.'

'Don't harass me, Mr Berger. Goodbye.'

He heard the click of the phone in his ear. *My nerves*, he thought. She was a cold one. Augustine wasn't going to open up to her, that was for sure.

Segert was at the grocery store, buying five kilos of dry dog food for Simba and Trigger. Rosalind snapping the phone down on him retuned his mood. He wanted some cases with action. He didn't say it to himself consciously, but his body was itching for a thrill ride. The storminess of a fist fight, the growling and adrenaline of some real drama. Or at least the salaciousness of catching a husband cheating on his wife with a pretty young thing. He enjoyed peeping through windows and seeing things he wasn't supposed to.

He reckoned Petersen must've been pissed at him, to give him a case this dull. This case was as dry as the dog food he was carrying on his shoulder. He called Petersen from the parking lot.

'Man, do you have any cases for me?'

'More? You have as much as you can handle. What happened?' Petersen asked.

'Nothing. Your office is full of situations.'

Petersen laughed at this. 'I count three jobs you're on for me.'

'No, man. Come on. They're all dry.' He hated working for corporations; the bureaucracy always slowed everything down.

'You mean you haven't got anybody to beat up yet.' Petersen laughed even harder.

'You know me. Why you give me cases like this?'

'I'm running out of favours at the municipal court, trying to keep you out of jail. There won't be any for myself. It's pure economics.'

'Economics? How come I'm the one living in a doghouse and you're living in a palace?'

'Come over for a *braai* tomorrow. Free booze usually piques you.'

'I've known you too long, you airhead. Is Doreen making you swallow a dictionary?'

'Don't you ever think of breaking up with me,' Wes said.

Segert made a loud kissing noise into his phone, and heard the click on the other end.

* * *

Segert Berger pulled up to Wes's Tuscan-hybrid mansion. The white walls shone like a lighthouse out from between the two large trees on each side of the entrance. He grabbed the cold six-pack of Windhoek lagers that he just bought at the grocery store down the road. It was almost twice the price as on Segert's side of town, and he wasn't impressed with the cashier when he handed over his credit card. Getting beers for a *braai* was the kind of thing his ex-wife used to be good at. She also made a mean potato salad. He straightened his shirt involuntarily at the memory of her and made his way to the front door. Before he knocked, Wes opened the front door, showing a broad mouthful of white teeth.

'Howzit.' They slapped hands on each other's backs and Wes let him in the house.

'We're sitting in the garden. Well, I'm sitting in the garden. The wife is in the kitchen. Don't ask me what she's doing in there.'

'I like the paint job.'

85

'Don't mention it, for God's sake. The whole street is up in arms about my house being the wrong colour. Like a bunch of vultures on my neck, squawking about hues of fawn.'

The house had a wide interior with large windows looking over the garden. He noticed that dark wooden beams had been worked into the ceiling and the large Persian carpet had been changed out recently. The new addition was a thick light-grey shag. Their kids were getting big now, if they could have almost-white carpets. He followed Wes to the kitchen to meet Doreen, who would inevitably be poised over a salad wearing diamond earrings, a half-finished glass of wine next to her. She turned from the sink to give Segert a kiss on the cheek.

'Bloody hell. Haven't seen you for a while.' She kissed him gently on the cheek.

Segert had always liked her; she was thin and attractive, but had a mind sharp as a whip. He never knew what she saw in Wes. She probably matched him in salary and came from money, yet had given him two children. She could've done better.

'*Ja*, man, it's been too long.' Segert smiled, genuinely happy to see her. 'How long do I have to carry these beers, man? I didn't come here for hard labour,' he said to Wes. Doreen tossed the salad again and poured herself a glass of wine.

Doreen and Janette, his now-ex-wife, had been sort of close. They got on whenever the four of them went out together. Truth be told, Doreen had been close with his first ex-wife as well. Probably still was now. Couldn't fault them, or Doreen, really. He just wasn't the commitment type.

'I like what you've done with the place,' Segert said.

'I'll send my interior designer over, should I?' Doreen joked.

Wes put the beers in the fridge and grabbed a cold Windhoek for Segert from the fridge door. 'Here you go,' he said walking out to the patio, leaving Doreen to finish in the kitchen.

They sat in the shade looking out at the pool and over the ridge to the suburbs below. The large tree they were sitting under had two vintage birdcages hanging not far from their heads. Fat white candles encased in plexiglass sat in the middle of each. Segert pulled a face.

'You know what Doreen is like. She's always hanging something somewhere.' Wes sipped his beer.

'Looks like you two are getting romantic out here,' Segert joked. He could imagine them sitting here at night having a meal under candlelight, drinking wine with the slow rustling of the leaves as music.

'It was a bloody headache to put there. And I have to get the ladder to light the candles. But OK, you need to keep the wife happy.' Wes winced immediately. 'Sorry about that, man.'

'No worries, china.'

'Oh no.'

'Oh no, what?' Segert asked.

'When it's china-time, it's problem time. When last did you see her? Janette, I mean.'

'A few weeks ago.'

'For what? To talk about old times?'

'Well, we did reminisce.' Segert smiled.

Wes shook his head. 'Oh no. Let me guess, when Janette tells Doreen the story, it'll sound like you promised her the world again. Enjoy our hospitality; it'll be the last time the wife allows.'

Segert changed the subject. 'This is all you.' He pointed his beer to the birdcages. 'There was always something Liberace about you.'

'I have the fine features for the stage,' Wes said, squinting his eyes as if looking into the distance, stroking the hook of his nose.

Wes wasn't an ugly man. He had a prominent long nose and springy black hair he wore in a ponytail to cover a bald spot. But he had a broad, sneaky smile that made anyone feel comfortable.

Wes and Segert met eleven or twelve years ago. Wes was still green and interested in working in criminal justice. He should've gotten a nice divorce attorney job. Splitting up assets and screwing people over when they were at their most emotional, when the only thing they could focus on was the soon-to-be ex.

But back then, there was a feeling that things were changing. Not just in the hinterlands, the places where the clouds had long been brewing. Things were changing in the suburbs. The international sporting ban delivered some blows. Nobody invited the National cricket team. Sanctions had spread to almost every sport and tour. Boredom of provincial matches became brooding, heavy fear pulling at everything.

And then a blonde teenager, her family recently transplanted from upcountry, had been found in some woodland. Stabbed and burned. It was all over the papers. The 'black terror' was coming late at night, killing innocent little white girls. The Boogeymen, the thick reservoir of a patient force of millions was ready to burst its banks. Either that, or devil worshippers were in the suburbs under the watchful eyes of their parents. For once, the entire country was united in one truth.

Wes got his nose wetter than a fish on that case. A little blonde with her face burnt off got through to the small soft core of Segert, too. The soft core that was left after he'd crawled on his belly out of the South-West and Angola.

Segert and Wes had been friends ever since.

'So how the cases treating you?'

'You got me a nice mix.'

'Something corporate, something domestic, this missing girl is ticking over slowly. Should be easy stuff. Beukes looks like he'd shell out some. The grocery store chain should be your bread-and-butter stuff from now on . . .' Wes took a sip from his beer.

'*Ja*, the Reader story seems like a lot of nothing. I just have to keep following this guy and seeing who he's meeting. Who's the client really? He works for SASOL; is it them?' He meant the South African Coal, Oil and Gas Corporation.

'Since when do you care? They gave you a whole month to follow him, give his whereabouts and steal his briefcase.'

'The advance is keeping me ticking over, but I'm not stealing his briefcase. It'll tip him off. I don't know if you want to tell the client that. I'm getting the contents another way.'

'I think that's OK for now. You've got time and if push comes to shove you have something to produce. Make a folder, keep it at your house. I'll speak to the client closer to the time. They're not expecting regular in-depth updates. I just tell them you're still on it.'

'Employment problem? Can I ask?' Segert said.

'Just want to know Reader's regular associates, and the contents of the case.'

'No problem,' Segert said.

'And what about Beukes?' Wes asked, wiping the dew off his beer bottle.

'That boy still needs wet wipes.' Segert laughed. 'I've got a few leads — one solid one — but it's not as easy as you would think for a runaway. I would've thought she's probably dead.'

'Really?'

Ja. I mean, don't reckon she can negotiate the streets. I could use a woman to talk to her when I find her. Make life easier.'

'Who you thinking of asking?'

'I'm not close to finding her yet. Anyway, the girl, Augustine — if she's still alive — doesn't want to be found.'

'You could leave her alone; give Beukes back his money.' Wes smiled and took an exaggerated sip of his beer.

'I've already invested it in stocks and shares,' Segert replied.

Doreen brought a platter of seafood and salads. 'What story you spinning now, Segert?'

'Nothing gets past her,' Wes said. His playfulness tucked away from his wife.

'I thought we were having a *braai*.' Segert loved the smell of coals and the sizzle of meat on a hot sunny day. Men standing in shorts, beer in hand, watching meat roast.

'Have to watch the cholesterol, I'm told.' Wes patted his small belly.

Segert watched them: Doreen's self-satisfaction, Wes's mixture of gluttony and love. Wes getting up to get more drinks. It was the looking after each other. It made sense in a small way, and Segert was content just watching the concert of it. Content and a little uncomfortable. He took a big gulp of Windhoek, burped loudly and patted his stomach. He missed his dogs.

CHAPTER 11

Kimberly Diamond materialised late one afternoon in the middle of September when spring was showing off all her colours. The sky was pink and orange, the clouds fluffy like candy floss. It was one of the first days that felt long but easy.

She sat in the passenger seat, a troubled look on her face. Her legs were wrapped in a light blue blanket. Her hair, which had usually appeared to have been whisked to a bouncy froth, lay greasy and lifeless on her head. She played with a hangnail as Martin parked the car and quickly walked to the boot.

The house at Number 68 with its raised *stoep*, stained glass library, remote operated black wrought iron gates, exuding the height of Transvaal elegance, had become the only hospital on Belgravia Road. The front room was a waiting room, where Augustine served tea while Martin made small talk with the latest round of visitors.

'Yes, she is very weak.'

'We mustn't keep her up too much.'

Martin fielded all the questions. He sat on the overstuffed leather chair, his feet at the three-panel fireplace screen, his right foot wriggling on the left. Behind the chair was a mantel displaying six fresh-cut lilies that Paulus brought with him every Friday. Next to the bouquet, a wedding photograph of Martin and Kimberly. It showed off Kimberly's petite frame, the tight fullness of the ivory satin train of her dress.

Augustine walked outside, chewing the last bit of her chicken barbecue sandwich. Paulus threw a load of dirt to the side of the wall. Behind him were a line of plants that he and Martin Diamond had picked up earlier that morning at a local garden centre. The thin black bags around the roots were open, the roots exposed.

'I thought you'd want a Coke.'

'Is there brandy in it?'

'It's too hot for brandy. Besides, it's bad for your blood.'

'Nothing wrong with my blood.' Paulus turned to take the tumbler of Coke. He could see into the living room. Martin had his back to the window, sitting at the dead fireplace. 'Who is it today?'

'I dunno. Maggie handles the register. I only serve tea and biscuits.'

'He's not very chatty these days.' Paulus sipped the Coke. 'You know what it is.'

'Everybody knows what it is,' Augustine said nonchalantly. 'I just never seen it with my own eyes.'

'They have it where you from?' Paulus asked.

'Obviously. I just never bothered about it. It was always some old uncle who got it. Then we had to go see him. If it was an auntie or a *lightie*, my mother and father went alone.'

'White people never get it. It comes pretty quick, though, if you don't catch it in time.' He bent down to his plants. 'I see he put up the wedding photo. That's bad luck, reminding everybody—'

'She can have a look at these flowers from the window.' Augustine tried to change the subject.

'It's too far for her now. She can't walk to the end of the top floor.'

The plants were a ground cover that flowered in spring and summer. The small buds were deep purples and lavenders.

'Nicholas will like it,' Augustine remarked.

'If she coughs up blood in tissue, bring it to me,' Paulus said, leaning on his spade.

'I'm not holding on to phlegm, never mind blood. That's disgusting.'

'I'll tie a piece of string around it, put it in a bowl of herbs and burn it. The ashes I'll mash with special red clay and bury with a pondo seed. When the tree grows, her sickness will be gone.'

'Yoh!' Augustine exclaimed. 'Do you want some Aromat for that a'so?' She laughed, referencing the light-yellow seasoning that was sprinkled on every dish in South Africa. 'Come have a sandwich and some tea. I dare you to tell Maggie this story.'

'She knows,' he said. 'She knows. Why don't you believe me?' he added, as he walked behind her to the kitchen. 'I'm an old man.'

This was supposed to count for a lot, but she paid him no mind. Her father had his own wisdom, more down to earth than Paulus's stories, and everyone knew he was under her mother's palm. Besides, Augustine had learned from her father and Teddy that a man was only wise when he was searching for an ally.

* * *

The boy approached Teddy at school on the first Friday of October. The top of the staff room door was hooked to the wall to create a cross-breeze. Like the rest of the school, it lacked heating and air-conditioning; the school preferred to spend any excess on the library, a place where homework and projects could be completed in relative peace. The school was already let out. Only a few students lingered on the sports field after volleyball and netball practice.

He peeped around the corner and raised his hand at the door. 'Sorry, sir. Mr Beukes, can I speak quickly, sir?'

He was wearing regulation grey school trousers and a white short-sleeve shirt under a grey pullover. His tie was missing but, as school was over, Teddy figured he'd put it in his schoolbag. Teddy didn't recognise the boy from any of his classes, but it was the beginning of the term and perhaps he wanted some extra tuition or wanted to change classes. He walked with the boy across the corridor to a railing that overlooked the school assembly area on the ground floor.

'Hello, sir.' The boy smiled. 'I want you to help me with some extra maths. I'm having a big problem.'

'Like I always say, *Maths is the key that unlocks all the—*'

The boy cleared his throat, interrupting Teddy, and from his back pocket revealed the edge of a photo that Augustine stole. 'Listen to me, sir,' the boy said respectfully. 'I need you to give me R200 a week, or this gets out.'

'More money? I'm not giving you anything. Where's Augustine?'

'Sir, I need you to remain calm. I want you to look out through the staff window, and I want you to see the group of boys standing across the road there. We know what car you drive, where you work and where you live.'

'I want to speak to Augustine.'

'That's up to her. I can't force a girl.'

'Where am I supposed to get more money?'

The boy laughed. A nonchalant laugh, more grown up than Teddy expected. 'I have my own problems. I'll be back here Friday.' He flicked the edge of the envelope and sauntered off.

He'd opened the letter when it came for Rosalind. He opened all her mail. Usually, she only had official letters from university. But the handwriting on the thick white enveloped piqued his interest. And there wasn't a return address. He thought maybe there was money inside, but it turned out it was even better. Augustine had given him a way to make some cash. Rosalind wouldn't do anything useful with this. She was too much of a goody-goody. She should keep her head in her books and not be distracted by Augustine's scandalous stories. Rosalind was there to look after him, she needed to get a good job one day as lawyer and work in an office. Move them out of Eldorado Park to a nice suburb. Not waste her time trying to rescue Augustine and her son.

Teddy's mind was racing. He was already putting money in Augustine's account. Who the hell was this boy, and how did he get that picture from Augustine? Was she just giving these to anyone, willy-nilly? At this rate, he'd have to go teach at a white school to afford all this blackmail.

The school secretary walked past him as he was leaning over the edge of a railing.

'You OK, Mr Beukes?'

'Yes, I'm fine. Just need to stretch my legs.'

'I know what you mean. Always good to keep your health in mind.'

CHAPTER 12

It was midnight. The last person Segert expected to hear from was Johnny, but, then again, drunks and druggies were like dogs. You had to treat them to what they craved, and they were yours. He'd left a message on the answering machine for Segert to meet him at ten o'clock on Friday morning.

But who was he kidding? He had nothing else to do and Segert knew no matter what time he turned up, Johnny'd be there, wearing his faded white T-shirt and jeans, sitting on the corner like an aged schoolboy on civvies day. Segert had to finish another job first.

He was just getting in from working on a light industrial espionage case, which involved breaking into the small first-floor office of Metro Cash 'n' Carry, a company operating wholesale stores selling groceries and fast-moving goods in an industrial block in Kyalami, just after ten the previous night. The windows weren't alarmed and the files hadn't been locked. He'd kneeled in the finance manager's office, adjusted the runner's lamp on his head and rummaged through the files for Christmas promotion, wholesale prices and offers. He was going to take photographs, but the finance manager, Danie De Kok, had his own printer.

'Thanks, Danie,' Segert said.

Being a private detective was always lonely work, but this was lonely and dry. The type of work his exes liked him to have. No women, no danger, no fist fights, no fun. Now they were through with him, and he could do whatever he liked.

Now he was finally doing what they wanted and there was no one around to give him credit for it. His mind trailed off at the irony. He threw the manila envelope of photocopies on his desk and went to get a shower.

'Fridays are paydays,' Segert sang to himself.

* * *

By the first week of October Kimberly had made a full recovery. Her cough was gone and she played it off as a seasonal allergy. She'd regained her bird-like appetite and gained some weight back. Martin worked from home for a week and drove her around to make social calls. Maggie went to the store every morning to pick up fresh flowers and chocolates. Kimberly took them with her, as if she was visiting the ill and she hadn't just recovered from a major respiratory infection.

* * *

Segert met the marketing girl from the rival company that hired him at a bakery and coffee shop downtown at nine thirty on Friday morning. He was paid cash in an envelope, because cash couldn't be traced.

'Thank you, Mr Berger. You've done a great job for us.' She eyed all the photocopies intently. 'I don't think we need you in the future, but if we ever do . . .'

'You have my card.'

She handed him the brown envelope marked *Receipts*, took a sip of her coffee and left.

Segert took the N1 to Noon and went down Flamenco Way. As he expected, Johnny was sitting on the corner, squinting in the sunlight, keeping himself company. The horizon seemed lower than usual, and the sun disappeared behind a cloud.

'Get in.'

Johnny picked up his radio and got into the passenger seat. The recess bell rang at the high school nearby, and groups of teenagers in navy-blue blazers, grey school dresses and slacks walked across the thin green pitch to eat their packed lunches and smoke cigarettes behind the benches.

'Johnny, Johnny, Johnny,' Segert said like a nursery rhyme. He doubted Johnny had any new information for him, but he would be a fresh vein for Johnny to tap dry if he wasn't careful. 'Did she come back?'

'No.'

Segert had stopped at a 7-Eleven on the way there, and had a six-pack of Castles, soft white government bread and a packet of sliced processed cheese. 'Then why are you calling me? Besides the fact that it's wage day.'

'It's not like that.'

They drove past the school, took a left at the New Apostolic Church that was next to a petrol station, and parked close to a bus stop along an auxiliary road that joined Noon to another township. There was no traffic, only a few old ladies watering lawns, watching empty streets and their grandchildren play in the yards. Segert reached across Johnny to the cubbyhole. The movement seemed to frighten the old man; he held his breath, pushing his spine into the back of the car seat.

'Don't get a *skrik*. I'm just getting a bottle opener.' Segert laughed.

'We can't sit here,' Johnny said.' I know a place.'

Segert followed Johnny's directions, and five minutes later they stopped at a library. The parking lot was immaculate, freshly painted. Three cars were parked close to the entrance. The only thing out of place was a black office chair that lay abandoned at a streetlamp. One of the wheels had fallen off, and it stood greyed under the intense sun, off kilter.

The bungalows around the library were large, bigger than Segert's. They were white or beige with large green lawns. Rock or tiled walkways led from the dropped pavement to the *stoep*. The fences were expensive, made of concrete and ornately decorated, but low and sun-bleached fossil white.

'This place is nice,' Segert said, cutting the engine.

'We call it Oz.'

'Why?'

'All the coloureds here always talking about moving to Australia, where they can, you know, pass.'

'Oh, makes sense,' Segert said nonchalantly, as Johnny passed him a bottle of Castle from the grocery packet that was now at his feet. 'And so? What have you got, Johnny?'

'How do I say it?' Johnny said slowly.

'You start by spitting it out.'

'I saw her face carved into a tree line at the edge of a field. It looked fresh too.'

Segert was about to bite into a cheese sandwich, but paused. 'Were you a bit drunk when you saw it?'

'Yes,' Johnny stammered, 'but it was still there the following day.'

'Keep talking, Johnny.'

Johnny gave him directions to the field, which was a circle at the entrance to a low-rent township. If the township around the library was heaven, for coloureds who could pass, then this was closer to hell. A lot closer. Johnny got out at the traffic light just before Segert turned left.

'I can't be here with you,' he said, and slinked out of the passenger seat onto the street without looking back.

Made sure you finished that Castle before you left, though, huh? Segert knew where to find him.

He parked his van at the edge of the field. At the opposite end, a clump of jackalberry trees bordered the main road. In the shade of the trees was a small orange-brown wooden shed. It resembled a tool shed for a neighbourhood fixer of transistor radios and old black-and-white TV sets, or a storage place for beloved grandchildren's keepsakes. It wasn't supposed to be out here in a public park.

A path of exposed white soil webbed from the road to the shed and criss-crossed the field. In the distance, Segert could hear a large group of small children shouting in play. He walked slowly towards the row of rounded crown trees. A woman was shouting in the distance and, without an answering call, she continued shouting in shorter bursts. She didn't sound panicked, but rather like a secretary bird calling her mate or chasing a snake. Segert looked in the shed, but it was empty but for a grey blanket, empty plastic bottles and a tattered black notebook. Sure as daylight, it was Augustine's face carved in the trees. When Segert turned around, he was met with a short, middle-aged woman was walking towards him. She was approaching cautiously, but had failed to change out of her red house slippers.

'Sir, can I help you?' she said.

Here we go, Segert thought. 'I'm looking for this girl. Do you know who carved this?' he said.

She swallowed hard. 'That's not a real person. It's just an artist's rendering.'

Segert thought he'd heard it all today. 'This is Augustine Pillay, and I'm looking for her and her son. Do you know who drew this?'

'What is this about?'

'Lady, this girl's face has been carved into this tree and might seem nothing to you. But she's been missing since July and that carving looks new to me. I want some answers.'

Across the road, a heavily bearded man was sitting on an old lawn chair selling chopped braai wood, neatly stacked into triangular piles. *R5 a pile*, a sign read. His feet were bare and black with ash and dirt. His matted hair was the same colour as his clothes and grew out of his head in spirals to the sky. Although he was tall and much lighter in complexion than this woman, Segert could tell from the way she looked at him that she was his mother.

'Did you throw him out?'

'No, Angelo comes over every night for his plate.'

The smell was a combination of wandering bush and walks down long hot roads and clear sky, and the wind caressed with coals and marijuana. His eyes were dark and intelligent.

'Can I help you?' he asked Segert.

'Have you seen Augustine? I'm looking for her, and you've carved her face here. I need to know where she is.'

'I don't know.' He shrugged.

'Tell him what you know, so he can go,' the woman told her son.

'I saw her in town. She was alone, carrying her bags. I would've offered to help, but she went into the post office. She looked good, too.'

'What do you mean?' Segert asked.

'Good-good, healthy, taking care of herself. It was just odd she had those bags. She went to the post office, the big one. I carried on downtown to pick up some pencils.'

'Pencils? And yet you ended up carving her face into a tree with a penknife.'

'It's a pretty face, and, I don't know, she seemed like she could look after me. She seemed like the type of woman I need. I can't explain it.'

'She'd grown up. She's a mother now,' Segert said.

'It's not a crime to draw pretty women.'

Segert told the mother to go for a walk, but she stared at him coldly. *Women. Plural*, Segert thought, but didn't want to push the point too far too soon.

'What you been drawing in that notebook in there?' He cocked his head towards the shed.

'Go inside. Have a look,' the mother said. And it became clear to Segert and Angelo that she'd been going through his things when he wasn't around.

'Where's the penknife?' Segert asked.

'I've got it. It's at home,' the mother answered, pointing at the house across the field. 'In case you hurt yourself. I took it with the crockery a few nights ago.'

'Mummy . . .' Angelo whined, and turned back to Segert, not quite meeting his eye. 'I really don't know anything about Augustine. She was a few years behind me at school; she was a looker but not my style. What happened? Why are you looking for her?'

'Somebody did something or something happened. And, Angelo, just be careful what you say. Tell the man what you know so he can go before he becomes fascinated with you,' Angelo's mother said.

A silver Camry had stopped across the road, and the driver had stepped out to inspect the piles of wood.

Angelo stood up from the stump he was sitting on, a new layer of smell rising up with him. Segert noticed another carving on the stump that Angelo'd been sitting on.

The woman patted Segert on the arm like she was dusting a cake with icing sugar, still with the aim of moving him along. Maybe his mother patting Segert's arm was code or maybe it triggered something, but suddenly he was pushing Segert away from his mother, and they fell down in the sand between the dried peels of jackalberries and sharp edges of exposed stones. A small creature scurried away from behind the shed.

'Get away from my mother. Stop it, stop it.'

The driver of the car turned around, saw the three of them scuffling on the field, and sped off, tyres screeching.

Segert pushed Angelo off, got on top of him and pinned his chest with his right knee. 'You need to straighten yourself out.' He held Angelo's hands.

'For what, huh? For who?' Angelo was struggling under Segert's weight, trying to get his hands free.

Segert shook him twice, then picked him up and shoved him against the shed. Angelo freed himself and pushed Segert away, then walked back across the road.

He swore under his breath as he left, dusting the sand off his dirty clothes. 'You interrupting a working man's business.'

He seemed the type of person who could proclaim he knew God's light then spit in your face. Segert pointed to the house and followed the mother to the family home, across from the field, in silence.

Angelo's father was standing in the sandy driveway, his body shielded by a white *bakkie*. He wore thick round spectacles and had a furrow between his thick black eyebrows. He was tall, and his blue checked shirt was tight around his large shoulders, but hung loosely past his waist.

'Come inside, please. We can talk.' The father had grubby hands with dirty fingernails. He rubbed his thumb and forefinger nervously. This was the original owner of the shed. 'I'm Roger. Roger van Hemel.'

'*Nee*, it's OK,' said Segert. 'Here's my card. Contact me if you can get more information out of him about Augustine.' He handed it to the woman.

Roger took it from his wife. 'He's harmless. Very bright boy once upon a time, full of promise, a bit obnoxious, but . . .' He trailed off, then finished. 'It's my fault. I used to be a real class act. Ask anyone, ask the neighbours. Used to beat my wife when I was drunk, and I was drunk a lot. One Christmas Day, at the lunch table, Angelo just couldn't take it anymore and he moved out there.'

'I'm looking for Augustine Pillay. Do you know her?' Segert changed the subject. He wasn't interested in getting in the middle of this, whatever it was beginning to look like. He guessed Roger was trying to humanise Angelo.

'Why are you really looking for her? When boere come around here . . . it's not to leave Christmas presents.'

Segert turned around to avoid the question. He had a clear view of the shed. Across the road, Angelo sat on an old lawn chair, selling wood. Angelo made sure his father could see him. He was obnoxious all right.

'Do you still drink?' Segert asked.

'No.' Roger put his arm around his wife. 'Look, I don't want any trouble from anyone.'

Segert looked at them, and didn't ask the other question. She was still there, literally by his side. 'Do you have any other children?'

'Yes, two younger boys. But they in Zim, working for her uncle.'

'Where does he get the wood from?'

'He scavenges around.'

'Where's the axe?'

Mrs van Hemel wiped her nose on her sleeve, and unfurled from her husband's embrace. 'It's in the back with our *braai* stuff. It never leaves here.'

'It must do. That stump over there, can you explain that?' Segert asked, referring to the tree stump her son had been sitting on. 'It had roots in the ground.'

'He comes to fetch it, but it's back every night when he gets his plate.' She turned to walk to the door. But her husband's eyes were burning on Angelo.

'It's like that a long time. Ask anyone.' Angelo's father nodded towards the park.

* * *

It was four o'clock when Segert went back down Flamenco Way, driving past Augustine's house, the curtains drawn and the windows dusty. He spotted Johnny sitting in his usual spot and parked.

'So, a minute?' Segert went to sit beside Johnny, passing him a beer. They sat side by side, looking down the road.

'Did you see it?' Johnny asked.

Ja. Angelo says she's pretty, that's all. What you think?'

'Me?'

'You know everybody around here, so you must've caught wind of Angelo's story. Is he the bogeyman, or just a bit schizo?' Segert pressed.

'I don't know much, but I heard he's been to jail for raping a girl. After he finished school, about five years ago. He went to jail quick-quick. There's a lot of stuff going on here, it's common. But he got picked up and put in jail, chop-chop.'

'Guess people think they can have a long career of rape before they get caught,' Segert said. 'Where's the girl?'

'I don't know anything about it, but she's not here any-more. Probably gone to Cape Town or P.E. Somewhere she can start over.'

'You could've told me some of this before.'

But Johnny shrugged and didn't answer.

'Tell me, what about Augustine's parents? What's going on there?'

'Not much. The mother's not one of those mummy types. Not hard, but family is not her favourite thing. The father's nothing special. Indian, out on his own.'

'You don't make it sound like it's a place she'll want to come back to.'

'There's nowhere else to park the bus.'

'And Teddy?'

'You know more about him than me.'

Segert noticed Johnny's leg start to shake. He was becoming restless or uncomfortable. He would have to wrap up this conversation quickly. 'Angelo only carved her face. Nobody else's. There must be a reason.

'Why would he tell me?'

It was too early in the day to *braai*, but smoke was drifting from the side of a house across from the school field. Three teenage boys were carrying orange bags of lamb chops and *boerewors*. One was carrying a six-pack of cider in each hand.

'If you go straight up to him and ask him, he won't tell you. Don't do that.'

Segert thought about this as he drove back to Solomon's. He was already three beers down the hole with Johnny and wasn't thirsty. He ordered a steak sandwich and a Coke. There was something about that day that kept bubbling in the back of his mind. He thought about the headless prostitute, and the axe in the backyard and Angelo's piles of wood. His stomach turned, and for the second time that day he couldn't finish his sandwich. The payphone wasn't working, so Segert asked to use the landline.

'I need to make a call, kind of urgent.'

105

'Go round to the office.' The bartender was a thin man with wavy hair down past his ears. 'Solomon's in a mood.'

Solomon was sitting behind his desk, watching TV and drinking a bottle of cider. He passed Segert the phone without saying a word.

'Hi Willem, it's Segert Berger.'

'Yes. Missing woman case. Haven't found her yet?'

'No. Tell me, did you get the ID on the headless one?'

'Still unclaimed. Don't think it's your girl. But keep in touch.'

Segert knew what that meant: there would be more dockets to look at.

'Who's headless?' Solomon asked, not taking his eyes off the TV.

'A coloured girl found on the dumps.'

'Shame,' Solomon said. 'Tell Lister I need another red cider. What kind of cases are you on now? Sounds a bit heavy.'

'I'm just trying to reunite a man and his family.'

Solomon frowned. 'And the Pope's an Englishman.'

CHAPTER 13

Kimberly Diamond was always generous. It was just in her nature. When she got well, she was even more generous.

She called Maggie into the garden early on Thursday morning. Nicholas was still sleeping and Kimberly was having a quiet breakfast with her husband.

'Go home early, Maggie.' Kimberly smiled. 'You're always here, take some rest.' Kimberly was giving Maggie the freedom to visit relatives who weren't ready to receive her. It was the middle of October.

Maggie didn't have any gifts. She couldn't turn up at home empty-handed.

Maggie looked to Martin. 'Take a month — we'll see you in December,' he said.

'Oh, I don't mean to mess up your *festive*, Maggie,' Kimberly said with punchy charm as Maggie walked back to the kitchen.

'No problem, Ma'am, sir, I will see you on the first of December.'

'Don't rush, Maggie, take your time, hey,' Kimberly said.

Augustine was in the kitchen but hadn't overheard the conversation. She'd noticed that Kimberly's orange juice was low and brought out a bottle, ready to pour out some fresh juice.

Kimberly turned to Augustine. 'I'd let you go on holiday, but I *know* you have nowhere to go.'

* * *

A bastard wind clipped Teddy in his ear. Augustine had left in July and three months had come and gone. Everyone around him was going on with their lives. But he was a hostage. He had to find her. A reunion was overdue. They could spend some time together and rekindle the past. He tapped his finger impatiently on the steering wheel as he entered Noon at 8 p.m. on Friday night. When the Casspir was out of sight he slowed down, cruising the corners looking for the boy and his gang that were blackmailing him. He parked next to the petrol station shop and scanned his rearview mirror for five minutes. Then got out and bought two Castle beers.

His tyres screeched as he reversed out of the petrol station. He adjusted his speed as he drove down the auxiliary road and turned right on Harmonica Way. It was the middle of spring and children were playing outside in the street. He leaned out the window as he drove slowly down the circular road looking for his blackmailer.

He heard someone shout, 'Stranger!' and then saw all the children start running home. Some cut across his headlamps to reach home. He'd thought it was a young woman but heard on the Saturday township headlines that it was a mother.

'A parent on Wednesday reported seeing a car driving suspiciously in the area of Noon as children were playing in the playground on Friday night.'

He had to stay out of Noon and keep folding to whoever came next.

* * *

Martin surged up the stairs in a frenzy of grief, tassels flapping on the roof of his shoes.

'*Bokkie, bokkie!*' he shouted, as he ran past Augustine standing at the edge of the staircase. Martin's voice was a shriek, a crack in a mirror that splintered across the wall. *Bokkie*, his pet name for Kimberly meant a baby antelope, the kind famous for its high leaps and tactical evasion of cheetahs and lions. And now, *bokkie* was down. Augustine couldn't believe how quickly Kimberly had been depleted. In the dusk of a summer kill, Kimberly was gone. In one month, she went from celebrating her new lease on life to the end of her life.

* * *

The next morning, a black Mercedes-Benz drifted past the electric gates. It was in good nick but for the small cloud of white exhaust fumes rising and disappearing as the car ascended the small incline. It didn't have any identifiers of an airport taxi, but the driver got a small leather weekend bag out of the boot and left it at the door. The woman who came through the front door was just taller than Augustine, and was dressed all in black, an ornate embroidered scarf over her hair, fluttering over a plum-coloured scar on her temple.

'I'm Martin's sister, Bessy. Where is he?' She was carrying a large tin of biscuits and handed them to Augustine.

'He's in the study.'

'Fix me a strong cup of black coffee.' She pulled her scarf down to her neck. 'I'm hot. Put some biscuits on a plate. What has he been eating?' Before Augustine could answer, she disappeared through to the study, her skirt flapping in the cross-breeze.

'Yes, sir,' Augustine said under her breath, and went to put the kettle on.

Augustine heaped Bessy's biscuits on a small lunch plate, along with two cups of black coffee, a sugar pot and a tiny milk jug that Kimberly had always favoured. She knocked on the study door twice, then heard Bessy answer.

'Come in.' She was on the phone, sitting behind the desk, and Martin was sitting on the sofa, averting his eyes. 'My sweetheart, that petite cup is not going to make it. Look at the size of me; I need a lot to sustain me. But leave it. And bring back two mugs and two chicken mayonnaise sandwiches. A nice size. Don't be shy.'

'I haven't cooked any chicken yet; it's only eleven. Can I offer you some scrambled eggs, maybe, with some toast?'

Bessy took the phone off her ear and put it to her chest. 'Nobody told me you were beautiful and clever.'

Augustine looked over to Martin, who kept his eyes unfocused, staring beyond the window that looked out onto the garden.

'And ham,' Bessy said, as Augustine reached the door. 'Scrambled eggs and ham.'

* * *

Augustine took a deep breath before she re-entered the study. Her tray was heavy with an antique white coffee pot and two mugs that didn't match the elegant milk pot. Two tiny teaspoons jingled in the empty mugs as she walked. She'd stuffed scrambled eggs and bacon between the toast. They were all out of ham.

'Leave it on the table,' Bessy told Augustine. 'Next time don't worry with a pot. I appreciate the sentiment. But I'm family. Just a big black coffee is fine.'

Martin had already disappeared upstairs.

'Should I take a coffee and toast up to Mr Diamond?' Augustine asked.

'No, if he gets hungry he must move from his room and come fetch his food. Grief is one thing, but there's nothing wrong with his legs.'

Augustine was unsure whether to agree or take it as authority that she should leave her boss to thirst and hunger.

She picked up the empty tray, feeling Bessy's eyes burning into her as she walked away. She was almost at the door when Bessy spoke.

'Grief can be a hole. I've been where he is.' Bessy held a biscuit close to her mouth but seemed to lose interest in it.

'If you need me, just call,' Augustine said. '

'When I need you, I will come find you.' Bessy smiled.

***

Bessy wrote a quick obituary over black coffee and wolfed down both sandwiches. Then she rushed up to Martin to get his final words on it. Augustine was in the water closet, spraying window cleaner on the medicine cabinet mirror. She heard Martin grumble as Bessy opened the door.

'The newspaper needs this by four p.m.'

Augustine could hear the curtains being pulled open quickly. 'Can't see anything in this light. Come now,' Bessy rallied. 'Let's get this done before we take Nicholas for a walk.'

'*We?*' Martin choked.

***

Over the next few days, Augustine noticed Bessy had an appetite for more than chicken sandwiches and morning ham. She made the study her control centre. Always on the phone, running between Martin and some vendor who had to be directed. She often started her conversations on the telephone with 'I understand . . .' then finished with 'Do you understand?'

Some nights Bessy would call a cab or a friend, telling Martin that she was tired of talking on the phone all day, and go out to goodness knows where. The car waited in the road, the brake lights visible from Augustine's window. Bessy walked down the allée quickly, holding a small black handbag she hugged under her arm. She'd arrive back after midnight, the smell of cigarette smoke and liquor lingering in the air as she padded upstairs. In the morning, Augustine would pick up Bessy's high heels from the bottom of the stairs and place them just outside what had been Martin's bedroom door when Kimberly was sick. Martin slept on the floor of the matrimonial bedroom now. Life had gone off the rails in Belgravia Road. Every morning, Augustine picked up the bedding from the floor and remade the bed.

The next Saturday morning, ten days after Kimberly's death, Bessy woke up at 5 a.m. to the sound of birds chirping before sunrise and tried to paint her birthmark white. She marched downstairs in a black crepe dress that defied her plump size, her strong calves bare and her feet in thick pink socks. She dropped a weeping veil on the side table at the front door and turned to Augustine, who had come in from the kitchen, carrying a bowl of seasonal fruit.

'I dusted this old thing off, thought I'd never wear it again.' She picked self-consciously at the pilling at her hip, but tried to smile. 'I'm throwing it out after this. Last time I wore it, was for my husband's funeral. Three years ago. Died in a quarry accident.'

'Sorry to hear that,' Augustine said.

'He used to work in Jo'burg. Driving all over collecting rent for absent landlords, you know. Real cowboy job. Windhoek was supposed to be a new start for us. Safe. Can't find anything at the shops that really fit,' she said in clipped speech.

Augustine watched Bessy's eyes glass over, and said, 'You look good, for the occasion.'

She left it at that, no need to offer further condolences. *This fat widow is free to go gallivanting at night*, she thought to herself. Then immediately felt ashamed. Had Bessy invited her to take part in her grief? She pushed the thought out of her head. 'Breakfast is ready,' she said, and put a smile on her face.

'Please . . .' She turned her palm to the small dining room and brought her mind back to her duties.

It was almost seven thirty and the table was laid formally with a stack of paper-thin pancakes, jams and cut rye bread for toast. 'I'll get Nicholas ready now. Do you need anything else?' Augustine scanned Bessy's socks and made a mental note to have her hosiery hung over the end of the bed, when she was finished dressing Nicholas.

It had been a very busy morning already. She'd deposited Justice at 6 a.m. with a kind old lady she met at a local charity shop who was desperate for the company. Then moved to get all Nicholas's accessories packed, before starting breakfast. Bessy gave Nicholas his first bottle.

Martin was in the bathroom when she went to pick up Nicholas. The shower was running. She peeked into his marital bedroom. His suit had been laid out already. His bedding folded neatly in front of the closet.

'Come baby.' She picked Nicholas up, wrapping him with an extra loving touch for the day.

Before they left, Bessy left her instructions for the caterers, who would be there within an hour. 'Make sure the food is cool and the drinks are warm. People drink mostly tea and water.'

Martin looked handsome — there was little real resemblance between the siblings. He was tall and slender, she was short with large diamond-shaped calves.

Bessy smiled as she sat in the passenger seat, the veil already pulled over her face.

* * *

The funeral was held at Linden Presbyterian church. Ten minutes' drive away. A modest stone church with an imperial white roof that reached far over the shade trees that sheltered the cemetery.

Martin had requested that the casket be closed. In his speech he said he wanted her remembered in her youth, in her

113

prime. As the perfect half of the wedding-cake topper couple they once were. As the casket was lowered someone started to cry, and Bessy's chest swelled. The last thing anyone would see before Kimberly was covered in dirt was the white and yellow roses that she'd bargained hard for.

* * *

The caterers had set up at Belgravia Road. They looked like students Augustine's age. This was their part-time jobs. Two of them arrived in their own cars. They would work and then drive off, blue trays of glasses in their boots. While Augustine would take care of Nicholas upstairs and out of sight, they would be the ones serving mini quiches and tea.

* * *

The next morning the weather had broken. The ground was wet in patches and insects were flying in circles around the flower bed at the far end of the garden. The house was quiet. Before breakfast Augustine packed a Tupperware of lefto-ver chicken wings and bundled Justice up and went to the city. She was going to meet Zula and her son at the Triple S printing works and board a minivan up to the Witwatersrand National Botanical Garden in Roodepoort for a family day picnic.

Local folk music was playing on a small radio. Augustine didn't understand the lyrics or what people around her were saying. Zula had taken hold of Justice and was playing a game of peekaboo. She had time to think of the bad luck that was passing over the Diamond house. She'd arrived there thinking she was the only person in the world with problems. And now, she was rushing away in the morning to show Justice black eagles and hedgehogs and eat day-old chicken wings.

* * *

A week and a half passed, and Bessy sat in the shade of the house by the back door, reading a newspaper. The vapours of last night's downpours curling in little mists into the bright morning.

'I'm taking Martin and Nicholas with me,' she said as Augustine brought her a mug of hot coffee. It was only 9 a.m. and already thirty degrees Celsius.

Augustine wasn't expecting the axe to fall on her job so abruptly and spilled a drop of coffee on her shoes.

'I need to get Martin out of here. Christmas is coming up, it's too much.'

'When are you leaving?' Augustine asked.

Bessy smiled, 'We have a small place upcountry, close to Hartebees. I think they will be back before New Year's.'

She understood that Bessy meant that they were leaving today, and that she still had her job.

'I called Maggie, and told her not to come back too soon,' Bessy said. 'The roads will be too busy and I think you can control things here until the middle of January. By yourself.'

'The gardener will be here,' Augustine said.

'Oh, I forgot about him.'

'But, I don't know anything about gardening. He's back around New Year's.'

'He can keep you company.' Bessy smiled.

* * *

Augustine was packing Nicholas's suitcase when she heard the buzzer from the front gate.

'Don't worry, finish what you're doing.' Martin ran downstairs to the study to lock the liquor cabinet and put his files away in a drawer. Then he left the front door open so the taxi driver knew they'd be there soon. Augustine looked out from Bessy's bedroom window, and saw her entering the back door.

Augustine carried the bags out to the front, then put it on the inside of the open door. Bessy stepped outside, enjoying the view of the runway of mansions and manicured lawns that gave the suburbs of Johannesburg a sheen of luxury just a few kilometres from the gold mines.

The same taxi came riding up the allée, and Bessy sidled up to Augustine before Martin came back downstairs from giving his house one last look-over.

'You know you're wasted here. I know it's safe, because of your son. But if you ever want anything more, just call me.' Her eyes scanned Augustine's face a tick too long, then she put her scarf back over hair. 'Must go as I came.' She laughed. 'Be a doll and carry my bag to the car. I'm going to use the ladies'.'

The cab driver was the same one as before, Augustine noticed, but today he wore a crumpled black trouser suit and white shirt, as if he were a low-rent chauffeur. He transmitted a raw physical power as he walked, and his complexion was damaged by heavy liquor drinking and smoking. *He lives for the night*, she thought.

She handed him the luggage at the boot. His hair was greased in black waves. A thick gold bracelet dangled off his wrist.

'Afternoon, pretty,' he said. He didn't open the boot, but instead deposited the luggage on the ground.

He smiled and put his hand forward. 'We didn't introduce ourselves properly before. I'm Cutman.'

That's a strange name, she thought. She walked back to pick up the rest of the luggage.

'That's the job I was training for,' he added, as if he'd read her thoughts. 'Fixing boxers during a fight. You like boxing?'

'Not really, not even in movies.'

'I don't like the fights in films either. It's a hobby now,' he said.

His answer was opaque, so she changed the subject as she walked to collect the last bags. 'You a taxi driver now or something?'

'Something. Used to work for Mrs Santos's husband. She inherited me with the business.'

116

Perhaps it had been his car lights she'd seen from the window, Augustine thought.

Bessy and Martin moved to sit in the back of the car. Nicholas sat on Bessy's lap.

Cutman stepped away and wished her a merry Christmas.

'See you,' she said, out of habit, and immediately regretted it.

As Cutman started the engine, Bessy unwound the window and passed her telephone number to Augustine on a neat piece of the late Mrs Kimberly Diamond's monogrammed paper.

'Behave, Bessy; behave yourself,' Martin said. He was agitated. Augustine guessed that power had been wrested from him by his sister. She was taking him against his will. But he was trying to remain playful.

'Never. I'll leave that to you, but I'm going to steal her from you one day. Believe me.'

'I believe you.' Martin laughed, but his face was sour. 'I've lost enough, can I at least keep my maid?'

'There, there,' Bessy said as she wound her window.

Augustine held the paper over her head for shade. It rattled lightly in the wind. She gazed into the horizon and saw the puffy white clouds wobbling like birthday balloons. Another thunderstorm was coming.

Nearby, a passing train signalled the time, 11.30 a.m. It was a small change of fortune for her. It was freedom time. The house was empty. Justice was keeping the old lady company down the road. Augustine didn't think too deeply about it — she made the most of the opportunity. Telling herself that it wouldn't last. Sometime soon someone at the complex would have a problem with Justice being there or Augustine going backwards and forwards for drop-off or pickup.

She turned the kitchen radio to the coloured station, listening out for the headlines as she made herself a bacon and egg sandwich. No one was asking something of her. Christmas was advertised as the silly season in jingles. A childish alliteration for the sunny excess that burned through everyone's thirteenth annual paycheque.

The salve for this cheerfulness was the road accident death rate. This time of the year, the roads were busy with people travelling to their ancestral homes. Maggie, returned home to Lesotho for a month-long break she'd taken ever since Kimberly was at high school. Bessy and Martin were on the road to Hartebees. The road accident rate was soap opera for those who had nowhere to go. Augustine could make herself feel better listening to the body count of unfortunate travellers. But in the news today was the story of a baby swept away in last night's flash flood in Alexandra township. He'd been malnourished and was probably already close to death when the waters came. His mother couldn't be located; she hadn't been seen for days. Everyone assumed he was with her.

Before she'd finished her sandwich, she remembered three things. Her idle vanity had gotten her into this trouble in the first place. She'd taken a job that was below her, just to have a roof over their heads. And, finally, she'd resorted to blackmailing Teddy to ensure there was the smallest of nest eggs for Justice. The breeze coming in through the kitchen fanlight wasn't cooling the room. Thunderstorms more often not broke in the darkest of night. When everyone was sleeping. She had time to do some cleaning and shopping. She thought of that baby, swept away.

She found a pile of Martin's soiled work clothes bundled up in the boot. She put them through the washing machine. It was 1 p.m. when she carried the basket of damp washing out to the clothesline that was in the narrow strip of the garden behind the garage. She hung Martin's shirts upside-down, the way Maggie taught her. Pegs close to the seam. She was thinking about dinner, and how she and Justice would be having Christmas lunch alone, but safe. That was the gift she was giving him. She plucked a light blue polo shirt out of the ball of wet clothes. As she pulled it up to the line, she noticed a faded bloodstain on the back, the shape and size of her finger. The hem flickered in the wind, and she put her thumb to it.

It must've been Kimberly's.

A dog barked deeply in the distance. A gardener or construction worker was being warned off a property by a heavyweight breed.

She finished hanging the washing, so that it could dry before today's stormy weather came.

This little big house with its secrets and stories. Kimberly, who had everything, lost it all to the same illness sweeping through the migrant hostels of the gold mines. How she got the disease of *moffies* and poor desperate men was a mystery. But she had it and then she was gone.

And then Bessy, the bubbly sister-in-law who had inherited a business in the underground economy. Collecting rent from landlords sounded like something that required the muscle of fighters, and here is Cutman. Every house in Johannesburg had its secrets from her little house in Noon that was cold and loveless, to Teddy's house that kept secrets of his filthy exploits with underage girls, to this mansion with its double dining rooms. Probably the most South African house of the time, she thought. House of the year with death and desperation for Christmas.

CHAPTER 14

Hours ago, New Year's fireworks had gone off around the neighbourhood. but had left the children undisturbed. It was the dogs howling down the street that woke Nicholas. Augustine ran upstairs to calm and change him, then he fell back into a deep sleep.

The fanlight of her window was open and she could smell the dry heat from the earth, and the burnt powders of flares and *braais*. The night outside was filled with the energy of New Year's Eve. Justice was sleeping next to her. That was all the excitement she could handle. Her tank was empty and she was tired. Martin had flown out of the house at bath time and still wasn't back. The Top 20 Hits of the Year segment was replaying on TV. She finished the end of a Smirnoff Ice and waited for sleep.

* * *

The beam came up through Augustine's curtains just after 3 a.m. She wasn't fully conscious, but noticed the sound of wet tyres. The air was cooler, but she hadn't pulled the blankets over her while she was asleep. The headlights were somehow different. She looked up as the light slanted towards the corner of the room. She sat up and watched Bessy's car sliding into Martin's space. The windshield wiper blinked once, as the car engine stopped. Cutman climbed out. She could tell by his footsteps that he went around the back of the car to the passenger seat. She was expecting to see Bessy, drunk and clutching her bag under her arm. Out from the small awning of the parking area appeared Cutman and Martin. Cutman was holding Martin up. His shirt pocket was torn and hanging slightly agape. He asked Cutman for a cigarette and began laughing in a high-pitched drunken way. Cutman lost his footing in a small puddle of water and Martin cursed at him. 'Hold me up, man.'

It was unnerving to see them entwined so closely. The slimy creature and her bereaved boss. She didn't move.

'Do you want to come inside?'

Her ears tweaked before the front door opened. The house creaked. She checked the bottom of her door for slices of light and shadows. The dimmest yellow glow appeared. Must've switched on the lamp close to the front door.

'Have some more fun?' Martin joked, in a voice she didn't recognise.

'I think it's been enough.'

'One more?'

They had stopped stumbling.

She imagined them, standing in the front room, upright and sober. No footsteps went into the study or carried Martin up the stairs. She would've been relieved for the sound of tap water flowing into a glass, or a fridge door opening. All she could hear was the engine ticking over and the dripping of rainwater from the pipe along the roof.

Her blood started to race in her ears. Was she drunk? She felt the beginning of a hangover. She looked on the floor and counted three empty bottles. Her skin became covered in a cold sweat and her spine felt pinned to the mattress. She felt capable of only moving her head.

'Don't have fun without me,' Cutman whispered close to Augustine's window as he walked back to the Mercedes-Benz.

She only took a breath again when the gate clicked closed.

* * *

'Happy New Year.' Paulus shook Augustine's hand at the back door in the morning.

'And Happy New Year to you.' She kissed Paulus on the cheek. 'Come have some breakfast and tell me about your holiday.'

'Ah, thanks, thanks. It was nice. My boy finished high school, and my daughter is getting big and pretty.' He sat down and bit into a melted cheese sandwich. 'I don't get this when Maggie's here.'

'Well, I just appreciate you.'

'What's he been like?'

'Like a captain,' Augustine said. 'All down and moody. This has been the longest month of my life. I can't wait for Maggie to come back.'

Paulus almost choked on his sandwich when she said that. She'd never thought she'd think it, herself. Paulus said, 'I always liked the missus. We must say a few prayers for her later.'

Just then, Martin cleared his throat and entered the kitchen. He was wearing dark blue jeans and a light-blue shirt that was neatly pressed. He looked wrinkled, even though there wasn't a line on his face. Both Paulus and Augustine inspected him without saying a word.

'I want to thank you two for working on New Year's. It means a lot.' He walked over to the sink and filled a glass with water and drank it in one gulp. Paulus nodded his head and made road for the garden.

'I have to pick up my car,' Martin said. He was watching Paulus inspect the weeds along the yard. 'Hope I didn't disturb you last night. I'm sure I made a lot of noise when I came in.' He turned to her, as if studying her face.

She suddenly felt that she should have something to do. 'No, no.'

'I'm taking Nicholas with me. Get his bag ready.'

Then the buzzer sounded at the front gate. 'That's for me,' he said. And hurried upstairs.

A spare bag was always packed and ready to go. She took it from the study and left it on the console by the front door.

A few minutes later, Martin returned and passed Nicholas to her as she was taking the vacuum cleaner out of the cupboard. 'I can't.'

Augustine and Nicholas watched on as Cutman revved the engine and reversed to the road, rather than turn in the driveway. He didn't look back, and almost reversed into a woman's car. The sound of hooting and fast-spinning tyres was uncommon in the area. Birds flew up from rooftops and trees in the commotion. Cutman and Martin jerked at the sudden stop. She may have been wrong, but it looked as though Martin, in the passenger seat, was laughing.

* * *

Paulus had collected dry leaves, twigs and weeds into a small mound. He got the spade from the shed and dug a small hole. Augustine watched his careful movements from the back window in the living room. The movements from his shoulders were lighter, and the movements from the bottom of his legs, not his feet but where the leg joined the ankle, seemed greased and fluid. He called her.

'Augustine, come here. Bring Nicholas with you.' He knew she'd been watching him.

She carried Nicholas out and the three of them stood outside in the shade of a pepper tree. The sun was climbing, and Paulus took any shade he could get, as if he could soak it inside his body and save it for later. Augustine was staring at the hole in the ground. Paulus had made three mud balls and laid them in the ground. Then he took the grass and leaves and placed them over the three balls.

'Missus Kimberly,' he said, without a hint of melodrama, 'we are here to say our goodbyes.' He extracted a curled-up piece of twine from his trouser pocket. Some blue fluff from his pocket drifted in the wind. He lit the twine with a matchstick and threw it into the hole. Augustine didn't know what do, so hummed to add some atmosphere to the performance. The fire didn't stay lit, so Paulus tried again with a small piece of newspaper he had in his back pocket.

'Now you are back with Mr Ryan,' he said to the small flame dying in the ground, meaning Kimberly's brother. The flame danced one little flicker in the breeze, then died out.

Paulus gave Augustine the first small spadeful of dirt. She threw it in while Paulus held the baby. Then did it one more time for Nicholas, before handing the spade back to Paulus.

* * *

The sun was a brass ball, and reflected off the windows in a white glare. The berg wind was low, drifting through the trees and moving the chorus of white flowers growing in the shadow of Martin's study window. There'd been a downpour in the afternoon that had taken the bite out of the heat, and Paulus had taken his leave before a second downpour meant that he was stranded on the highway, waiting for a minibus taxi in the rain.

It was five o'clock and there was still a good three hours of sunlight left. Augustine peeped in through the narrowness of the open door, and asked Martin if he wanted something to eat. He wore the expression of the sick who are tired of being infirm. He stood up, came to the door and touched her face. Expanding out from loneliness, the fatigue of grief and survival.

Augustine didn't resist. The touch was a fingertip of sadness, a cupped hand holding her face. She heard car doors opening and closing, saw bubbles floating behind her closed eyes, and felt two cold dewdrops on her nipples. A tingle on her neck when he touched her back.

When it was done, they separated like strangers but spoke softly to each other.

* * *

The next morning, a bright yellow weaver sat on the windowsill, filling the air with his swirling chirp. The boys were feeding themselves breakfast in the first dining room. It was a creamy white porridge and mashed soft bananas. The bird made the boys laugh and spit out their porridge. Augustine had never seen one alone and wondered if he'd gotten lost in a downpour last night.

Martin came downstairs. His hair was wet and he smelled of Old Spice and shampoo. Augustine greeted him as he sat to feed his boy. He only nodded.

Something inside her bounced lightly. This feeling was familiar. She'd read in one of his digests that bats can hear shapes, bees can dance maps. And she was trembling lightly at the edges of her rut, ready to be tangled in a flood and a waterfall. She bit her lower lip in anticipation, reckless and desperate again.

CHAPTER 15

Maggie and three other ladies sat on stools that Bam claimed were hand-carved by her husband, even though they all knew it was more likely that he'd bought them for her at a market, on the way home from the mines last year. His knuckles were thick from drilling holes for explosives, excavating rocks and holding up wooden posts. His fingers were good for cutting apples and poking sticks with his grandsons, but not patient enough for carving furniture. Bam grew marijuana in rubber tyres on her thatched roof and sold it to the backpacker hotels in a thick pumpkin soup with cornbread.

Bam wore a pastel blue floral dress that was too tight over the bosom and, when she bent over to refill the teacups, Maggie could see through the straining buttons to Bam's white bra, stuffed with R10 notes and toilet paper. Bam was always the smarter of the two. She only went as far as grade four, but she was sharp and hardy. She had sheep in the *kraal* and her children never went without food. She'd always dreamed of owning chickens, but knew it would attract sour smiles and pleas for eggs, gossip, jealousy and chicken-theft.

Maggie's brother, Cebo, shouted for her from the bottom of the hill. He was standing half-naked in the grass. He stood behind a baby palm tree, his belly protruding over the fanning leaves like a large heavy coconut.

'Phone call, Maggie,' he shouted, elongating the syllables of her urban name.

She knew it had to be the bank, Mr Diamond or one of the shops where she had an account. She put the tea mug down and said her goodbyes to the ladies. She wouldn't be walking back up the hill this afternoon.

When Martin said hello, she knew what he was going to say. And she sat down on the two-seat sofa to be comfortable for the bad news. Kimberly was gone now. What use would he have for her?

He'd been happy with her service over the years, he said. She'd been a great aid to Kimberly. She couldn't take in every word he said, although Martin was making an effort to speak slowly. She concentrated on the emotion in his voice instead. A sadness in him had lifted. A little of the thick fog had left his voice. A woman of fifty-seven reads these signs. She had seen them before, with the men who went to town and the migrants. A type of solid foolishness that only a man or a spoiled child could possess.

He knew how difficult it would be for her to find another job at her age. And he would look after her, for a time, he said.

Her brother had pulled a light cotton leopard print vest on and shuffled to put a kettle over the open fire in the front room. He looked over his shoulder at her as he bent to arrange the kettle on the flames.

'For how long is "a time", sir?' There was no need to call him 'Mr Diamond'. He'd just become another distant figure who could make life-and-death decisions for her.

'Until your pension starts. That is eight years, Maggie. I think that's enough.'

'That is not too bad, Mr Diamond.' She didn't want to betray negotiations about money in front of her brother. She'd be a magnet for aged womanisers, loafers and the abandoned. She sat back in the sofa, feigning ease and comfort. 'We can make all the arrangements another time. Everything is so difficult for you now. You must rest.'

'Thank you, Maggie,' Martin said. He sounded relieved she had taken that well. It was better for her anyway; she could spend more time with her family.

* * *

'How did she take it?' Augustine asked him.

'She took it better than I'd expected.'

'What are you going to pay her?'

'Her salary for eight years on a sliding scale, until her pension starts. If she finds another job, then she'll still have money she can save for her old age.'

Augustine pretended to know what 'sliding scale' was. She was so-so with English and never good with maths. Teddy could attest to that.

'She wasn't paying for rent or food here,' she pointed out.

Martin wasn't sure what precisely she wanted. It was her idea to get rid of Maggie.

'Oh, Judas, a sensational lack of remorse.' He pulled her in closely, and rubbed his nose against hers, teasing her for a kiss. 'You've impressed me, my little gazelle.'

'She deserves it, Martin.' She kissed him quickly, but he held on to her.

'You're right; I should never undersell my staff.' He slapped her on the bottom as she left the room to take care of the rest of the house.

* * *

Maggie picked up an old torn-up magazine, turned the first few pages pretending to be interested in it. She knew Augustine was behind this somehow. She and her son had burrowed their way into the house and, now that both she and Kimberly were gone, Augustine could manipulate Mr

128

Diamond any way she wanted. The sorceress, the she-devil, the unskilled beggar.

Kimberly would turn over in her grave, she thought. Turn right over.

'I hope she haunts that house,' Maggie said out loud, betraying her line of thought.

'What did you say?' Cebo was back at the stove now, holding the kettle by its cast-iron handle, pouring himself a mug of tea.

'Yes, please,' she said, pulling herself together and standing up, wiping the fluff off the back of her skirt. 'Yes, I'd like a cup of tea.' She beamed at her brother.

Cebo's nose twitched. 'There's not enough water for another cup,' he said. 'But here, have mine.'

She took the mug without thanking him. After a sip, she twisted her face. 'This is too sweet. You're going to get sugar.' The last thing she needed was to take care of someone else and their medical bills.

CHAPTER 16

At 9.39, when the telephone rang, Segert was sitting on his *stoep* drinking a cup of dark coffee. His head was against the window, his left bare foot resting on the right on the *stoep* wall. The summer sun was on his unshaven face, and he was listening to the sound of traffic while considering taking the dogs for a walk.

'There are two new girls, Mr Segert, and one of them looks like yours,' Willem said, on the other end of the line.

Segert was still on the Richard Reader case. He hadn't made any headway in the disappearance-of-Augustine case. He wanted to know where she was out of curiosity, why had she gotten caught up with Teddy and where her decisions had led her to.

In the meantime, he followed Reader and took pictures of his out-of-office business meetings. The men met in dark leather cigar lounges, drank whisky that sang with elegant *rancio* notes. The whisky part was easy. The rest required some work. Segert took care to never look alone. Buy two women a drink, try to avoid a woman on her own, unless as a last resort. Offer them compliments and some conversation. Pretend to be a tourist, take some pictures with Reader in the background.

He got their car registration numbers from the valets and linked it to company and persons of interest.

So far, it'd been what he expected: coworkers from SASOL, industry professionals from Shell and the like, although Wes hadn't made it out to be a Big Oil case.

'Don't think Big Oil issues would land on Wes's desk,' Segert ruminated time and again. It was definitely something deeper than fraudulent company expenses.

The case had another layer that was veiled from Segert. Wes paid him for it directly every Friday, and that was unusual. He hadn't gotten his lenses out for an adultery case for a long time. Maybe the sleaze was over for him, for good this time.

But now Willem had called. And curiosity was an itch that needed to be scratched.

**

Willem met him in the grief room, with a police docket and a crime scene photo he'd left out on the top. The picture had been taken early in the morning. She was covered by a tarp, lying in the dirt of an abandoned factory or warehouse. One white high-heel shoe peeped out from the blue tarp. She was lying face down, and the tarp concealed a pool of blood. From the ankle, Segert could tell she had the same colouring as Augustine. The top of her head was exposed, and Segert could tell that her hair had a loose curl that had been cut bluntly into a bob, but in the picture it was held in place with her own dried blood.

'Why are showing me this?' Segert sighed.

'You know why.'

'What colour are her eyes?'

'Hazel.'

'She doesn't look like my girl.' He'd come here to find Augustine, but was defensive about finding her this way.

'You can tell that from this photo, where she's completely covered? You want to see the autopsy photos?' Willem held the docket up above the table. He was upset and taunting Segert at the same time.

'She's not the one,' Segert said, not wanting to know, but not regretting being there.

The photos spilled out of the docket onto the table, and even though Willem had seen them before, he didn't attempt to recover them.

The body was almost decapitated. A large gash across her neck, and, as Willem pointed out with subsequent pictures, above her right knee, arm and hand. She was a young prostitute, with small lips, a button nose and wide forehead. She was small, without any meat or muscle to her. Easy to overwhelm with physical force.

'He split her leg open while she was still alive,' Willem said.

But she wasn't Augustine Pillay.

'If I bring you something, can you test it?' Segert asked. This was the case that wouldn't go away. He needed to make some progress.

'It's just the two of us.'

'I need a stack of newspapers and a good three metres of plastic sheeting.'

'I'm not going to bother asking.'

'Good.'

* * *

It was lunchtime when Segert got back in his BMW and gunned it down the M1 to Noon. The M1 was the best call for this time of the day. He took his foot off the accelerator and cruised down Flamenco Way, heading straight to the omniscient man on the crate.

'Like a boomerang, you're back,' Johnny said.

'Get in.' Segert nodded towards the passenger seat.

'Where you taking me?'

'You'll see.'

'I don't like the sound of that,' Johnny said.

'I'll get you a six-pack. Put your radio in the back.'

Segert did a quick U-turn and headed in the direction of the library.

Angelo was sitting on the verge of the arterial road that ran behind his shed, next to four or five piles of logs carefully placed in neat triangles.

Segert stopped his car, and spoke through the passenger window that Johnny had rolled down. 'Can I get a pile?'

'Look it here, what you two up to?' Angelo asked. He was surprised, but enjoyed seeing Johnny and Segert as a pair.

'Johnny's doing a ten-beer *braai*.' Segert popped the trunk of his BMW and got out of the car. 'Can you put it in the boot?'

Angelo dropped the logs in the boot. 'Hope you have firelighters.'

Segert was looking around him. 'Where's your axe?'

'At my mother's house.'

'Let's get it, then. Get in.' Segert nodded towards the open trunk.

'No, man, I'm not getting in there.'

'In the boot.'

'Bloody *Boere*,' Angelo shouted, as Segert pushed him off balance. His head knocked against the wood he'd thrown in carelessly. He shouted as Segert closed the trunk on him.

Segert drove down the road and pulled up at Angelo's parents' house, right up to the front door.

Johnny stayed in the car. So far, he didn't know why he was there, but he wasn't happy about how his day was panning out. 'What are you doing?' Ever since Segert lied about the ten-beer *braai*, his mood was more severe.

'Get out and stand guard,' Segert said, as he got out of his car.

'Hello, it's me,' Segert said to Roger, Angelo's father, when he opened the door.

Roger looked from Segert, across the field and out on the road for Angelo. All he saw was an empty old garden chair and

Angelo's *braai* wood and sign. Johnny was standing at the back end of the car, looking out into the street. Segert could see Johnny's reflection in the bedroom window next to the front door. He was facing out into the street. Too embarrassed to make eye contact with Roger. His position worked well for Segert. There was strength in numbers.

'How can I—' Roger began.

'I need the axes that Angelo uses for the logs.'

'There's only one. Why?'

'Just give it to me.'

'What's going on now?'

'Just give it to me and there won't be any problems. I'm not a problem you want to have,' Segert said.

The sound of screaming and kicking came from inside the trunk.

'I'll let him go as soon as you give me the axe.' Segert smiled.

* * *

The front room was a narrow rectangle with the TV as the focal point, just opposite a bow window. The settee below the windows had a large brown crochet blanket across the seat cushions. There was a fan on the side table.

'Where's your wife today?'

'She's gone to work.'

'Must be nice to have her out the house.'

Roger had stepped through to the kitchen and was walking to the back door. 'I don't know what you mean.'

'Never mind,' Segert said, surveying the kitchen before following Roger outside.

The small house sat on a corner lot with a large well-kept back garden. A high vibercrete fence was on the back perimeter, offering some privacy, although the upstairs neighbours could see and hear everything. Straight ahead from the back door was a hand-built brick *braai* stand, three white garden chairs, like the one Angelo had on the road, and a matching table. A pile of logs under the *braai* stand, an axe nestled in the corner at the back of the wood. Roger's tool shed was open. Broken TVs and radios littered the workbench.

Roger reached for the axe, then shifted his grip on the haft with his palm and looked at Segert.

'Think about it. You don't want this kind of smoke,' Segert said, looking around for something to use as a weapon in case Roger decided to fight. 'Put it down on the table and walk back to the house.'

'I can't until you let him go,' Roger said.

'You think I want to hold on to him? Just let me leave in peace and I'll drop him off.'

'What are you going to do with the axe?'

'Don't worry about it. I'll let him go.'

Roger didn't surrender the axe to Segert, but left it on the table. It lay between them, like a poisonous snake.

* * *

Segert kept an eye on Roger in his side mirror as he drove to the two-way stop sign. The older man's fist was clenched as he stood at the end of the driveway. Segert turned left at Angelo's log pile, and that's when Roger started running. The loud kicking in the boot was damaging the brake lights. Segert skidded up the road and stopped at the verge of the highway. He yanked the boot door open and hauled Angelo out.

The word Angelo shouted at Segert described the act of unbathed wild animals procreating in a dusty heap.

Segert looked back towards Angelo's parents' house. Then fixed his black eyes on Angelo, straining to make him feel the size of a dung beetle.

'I can get to you any time,' he warned.

He got back in the car as Roger came running round the corner. The car peeled off, leaving Angelo in an insolent, angry heap on the side of the road.

Segert drove back towards Flamenco Way. The only sound was Johnny's radio rocking in the footwell of the passenger seat. Johnny had a head sweat that started at his grey hairline and ran down his temples to his neck. He wiped his hands on his jeans and sighed.

'You should learn to breathe properly before you suffocate,' Segert said.

Johnny looked out his window.

School children walking home looked back at him, then at Segert sitting next to him. Johnny pushed himself down in his seat, as though trying to disappear. Segert stopped the car, turned the ignition off and handed Johnny a folded R50 note.

Before he took the money, Johnny said, 'I didn't want to be involved like this. Now, I'm a'so dirty.' He swallowed to deepen his voice. 'Don't come here again.'

Segert laughed, but not for the reason Johnny thought. This reminded him of his ex-wife, and her futile expulsions. She took him back every time. He still lived in their house, although she'd run off to God-knows-where. One way to make sure she never took him back.

He parked the car and walked over to Augustine's old house. He didn't bother asking Johnny if anyone would be there today.

A woman with sharp brown eyes answered the door. She had an acidic presence that gave him the sense that she dissolved and discarded people.

'Mrs Pillay, have you heard from Augustine?'

'No. Who are you?'

'Do you know where she is? Can I come inside?'

'No, we can talk here on the *stoep*. I haven't heard anything from her.' She took out a cigarette and started smoking.

'Aren't you worried?'

'She got shacked up with Teddy Beukes, then landed here with a baby. Who are you, by the way?'

'Teddy hired me to find her.'

'Then you probably know more than me.'

'You telling me you don't know if she's alive or dead?'

'I'm telling you I don't know where she is. She's like a cat; she's got nine lives. She'll turn up, and I'll have to take care of her and the baby.'

* * *

A draft blew in with Segert as he walked into the coroner's building. The bottom of his shirt was undone and it wafted limply above his khaki slacks as he closed the door. His hair was flat on one side and his thick eyebrows met in a furrow.

'I need you to ask Willem to come get something from my car.'

Beverly looked up over her glasses and picked up the phone.

CHAPTER 17

Light. Sunlight pierced the old floral curtains, cutting across the bed, waking Augustine. She sat up rubbing her eyes and looked at Justice, grateful he was still asleep, and then looked at the radio clock. Six o'clock. Light meant something different to her now. She got up, put the kettle on and enjoyed the view from the kitchen window. She stood in the tender shadows wearing only her T-shirt and pastel green cotton briefs. She knew Martin wouldn't be up for another forty-five minutes. She sipped a half-cup of sugarless white tea, dipping Marie biscuits in it, and kept an ear out for Nicholas and Martin.

Martin didn't pay her any more, but he didn't disturb or second-guess her either. The leaves were browning. This morning red, yellow and orange leaves drifted in the light wind across the lawn and the pool tarp. She watched the leaves roll over each other. The sun went behind a cloud and a dust devil swirled the grass and leaves into the air.

They'd been entangled for three or four months. When the boys were down for a nap, he'd come to get her. He wouldn't fuss around with words. If she was downstairs, he took her hand and led her upstairs silently. She didn't complain.

His bedroom was bare and rustic, unlike the rest of the house. The curtains and duvet set were in light blue and his double bed had a thick unvarnished frame carved blunt and unevenly, to resemble the petrified trees of the Kalahari.

Generally, meaning always, when he was finished he would sigh, give her a kiss and then turn his back and fall asleep. In the afternoons, she could be the only person awake in the house, and she would count the freckles and the thick hairs on his back; drift away to three summers ago when she was with Teddy and scold her past self for her foolishness, or travel to her future self, in her flat with Justice or driving her car to her job. But today, Martin was awake and making conversation.

'I would like to, but I can't buy you any gifts,' Martin said, catching Augustine off-guard.

The sun was sloping to evening, the room lit in the last few embers of the day. She rubbed the side of her neck, then pulled his woollen cardigan from the chair and draped it over her shoulders. 'Don't worry about it.' She'd taught herself to expect nothing. Augustine couldn't be disappointed, not again.

'No, I mean it.' He stroked the middle of her back with his forefinger. 'It's just that it's so soon after, you know . . .'

She shook her head slowly, patiently. She knew. Besides, what would he buy her, lingerie? He couldn't walk in the department store and buy bra and panties. Perfume? Any visitor could smell it on her. A dress? Dresses were for women who commanded the attraction and unquestioning loyalty of a man. That man lived somewhere in the chorus of a pop song or on a TV show. Some stockings for winter maybe, a little purse to hide your little money. An umbrella for the deep strong sunshine and the summer rain. 'Don't worry about it,' she said again.

'Don't put your sad face on.'

She turned to look at him. His eyebrows were close together, his lips pulled in an inquisitive pout. But he wasn't looking at her. He was looking out the window over the neighbour's black roof, off into the distance of an almost empty sky, watching a bomber.

'My favourite soap is on TV.' She got up, pulling up her underwear.

Martin was ready to drift into a dreamless sleep. He kept his eyes open long enough to see her breasts wiggle in her bra as she bent to put her shoes on.

'Is it OK that I warm your food for you, or do you want to eat later?' Augustine knew it was pointless warming his food. Still, she played her part.

The bomber was out of sight and Martin lay down. His eyes heavy.

'No, no, you run along to your beloved soapie,' he gibed as he closed his eyes. She looked at him, so comfortable in his bed. His face framed by the white-and-blue flecked continental pillowcase.

Below the surface, she thought, underneath his sadness was a cool meanness. A selfishness that excluded every living thing. A few seconds ago, he'd wanted to buy her gifts; now her TV habits were too much.

They suck your energy, she told herself. *They're worse than children.*

Justice and Nicholas were watching a cartoon video in Nicholas's playroom in the room next door. Daffy Duck and his nephews were up to a captivating prime colour adventure. Nicholas was asleep on a big pillow on the floor and Justice was lying next to him. She poked her head in, and Justice smiled at her, drool falling from his mouth. It was the smile she lived for.

'What is Daffy Duck doing?' she asked him, in the high-pitched motherly voice she always put on for him. He reached out his arms and she sat on the floor and put him on her lap. She was bobbing him up and down when she noticed Nicholas's heavy breathing. She put her hand on his head. He was warm.

'Martin, Martin!' she shouted.

He didn't like her calling his name like that. 'Don't shout like that—' He couldn't finish, because she was rushing into her bedroom with Justice on her hip. He didn't like this image. This was getting a little too comfortable.

'Nicholas has a fever, and he's breathing heavy.' Her eyes were big.

Martin started towards Nicholas's room. He put his boxers on in the passage. Augustine stood outside, looking at Martin picking Nicholas up. He felt Nicholas's warm head on his bare shoulder. 'I'm taking him to the doctor right now.'

'Get dressed. I'll get him a cool towel for his head,' Augustine said, taking charge.

Nicholas opened his eyes slowly. It was obvious he wasn't well. Martin left within ten or so minutes, with Nicholas strapped in a baby seat Augustine had gotten out of the boot. She stood at the front door, on the brick-faced top step, and watched the back of the old white Benz drive through the black wrought iron gates. She stood in her maid's uniform, her hair a mess from tossing against him. She held Justice close to her, knowing not to wave to Martin as he exited, in case one of the neighbours saw her casualness. She looked up at the sky, seeing the dark clouds approaching for an unseasonal rainstorm. But it meant tonight would be warmer, and they could snuggle together listening to the rain on the window.

'Are you hungry, my lovely man?' She closed the door behind her. She warmed his food in the kitchen and heard a thunderclap in the distance. She worried about Nicholas, a child quietened by the death of his mother. Looking after him was hardly anything extra. Justice was the busy and wild one, and she always thought that the mixing of the blood made him that way. He would wake up at six in the morning looking for her, talking to her in baby language, in a possessed way that made him look like a miniature drunk cursing at her. Then he'd go back to sleep with his bottle. He pulled to his father, she thought. There was truly little she could do about that.

They sat to watch her soapie, and wait for Martin and Nicholas to come back. She just hoped Justice didn't catch whatever bug Nicholas had.

CHAPTER 18

Willem had called him last night and told him Angelo's axe was negative for human blood.

'When are you coming to fetch the axe?' Willem asked.

'Hold on to it.' Segert felt Willem would try to draw him into something else that he couldn't fix. Besides, what was he going to do, go round to Angelo's parents and give it back? For now, Angelo and his little carvings didn't amount to anything for him.

Segert was still ruminating over that development as he walked towards the train station, where he'd arranged to meet Augustine's friend Rosalind.

This girl is a piece of work, Segert thought. Before he'd set eyes on her, he'd already developed a firm dislike of Rosalind.

The entrance of the train station smelled strongly of damp and cat urine. Segert trampled sand and dust under his old tan leather boots and unconsciously rubbed his hands down the front of his faded jeans. He ordered a coffee from the bored-looking cashier and looked out the window at his van on the otherwise empty parking lot. No one left their cars at the train station. The ones that had cars either drove to the city to work or left their cars at home to commute by bus or train.

Either situation had its challenges. Traffic, parking, pesky neighbours asking for lifts, or the banality of weekend driving that commuted the beautiful act of driving into a death sentence of grocery shopping and Sunday family gatherings. But besides that, it was too dangerous to leave your car here. You could come back in the middle of a spontaneous riot and find your gleaming Corolla stoned or bullet-ridden. What would you tell the wife?

A large Casspir was stationed across the road. A soldier crouched at the top, posing like a sharpshooter all day, back-up squads mere minutes away. If a throbbing disgruntled mass thronged from the station, chanting in deep voices and throwing stones or petrol bombs, they could easily be decimated. All the trees had been cut down on the street. Not many had been planted around here in the first place, but all been sawed at knee level. The street was a killing alley.

The train from Witwatersrand was five minutes late. The large rectangular clock over the doorway slowly ticked to 15.48. The ticket inspector, a middle-aged man with a full head of salt-and-pepper hair and a soft round belly, paced slowly in the empty corridor playing with a silver coin he let drop on the back of his fingers. It was one way to pass the time. Segert took a sip of his coffee and nodded at him. The ticket inspector nodded back, idly absorbing Segert's demeanour and dress. Segert sitting there was curious and out of place. His muscular arms, thick neck and strong chest and tanned skin made him an alien in the coloured part of town. Even so, the inspector seemed to decide he wasn't a serious threat and started playing with his coin again.

A low voice crackled loudly over the tannoy, announcing the train from Witwatersrand. The sky was speckled with grey clouds and a light wind was blowing. Pink, blue and orange pieces of plastic beat gently against the railway fence as the train pulled in and stopped. The passengers were mostly school children, students and a few gangsters and town loiterers — men with nothing else to do but go into town looking for work, looking for a beer, or for women to pester. Segert searched the crowd for any signs of recognition, but everyone seemed to get off and walk back to the end of the train to the exit furthest from the Casspir. Segert was distracted for a moment by the plump inspector, who nodded at the train driver, who shouted something quickly, his voice as high as a whistle. Segert couldn't make out what he said, but it clearly tickled the plump inspector, who cupped his right hand and pretended to drink water from it, then raised his hand and made an exaggerated wink. A sinister smile in his eyes.

Segert felt a tap on his shoulder. A small woman stood behind him. She wore stonewashed jeans and a black polo neck, and a purple backpack hung on her tiny shoulders. Her hair was pulled back in a tight bun, dyed brown at the tips, escaping in strategic tendrils. Segert noticed the cheap but elegant silver and black leather watch on her wrist.

The train had started and the inspector turned, still in his playful mood. But his eyes went dead when he saw her, and his right hand demanded her ticket through the glass. She pointed at Segert. He looked, upset he hadn't had a chance to watch her bottom as she passed him.

'You Berger?'

'Rosalind.' He faked a smile. 'What have you got for me?'

Her face gave Segert the impression of a goldfish bowl. Large, round and blank, with maybe one interesting thing in it.

'Not that much, really. Can I have a white coffee?' she asked softly, as she sat down, putting the backpack on the chair next to her.

'What have you got for me?' Segert repeated, looking at the bag.

'My neighbour saw them. Augustine and the baby. At a nature park or something, over Christmas.'

'So where is your neighbour?'

'She doesn't want to get involved. It's a relief.' She blew on the coffee as she stirred it. 'It's none of her business.'

'Nothing's going to happen if I meet her.'

144

'She's not hedging her bets. I don't blame her. Meeting you is like telling everyone around here you some collaborator.'

'I don't work for the government.'

'Maybe not now. You used to. I can see it, everyone can.'

'OK.'

'My cousin is more my business than hers anyway. The only industries for us are catting around, childrearing and gossip.'

Segert sat slightly back in his chair. 'Tell me everything she told you.' He noticed the inspector coming up to the window, pretending not to be nosy.

'We need to make a deal,' Rosalind said.

'A deal? What kind of deal? You've been watching too much TV.'

'When you find her, I want you to tell me where she is.'

'Sure. Of course. Is that it?'

'I'm serious. Is she in trouble? Maybe I can help her.'

Segert tried to convince her that her friend wasn't in any trouble with any authorities. She wouldn't be locked up in detention, jailed or separated from her baby.

'Is this just about the baby's father? He is going to a lot of trouble to find her. Now.'

'People are full of surprises,' Segert said lightly.

'Can I talk to him?'

'I'll tell him you asked, but I wouldn't get my hopes up.'

'Why? You just told me people are full of surprises.'

'I'll give him your details after I find her. That's all I can promise.' If Teddy wanted to talk to Rosalind, he would've done it already.

'All right.' She gave him the rest of the details that the mysterious involvement-averse neighbour had given her.

Segert wrote them in a small navy handbook. His thick black eyebrows furrowed together at the mention of African Zionists. *Did Augustine join a cult?* Segert asked himself.

'It's a type of religion,' Rosalind added unnecessarily. 'Like Christianity.'

'Thanks for your help.' He nodded.

'Good luck with the churches.' Rosalind picked up her backpack and stood up. 'I don't know if a bunch of Africans will like another Afrikaner poking about their godly business. If you need some help, call me. I might be able to talk to them.'

She definitely had some theatre about her.

'Would I be the proverbial last straw?' Segert said, the idea completely preposterous to him.

Segert got into his van and started north towards Orange Grove. He turned out of the car park and drove down the main road that connected all the stations along the train track. The Witwatersrand basin stretched from Welkom two hundred kilometres in the east to Johannesburg. It was a shallow sea once, millions of years ago. Pockets of ancient granite undulated in small hills at his back. He could see three, maybe four kilometres down the straight road. Then the road curved through cookie-cutter houses in manageable perpendicular blocks.

Each station he idled past, a heavy inert Casspir was set like a piece on a chessboard. Every block was poorer than the last. Large four-bedroomed houses gave way to little cluster homes to community houses where the narrow doorframes foretold how small the possibility of love and peace and happiness can be.

The only places with tall trees were the cemeteries; in death, you would find eternal shade from the relentless Jo'burg sun. The birds were cooled by leaves and stood on thick rhythmic branches watching coffins being lowered into the ground. Above, three jets traced the sky practising military manoeuvres.

Segert thought that he loved the winter in the Highveld. When the mornings were dry and cold and the sky a chalkish blue, and he'd amble around his house waiting for midmorning, for the heat to bite through the frost. The perfect time for a cheap oily steak in a floury Portuguese roll and a can of the

146

best. He rubbed his lips together. There was almost nothing that couldn't wait till after he went to his local, Solomon's Saloon.

He carried on the Golden Highway, heading north, but then split off at the exit to Braamfontein. It was late afternoon, and the streets were full of meandering sedans and unloading trucks. He turned left onto Carr Street and parked outside a low-rise called Brickfields, the name of the old town before it was razed to stop the bubonic. He jogged to the shop for a Coke and was squinting in the doorway when he heard a voice.

'Hello, stranger. What you doing here?'

'Looking for you.'

'I like to hear it.' Brown Sugar smiled, her buckteeth protruding slightly. 'Nice car. Are we going for a ride?'

'What do you know about Zionists?' he asked.

'What is it now?' Her voice was wary. He'd broken the spell again. 'Do I look like an encyclopaedia?'

Segert laughed and realised her posturing was designed precisely for this. He offered his Coke. And got out his wallet.

'I don't know anything about Zionists. Never heard of it.'

'I believe you.'

They stood side by side, leaning against the shopfront window. The sun was low. She sipped the Coke and passed it back to him. He told her to keep it. It was that time of the day, when people who didn't have children could make friends over a drink and chat.

'Scared for my germs? You all nice, and then you act like this.' Her eyes were sharp. 'Why you bother me at work?'

'If you don't want the Coke, then just give it back.' He raised his voice.

An old white woman walked out of the shop at the time, stopping long enough to give them a look of distaste. She walked down one step, then turned around to say something.

'Shut up,' they said to her in unison. The lady kept her mouth shut and walked off in a huff.

147

'It's not safe these days,' Segert said to Brown Sugar. 'Be careful.'

'Hello,' she said, as a greeting and a warning. And walked down the stairs to the hotel at the other side of the road. The fat Coke can balanced casually in her right hand.

* * *

The next morning, Segert tasted evil. A family of small furry rodents had died inside his mouth. His breathing was low and dry, and he hesitated to open his eyelids. The usual reel of regret flashed in his mind. His wife's broken, disappointed face, the forbidden naked curve of his lover's shoulder. Ultimately, the recurring nightmare that was the memory of his wife sobbing made him lift an eyelid to witness a sunbeam capable of scorching the earth tunnelling through the break in his curtains. Hell was upon him today, and Trigger and Simba barked loudly to herald the devils.

'Sorry, babies,' he whispered to the dogs as he opened the back door.

There were indications that he'd fed them last night. How much and what, he couldn't remember.

When they were starving because he'd neglected to come home or feed them, their bowls would be overturned in protest. It didn't happen that often, but still, once was too much.

'I'll be good today.' He rubbed their heads and bargained for forgiveness before he threw up in the drain by the hose pipe. He'd rather think about what a lousy dog-owner he was, instead of the lousy husband he'd been.

He drank from the garden hose, then filled their water bowls.

Segert walked his dogs one and half kilometres, then ambled back up the avenues. He was wearing dark sunglasses and sipping a *naartjie*-flavoured Energade. He hadn't shaved. The dogs pulled slowly ahead of him on their leashes, sniffing trees and investigating wall cracks. He was mentally scratching people off his help list when he remembered a pimply man-boy who blinked too much when he talked. They'd met once at a neighbourhood *braai*, and he'd been an African Studies major. Now he worked at the post office.

Jonty was on the loading dock at the side of the Observatory Post Office. The floor was strewn with cast-off cigarettes and chewing gum like the corners of a grammar school playground. He was wearing standard issue grey slacks and a dark blue shirt with a post office logo on the right pocket that hung loosely over his small shoulders. He'd added thick black spectacles and a pair of old *vellies* to his ensemble. He fidgeted constantly, push-ing his spectacles higher on his nose. Segert had left Trigger and Simba tied up at the lamppost at the end of the street. Better not to bring them. They'd make Jonty even more nervous.

'What are you doing here?' Jonty lit a cigarette.

'I have a question about Zionists. African Zionists.'

'You told my supervisor you're my brother.'

Ja, well, sorry. I couldn't wait till lunchtime.'

Jonty took a deep puff of his cigarette. He looked up into the sky.

Agh boy, Segert thought, *this is going to be a long one*. His loose stomach shook the rest of his entrails as he tried to focus on what Jonty was saying.

'. . . not from Zion in Israel. It's based on faith teaching from Zion in America.'

'Do you know if there's any churches in Jo'burg and where?' Segert interjected.

'There's a few around here. Melville, Berea, downtown maybe; most will be in the townships. I'm with His People. You should come join us on Sunday if you're looking for a church. We do house church on a Thursday down in 14th Avenue.'

House church? Down the road, Trigger yawned, and Segert felt the kinship of spirit animals. 'No, no, it's not for me, but I'll let my friend know,' he said quickly.

Church people were freaks of nature. House church in the week — what were they talking about, every Thursday?

'We start with a free meal, so feel free to come.'

Segert appreciated the hook. '*Ja, ja.* OK.' He was already edging away. He coughed, nodded and turned towards his dogs. 'I have to get them back.'

* * *

At eleven o'clock Sunday morning, Segert watched a group of Zionists ranging in age from mid-teens to late sixties, walking in twos along a slip road along Boom Street. Jonty was right. They dressed in distinctive green, blue and white. The women were in knee-length duke blue dresses, their heads covered in elegant white hats and wraps. The leader was a tall man in his early thirties, his chestnut skin sleek with a light sheen of sweat. He wore blue robes that flapped in the breeze, a grey feather behind his right ear, a Bible in his right hand. Segert parked his BMW in front of a row of exposed brick shopfronts. He went to sit at the window of a small café.

A low breeze cooled the morning, rippling the candy-striped awning of a pastry shop. The group of Zionists had gone off road at the willow across the road, about twenty-five metres from where he was sitting. He ordered a black coffee and took the thick Sunday newspaper from the empty table behind him. The last of the older women Zionists were struggling to negotiate the terrain of the riverbank. Their heads disappeared from sight in a stammer. The café owner was an old man with a turkey neck who wore a blue short-sleeve shirt, brown bowtie and jeans. The front of his shirt had a dried-out tomato ketchup stain that he'd tried to wipe off.

'Beautiful day,' he said, as he put the coffee down.

Ja, nice.' Segert didn't look at him.

* * *

The leader emerged two bitter coffees later. His gown was wet from the bottom of his sleeves. He'd performed baptisms in the shallow river. Two men behind him were blinking water from their eyes. Their cloaks completely soaked as if they had gone swimming. Underneath, their tan trousers clung to their legs, and their feet remained bare as they negotiated the embankment. The group walked in twos alongside the pavement, back the way they'd come. Segert scanned the group for Augustine's face. He didn't find it, but took pictures of all of them as he drove out the car park. The group walked eight hundred metres to a ramshackle minibus and an equally old but well-panel-beaten white Toyota Corolla. Segert took a note of the registrations, then drove to downtown Johannesburg looking for the other congregations Jonty'd told him about.

The Berger family was Methodist, and as a child Segert had felt that church burned him inside his bones. The singing and then being quiet, the listening and the nodding. His father's singing and the clothes that felt like a Monday morning before school. Maybe he would've liked church more if he could be outside, sitting barefoot by the river.

He took photographs of as many congregations as he could find. Six. As the sun began to set, and the temperature dropped, he drove home to feed his dogs.

* * *

Tuesday afternoon Segert was back at the Langlaate train station coffee shop. He passed Rosalind a thick wad of photographs tucked inside a neon pink school diary.

'Do you have an eight-year-old daughter? What is this?'

The diary was obviously overkill.

'I'm not sure you have a neighbour.'

Ja, I live in the woods. This diary will come in handy, though. *Dear Diary . . . today I met a strange man at a train station.*'

'I think you saw her yourself.'

'You think I saw her myself? I'd just go over and say, "Hello, what are you doing?"'

151

'Maybe something stopped you. Maybe you were with someone else, or friends, and you were embarrassed.'

'Like she'd ruin my vibe? It's not like she's an aunty or something that I don't want to see on a Sunday because I have a hangover.' She put the diary in her bag. 'I'll call you if my neighbour recognises anyone.'

'OK, thanks.'

'Yes, thanks.'

He watched her cross the road and hop into a minibus taxi. He got up quickly, spilling coffee on the table. He was never coming back to this station. There was something about Rosalind he didn't like. It was a dislike he couldn't describe, didn't want to find the words; she wasn't worth that. He knew the racial slurs, and the words for difficult women. But she was both, and worse, and much less due his energy.

***

She called him back at lunchtime on Friday.

'Hi, it's Rosalind.'

He could hardly hear her over the background noise of shouting and excited talking.

'Mr Berger?'

'Where are you? Did she recognise anyone?'

'I'm using the campus cafeteria payphone. And yes: the man and woman in the white Toyota.'

He knew exactly who she meant. 'Is she sure?'

'Yes, she is. God. Remember what you promised me?'

'I won't forget. I promise.' He sighed. He hated owing anybody anything. But he knew if the pastor didn't want to speak to him about Augustine he might just be inclined to open up to Rosalind. She could be useful in the future.

Saturdays were his best time to work. He could catch people relaxed, without any type of formality. But this time it was a bit different. Sunday was the pastor's professional day.

He was more likely to open up on a Saturday, before God inspired resistance in his humble servant.

The pastor held his small Bible tightly when he saw the man with the taut muscles standing in the church doorway. He hoped that this man remembered he was in the house of the Lord, but Jesus and Black Gods were as meaningful as mud piled into ant hills to these people.

The pastor dabbed a trickle of sweat at his temple. Bristling against the heat of the small circle of hell visiting his church. 'Good day, sir. Welcome to the house of the Lord. Come, let us sit down.' He kept his speech slow. They sat down and, instead of leading the conversation, he waited for the man to talk. Men like this, with whatever agenda he had, never travelled alone.

'I was wondering if you could help me find someone.'

'Are you talking about Jesus?'

'No, no, I'm not here looking for Jesus.' The man looked around the small church.

'Are you looking for . . . yourself?' The pastor smiled.

'I haven't introduced myself. My name is Segert Berger. I'm looking for a young woman. I think you might know her.'

'What makes you think that?'

'Someone saw you with her.'

'Are you looking for a Zionist woman?' The pastor looked at the folder in the man's hand.

'I am looking for this woman.' Segert took out a picture of Augustine from his folder. He noticed a flicker of recognition register on the pastor's face, but as soon as it arrived it disappeared behind his eyes.

'She doesn't look like someone I would know.'

'Yes, I know. But you were seen with her.'

'I am a pastor. I counsel lots of people. I am a shepherd of the Lord. And a married man.'

'Look, no one is looking for any trouble. She has a baby. I know you know her.'

The pastor was quiet, considering his options, his religion.

'The baby's father wants to make sure his son is safe.'

'Are you sure this is all it's about? Give me your number. I will try to get to the bottom of this.'

Segert readjusted his level of authority. 'You don't want any trouble. It's easy to get into trouble these days. You can understand this.' His voice was slow and thick. The threat clear.

'I don't know where she is. I only saw her twice, but someone else might know who she is.'

'Who?'

'This I can't tell you.'

'You are a married man. And a man of the cloth. You know what's the difference between you and me?'

The pastor wanted to say, *Yes. The difference is my skin. The Lord loves us both and I must love everyone as he loves us. But I must put up with maltreatment by your ilk because of the colour of my skin.* He remembered his prayers, and his wife. He remained quiet.

'The difference is you have a lot more to lose than me. I'll come see you tomorrow.'

Segert got up and walked away. Somewhere in his subconscious, he knew he left the pastor with a face burning with shame. He hoped it was shame. But when he got outside, he got in his van and thought instead of the beer he could drink and how much he spent on the Windhoek lagers last week, and how Wes Petersen was probably drinking them lounging around his house. He'd burned up Teddy's money faster than he was making progress, and he needed results before he could hit Teddy up for some more money.

The following day, Segert parked his van in an empty industrial car park opposite the church. He bribed the security guard with a crisp R20 note.

'I won't be long. I'll be gone in an hour.'

The security guard abandoned his post immediately, quite possibly to buy beer and porridge.

It was 3 p.m. and the pastor had hung up his gown to dry on the back of a chair close to an open window. An older

154

woman was talking quickly in Sotho as she poured boiling water into a cup. Segert wiped the gravel off his boots at the door, and she turned to him, appraising him slowly. The only sounds were of the birds chirping on the telephone lines and the hum of dense electricity cables. This must be the woman Rosalind's neighbour was talking about.

'I hear you have been looking for a young woman.'

'Yes, I am looking for Augustine and her son. Do you know where they are?'

'I met her on a bus; she had nowhere to go. Why would a girl with a baby not have anywhere safe to go?' The question hung in the air.

'I'm not the baby's father. I've already told the pastor.'

'We're not sure what you want from us,' the pastor said.

'You know where Augustine is, and I need to find her. It's not any more complicated than that.'

CHAPTER 19

It was an average summer's day for Augustine. For everybody else it was Valentine's Day. The house had the usual daytime quiet she had come to enjoy. No arguments or deep swallowing of a thousand tiny resentments. It was a quiet place where she had almost everything. Clouds had been climbing into the blueness of the sky and swallowed all the colour. Now they were turning a stormy grey. Augustine and Justice had been out in the neighbourhood for a short walk. She got some groceries at the Spar supermarket and the cashiers gave him admiring looks. He smiled at them, and Augustine knew she had a budding little flirt on her hands. He did like the ladies already. She propped him in front of the TV after lunch, and he fell asleep.

Augustine went outside, thinking about the friends and the conversations she missed. She leaned back, remembering the time she and two of her friends danced around a coffee table at her parents' house. Drunk on cheap liquor and listening to Afro house music on the radio. *On the radio*. She laughed to herself when thinking about it. The cops walked in and caught her friend, Ludmilla, in her bra dancing on an old sea-green floral sofa. The two policemen were surprised that

156

there were only three girls dancing in the front room. From the neighbours, it sounded like a wild party.

She heard the sound of gravel lightly churning, and knew that Martin must be home. Everything was more or less in its place, so she got up slowly to meet him at the front door.

'Hello, sir,' she said quietly.

She looked a beautiful picture standing there. She was calmer now and had fewer anxieties. Young women still itched for life and excitement, but she had calmed down in the days he was away while Nicholas was in hospital. Her eyes searched for Nicholas in the car. But there was no one.

Before she asked, he said, 'Nicholas is still with my sister in Pretoria.' He walked past her to his bedroom, carrying two leather travel bags.

'I'm sorry to hear that, sir.' She felt relieved that she had put Justice down in her room, his health not on full display for Martin to resent.

'Is there anything I can get you to eat?' He was already in his bedroom and she had to shout.

Martin spent the rest of the afternoon in the library. Listening to slow melancholic music that she felt described Nicholas's health.

* * *

The weather had broken when he called her into the study, after. Rain was pouring on to the window and the floor lamp was shining onto a book he was reading on his desk. The pages were bright like laminate. When she came closer, she saw it was only the pages of an architectural magazine.

'All this, that's happened to me, made me think of you and Justice. What's going to happen to him if anything happens to you?'

'I don't know. I don't think anything will happen to me.'

'I thought the same thing. The same. Your family?'

She got up to leave. 'Thank you for your concern, Mr Diamond.'

'I am concerned.' He shifted in his chair. 'This isn't easy to talk about. I don't want to ask your personal business. But your child is living in my house.'

'I have a way to make sure he will be taken care of. There are people who will be able to help me.'

'Your parents?'

Augustine chuckled lightly. 'No, but people just as good. Better. Church folk.'

'If anything happens to you, how will we — I mean, how will I — get in touch with them?'

'Ms Maggie and . . .' she hesitated saying the name, 'Mrs Diamond made me fill in some forms. All the details are on there.'

'Oh, good. I was just wondering if there was any change in arrangements, maybe now . . .' Martin trailed off.

'I won't be a burden, don't worry.' She smiled, satisfied with herself.

'I can take care of him, you know. Me and my sister. I mean, not here, obviously. But my sister can have him. If anything happens to you. Right?'

'Nothing will happen to me.' Augustine was shaking her head. 'And there are some people from a nice church who can look after him. I know you're worried about Nicholas, but you don't have to be worried about me, too.'

'I'm just trying to help you out. That's all.' Martin stood up and came to sit on the edge of the desk, next to her.

He's just sad, she told herself as she stood up.

'I can help you get out of here,' Martin said.

'Here? Why would I want to leave?'

'Bessy needs help, and the two boys can be together.'

'Do you want me, us, to leave?'

'Without Nicholas here . . .'

'I thought your sister lives in Windhoek.' Augustine heard her heartbeat in her ears.

Martin took her left hand by its fingertips and pulled her closer to him. He put his right hand around her neck and kissed her. She leaned back and he caressed her ear with his thumb. She knew more than anything that is what he wanted most. A kind of submission that for her was easy to give. She kissed him back, and he unbuttoned the cardigan she was wearing. He recognised it, but said nothing. It belonged to someone else, but then so had Kimberly. That is how all the trouble started. It was spilt milk. He pulled her in closer. The best thing about Augustine was that she took your feelings upon herself. Like it really was her job to make him feel better. He put his hands on her buttocks, then her back. He cupped the back of her head and she leaned back against the window. The rain falling heavily behind her.

Her eyes opened in shocked surprised when he put his left hand around her neck, then squeezed. She mouthed for him to stop, but she could see in his eyes that hurting her was precisely his intention. The storm was heavy but all she could hear was the sound of her heart beating thickly in her ears. She couldn't breathe and fought so she could get to Justice, who was still sleeping on her bed.

'Come my darling, give up,' he whispered like a secret. She saw one thick sharp white light across his face, and her last thought was her realisation that she had been a fool to think that she could live in both worlds.

The lightning hit a tree in Martin's back garden. He would have to move it.

* * *

After the storm cleared, the ground was thick with water. Martin sweated in the mud for hours. The neighbourhood was dark and quiet. The only noises were from nocturnal birds and the muscular black cat that stalked up the cypress, watching Martin exert himself. His shirt clinging to his body in sweat.

CHAPTER 20

The church was a large room, green paint cracked and chipped across the walls. Broken windows were covered with toilet paper boxes, black tape and rubbish bags. The room was once the administration office of the Triple S Printing Works. The back door of the church was a lacquered oxblood red, repurposed from a club or shebeen. A brick held it open, and you could see into a large workshop with disused printing machines in the foreground. In the distance, it was well-lit with natural light and Segert could make out small stacks of printing ready for collection, perhaps early tomorrow morning.

Zula Moloi was wearing a turquoise dress with yellow daisies in fine print, a thick yellow cardigan and white heels that were slightly scuffed. Her hair was smoothed in a practical yet elegant manner. She took a deep breath while stirring her cup. The steam rising in spirals. For a time, no one looked at each other. The pastor rubbed the spine of his Bible with his thumb while Segert paced the empty space, picking at the paint chips, then touched the pastor's wet gown that was drying under an open window. He walked over to the kettle.

'Do you have any coffee?'

'If tea doesn't suit you, there's water,' the pastor said. 'We are humble people.'

'No matter,' Segert said.

The pastor was wearing the typical ensemble of black shirt, black trousers and shoes with a tan leather belt.

'Where's your feather today?'

'Excuse me?' the pastor said, surprised.

'Last week. You were wearing a feather in your hair last week.'

'One of the youngsters gave it to me. I entertained him. How long have you been following us?'

'Just that one time. Honest.' Segert held his hands up in surrender, then switched on the kettle.

Mrs Moloi's chest moved up slowly. She was a short woman with large legs and breasts and a big low stomach, without any unnecessary rolls of fat on her neck and arms. She was strong fat. A group of women like that in this space, and Segert would've thought twice about coming in. Even if they were in their fifties and sixties. Batons and bullets couldn't stop them advancing. And if it weren't for the fact of each of them being the only barrier between their families and the abyss, they'd be an unstoppable force. The government used the pass system to keep them separated from their men. Their men on the mines, the woman in factories. Segert remembered a piece of graffiti that seemed apt now. *Fat strong thighs give life*. At first, he'd thought it was innuendo, but he saw now it made sense.

'Let's start from the beginning,' Segert said. 'I'm trying to find Augustine and her baby. The baby's father wants to see him. I know you were with her up north. Let's start there.'

'I met her on a bus from Rosebank or Parkhurst. I can't remember. But she was with the baby and I helped her,' Zula said.

'What was she doing that side of town? Was she with anyone else?'

'She wasn't with anyone besides the baby. I didn't ask questions because I'm not nosy like that. I'm a good Samaritan.'

161

'But what about the park? You had plenty of time to talk. Didn't you try to convert her? You must've wanted some background information.'

The pastor answered. 'No, we didn't try to convert her. She doesn't speak the language. We could tell she needed some friends, and so we were just around.'

'So, what did you talk about? You must know something. Where was she living, did she have a job or a new boyfriend? Anything?'

'We spoke mostly about the Lord. But it looked like she landed on her feet. Her baby, Justice, the cute thing, looked well. She was wearing nice slacks and a soft cardigan, like from Edgars. She smelled nice,' Mrs Moloi answered.

'The Lord hears everything, Mama,' the pastor said. 'My mother did prod her for information, but my wife and me stopped her. It wasn't right, especially in front of everyone.'

'Why do you talk about me like that? Oh-oh. I am prodding people like they are cattle? I am the main actress on the stage asking questions in a drama? Like I am making a performance. You talk about me like this. Your wife, I can understand. But you? My own son—'

'You always ask questions, but I overlook it.'

Her son spoke directly to Segert. 'She was grateful for our help. Everyone is welcome. We don't ask too many questions. In these troubled times . . .'

Pastor Moloi's voice was warm, and for some reason reminded Segert of Old Brown sherry on a winter's night. Janette, his ex-wife, used to drink it. But the calm words weren't what he needed. 'Your philosophy is not helping me very much. Where do you live, close by here? Here?'

'Soweto.'

'What did she do that night? Where did she go?'

'We gave her some money,' Pastor Moloi lied. 'We don't have much, but we made a collection for them. Then she walked to the taxi rank before it was too late and too cold.'

* * *

162

Zula wanted to avoid connecting Segert with her son's home. She didn't want Segert there, or anywhere in Soweto. Nobody's reputation could afford a man like Segert around in the townships. All it took was a jealous neighbour reporting her to the local Apartheid resistance, and that would be a match to set both her and her son alight. She kept her mouth shut and lied alongside her son. White people do it all the time, she told herself.

'I might have to come back here, if I can't find her soon enough,' he said.

'I remember now,' Zula said. 'We met in Greenside. I think she works nearby.'

***

Segert was in two minds about what to do. All he had was the photographs from Beukes. What was he going to do, stake out the whole of Greenside? Though it wasn't big. He could drive around there in thirty or forty minutes. But all he would see were houses and cars.

Maybe she'd found a rich leftie university student whose parents had emigrated and left them with a big house. She could be living with him. Students liked to experiment and think they could change the world. Do drugs, listen to music. Still, it was unlikely. Augustine had a baby in tow — an instant student-party repellent.

Segert was convinced that all students did was smoke weed all day, drink and have sex.

Unless you were poor, like Rosalind. Then it must be some serious business, because you were scared of the world and the world didn't care about you. And you couldn't afford all the booze you wanted to drown it all out, either.

No. No matter how open-minded these college types were, they wouldn't want to turn their house into an actual kindergarten. So, she wouldn't be shacking up with someone, unless she'd gotten rid of the baby. And the last time she was seen, she was with the baby, so chances were she hadn't dumped it. He hated to admit it, but he needed Rosalind's help — or, at least, her opinion — on Augustine's habits.

* * *

'Rosalind.' He didn't bother saying hello. He wasn't interested in getting into a drawn-out conversation on the phone with her.

'Hello. Did you find her?'

'Sort of. The lead checked out.'

'Really?'

'You sound surprised. Listen, they met her in Greenside. Do you think Augustine knows anyone there?'

'Whatever you do, don't tell her boyfriend. He'll go out and hunt her down.' There was that dramatic flair again.

'What boyfriend, Teddy? She ran away. I don't think they're a couple anymore.'

'Even more reason not to tell him.' Rosalind was sitting on the brown and cream carpet in the lounge. Her legs hugged to her chest. She'd just vacuumed and cleaned the living room while a chicken curry was cooking on the hob. The scent of garam masala and onions filled the small house.

'What do you think, I'm doing this for my health? He is paying me to find her.'

It didn't take much to set him off, she thought. 'Fair enough. I forgot about all that. So, what are you calling me for?'

'Do you know if Augustine knows anyone in Greenside?' he repeated.

'No. That crowd don't mix with us. You know that. Where you calling me from? It's noisy.'

'It's raining.'

Segert hung up. He was standing at a busy intersection downtown. The payphone had a short roof to shelter from the sun and the rain, but was otherwise open to the elements. The chain that was meant to hold the telephone directory was

164

empty and rusted. The place smelled of urine and faeces, and he wanted to get out of there.

Segert's next call was to Teddy. He was due an update.

'I thought you'd forgotten about me,' Teddy said.

'Why you sound so nervous? What happened?'

'Nothing, nothing. Maybe you should leave things as they are.'

'If that's what you really want, I can send you your last bill in the post. But this is your son.' Segert tried to hook him once more.

'She's been in touch.'

'Congratulations,' Segert said.

'It's complicated.'

'Show me a woman that isn't. If you need to see me, you know where I am. Consider the bill in the post.'

* * *

Segert was disappointed. The Beukes case had stalled, if not stopped altogether. Meanwhile, Richard Reader was just a man of business now. He'd stopped going on dates, and the cigar lounges and whisky drinking had dried up. Keeping tabs on him meant tedious nights in the parking lot, dressed in Wes's suit in case he stepped out somewhere in Sandton. It was dry times. The flask of black coffee and *boerewors* sandwiches weren't sitting right in his guts anymore.

On Saturday morning, Segert got up at 7 a.m. He'd decided to follow Reader from his flat in Killarney. Weekdays made no progress, and he had nothing else to do.

The dogs sniffed the dew on the grass, excited by a change in their routine. Simba rubbed his nose against Segert's leg as he opened the front gate. The two dogs were ready to run. They didn't even stop to sniff the first paperbark tree on the pavement. They paced playfully, bodies confident and tails relaxed. Segert was glad he was hydrated. They waited at the edge of the pavement further down the road.

'Slow down, boys. We need to stretch first.'

Segert put his foot against the pavement base and leaned forward to stretch his calf, then the other. Rolled his shoulders, patted the dogs on the back and started a slow jog down the gentle slope towards Orange Grove Park.

It felt that the day was opening up like his lungs. Saturday mornings in Jo'burg were the best mornings in the world. The sun was always shining on your head, whether you were rich or you had nothing. Jo'burg had Saturdays and a hustle spirit; even the dogs had it.

An hour later, Segert let himself back into the backyard, filled the water bowls, stripped and hosed himself down outside using a green Sunlight soap sliver he always left on the back retaining wall. He sighed, enjoying the cold water and his nudity. The dogs waited for breakfast.

* * *

At ten thirty, Reader got in his car that was parked in the driveway and reversed out and headed north. The morning was warming up nicely. The sun was over easy and Reader drove with the window down, the scent of acacias and blossoms breezing through his vehicle.

Segert cruised behind him, unnoticed. This was a residential road with light traffic. If Reader turned off left, Segert could miss a turn and circle back or take the next auxiliary road and try to catch up behind him later. Reader crossed the R25 and then turned right slowly, without indicating. Segert kept straight at a slow place. The right turn led onto a short road that was the entrance to the Killarney Golf Club. Reader wasn't dressed for golf. He hadn't carried a set of clubs down the stairs. Reader was in his Saturday casuals, a straight pair of navy shorts and a white T-shirt. He wasn't dressed to tee off. He was meeting someone for brunch, maybe.

Segert parked on the side of the road, climbed out and inspected the fence. Even if he snuck onto the grounds, he'd be spotted by some golfers. He was too out of place. He needed higher ground. He got back in his car and drove up to Linksfield ridge.

A brother and sister of about six and eight were playing in the park, close to homes designated for lower-level embassy staff. All the properties had high walls and cameras, but the park seemed to be neutral ground. Their chocolate-and-white springer spaniel puppy was running between the two of them excitedly, deciding who to be the most loyal to.

'Protestant dogs,' Segert tutted under his breath, for no reason, and then ducked to get his binoculars out of the cubbyhole. This was not the area to be caught with a long lens. He stashed his long lens on the floor and covered it with Wes's old jacket that now lived in his BMW.

Further down the road, a path between two houses led to a clearing that was the home for a short radio mast and looked out over the eighteen-hole green. Segert walked around the mast, looking over the holes for Reader. The course was busy. Segert scanned the buggies emerging onto the course, then walked a few steps down the slope, to have a better view to the country club restaurant.

There he was. Segert was expecting Reader to be with a young lady or perhaps his mother, but he saw Richard talking to one of the men he'd seen him with at one of the cigar lounges. They were at the edge of the infinity pool on the first floor.

'This got interesting.' Segert sat back on the slope and peered through the binoculars, watching. He'd been sure that Wes had sent him on a dry case, but this was making him curious.

They seemed relaxed, but there wasn't any swimming going on. Their expressions seemed too serious for a swimming pool. Then Richard got up and walked away from the pool and the other man followed.

As the morning shadow receded from the mast, Segert went to stand at its base.

By the edge of the park, an ice-cream truck was yelling its business in a persistent jingle. Segert looked at his watch. He'd been out here in the sun for two hours, but he hadn't seen Reader again. He stopped the truck for a Coke, but they were out.

'Don't have any drinks today?'

'Just ice cream and bunnylicks,' the ice-cream man said, nodding to the rows of frozen glucose-syrup sticks bike-riding children seemed to like the best.

'Give me a soft serve, then.'

The man eyed Segert's binoculars and handed him his cone.

'Bird watching,' Segert said.

He licked his ice cream and looked back at the ridge behind him. It would be a good place for the dogs. The terrain was unpredictable in places, and the dogs could separate and then pair up again. Long thin grasses and rocky paths would break up the monotony of running in streets and sniffing the same trees.

He went to Solomon's for an early lunch and called Wes.

That was one of the last things he remembered before waking up in the hospital.

* * *

'This is the worst hangover,' Segert said.

'It's worse. You don't know what happened? You called me from Solomon's. You were drunk. Cheerful, not at all maudlin. I found you in the backyard on Sunday afternoon passed out.'

'Why is my mouth still sandy?'

'You were outside. I sprayed you down.'

'What about the dogs?'

'Me and the kids are feeding them and taking them for walks.'

'But, I mean, I didn't drink *that* much. It must be food poisoning. Shoot.'

'And lots of it.' Wes laughed. 'I'll tell the nurse you're awake. I'm going back to the office. Solomon's was closed by the Health Department, by the way.'

'Best prego steak roll in town,' Segert said to Wes's back.

Wes turned and chuckled. 'How can you still say that? Don't expect flowers, though. The wife won't be happy.'

'Just make sure Simba and Trigger are OK.'

The nurse glided in. 'Glad you're awake, Mr Berger; how are you feeling?' She started taking his blood pressure. 'Mr Berger, you have cholera. You lost a lot of fluids. Very unusual case. We'll keep an eye on you,' the nurse said, putting the stethoscope tips into her ears.

CHAPTER 21

Segert was standing in the hollow of the front door drinking a cup of coffee. His usually short dark hair had grown out slightly and he was pushing it up over his temple. The water loss from his stint in the hospital gave him the appearance of cut muscles, which was the only benefit, after the Reader case that had gone sedentary for close to a month. Segert was beginning to feel back to his fighting weight. It'd been a rough couple of weeks.

'Déjà vu, hey,' Segert said to himself, as Teddy parked his car. He stretched himself out like a cat as Teddy approached.

'Afternoon.'

Segert searched Teddy's hands for a cheque, then remembered he'd already been paid. 'Howzit. Always nice to have a repeat customer. Do you want to come inside?'

'No, I need to walk, do you mind?'

'Let me grab a shirt.'

When clients wanted to unburden themselves of their grief or problems, Segert let them take the lead. He let Teddy walk out the gate ahead of him. Teddy turned left and walked down 16th Street, crossing 8th Avenue towards Linksfield. School children were playing a game of cricket in the street.

170

A tall girl started running up to bowl and flexed her trunk forward before releasing a fast ball to a smaller batsman, who was holding his nerve.

'You're probably wondering why I'm here, Mr Berger.'

'Of course. There's nothing around this side of the neighbourhood, just a swimming pool.'

'I need your help,' Teddy continued, ignoring the joke. 'It's about Augustine again.'

'My man.'

'I'm afraid I haven't been completely honest. Well, I was at the start, but it got complicated.'

'Go on.'

'Someone is blackmailing me.'

'About what?'

'About something Augustine took from me.'

'Other than the baby,' Segert said.

'Other than the baby.'

'I don't know who it is. It was a schoolboy, I thought. And I could handle it, but it's become more complicated.'

'Tell me everything. That's the only way I can help you. What are you being blackmailed about?'

'I can't tell you, it's embarrassing.'

Segert guessed. 'Naked pictures.' He appraised Teddy quietly. *I didn't see that one coming.*

'So, it's dirty pictures of both of you, or just you?'

Teddy looked at him. 'Does it matter?'

'I need to know what I'm looking for. It's for context.'

'It's just me and some . . . other people.'

'Oh, you dirty dog.' Segert slapped him on the back and laughed.

'It could destroy my career, my life.'

'Augustine gave him the pictures?'

'She was blackmailing me first, and I needed it to stop, so I came to you. Then this other boy also started blackmailing me. I don't know who he is. He has some of the pictures; she must have the rest. He only showed me one. I don't know.'

'So, I really wasn't looking for your son?'

'Of course you were. But I want the blackmail to stop.'

'The boy came later?' Segert understood. 'So, that's when you said she made contact.'

'I thought I could manage him. He was asking me for a few hundred bucks. I could handle that. Then it started to get out of hand. Someone else started turning up with him, someone scary-looking, and I didn't want to pay three people. It was too much.'

'Who's the third?'

'I don't know. I don't know who either of them are. The kid's not from the school, and Augustine doesn't have any brothers. Small family. Her male cousins are Indian. These two aren't,' Teddy said.

'Look, I can't break up gang blackmail or whatever this is. It's not my speciality. I know you can't go to the police, but I don't have the manpower for this. I'm a one-man show.'

'The only way to get it to stop is through Augustine, then.'

'For once, I agree with you. Where do you think she is?'

'I still don't know.'

'But you said she'd made contact.'

'She called me from a public phone, and now I deposit money into a post office account.'

'Her account?'

'Justice's.'

'I think she opened that account at the big post office in town. Dead end.' *Well, she's alive then*, Segert thought. *I should tell Willem.*

'So, we'll have to go back through her history, then,' Segert said. He couldn't understand his own reasoning now. Was it easier to deal with dead bodies or the prospect of real live coloureds?

'I remember some of her high school friends,' Teddy said. And he was right about one thing: those types of girly friendships tend to endure in one form or another.

Teddy described the girls in a meticulous detail that made Segert shiver. He heard a bit of himself as Teddy described their bodies and limbs, in the classification of physiques and smiles. But Segert was a creep by trade. Teddy was a schoolteacher.

Segert asked him for last names or addresses, but he didn't have any.

'Can't you get the numbers from the school records?'

'It's guarded by a pitbull of a woman. Otherwise, I would've done it a long time ago myself. But,' Teddy continued, 'there must be yearbooks lying around the staff room cupboards. I can get one to you tonight.'

Ja, that would've been a good place to start.'

It was interesting to him that the school would go to the trouble to produce a matriculation yearbook. Who were they ever going to be? What was there to look back on?

When they walked back, Segert led Teddy through Orange Grove, making sure to avoid the young girls playing cricket in the street.

* * *

Teddy knocked on the door, three days later. Segert looked like he was just getting up. He was shirtless this time, and squinted in the afternoon light. He coughed as he opened the door.

'I don't need to come in,' Teddy stuttered. 'Just wanted to bring you the yearbook.'

'I was busy sleeping. Sit,' Segert said, in the same tone he used with his dogs. 'Had a late night.'

Teddy heard a kettle boiling and sat on the chair, fingering Augustine's class yearbook. Segert walked out the door carrying two steaming mugs of coffee. He'd thrown on an olive-green short-sleeved shirt. His belly was still thick with muscle and protruded slightly over his shorts as he sat down. He hadn't bothered buttoning them up.

'Hope you like it black.' He chuckled. 'Look who I'm talking to. Tell me . . .'

On the first page was one photo of the entire faculty. Teddy stood out like a night light. Underneath it, the school motto — *To those that are willing, nothing is difficult.*

Teddy leafed through and pointed out Rosalind. Her hair tied back. She smiled, revealing braces and two descending eye teeth. What a nerd.

'What you know about this one?' Segert asked.

'You told me you've spoken to her already.'

'Yes, I am asking your opinion of her. Please.'

'They call each other "cuzzie". Doubtful they're related. Rosalind was studious, smart. Slightly emotionally detached, but that's a survival mechanism.'

Ja.' Segert just wanted Teddy to talk.

'If you are smart, this system will crush you and spit out your bones. She doesn't know what's coming.'

'What do you mean?'

'Do any of us? There's a degree of uncertainty in all of our lives. But chances are it'll be bad for her. The odds are against her.'

'I think she's just hardwired that way. A drip.' Segert thought for a moment. *Ja*, wasn't much help. Any other friends?'

Teddy pointed to three faces across the page.

'What do you know about them? I mean, any of them who she is likely to keep in contact with generally, or in an emergency. Everybody has emergency friends.'

'What do you mean?'

'Friends you call when you're in a tight spot, but otherwise you're busy living your life.'

Teddy didn't answer him, so Berger just carried on. 'What do you think they're doing now?'

Teddy looked up into the gold light peeking through the trees.

'No, man. Focus, *asseblief.*' Segert laughed. 'Do you think they're working, moved away or still living with their parents?'

'If they're not at university, they're still home with their parents. Culturally, they stay at home until they get married, generally.'

'Like normal, then.' Segert took a black pen and crudely circled her friends. 'Did any of them have boyfriends their own age?'

'This guy here, nicknamed *Perd*.' Teddy pointed to a young man with a strong neck, a wide happy smile, a little dark fluff on his upper lip and a massive spot erupting on his nose.

Segert burst out laughing. 'That's unforgettable. *Perd*, of all names . . .' *Horse.*

'He was a great athlete, a good hurdler. Long legs.'

'He's gold, that's for sure. He wasn't called "Perd" because he was hung like a horse, or thought he was?' Segert slurped his coffee, his shoulders releasing one last wave of laughter. He slapped his bare belly, then fished a small grey piece of fluff from his navel.

Not for the first time, Teddy wished that Segert Berger was properly dressed. 'They were just kids.'

'All the same. What do you know about a young guy called Angelo?'

'Angelo van Hemel? He was a few years ahead, two years. Loud, intense guy. I don't think they would've been in touch. I mean, he went to jail. Perd had a clique. They're just the type, actually, to know where she is and be blasé about it.'

'OK,' Segert said. 'You can go now.'

He looked down at the picture of Perd. He had a face like a million others, and when Segert saw him he felt he'd already met him. Nothing distinguishable about him but his nickname. You remember someone with a nickname like that. They were never incognito.

CHAPTER 22

The edges of the newspaper fluttered on the dashboard as Segert set off. He'd met Rosalind at a four-way stop opposite the Eldorado Park police station.

'I'm glad you called,' Rosalind said.

'Really?'

'I'm glad you haven't given up.'

He leaned over, grabbed the newspaper and tossed it on the backseat. There was nothing about the Mine Dump Murders. 'This is my job. Let's find your friend.'

* * *

Perd was leaning against the doorframe of a darkened Wendy house that was at the furthest edge of his parents' large backyard. He was flirting with a young woman, who seemed interested. Her back was turned to Rosalind and Segert. The tiniest ripple of distrust moved over the party. She turned around, then walked towards a small group drinking beer under the security light. Perd nodded when he saw them, but didn't smile.

'Howzit, glad you could make it. Who's this?' he asked Rosalind.

'Happy birthday, Dave. He's nobody. Needed a lift.'

'Boss.' Perd laughed. 'How's your cousin, haven't seen her for a long time. What she up to?'

'I don't know. Haven't seen her for a while.'

Perd hadn't been introduced to Segert but offered them both drinks.

'I'm working,' Segert said.

The voices inside the Wendy house stopped, and all that Segert could see through the darkened windows were red cigarette embers. It reminded him of the shot houses he used to visit with Rousseau, his contact at the traffic department when they were teenagers.

'He's helping me find Augustine,' Rosalind said. 'He's not police.'

'The last time I saw Augustine, she was working at Khan's as a cashier. You know, girly didn't even want to talk.'

A woman appeared from behind Segert, and walked in between Perd and Rosalind.

'My mother waited twenty-one years for this. She ordered the cake from Tita's in town. We can't rob her of this moment. Here, have something to drink.' She eyed Segert with suspicion.

'Augustine had a baby. Both of them are missing,' Rosalind said.

'With this guy?' the older sister asked.

'No, Beukes is the father,' Rosalind said.

Segert took his cards out from his front shirt pocket and gave one each to Perd and his sister. 'If you hear any information about Augustine or her whereabouts, please contact me. Just a quick question. What do you know about Angelo van Hemel?' he asked.

Perd took a step to his sister until she was stood in front of him, her head just under his chin. 'The cake and candles are ready.'

* * *

Berger and Rosalind disappeared when Perd was posing for photographs with his ceremonial twenty-first key.

Twenty-first birthdays weren't a huge celebration in Segert's culture. Men that age had generally been conscripted. The boys here were allowed to be teenagers until they were twenty-one and then still lived at home. No army or burden of marriage.

Segert drove off towards Eldorado Park. It was barely eleven pm.

'They going to church tomorrow. They drink, smoke, have sex. Tomorrow, they are showered and fresh in the front row.'

'Sounds normal.'

'Really? Guess it is. I don't get it, though,' Rosalind said. 'What about Angelo?'

'He's a dead end. But the last person from around here to have seen her.'

'He lives around here, I need to talk to him.'

'No. I'm taking you back home.'

'Then tell me, what did Angelo say and how did his name come up?'

'He saw Augustine at the Central Post Office. It must've been the day she collected her things. She didn't have the baby with her.'

'Oh my God. You weren't going to tell me. No wonder you think she's one of those girls. Maybe she just left the baby with someone for the day. It doesn't mean . . .' She stammered, trying to collect her thoughts. 'If you don't take me, I'll go by myself.'

'Both of us know that's not wise. You can't go by yourself.' Segert wanted to close the subject.

'Then take me, if you're so concerned.'

The streetlamps were sparse, and only lit the furthest edges of the semi-circular field. A lot could happen to you from one streetlamp to the next. The only shapes you could make out were the three young jackalberry trees, and the roof of Angelo's wooden shed. The glimmer of a torchlight shone through the shed window. This side of the neighbourhood was quiet, unlike Oz, which had a suburban heartbeat. Segert parked his BMW on the curb at the van Hemel house, facing the closest exit.

A young street boy kicking a football recognised him from the Musical Section in Noon. Threw away his cigarette and crossed the road. Now was the time to jump concrete fences or get lost behind old cars. Trouble was coming.

Segert walked up the driveway to check through the front window, then came walking back to Rosalind, who was still sitting in the car.

'He's not there. Let's go.' Segert was standing in front of the bonnet.

Rosalind thought he meant Angelo, but he was talking about Roger, his father.

'Over there.' Segert nodded towards the dark field.

A shiver travelled down her spine when she looked across and saw the field, the size of half a block, and the small wooden shed, in the shadows of swaying jackalberry trees.

She wanted to come here. Segert laughed to himself, letting her stumble ahead among the grass and flattened beer cans.

The traffic on the arterial road was light, and Rosalind watched the car headlamps approach and disappear. She was aware that she couldn't be seen and that whatever happened here would always stay here, if she didn't get out. And stay with her, if she did. She was about fifty metres to the closest compact council house and counting. She wanted to turn and look back at Segert. Instead, she rubbed her tongue against the right side of her lip, then wiped her chin against the soft fabric of her cardigan.

When they approached the shed, Segert checked the tree trunks and could see by the streetlight that the carvings had been scratched out.

Mommy's handiwork, Segert thought.

He knocked on the window, and the torchlight swirled on his and Rosalind's faces and then fell on the floor.

'Angelo, it's Augustine's friend Rosalind. I need your help. Please.'

Angelo opened the door and held the torch on Rosalind's face longer than necessary.

'You know it's me, man. Stop shining that thing in my face.' Rosalind tutted.

Angelo was wearing his blanket and his feet were cracked and black with dirt. He smelled of beer and cheap sour liquor, mixed with the sweet smell of body oil, the sweat of long days in the sun and sand.

'You have a nerve showing your face here,' he said to Segert. To Rosalind: 'I've never had the pleasure.'

'Good evening, Angelo. I don't know if you remember me. I'm Rosalind; I'm friends with Augustine.' Rosalind sounded calm, but she'd unconsciously taken a step towards Segert.

'Good evening, now I remember you,' he said to Rosalind. 'When you going to bring my axe back?' he asked Segert.

'I thought I'd hold on to it for a while. Besides—'

'Besides, nothing. Always being so unnecessary. What you want now?'

'Rosalind here wants to talk to you, and I can't talk her out of it.'

Angelo smiled at her. He liked having a woman to talk to.

'I heard you saw Augustine in town?' Rosalind said.

'Like I told the man. She had her bags and she went to the post office. I didn't talk to her.'

'Do you know where she went after that?'

'I was doing my own thing. I didn't talk to her. I already said. Then he comes back, puts me in the boot, attacks my father and takes my axe.'

'I thought it was your father's axe,' Segert said.

'Same thing.'

Rosalind heard the deepening of Angelo's voice and the pacing of his words. She considered running to the arterial road, but that would mean running right past Angelo. She felt he would raise his hands and, like a giant moth beating in the wind, cloak her in that blanket that stank of hell and wet dreams through the narrow door into his shed.

Angelo walked out of the low doorway, towards them.

'Where's your father tonight, by the way?' Segert asked.

Angelo threw the torch at Segert's shoulder, but Segert flung it aside and it hit Rosalind on the head.

'Sonofablood,' she shouted, and started running to the car. The torch light illuminated a small patch of sand and berries and a tiny drop of her blood.

Segert was ready for a blow, but instead Angelo charged him to the ground. Smothering him with the blanket. He held him down, breathing hard in Segert's face, then wriggled to get his knees on Segert's arms. The edge of the blanket was straining and he hunched himself through the cavity. Segert tried to push him off balance. But Angelo was heavy and stubborn. He wriggled his weight so he could hold the blanket over Segert's face with his left knee and punch with his right hand. For Segert, it felt like a big cat was wrapping itself around his body. He got his left foot in position to lift him off the ground, but his heel fumbled against a jagged stone. Angelo sounded like his mouth was foaming with wild happiness. Segert took a big breath of pungent air, tensing his shoulders to push Angelo off. Then there was a dull smash and Angelo fell on top of him.

Rosalind had been halfway to the car when she turned around to see Segert's situation, then she ran back and hit Angelo over the head with the torch as hard as she could. He was still conscious, but it gave Segert enough leverage to push him off, pin his knee on his chest and punch him in the face.

They ran through the grass towards the car.

'You can't just leave him lying there like that.'

'Me? You wanted to come here. He's an outdoorsman. It'll suit him.'

* * *

Segert turned down the M2 and searched the horizon for the bright lights of a petrol station.

'So, can you fill me in about the axe story?'

'*Nee*, not really. Do you want a guy like that to have an axe?'

'Does it really have to do with Augustine, or . . . ?' Rosalind's head was throbbing.

Segert still smelled like a vagrant and, as he turned into the petrol station, Rosalind started to feel claustrophobic. She scratched the door panel to open the door or window.

'I don't think so.' Segert was parking in front of a petrol station shop. The bright lights gave his skin a green tone.

The load was stacking up. One thing on top of another. Constant and relentless pressure of losing people and things, and being on the receiving end of bad news.

'Go clean yourself up. You can't go home looking like that.'

She walked over to the ladies toilets, at the side of the convenience shop. There was no one in the cubicles, so she closed the exit door. Took her cardigan out of her bag and stood with her back against the door as she screamed into it. She heard footsteps on the other side stop, turn and run away. That made her feel better.

She splashed water on her face, inspected her head for bruises, then rubbed the sand out of her hair.

* * *

'I got you a *boerewors* roll,' Segert said, when she got in the car. *Some women can't handle the things they demand, and then now look . . . She'll have to learn that sooner or later*, he thought. He passed her a Coke and joined the traffic to south Johannesburg. 'Thanks for coming with me to Oz,' he said.

'It was fine. I'm not sure if I should thank you about Angelo.'

'All in a day's work.'

'And the axe?'

'I'm still holding on to it. I don't have anything. Honest.'
He reversed out of the parking spot, not looking at her.

* * *

Segert dropped her off the same place he'd picked her up.
The police station looked like it was doing good business.
There was only one police van in the parking lot. A couple
was stumbling out through the front door, holding each other
as if they'd just survived the sinking of a ship or the rush of a
flood. Wet with alcohol and tears. The expression of an end-
less argument etched into the muscles of their faces.

'You know I can drop you off at home.'

'Yes, but this is for both our safety.' Then her face turned
serious as she sniffed the air. 'How long has Angelo been like
that? A while, right? No way Augustine'd be caught with a
guy like that.'

'I think that's enough drama for one night,' Segert said.

She took her chance. 'But why'd you ask where his father
was?'

'Goodnight, Rosa,' Segert said, and pulled off Turf Road
towards Orange Grove.

CHAPTER 23

Segert idled the length of the suburbs to Greenside, enjoying the lazy pace of the late Monday morning. He had the radio on, but there was no news on the Mine Dump Murders. He'd washed the stink of the weekend off. Rolling around with a rapist in the dirt, all eyes on him at a twenty-first of a young coloured man who had a kind of freedom like a mayfly. Here today, gone tomorrow. Rosalind coming undone in a petrol garage. Augustine was close. He was almost there. She was in the middle, just in the cut. He just had to push over a few rocks to find her.

He pulled into a parking spot in a ribbon of two-storey shopfronts. Most of the parking spots were empty. Only the purple-rinse and domestics crowd strolled through the shops, inspecting avocados or selecting birthday cakes. He walked through the aisles of the Spar Market, holding the red basket firmly in his left hand. The clenched hand pumped his forearm to prominence, and he liked looking at it in the frosted window of the beer fridge.

Not bad for an old man, he thought to himself.

He filled the basket and took it to the cashier at the tobacco counter.

The checkout girl rang up his groceries on her large till, entering every number and matching it with a type of produce on the other side of the thick plastic console. It looked like highly concentrated work from where he stood.

She still hadn't looked at him.

'Actually, can I have a Rothmans Mild? Twenty.'

She turned around to get them.

'Give me a cheap lighter as well. The one in my car's broken.' He put a smile in his voice.

Cigarettes always made people talk. It was a fact. Whether they were smoking it, selling it or standing next to an ashtray with a singular lit cigarette. They talked.

She packed everything in the white-and-green plastic bags, but, well acquainted with smokers' requests, she left the pink Bic lighter on top of the red-and-white Rothmans packet on the counter. He unwrapped the slim cellophane, then paid her in cash.

'Have you seen this girl around here? She went missing. Her parents are looking for her.'

She placed the change in his hand, and tossed the plastic film in the bin beside her feet in a casual motion, like a bartender. She wiped the counter with her right hand and leaned over. *Ja*, well, can't say I know her face. When did she go missing?' She looked up at him, wearing an expression of child-like inquisitiveness.

'Around July, August.'

'I've only been here since December. Christmas cover, but I think I'll get permanent.' She wiped the counter again and leaned back, looking for other customers. Lucky for Segert it was a quiet day in the store.

'Well, she's missing from home that long. But she was last seen around here.' He made a small circle with his hand, which had the packet of cigarettes in it.

'Do you want to put her picture up in the local ad section on the wall? You can ask the manager. His office is in the corner over there.' She pointed to a small white office. A silver blind in the office window fluttered as Segert turned around.

'You did that on purpose.' He smiled at her.

'I'm not getting fired, Mister. No, thank you. The manager won't spy now; he'll be embarrassed. He's only a year or so older than me and wants to boss everyone around. Not smart enough for university, I think, and he's got vitiligo. No army.' She pursed her lips together and looked at him, ready to tell him all the Spar Market truths. 'OK, let me look at the picture again.'

Segert just held up the small photograph without saying anything.

'She does look familiar, but that's a bad photo. You should try down Fourth Avenue and Gleneagles Road. Not far.' She pointed to her left, but there was nothing but a door next to her.

She was pleased with herself, smiled at him and said, 'I hope she's happy to see you.' But the smile was turning into a frown as she began questioning her earlier zeal.

It was too late, no take-backs.

He thanked her and picked up the bags. The thin plastic bag straps bit into his hand and forearm.

His BMW was still ticking over when he got back to it, a small pool of water collecting under the engine. He made a mental note to go to the mechanic down Louis Botha Avenue, after one of his famous *boerewors* sandwiches with avocado and tomato saus.

'I shouldn't've bought this meat now,' he said aloud, as he started the car, but his eyes were settling on the six-pack of beers. *Have to get everything in the fridge soon*, he thought to himself. He fished around in the plastic bag, pulled out a packet of chips and cracked open a can of Coke.

At the north end of Fourth Avenue, Segert parked under a clump of birch trees. Risking the high possibility of bird poop on his windshield, to keep his meat and beers cool. He wrapped the half-eaten packet of chips in on itself, then put all the groceries behind his seat, looked in the mirror, checked his teeth and dusted away any chip dust.

The street was empty, suburban-empty, and, if Segert hadn't been run-down with a slight cold, he would have smelled that it smelled rich. Not orange blossom rich or bleached-and-sterilised rich. It smelled of thick slightly damp grass, so thick it weaved between your fingers like a baby blanket. So thick you could lie down on it, fall asleep reading a luxury car catalogue dreaming of smooth silent rides. A rich that sent a ripple of wide blind acceptance. He knocked on doors, spoke to maids and gardeners.

Bored, long-legged housewives said, 'I can't say . . .' when he presented Augustine's photo and told his story, and then invited him in. Big dogs stood in their lobbies and eyed him suspiciously.

Eventually, the trail led him to Beech Street. He drove there slowly, the grocery bags forgotten. His mind was on the women he'd talked to, and the discreet services they had hinted that they required. A real lady never said outright she suspected her husband of being a cliché. A real lady planned on playing chess with her cheating spouse's real estate.

The housewives offered him coffee, beer or something stronger, and one of them held her manicured hand on his arm as they stood at the front door, and he'd gotten a stirring in his dark blue jeans. He was up for it; it wasn't just her meek heart-shaped face, but the exquisite delicateness of her wrist that made him want to stay. She needed to be taken care of, and he could imagine them upstairs in her three hundred-count Egyptian-cotton-sheeted bed. Imagine her hair falling on her pillow and framing her face. She had an air of desperation about her that wouldn't usually put him off, but, looking around, he concluded she had the means to pursue him a lot longer than he was comfortable. He wasn't interested in a fling that could turn into every other weekend, then into every other evening.

He made a three-point turn, absentmindedly hit the curb, and slid slowly down the road. Figuring he'd park on the road;

Segert drove past 68 Belgravia Road slowly, then circled back and parked down the road. The large black gate, Mercedes-Benzes in the driveway and dark green ivy creeping up the modern and stately security walls made him want to leave his dirty seven-year-old BMW far from the eyes of anyone in that house. He buzzed the small black box at the pedestrian gate, then walked the thirty or so metres alongside the gravel driveway to the open door at the far side of the house, where a man about his age, or younger, was standing.

'Are you OK?' Martin was surprised to see him walking up the driveway.

'Yes, I parked down the road.' Segert didn't break his stride.

'You needed help?' Martin noticed the strength in the stranger's body when Segert reached him at the door.

'Hello. Yes. I'm going from house to house looking for this missing girl.' Segert exhaled heavily, exaggerating the effort of his day. He held up the photograph of Augustine he'd produced from the thin black folder he was carrying.

Martin looked at the photograph in Segert's hand. 'Please come in. Would you like something to drink? Looks like thirsty work.'

He squinted as the sun caught his dark-rimmed spectacles. He extended his arms into the house to welcome Segert in.

'No, no trouble,' Segert protested, low-voiced, but moved his foot towards the door.

'Come in, so I can have a closer look at the picture. Can't say I've seen her before.' Martin walked slowly behind, and past the leather sofa to the study.

Segert heard the clink of a crystal decanter. His lips curled slightly.

'What's this about?' Martin asked, as he passed Segert a glass. 'I don't get so much company now. Drink, drink. Otherwise, I drink alone.' Martin crossed his legs at the ankles as he raised his arm in a silent toast. His exposed socks had a large argyle design.

Segert showed him the photo again. 'Her family is looking for her.'

'I thought it might have something to do with the break-ins around here. They go after the jewellery. Big-ticket items. La Mude down the road had her great-grandmother's ring stolen. They were Huguenots running away from persecution—'

'No, it's nothing to do with that,' Segert interrupted. 'This is a missing persons case.'

Martin pulled a face. 'Must be a special person.'

'Can I ask any of your staff if they've seen her?' Segert had finished his whisky and put the glass down on the side table. The ice danced loudly in the thick lowball glass.

Martin sat up in the oversized caramel leather seat, but his legs remained crossed. 'No, I let everyone go after my wife died. No point, really.'

He looked to Segert like he wanted to lie down in his dark grief. 'That's a shame. I'm sorry for your loss.'

They sat in silence for a moment. Martin stared out across the room, through the window and out into the afternoon with its dark orange and blue sky. The winter cold was beginning to unfurl its frosty cloak.

Segert wanted to ask, *Why did she die, how old was she, how long were you married?* Instead he pointed at a stuffed purple teddy bear lying under the coffee table. 'At least you're not alone. Looks like you have children for company.'

'Yes, a boy. He's napping. My sister comes to help me whenever she can. But I manage. I shouldn't let him sleep now, really; he won't go down tonight.'

They filled some time talking of sport, the break-ins and this year's frost.

'Do you mind if I use your bathroom?' Segert got up and started to walk to the back of the house.

'No, no,' Martin insisted. 'The downstairs bathroom isn't fit for civilised people since my servants left. Please, please . . .' He gestured upstairs. 'The second door on the left.'

189

Segert left the photograph lying face up on his black folder on the sofa, next to the indentation where he'd been sitting, as he walked upstairs. He climbed the stairs and walked to the bathroom. He peeked into the bedrooms, careful not to slow his step. The baby snored faintly to the left. Berger went into the bathroom. Riffled through the Gillette shaving cream, razors, clippers and soap. Nothing. He checked underneath the sink, but there was nothing behind the empty bottle of Handy Andy and rolls of toilet paper but dust. To keep up the pretence, he flushed the toilet and washed his hands.

'You OK? Thought I'd check on Nicholas. Do you have children?' Martin called up the stairs. His footsteps turned into Nicholas's room.

Ja, no,' Segert said, wiping his hands on the back of his jeans as he closed the bathroom door behind him. 'I mean, no, I don't have children.'

He came to stand in the doorway to the nursery, watching Martin bend to smell the boy's nappy, then rub his head.

'I'll wake him up in a bit. Let me walk you out.'

Segert side-eyed another bedroom as he headed towards the stairs. The straightened lavender duvet cover hiding the suitcases housed beneath, the plush beige carpet, the dust motes drifting in sunlit spirals. Was it the dead wife's?

Martin walked a few steps behind him, as he descended the stairs. Martin had a soft walk but for the crack of his ankles.

Segert looked towards Martin's empty chair, and the two brown shoes sitting one foot in front of the other, the short laces still tied in tight bows. He picked up his folder as Martin walked to the front door. 'Thanks for the drink.'

Martin adjusted his spectacles and handed him a business card. 'You can contact me anytime.'

'Sure. Thanks. Might have to follow up about the case again.'

Martin smiled. 'Give me yours, in case I hear anything. Save you a trip.'

Segert produced a business card and gave it with the photograph to Martin. 'Can you give this to your sister? Just in case she knows anything.'

'I'll buzz you out. I have to change my son's nappy. Small man, big poop.' He laughed, and Segert smiled at his little joke.

Segert walked back across the gravelled driveway and shivered slightly in the cold, trying to shake the feeling something was up. His car purred like a disgruntled housecat. The sound didn't comfort him from the low coldness of the leather seats. Leather seats. Cold in winter, burning hot in summer. The extra expense was of no use. It was just another symbol of luxury.

Then it hit him, sharp and clear. The worn-out cases under the bed in the front bedroom. They didn't belong in that beautifully kept room. And he remembered Johnny, Noon's neighbourhood uncle, saying that Augustine had left with two vinyl suitcases.

Driving past the German cars coming home from work, he thought of stopping at one of the housewives' houses and using the phone. But that would risk overexposing the situation. He put his foot on the accelerator pedal, and drove to the group of shopfronts he was at earlier that day.

He hadn't smoked in two years. Just bought the cigarettes as a conversational device. But he'd already had two whiskies, two coffees and a milk tart. Abstinence was far gone. He pressed the lighter button on his console and reached across the gear stick for a cigarette. He rolled down the window and exhaled a small circle of smoke.

***

Back inside the house, Martin listened out for Nicholas. The boy was still asleep. He looked out at the street, and didn't see any sign of the detective. He put the business card in the console drawer. Went into his study and unlocked the large

191

three-drawer cabinet behind his desk, looking for Augustine's file. He hadn't bothered to destroy it. She'd never spoken of anyone, just some people from a church that one time. Not her family, not the baby's father. It'd suited him, of course. She'd had no attachments besides the baby, and, well . . .

Augustine had written two addresses for next of kin. A primary address in an area called Noon, and another address in Soweto. A Pastor Moloi and his wife.

He looked out the window at the burial site.

The mound was completely flattened now and the lawn was almost even. The whole little episode was over as far as he was concerned. Maybe it was time to get Paulus back. He'd been interviewing nannies, but perhaps now was the time for a change of plan. He picked up the phone to call his office and left a message for his secretary, Sharon.

'I'll be out of the office, but I need someone to drive me around to have a look at a few sites around Jo'burg and then further afield.' He liked Sharon; she was hardworking and divorced and was always available to stay late. She always wore slacks to work, no matter the weather. She'd been married for five years in her twenties and didn't produce any children. It was time to consider doing something clichéd, like having an affair with his secretary, someone who didn't have children of their own and who could look after Nicholas one day.

* * *

Bessy climbed the stairs to an apartment block that was over a cluster of stores in Parkview, a religious conservative part of town, close to Parktown. She hardly came out to see the sites anymore and usually left most of the work to Cutman. She'd expanded the business, but the promotion didn't suit him. He was dedicating more time to his hobbies. He was howling for trouble.

This afternoon of all days, Cutman was with her brother, when she needed him at a site as big as this. Driving Martin around Johannesburg. If it wasn't for Nicholas, she'd make both of them pay.

The landlord moved back to Portugal over a year ago to retire and had been left in the lurch with this. He'd given the tenancy to a maintenance company who promised to break it into smaller high-yielding parcels. The interior had been demolished and the interior was 'not yet habitable' and left with six months' rent in arrears.

Bessy unlocked the grille door at the top of the stairs, leaving it unlocked behind her. The paperwork in her hand stated that part of the interior had been demolished to make way room for smaller apartments, and the outside would appear completely intact. The first door to her left was a back door to an apartment. A red steel tube was mounted across the door. She found the barrel key in the set and unlocked the mount and opened the door. The first thing she smelled was light dust; she could almost taste it. Then the smell of leather. Her sandal got caught in some dust and sticky fluid as she walked over to the far wall to put the lights on.

She could sense the room was larger than the average flat, but she was expecting some renovation airflow.

When she pressed the switch, a disco light lit the space. She walked through the blown-out walls to the next room. Her mind was rushing and she didn't stop to search for the lights. The disco light tweaking through the doorway was enough. The next room had a roulette table and two blackjack tables.

This could have happened to anyone else. But she could do so many things with this. There was a reason she was a woman alone when she opened the door and found this.

CHAPTER 24

When Segert Berger opened his front door, he noticed the blinking red light on his dusty white answering machine. He listened to the message on the machine as he pulled off his black boots and socks and slipped his feet into a weathered pair of house slippers.

'Man, it's Wes. I've got something for you. Call me back.'

Segert fed his dogs dried granules in their scratched-up old stainless-steel bowls, changed their water bowls and patted them on the head.

'Sorry about the dry food.'

The two Alsatians accepted his apology with small sighs.

He opened a beer, still cool even though it had been sitting out in the car for the last hour of the afternoon, and left the rest of the groceries on the table. The yard light attracted winter moths that either stuck to the wall or danced around the glowing hot bulb. He watched the dogs eating for a beat, then called Wes.

'Howzit? What's going on?' Segert asked, absentmindedly eating the *boerewors*-flavoured chips, too lazy to cook.

'What in the name of all that is holy are you chewing in my ear?' Wes asked. 'Listen, I got a job for you.'

'Anything heavy?' Segert asked.

'Usual cheating stories. Some fun for him; some money for you.'

They chatted about it some more.

'Anything else, just call me or come round,' Wes finished; his mood soured by Segert's casual indifference.

Ja, I have a few things to push around in my head with the old Beukes case. Might come around for a chat soon.'

'OK, no problem. My wife says to take the dogs out for a walk.' Segert's loud crunching stopped abruptly. It was the way Wes said *the dogs* that let Segert know that Janette and Doreen had been talking, and they'd been talking near Wes's ears. If Wes ever spoke about Simba and Trigger, he'd call them *the boys*. *The dogs* were Janette's words. She'd complained that their marriage was dictated by the dogs' eating habits. She'd had strong feelings about his commitment to his animals' welfare. Even in divorce, she was controlling him.

The back garden was a mess of sand, dog hair, urine and faeces. He'd have to clean this up and wash the dogs before they developed some disease that was going to cost him money he didn't have. The dogs whined gently when he whistled for them, but went to him. They could tell he was in a bad mood.

The air was crisp in his lungs as he ran. Segert was wearing dark blue jogging bottoms, a white vest and a cheap pair of running shoes. His white socks pulled high towards his knees. His burp tasted of beer, Rothmans Mild and salty meat-flavoured chips. His arms strained under the force of trying to hold the dogs back. They pushed ahead, eager to exercise their legs. They ran towards the public swimming pool on Dunvegan Street, then circled around three times before running back up parallel to Louis Botha Avenue, up the hill. Their ears pulled back as they struggled against Segert's weight. He couldn't keep up; either he needed new shoes or new ankles. The dogs gained energy, breathing heavily and with purpose. Segert couldn't hear anything over the sounds of the dogs' breathing. His feet landing too quickly to articulate a proper running step.

'Slow, slow.'

He pulled the dogs lightly on the leash as they ascended the hill. They slowed down, but Simba had to be told a second time.

'Simba,' he yelled.

And the dog slowed down. His tongue hanging out of his mouth.

The roads in Orange Grove were almost empty. Everyone was home for supper, a bread-and-butter pudding with smooth yellow custard and the seven o'clock news.

It'd been two weeks since he'd taken the dogs for a run. Trigger and Simba sat one on either side of him as he leaned against a post box, catching his breath. He let go of the leash so they could cool their muscles. Trigger sniffed the ground and moved quickly, muzzle down, across the lawn. Simba stood back, looking defensively around Berger, then followed Trigger and came to a rest five metres away against the outside wall of an unlit house. In the darkness, Simba looked like the dark shadow of a small tree under the window.

Segert thought about Martin Diamond. He needed to investigate his background. He was hiding something: either he was a sympathiser or a profiteer. And Augustine wasn't involved in any movement. She wasn't the type. She was barely able to look after herself before a baby arrived on the scene. Did Augustine comfort Martin after the death of his wife? If so, there wasn't real shame in that. Segert wasn't going to tell the authorities.

Trigger sat up in the middle of the lawn.

'Come here. What are you doing?' Segert asked him.

Trigger strained to defecate.

'Looks like you've been backed up, old buddy.' Segert rubbed Trigger on the length of his body and turned to head home.

* * *

196

An hour later, Segert parked his car in a short road almost perpendicular to Belgravia Road, within good view of the Diamond house. Greenside was silent. The wind rustled the trees gently. In his rearview mirror, he caught sight of two teenage boys cycling side by side. One took his hands off the bar, impressing his friend with his balance. At the end of the street, they separated without slowing down. One turning right, the other left. Segert imagined that they sped up as soon as they split. He pulled the red tartan blanket from the backseat and covered his lap. He didn't know what he was going to find out from watching Martin's house, but he knew he had to come back.

A cop van would be cruising the suburban roads soon. Patrolling for errant children and dangerous elements. He sat low in his seat, ready to duck down. It was about ten thirty when a black Mercedes-Benz stopped at the driveway gates briefly, then drove up the allée to the Diamond house. The black van that had been following stopped on the road, obscuring Segert from seeing who was getting out of the stopping car. All he could see was the headlamps splashing the roses with light. Segert waited two minutes for someone to get out of the van, but the engine idled as the lights were dimmed. Segert started his car and slowly drove to the end of the road, trying to see the driver of the van, but the windows were tinted. He turned right, drove up two blocks, then came around so he would be behind the van. He switched off his headlamps as he came around the corner and came face-to-face with a police van.

'*Boet*, what are you doing?' the policeman in the passenger seat asked as he unrolled his window.

'Nothing, man, my brights were on.'

'Do you need a jump?'

'No, no. I'm just turning the radio on and the brights off.'

'You not from here,' the policeman said. His eyes pinched the question. 'What are you doing here?'

'I came to fetch Verna from down the street,' Segert lied.

Verna was one of the married women who'd made herself available to him this afternoon.

'It's getting late for chatting and romance music, hey.'

'I can't wait till tomorrow.'

The policemen laughed. 'You're going to be hanging around a long time.'

'I'm used to it,' Segert said, looking off into the distance.

The policeman behind the wheel laughed, but stopped abruptly. His ribs jabbed by a sharp elbow. He cleared his throat. 'You should meet Verna somewhere else. You can't be hanging around here like a lapdog.'

Ja, you're right.'

'Don't stay here all night. By quarter past eleven, we don't expect to see you sitting here with a hard-on anymore.' He pulled off, laughing.

***

By the time Segert got back to Belgravia Street, the van was reversing slowly. It let the Mercedes out in front. Segert took down the number plate, and got ready to follow. Four blocks down, they would turn out onto the main road out of Greenside. He took the third left, hoping to get a view of the Mercedes number plate, but the road turned out to be a cul-de-sac with double-storeys and mature oak trees. No luck. He'd give what he had to Rousseau, tomorrow. Then he'd pop in to have a catch-up with Wes.

It was a moonless night. The sound of dogs barking carried on down the road. Motion-triggered lights were switching on in a straight line from house to house. Then Segert saw a short black man walking across the lawn to a house that he'd been to earlier that day. He'd talked to the domestic and the housewife, but this man hadn't been there.

'Psst, hey,' Segert said, leaning across to the passenger seat window.

The old man's spine became taut and he turned around robotically, his body shaking in an almost imperceptible rhythm, a yellow plastic bag crinkling against his grey trousers. The first thing he said surprised Segert. 'I'm tired.'

For a moment, Segert wondered if the streetlight was broken. The old man's lips were bloodied, and his left temple had a small bruise across it. It would swell and turn blue.

Segert knew what had happened: the two policemen had interfered with him. 'I just want to ask you a question.'

'Boss, I'm tired.'

Dogs started barking next door, and the hall light turned on in the house behind him. The old man edged away. He didn't know what his boss would say. He was already late. Staying out here talking could lose him his job, his pass to the city. Then he would have to go back to his homeland, and he would be a drop in a reservoir of desperate workers. It was better to die than lose your job. His first grandchild had just been born. He was ready to be an ancestor.

'I was here earlier today, looking for a girl.' Segert waved the photo of Augustine at the old man.

'I don't know . . .' The old man took a step closer.

'You've never seen her?' Segert put the gear down from first into neutral and pulled up the handbrake.

'Don't know her face. From where is she?'

'Noon.'

'Now, why you asking around here, and at this time of night?'

'She used to work around here.'

'Doing what?'

'I can see how you got that fat lip. Who is asking the questions?'

At that moment, his boss opened the front door. A middle-aged white man, with a flabby belly and skinny bare ankles.

'Booky, how come you're so late?'

'Hello, sir,' Segert said from his car. 'Sorry he's late, hey, I'm just dropping him off. He helped me with a flat tyre.'

'Oh, all right. Booky, what happened to your lip?'

'That's my fault, hey. I'm no good with a lug,' Segert said, in good humour.

The boss was suspicious, but let it go. 'That's quite all right. Go to the back now, Booky.'

The man went back inside his house, and Booky took the opportunity to hurry across the lawn to the back gate.

Segert left his car door open and padded softly across the lawn after him.

'Do you know her?' Segert persisted, as soon as the front door shut. . 'You know it's dangerous to walk around here at night. What you got there in the bag?'

Booky fished for his keys in his front pocket. 'Pap, maize flour.'

'Why you walking around at night with that? Don't you have bread or rice at home?'

'Mister, I must go,' Booky whispered in urgency.

'Or potatoes or spaghetti? You risking too much going out just for that.'

The tension in Booky's shoulders lifted, but he didn't turn around. 'My son gave me this. He just had a baby girl at the hospital.'

'Congratulations. A granddaughter, hey. Do you know the girl in the photo? I think she used to work at the Diamond house on Belgravia. She and her son are missing.'

Booky unlocked the chain and slid back the gate just wide enough for him to slip into the backyard. 'Shame, man, I don't know. We don't get a chance to socialise much. Do you see any tennis courts for us?'

'What's this got to do with tennis courts?'

From behind the gate, Booky whispered, 'Come back tomorrow morning at eleven. The house will be empty.'

* * *

The following day was Thursday. Segert parked his car around the corner and knocked on the gate. Booky unlocked the chain and let him in. His lip had doubled up in size. It was shiny with Vaseline and camphor cream. The old man touched it unconsciously and mumbled for Segert to follow him.

The garage had been levelled, and a concrete slab shiny with rust and stained with oil put in its place. It was big enough for two cars to park side by side. There was extra space for roller skating. On the left was a frosted window of a bathroom. At the end of a lot was a mature English oak tree with three wide climbing posts nailed in for the children.

He followed Booky as he turned left past a large flat lawn, then a swimming pool, past the deck, which must've come round off the main house's living room. They kept walking round the house and then to Booky's small living quarters. The door was at the far side, so you had to go down an alley that was made by the neighbour's concrete fence. It felt colder in the shadows.

They walked into an open space with a kitchen area that had a two-plate gas burner. An old torn-up floral sofa against the wall that touched the end of the bed. Two young black women were sitting on it, talking to each other in two different dialects. Segert recognised one of them as the maid he'd seen at the house yesterday. Another older black man, about Booky's age, was sitting on a cozy chair that was too big for the space and dominated the room. He looked at Segert, not sure whether to offer him a seat or leave the sofa entirely.

'I'm guessing you didn't tell anyone I was expected.'

'Oh, you're always expected,' Booky said. Implying the law and the multitudes of white people that upheld it.

Something about having Augustine and Justice's photographs in his pocket gave people the power to say things they would never usually say. It was a bell ringing over his head. He knew he should be ashamed for wanting to explore this new feeling, but it twisted his insides and made him feel more himself than almost anything else.

'Just, this time, you're here by invitation for samp and beans.' Booky took the lid off a black cast-iron pot and poured in a generous amount of Cerebos salt. He winced as he tasted it, the salt stinging his wound.

'I'm not from the police, or anything,' Segert started. 'I'm just looking for this woman and her son. That's my job, to look for missing people.' He sat down and showed them the photographs.

'Really?' said one of the maids on the bed. 'Maybe you can he'p me find my boyfriend. He's been missing since I gave him my panties.'

The two maids giggled on the bed, rubbing their feet together. There was a gag going, and he didn't want to know what it was.

'The boyfriend wants to see his son; he's about a year or so now. She maybe used to work at the Diamond house on Belgravia.'

Booky brought Segert a Coke in a scratched-up old glass.

'Don't mind them. They already been drinking from a stash. Talk to him.' Booky nodded to the man about his age, sitting next to Segert on the sofa. 'Everyone likes him. Don't ask me why.'

'I'm Moses,' the old man said. 'I don't know her or the boy. It's a nice day. Let's go outside.' Blood had pooled in his feet and he shuffled slightly to the door.

Segert followed him to the narrow strip of garden along-side the kitchen window. Moses was dressed in faded blue jacket and dark trousers, scuffed work boots and a frayed orange baseball hat. He took a black pipe from his pocket, held it between two fingers and brushed the lip of it back and forth with his thumb. Then he put it back in his pocket.

'What's this really about?' Moses asked, squinting at Segert sideways.

'Like I said. All I need is to get contact between the man I work for and his child.'

'Do you have a photo of the father?'

'No. And to be honest, even if I did, I wouldn't show you.'

'Some people believe that babies look like their fathers, so they don't run away.'

'Well, he doesn't look like me, thank you.' Segert put the picture of Justice next to his face.

'Do you have any children?'

'Why, have you seen some babies that look like me?'

Moses didn't like the joke. He bent down and pulled a white sparkle flower from the ground, pulling the stem through his teeth.

'I'm not married,' Segert said. 'So . . . *ja, nee.*'

'A man should be married. You're too old to be single. It's hard for us, you know, to be away from our women. But a man should be married.'

'That's not for me. I tried it. It didn't click.'

Moses shook his head, then tossed the flower back in the garden. 'Maybe you should try with a different woman. We can go and find Paulus, the gardener who used to work there. I used to see him in the taxi, but no more.'

'The gardener from the Diamond house? Are you sure? OK, just tell me where you think he is.'

'Not now. Sunday is better. I'll take you. He's in the loc'tion.'

Ja, you better come with me,' Segert agreed.

* * *

Sunday morning, the two of them drove in silence to Alexandra location. A large mound of shacks about a half-dozen kilometres north from Segert's house. He changed the radio station from Radio 5 to Metro FM, and tried talking about the weather, but Moses wasn't big on small talk. A large yellow Casspir was stationed just off the M54 at the entrance to the township.

There's no need to be nervous, Segert told himself.

But the terrain was bad. The road was bare and full of potholes. Foot traffic streamed alongside the road. Women of all ages carrying shopping and feral dogs sniffing for food. There weren't any pavements; the shacks sprang out of the dirt in a straight line, like corrugated iron ant hills. Behind a parked school bus, two dogs were attacking a feral cat. Young children were playing with long sticks and older girls were hanging washing out of their windows or on a line that went high above street level. His BMW caught a lot of attention; little boys ran alongside them smiling and laughing.

Moses lifted his hand and waved, laughing with them. 'I'm famous now. I'm in the front seat.' He laughed.

'I'm not a cab driver,' Segert said, sounding more serious than he intended. He cleared his throat, but said nothing else.

'I like your hat,' Moses said.

Segert had put on a blue newsboy cap this morning, so he could be perceived as less of a threat. 'I took my cue from you yesterday. No hat today?'

'No, I'm not working.' Moses smiled and made a sound that was adjacent to laughter, but in any language translated to, *you know*.

The shacks and shebeens were all on top of each other. Dark brown brick government bungalows were next to two-storey shacks. Lean-tos hung precariously along small trees. There were irregular spaces between the houses, and as they drove past each alley Segert scanned them quickly. There were plenty of places to hide.

'How much further?' Segert asked, scanning the rearview mirror.

Before Moses could answer, a stone hit the wheel. Segert slowed down.

There's no need to be nervous, he thought to himself again. He scanned the rearview mirror. Nothing had changed. The stone had probably been thrown up by the road.

'Stop here, here.' Moses pointed at a well-kept bungalow on a corner three doors down. He climbed out slowly and told Segert to stay in his car.

* * *

Segert turned down the radio and checked all the mirrors. This road had brick houses, but seemed quieter than both Noon and Orange Grove. No trees swayed in the wind. No children walked from the football field. Wire electrical cables were connected to the house Moses went into. Segert didn't know that there were actual landowners here. He'd always thought it was just an empty piece of ground where people had built informal houses. The clouds were drifting high above a treeless skyline. He waited in his car five, then ten minutes. In the rearview, he saw a tall, lean black man turn into the road, then quickly step back behind a shack.

The thought flickered that Moses had led him to be ambushed. Just for his amusement. For revenge for Booky getting beat up last night. Leaving him to be pulled from his car and necklaced. His burnt and blackened body torn to pieces by an angry mob.

He switched off the ignition, threw the cap on the passenger seat and scrambled out of the car. Strode quickly to the front door, checking left and right quickly, then knocked and pushed the front door open in one motion. The feeling of being fresh bait pulled at his innards like a drawstring.

The old man was sitting on an armchair, laughing, with two little girls on his knees. A young woman, perhaps in her late twenties or early thirties, was sitting opposite them on a sofa, also laughing. It was as if Segert had taken a picture the moment he stepped in. Everyone had stopped moving.

'Oh, I was just wondering where you are, Moses.'

'I'm here. How far can an old man disappear to? Come, let's go to the shops.'

Segert looked from Moses to the young woman, putting the pieces together. She had the same sharp eyes. He scanned the room for family photos. On the small table next to the sofa was only photographs of the young girls. This was probably his daughter and grandchildren, even though no group shots were on display anywhere.

He had to be careful not to mention Paulus now and spook Moses. He could change his mind, or come down with a case of amnesia. For now, he played along. Nothing would be worse than embarrassing an old man in front of his family.

If he wasn't bait before, things could still turn. No one offered for him to sit or a cup of tea, so everyone stood up. Moses spoke to his daughter in Sotho, then the girls' eyes went big and they shouted *all right* in unison. The oldest exposing her descending front teeth in excitement.

The two girls climbed in the backseat, excited to go on an adventure with their *mkhulu*, grandpa.

They cruised to the end of the road, about two hundred metres, to a large shack with a colourful decoration around the window and a hand-painted sign of fruit and vegetables. They could've walked, but Segert understood the children's excitement for his car. It was an exciting car to drive. His van was functional; he could carry the dogs in the back. But his BMW was a beautiful piece of machinery.

A woman wearing a black scarf tied in an elaborate knot at her forehead peeped through the opening. Her eyes were cut like diamonds into her face. Her neck was long, and she had a warm breezy attitude that Segert thought was at odds with her surroundings. When her gaze met Segert's briefly, she smiled confidently. Moses looked at Segert and laughed. Beauty was currency, even here.

The little girls had jumped out the car and were standing below the window. The shopkeeper gave them a bag of sweets and cans of fizzy drinks and teased them as they left. She winked at Segert. Moses smiled as they drove away slowly.

'Are we going to Paulus now?' Segert asked.

'Not yet. We have to go to the grocery store.'

They drove to the far end of the township, close to the large towers and shopping malls of Sandton. They bought two loaves of unsliced white bread, potatoes, mutton, onions, beans and 1.5 litres of Stoney's ginger beer. The girls got another chocolate each. It was like Christmas. As they drove back into the township, Segert got used to the rhythm of driving and chaos. He felt more comfortable with the children in the back. As if they were some type of insurance. They drank crème soda and ate puffy chips that left a bright yellow residue on his seat, but they were respectful children who didn't talk to Segert, and only spoke to their grandfather when he addressed them. The old man asked Segert to stop along the way as he asked for directions.

* * *

The sun was high in the sky as they approached the incline to Paulus's shack. It was right up on the banks of the Jukskei River. He was sitting outside on a five-litre paint drum, talking to a neighbour who was inside her shack sweeping. Small clouds of dust and sand sailed out the front door. Paulus stood up as he saw Moses, a smile on his face.

'Stay here,' Moses said to Segert.

From the car, Segert watched as the old friends shook hands and exchanged sombre greetings. The children made their last violent slurps in the backseat, dropped the empty cans in the footwell and picked up the groceries.

'Don't slam the—' Segert said, too late.

Paulus's neighbour peeked out of her shack and took inventory of the grocery bag, then stared down the road at Segert, and then closed her front door. The two girls gave Paulus the bag silently, then, errand done, ran off to play hide-and-seek in between the shacks. Paulus appeared serious in his thanks and left the groceries just inside his front door. Moses jerked his head towards Segert and said something he couldn't hear. The two men looked at him, then Paulus walked over to the car.

'Thank you for the groceries. You are looking for a woman and her baby?'

'Yes, Augustine and Justice. Was she at the Diamond house?'

'She used to work there, looking after the cleaning and household things.'

'How long was she there?'

'I don't know, not long. She was still there two months ago.'

207

'Why you not there anymore?' Segert asked.

'The boss got rid of us, me and Maggie, soon after the missus died. He said he was keeping Augustine a little longer until she could find somewhere else, but it was difficult, because of her baby.'

'Did you believe that?'

Paulus rubbed an invisible piece of twine between his thumb and forefinger, thinking carefully what to say next. 'It looked easy for him to throw me out, and I'm an old man. He didn't care about what I have to do next, but suddenly he cares about a coloured girl and her child? I don't know. It was, how do you say, fishy. Do you have a gardener?'

Segert adjusted to the hairpin turns conversation without changing his expression or tone, but wanted to bring Paulus right back to why he was here. 'No, I don't need one, thanks. What about Maggie, is she around here, too?'

'No, we don't all live here. She went to the Transkei. I don't think she'll come back to start again now. She was with that house since years.'

'Do you have her number?'

'Maybe someone you know needs a gardener? You can find me here.'

'Give me her number, and I will pass your number to my friends.'

Paulus went inside and scratched around in his shack. Segert looked around for Moses, and caught sight of him playing hide-and-seek with the children between two shacks.

Paulus reappeared with a small piece of paper he'd crinkled out. 'Here it is. It's the phone by the shop; just leave a message. And I put Maggie's phone number on the back.'

* * *

Segert reversed slowly down the incline, putting his left hand on the back of the passenger seat and turning to have clearer sight of the road, instead of relying on his rearview mirror.

The children scratched the last flecks of any lingering flavour from the chip packets. Sunlight bounced off the boot into his eyes. He had to blink a few times to make sure his eyes weren't deceiving him. A black cloud was enveloping a packed clothesline that was across the road. The smoke rolled quickly between the shacks. Tyres must have been set on fire by or behind the curve of the road. Judging by the size of the cloud, petrol or paraffin was the accelerant. But it was still quiet. He couldn't hear any chanting or screaming. The blockade could be intended for someone else.

Even if it was, he was too close to it now, and a casual cap, low on the brows, couldn't help him. He was in the wrong place driving the wrong vehicle. The van's shock absorbers would've handled this terrain at speed better. He had to keep as much distance between himself and what was happening down there as possible.

Moses sucked in his breath as Segert turned his steering wheel hard to the left. The bumper grazed a shack as he changed gears, then put his foot almost full on the accelerator, driving up the small alleyway that ran perpendicular to Paulus's house. He just wanted to get out of there. Now. Behind Paulus was nothing, just a dip into the river. Segert sped round another corner. Moses held onto the dashboard as they bobbed in and out of potholes.

'Stop!' Moses shouted.

'Are you crazy?' Segert said, speeding past a corrugated iron shack. Chicken feathers flew in the air as he bumped through the backyard. A young woman stood alongside a falling wall, holding her child, her hand fanned across his chest. Chickens and guinea fowl dashed across the tiny backyard.

'They don't want us,' Moses said, referring to himself and his granddaughters.

'*Ja?* But you're with me now. For better or worse.'

The wireless didn't do justice to the sound. Segert had heard it as snippets on the radio or the TV news, and he'd always paid attention to the newsreader, dismissing the crowd.

This war cry made the air humid with the chanting of young voices. A rolling thunder, charging to attack.

He sped through a narrow alley. Children scrambled through neighbours' doors, and youngsters pinned themselves against corrugated iron walls, watching the white man's BMW disappear, destroying Sunday street games. Then they picked up a stone or any instrument nearby and gave chase.

Moses scrambled between the two front seats and sat between the children when the first stones hit the car roof. The girls tucked their heads under his arms, their cries muffled by his jacket.

Segert drove four hundred metres, cut across traffic exploding into the sunlight. Beeping at a pedestrian as he joined the road.

A thin boy was casually pedalling an old bicycle in circles in the middle of the road, a plastic bottle in his back pocket. Segert hit the brakes. The boy put both his feet on the ground and reached inside his pocket. The clutch screamed for mercy as Segert changed gears quickly. Here was the one who'd set the tyres on fire. The boy looked intently at Segert as he lit the rag. He pursed his lips together in concentration, put the lit rag in the bottle and took chase. The rest of his mob had come out of the alley by now and ran behind him. He threw the bottle at the bonnet. Segert swerved and the makeshift bomb hit the road. Petrol and flames spilling across the dirt. The mob from the alley came up and splintered around it. Segert sped up and joined the main road. It would be the quickest way out of here.

Men, children, dogs and goats who'd been luxuriating in the monotony of the Lord's day ran deeper into the township. A woman holding two grocery bags and a baby on her back was crying on the side of the road. The two children stared at her from the backseat as they blew past. Moses tried to shield their eyes, but the eldest pulled his hand away.

A white minibus taxi drove quickly towards them, jerking on the road with malign purpose. Straight for them. A boy, not much older than the one on the bicycle, was hanging out of the front passenger seat. He couldn't be older than twelve, a chipped rock in his hand. The rock landed on the windshield, and the cracking sound of glass made the girls cry. Segert didn't brake.

'Which way now?' he yelled.

The mass that had formed from two separate groups was about one hundred metres behind them, and then splintered into three groups, maybe more.

'That way, right.' The eldest girl pointed.

'What's there?'

'A field by the highway.'

In his side mirror, Segert saw that the taxi had stopped abruptly close to the low flames that remained in the street. The boy held his arms high in triumph like a bull fighter. Then bullets started flying from the west, where shacks were built on a small hill. Opposite from the road that led to Paulus. The plume of thick black smoke clearly visible through the passenger seat window was Segert's only landmark.

The taxi lurched forward, turning away from the gunfire, but drifted away into an alley. It wouldn't get far; it was too wide to go down those small roads. The gun was short range, the intervals between shots erratic, and whoever was firing couldn't hit them. If it was going to hit anyone, it would be some pedestrian who still trying to get home in all this chaos.

In the distance, Segert could see the Casspir moving in and heard the boom of tear gas canisters hitting iron roofs. People and rats were scrambling out of shacks, shebeens and spaza shops, holding their heads and rubbing their eyes.

Segert sped across a small field littered with broken bottles and plastic bags and drove down a sharp ledge into fast-moving traffic. Horns hooted, and he almost hit two or three cars. The back wheel hit the island. He skidded, then drove back up the freeway.

When he joined the pace of the other vehicles, he felt his breathing was deeper and quicker. Like he'd been holding it a long time.

Traffic was light towards the city centre; people would be travelling home from work in a few hours. Segert stopped close to a bus stop on Louis Botha Avenue. It was a clear wintry day. The air was clearer just ten minutes away from the township. The oak trees were swaying gently as Segert passed each avenue in Linksfield and Orange Grove. Moses and his grandchildren climbed out the backseat. The youngest clung to Moses's slim leg. Segert gave them R30 bus fare to Greenside and back to the township, then topped it up with another R20 note. The old man would have to go back; the girls needed food.

'*Ke a leboha*,' Moses thanked him. He was still shaken from the chaos in the township and unsure how he was going to get the girls home.

Segert looked at his car. The back bumper was dented. A hubcap was missing and the windshield was busted.

'Don't let worries get you down,' Moses said to the children.

'What? This?' Segert laughed. 'It's just a scratch. Nothing some tape and elbow grease can't fix.' He was avoiding the deeper conversation about why he'd been targeted by young boys in the township. And the buzzing feeling that he was discarding them like luggage on the side of the road.

Moses and the two girls looked at him with blank faces, then walked to the bus stop. Moses would figure out how to get them back home, then travel to Greenside by himself. It had cost him the whole day, this free ride with Segert to Alexandra.

CHAPTER 25

'What happened to your car? Were you in an accident?' the chatty old lady at the bakery at the top of 8th Avenue asked, as she counted out change for the parking meter and directed him to the Telkom public phone at the far end of the row of shops, close to an empty green.

When Segert didn't answer, she just kept talking.

'Don't mind the teenagers sitting there like a bunch of crows,' she said.

But there were no teenagers there when Segert inserted his coins into the box and dialled.

'Hello, I'm looking for Maggie. Is she there?' he asked, as cheerfully as he could.

'Hello, Mister. She's not here; must I call her for you? She's next door.' The boy didn't wait for an answer, putting the receiver down hard on a table and running off.

Segert could hear a collective complaint from children of various ages near the phone. Less than two minutes later, a heavier, older female voice answered the phone.

'Hello?' She spoke slowly.

'Hello, is this Maggie?'

'What is this about?' The corrugated sound of suspicion came into her voice.

'I'm looking for a girl called Augustine. I heard you used to know her.'

'Who is this?'

'I'm Segert Berger. Her family is looking for her—'

'How did you get my number?' she interrupted.

'Paulus gave it to me. He was the gardener at the Diamond house. Don't know his last name, sorry.'

'And what did Mr Diamond say? I used to work for him and his late-late-wife. I don't know any August.' The grooves in her voice straightened out to steel. 'Tell me what she looked like.'

But Segert had already used his cultivated manners for the day. He looked over at his battered car. He held no reservations now; he could be himself. 'Don't play with me. Some people have dogs outside in their yard. Some people bring their pets inside the house.'

'Mrs Kimberly was the lady of the house. There were no dogs, Mr Berger. And Mr Diamond was always busy with Mrs Diamond's business.'

* * *

'Are you OK?' Maggie said to the children watching TV. Piling their legs over each other like logs to keep warm. She'd become a new favourite in the neighbourhood. Her rondavel was now connected to electricity, and she'd gone big and splashed on a colour TV.

None of them turned to answer her, and she wondered about this generation that didn't listen to anyone. The older ones burning tyres in the street in the cities all over the country, throwing rocks at parked cars, wanting to accelerate that fast feeling of dying. No slow-motion death for them.

She let it be, them sitting in the quiet, the light bouncing in their eyes. She looked forward to finishing the cold

214

remnants of her favourite dish, an oxtail stew that her neighbour cooked special for her. It was a celebration meal now, because — she didn't know how, and she didn't care how — but she was satisfied that Augustine and her lazy bones weren't in the house anymore, that she'd been driven out like a goat.

***

Segert'd made a rookie mistake. He should've brought someone to the suburbs with him. His only friends besides Wes were at Solomon's and at the police station. He couldn't bring any of them. He needed a middle-ground person. A woman. Janette had always been his saving grace. And convenient, in a situation like that.

'Bloody hell,' he shouted at the memory of the luggage under the bed in the Diamond house. 'Where is she now?'

But even Rosalind could've helped. Her big round eyes in her coffee-coloured face were enough to annoy him, so she surely would've provoked even a small reaction from Martin. Rosalind was defying a rule of nature. She was supposed to make her eyes smaller, never ever bigger.

He hit the steering wheel hard out of frustration. He had to get more information from somewhere.

215

CHAPTER 26

At about noon the following day, Segert met Rousseau, at a Bird's-Eye chilli chicken restaurant close to his office in Marlboro. They ordered a whole chicken, peri-peri, chips and Cokes.

'Hot,' Segert ordered, meaning spicy.

'Medium,' Rousseau countered. 'I can't have half a spicy chicken in here for the rest of the day.' He patted his small paunch.

'Rest of the day? You finish at three.'

The restaurant was crowded with office workers, and Segert and Rousseau sat in a booth in the back that was framed with local black art and sculptures. Rousseau knew why he was here. He and Segert had grown up together. Stealing cars, dicing on empty roads. Abandoning the cars on mine dumps at dawn. That was when they were in their teens and twenties. Now, Segert only called him to trace number plates or get rid of his parking tickets. Segert gave Rousseau the number plate of the black van, as he slurped loudly on a Coke.

'What type of case is this, hey, Iceberg?'

Segert grinned at the use of his old nickname.

'Is the plate number for the other woman? Or are we talking murder and kidnapping here?' Rousseau's job was tedious.

He spent most of his day supervising the licencing officers and traffic wardens. His branch hardly ever saw any vehicle testing, because in Marlboro everyone traded in their cars within the first three years.

'No, not this time. A missing persons case. A girl.'

'I figured. No one seems to hire you for a missing boy. I guess we can look after ourselves.' Rousseau sucked on a chicken wing. 'I don't keep up with the papers. Is it a big wig? Any reward?'

'You wouldn't read about it in our papers. It's on the radio, and bits and pieces in magazines. So, no reward. Just a case. Not sure this has anything to do with it, even.'

'What exactly are we talking about?'

'It's a missing girl, like I said. I hope she's alive, but I don't know.'

'And the tabloid magazines?'

Rousseau isn't giving up today, Segert thought.

'How's your legs from making that big leap?' he said.

'You said radio and magazines. It's sordid.'

'Could be a serial killer in Johannesburg, dumping girls on the mines.'

Rousseau put his chicken down and cleaned his hands on a napkin.

'I'm just looking for a missing girl, that could be permanently missing,' Segert said.

'I'll get it for you. Call you later.'

'Man, thanks.' Segert looked out at the midweek lunch crowd. The daily world of department lunches that was magnetic for the day people was a foreign country to him. He needed to change the subject, so that Rousseau could get back to finishing the peri-peri bird in front of them. 'How's the family?'

'The same. Bigger. They're popular, they go to a lot of birthday parties. There's a lot of birthday cake, lot of presents. Young ones have expensive taste,' Rousseau joked. He was always fishing for money. He'd been that way since they were small.

'We used to be happy playing with sticks and stones. But not this generation.'

'I tell you, hey.' Rousseau nodded in agreement. A smile on his face.

'What's got you thinking so deep?' Segert asked.

'Nothing, nothing,' Rousseau wiped his mouth vigorously with a serviette. He'd felt a bit stale lately. It'd been his thirty-fifth birthday two months ago and his life felt like a puff of smoke. He'd invited Segert to his birthday *braai*, but he hadn't turned up or called to make excuses.

'So, give me a call when you have anything. We can go for a drink.' Segert was getting up to leave.

'I'll call.'

'No, I mean it. I still owe you for your birthday. We can call the boys.'

Rousseau knew he was lying, but couldn't help getting sucked in. 'Make a plan.'

* * *

The phone rang at eleven the next morning. Rousseau gave Segert the details. 'Your van doesn't have outstanding tickets. Parking or speeding. Owned by GDB Pty Ltd, since early last year, '82. Owners are in the Copper Mountains close to the border with South-West, up at the end of Namaqualand.'

Segert took down the address, convincing himself it had nothing to do with Augustine, that those vinyl suitcases were an apparition. That they were just old cases full of keepsakes of Martin's wife. But Paulus had confirmed Augustine was there. Maggie was defensive about Augustine's existence.

He wanted to put the pieces together. Anything shady that Martin was dealing in was bound to lead him to Augustine or to something lucrative. Two birds, one stone.

'Your social calendar full?' Segert asked.

'You joking?' Rousseau's voice went loud.

'How about next Friday?'

218

'I can't Fridays.'

'You see?'

'Next Saturday? I'll call the boys. All the boys.' This meant even Segert's elder brother. 'Hope this helps your case.'

'We can mull it over next Saturday.' Segert threw Rousseau a morsel.

He hung up, then called Wes for a late lunch date and asked him to look up GDB.

* * *

They both ordered a bottle of Windhoek as they sat on high stools overlooking St Andrews Road.

'You eating?' Wes asked.

'I can't eat just anywhere these days, china.'

'Don't blame you.' Wes chuckled. Cholera definitely had made him *delicate*. Wes decided to just leave the china saga alone. He just hoped Segert would stop playing with Janette as if they were teenagers. 'I'm glad you called actually. I have a quick case for you, just some work for a divorce. Getting concrete proof of infidelity. Stuff like that.'

'I thought you're out of family court drama?'

'I owe someone a favour.'

* * *

A traffic cop parked his white motorbike across the street and sauntered past the parked cars, checking parking tickets and eyeing the meters. A black BMW was parked in the last parking space, and the passenger, a lean man in white shirt and black suit trousers, jumped out and fished for coins in his pocket and smiled at the traffic cop. The driver hid his camera under a black jacket on the passenger seat. They'd had a busy afternoon, finding Segert's address and then following him here. They'd have to split up to follow this other fellow that Segert'd met.

His gold bracelet scratched the dashboard as he put the ticket down, and both of them crossed the road to the bistro for a beer and a sandwich.

* * *

It was three o'clock and the restaurant was mostly empty. Jazz was playing on the audio system, and someone in the kitchen was banging coffee granules out of a portafilter. The slow bubbles rising in Segert's long glass was like a meditation.

'I sent Helen down to CIPRO to ask about GDB Pty Ltd. She got company director info and everything. It's a dormant company. They have it listed under logistics, but they've had zero earnings so far,' Wes said.

'Make it make sense, Wes. Simple English.'

'It's easy to put assets in dormant companies. They can say it's for future use while the assets either appreciate or depreciate. In this case, the van will depreciate, but they can still claim capital allowances, and, since they aren't trading, won't need to pay tax.'

'But what does that mean?'

'They're giving themselves a tax break. It's one of those loops. The government isn't going to change the tax law, because it incentivises big-ticket purchases, which stimulates the economy. Once everything stabilises, maybe there'll be a change.'

Segert signalled Wes to stop. 'Can you just drill down to the important facts?'

'I was just giving background.' Wes took a sip of his beer. 'But you know I get weirdly excited that I know stuff like this.'

'I can see it.' Segert laughed.

'The two directors are from upcountry. My guess is, they are unconnected to this van and company, and are just paid a fee to sign forms every year. Go talk to them if you really want to know. But . . .'

'But what?'

'That won't have anything to do with your missing girl.'

'The girl was there. The gardener ID'd both of them. She and the baby. And I don't know why he would lie about it. Unless . . .'

'You were born to scratch where it doesn't itch. Suit yourself. Tell me how it goes. And the paraffin boy, Reader, are you still following him?'

'*Nee*, that's wrapped up. I was doing that before I got sick. I need to get out again. I can't be in cars all day. Any follow-up your side?'

'No, seems like what you gave before was enough. But when you ready, I can shake that money tree again. If you want. I have another case for you anyway. Easy. Adultery. When is the wife ever wrong?'

'Wives make the best detectives,' Segert said. Their laughter was deep with battle scars. 'What you up to next Saturday?'

'Nothing. Why?' Wes asked.

'Rousseau wants to get the boys together.'

'As much as I would like to watch you and your brother act all dark and broody over a snooker table, then get into a drunken fist fight in the parking lot, I can't deal with Rousseau.'

'He's not that bad.'

'He just reminds me of the type of criminal mind that'd end up being a prison warden.' Wes was already simmering with *dronk verdriet*.

Segert recognised the mental video when it played in Wes's glass, the visions of youth and women, sport and bitterness. But they were only on the second beer. There was something else.

'I know you. You're a bit jealous of this Diamond character. You can smell on him that he was a poor little barefoot white boy like you once.'

'He isn't somebody. He married somebody.' Segert couldn't be hurt by what Wes said. They knew each other too well.

'That's enough, usually.' Wes sipped the last of his beer. 'What about Beukes, the girl's ex? He's a character.'

'I checked him out. Turns out his pa died two months ago. He has some money to tie up a loose end. He wants to get some naked pictures sorted that she took with her when she left.'

'He doesn't want her back, does he?'

'No, but in general he's suspect.'

'But everyone is suspect if you look close enough. You're going pro now. Pretty clean. You don't need to do these dirty cases anymore. Missing people, dirty pictures. Soon you'll be able to give that all up.'

'So, you want me off the adultery case you were just offering me? Or is that fine because you can still make money off a divorce?'

'That's a win-win, different situation. I have children to put through school; make hay while the sun shines. But you, your house is almost paid off, you don't have to pay alimony.' Wes quickly brought his argument back on track.

'How you know that?'

'Women talk. I just listen.' Wes drained his beer and paid the bill. 'Or is this about your car?'

Segert winced. 'That cost a small fortune.'

* * *

When Segert and Wes left, the bar was almost empty and the staff were cleaning up, getting ready for a shift change. Their waitress stood at the door, sunning herself and applying coconut chapstick to her lips.

The two men who followed Segert were sitting at a table opposite a small stage and a TV that had a rerun of Saturday's rugby union game, the Boerbulls vs Western Province. When Wes and Segert were out of sight, they left a twenty-rand bill on the table and split up at the door. Cutman went with Segert. The younger followed Wes. He could tell that Wes would be easy to follow; he didn't have any sense of anything

222

but himself. Wes stopped once to buy fruit from a hawker, inspecting two colourful plates of apples before choosing one, then walking off with a single-minded sense of immortality. He didn't even notice the hawker glaring at him. The type of mark he liked. He must be in control in his professional life — likely either a finance prick or a lawyer dick.

Wes walked around the corner and into a short blue-grey building on Commissioner Street. He smiled at the receptionist and nodded at the security guard who stood at the lifts. The tail would have to sign into the building. He looked at the board to check the floors and signed in for the penultimate floor. Aesthetic dermatologist and a proctologist. That was unfortunate.

The passenger pretended to be a lost tourist and walked over to the receptionist, asking for directions, watching Wes's lift go up from the corner of his eye.

The lift had two other occupants. Two young co-ed colleagues who looked like they were hiding a budding romance, or flushed from a run to the magistrates. Wes joined them, holding up his bag of apples like a prize. The lift stopped at the third and seventh floor.

'Thank you,' the tail said to the receptionist, in his best fake Italian accent. He eyed the directory on the way out and walked back to the parking spot, not sure whether the driver would be there or not.

'Who was that?'

'A lawyer. Small time.'

'I'm guessing he feeds Berger.'

'That's good to know.'

They both checked the rearview mirror, then the driver backed out quickly and did an illegal U-turn across the busy street.

* * *

Sometime, close to midnight on Sunday, Segert reversed his BMW and backed out into the road. He'd drunk four of the six-pack, bingeing on *boerewors* and mashed potatoes while watching an Afrikaans folk bandshow on TV.

He swerved quickly as he changed into first gear. The roads were empty, all the houses on the block now darkened. Before he'd left, he'd filled the dog bowls with water.

Lately, the dogs had been disturbing the neighbours, barking late at night. He checked on them; maybe it was a feral cat or mole that bothered them. He woke up in the darkness one night, his senses exploding like a minefield. His breath fogging on the windowpane as he looked for intruders, but there was no one. As he fell asleep, he heard the piercing cries of two cats, then the soft padded sound of paws jumping from the eaves and the clapping sound of a pair of wings.

CHAPTER 27

Letters in gold vintage font ornately spelled *Café de Paris* on the black awning. There was a table and two rattan café chairs set in front of both windows at the corner of a cobbled square that led to the Majestic Hotel. Popular with visiting diplomats, politicians and moneyed tourists, the hotel was a throwback to the colonial era, complete with a night watchman in safari hat.

Segert was underdressed in his worn-out blue jeans and grey short-sleeve polo shirt. At least he'd pulled on his dress shoes.

That has to count for something, he thought. He was having a bad day. The windshield had cost a fortune. And now his breath, wet eyes and snow-washed denim jacket cancelled out his intention of slipping into the café unnoticed. A long-nosed Italian in a black suit stood in front of the solid black door.

'Let me in, man. I'm here to see Carol,' Segert said coolly. The bouncer looked him up and down, shook his head but let him in.

The small commercial kitchen was cleaned up. Lemons and limes neatly piled in a two stainless bowls in the corner. The grease spatter sprayed from the jungle green tiles. During the day, the restaurant served reasonable minute steaks and seafood pasta. In the summer, it was famous for its thick strawberry juice.

He walked up the wooden stairs to a platform that overlooked the downstairs restaurant and kitchen, up three wooden stairs and through a small door. The corridor sounded of quiet chatter, and a child playing with chopsticks. The hallway opened to a room about twice the size of the downstairs restaurant. Lacquered tables and chairs were lit by antique ceiling lamps. The small stage was straight ahead of him; on the sides it was packed with an upright piano and a large gramophone.

Carol was sitting on a black-and-gilt tub-style two-seat sofa close to the stage and just out of the stage light. The gilt on the swan arms was damaged from repeated polishing, and flecks of paint and smooth wood peeked through. A young couple sat on two chairs next to her, looking out at the stage. A much older man was sitting at the opposite end to the couple, trying to keep Carol's attention. They were all sharing a bottle of red wine in small tulip-shaped glasses.

She saw Segert, and blew a kiss dramatically in his direction. Her companions stopped to turn to him. The older man in his pressed grey slacks seemed visibly bothered by Segert's presence.

'Berger.' She air-kissed him on both cheeks. 'This is Francois, Joseph and Nandi.' Segert sat down next to Carol, displacing old man Francois for conversation.

'Nandi, like Candy,' the woman said, correcting Carol's pronunciation.

Segert ignored her.

'To what do I owe this pleasure?' Carol purred.

'You know how much I like your company,' he teased back, moving in close to her. She gestured at a waiter to get him a drink.

'When will you stop drinking beer, Segert? It makes you fat.'

He hit his flat hard stomach. 'I'm not fat. It's a bit close in here tonight.' He changed the subject. Already they were back to playing cat and mouse games.

226

She didn't look at him, but ordered a whisky on the rocks from the waiter now standing at her side. 'Are you married again?' she asked, staring into his eyes.

'Very funny.' Segert sat back in the sofa.

'You only seem to like my company when you're married. So, I'm surprised to see you.'

'I'm very much single.'

'You're not here for the jazz?' She moved her short right leg over the left one.

Segert didn't like *the* jazz. It wasn't entirely chaotic; it just didn't get to a point. 'I've come over to see you. There's nothing like this place.' He looked around the room. The maroon stage curtains, and the flickering tea-lights, glowed with the intimacy of a romance that could grow into a fire. It wasn't completely weak. It just wasn't for him. He drank a gulp of the whisky. 'Do you know anything about a Martin Diamond?'

She raised her eyebrows.

'Or anything very new going on?'

'Why?'

'Never you mind. I have a situation with a missing girl.'

'Missing. How missing?'

'Not *that* missing. Just you know, missing,' Segert whispered.

Carol wasn't in the hospitality trade. Just a young woman kept up by her family connections, who got a thrill complicating other people's lives. 'Carrying on', as her mother called it, was firmly cemented in Carol's persona now. She'd made some powerful connections locally and overseas. She could set up a round of golf for you with a CEO of a top bank to chat about your business ideas. She was Daddy's little golden child, so she'd always had a penchant for older men, with soft necks. But then there was also Segert.

She took another sip of wine. 'Something must be going on. Look around here, it's almost empty.'

Segert looked around, but saw it mostly full, for a jazz club at the end of tourist season.

'So, what do you know?' he asked.

'What I've heard is that they have some out-of-town talent. Portuguese, maybe. Things must be really bad there, that they're here in Africa,' Carol said, without a trace of irony in her voice.

No ancestors of hers had cramped with their small boxes of belongings on boats or in wagons. They'd arrived in Africa by limousine. The paedophiliac impulses manoeuvring from old country to the new land. Pressed tight under suits, in expensive cars and with framed certificates. Her father and uncles were on the boards of orphaned girls' and boys' charities. Lavish Christmas parties were arranged at the family home. Kids could swim and eat and enjoy themselves, even though the six-week summer break was heavily monitored. No riding bicycles in the streets, or visiting school friends, holidays overseas or the beach. This was it, their Shangri-la. But some poor kid always had to pay the bill.

'Tell me something. I'm looking for a missing girl,' Segert said. 'Anything you've got.'

'I don't have anything now. Let's talk in a few days. The whisky's on them.'

The two men turned to nod their heads at him. He was dismissed.

A saxophone hummed in his ear as he got up. The C-melody didn't move the audience. They were consuming it without taking it apart, without perhaps recalling memories or feeling emotions. Carol's world was surreal and elusive. The money, the sex and the stories. The stories didn't so much surprise him, but something intangible unfurled like a mollusc in and out of its shell. Moving slowly, leaving a residue. He decided he'd drunk too much.

CHAPTER 28

It was ten o'clock and Segert was standing outside under the long shadow of the eaves, drinking a mug of black coffee on his red stoep. The lawn was unkempt and overgrown. Small soil ridges with exposed stones and roots appeared around what was once the flower bed and across the lawn. Molehills had sprung up overnight.

There was a hint of smog in the air from open fires. In the east, the sky had a greyish-brown light. Segert considered the day warm enough for bare feet. The circles around his eyes were dark and sunken. He sat on the low wall of the *stoep*, enjoying the sun on his skin. He'd have to get rid of that mole, but not today.

After he'd fed the dogs and cooked boerewors and scrambled eggs for breakfast, Segert went for a walk. He needed to clear the thud in his head, and think about his cases and prioritise leads. He popped two aspirin, put leashes on the dogs and set off. Nothing he was working on warranted last night's attack. He'd done some corporate espionage, but that was small stuff. Marketing and alcohol licencing. Was he really getting hit over the head for stealing the promotions calendar and calculations for drinks and spirits? The Reader case

229

was nothing; he'd stopped that weeks ago. He'd taken some photos of his briefcase. He was just getting background information for Wes. The most he got was some oil and gas prices. Not exactly anything worth fighting over.

The prostitute game had yielded him nothing, even though he kept the photographs in his cubbyhole.

* * *

There was nothing on TV, and Segert was coasting between agitation and frustration. Usually this led to a can of beer. Anytime was beer time this time of year. But the beer could wait thirty minutes. He had to face facts, and confront his bills. He walked blindly to his office that doubled as a dark room. The blinds were down and the petrol smell of the photographic chemicals gave him the feeling of isolation from the world he often craved and hated himself for.

He pulled the light cord and got the concertina file stuffed with bills out from the bottom drawer of his desk. He would get into serious debt unless he caught some more bread-and-butter cases. But, at that moment, all he wanted was to go outside and feel the wind on his neck and hear the paperbark rustling its leaves.

Accounting wasn't his strong suit; he could hire someone to sort this out for him. That was an expense he could write off. What he hated was strangers going through his business. For a time, Wes used to get his secretary to sort the bills, but Segert was skating on thin ice if he didn't get his act together. He didn't have the courage to look through them today. Instead, he went to put on the kettle while he listened to messages. He was half-expecting a call from Rousseau, shaking him up for that reunion. Maybe next month, he thought.

Carol's voice came crackling softly through the machine. The hair on the back of his neck stood up. Residual arousal and guilt. She'd never called his house. In the past, his wife, Janette, would've become suspicious. They used to have two lines, one in the office and one in the lounge, because he preferred to keep the two parts of his life separate. But he was sure Janette would've checked both lines. Because women are nosy.

'Segert. I have some information on that house you were talking about. I'll come over around lunchtime.'

'Can't you just tell me what I need to know?' he asked, to no one.

He wished for the old days, when they met outside Johannesburg and drank whisky and they'd spend the last part of the afternoon in a dark hotel room. She liked the cheapness of the bed linen and drinking out of the bottle as much as she liked him. It was like starring in her own little production. They left a mess of dirty sheets and cigarette butts for somebody else to clean.

Confronted with the prospect of having to straighten up and clean his house, he decided he wasn't that interested in seeing Carol. He put his hands through his hair. Mentally, he was picking up the black towelling socks and boxers from the edge of the bath. Pouring bleach down the toilet. For the first time, he wished he had air freshener, and thought about checking under the bathroom sink, then remembered the sink full of dirty dishes and felt hopeless.

When his wife found out about Carol, she was speechless for two days, Friday and Saturday. Sunday, which was traditionally her day of calm cheeriness, was the day that she went crazy. Janette had always been sort of traditional. She took the traditions that suited her, like home-cooked Sunday lunches, but she utterly refused any form of worship. It suited Segert fine. He spent Sundays catching up on sports, taking care of his cars and the dogs. Sometimes, when it was needed, like now, he did some gardening.

* * *

It had been on one of those glorious Sundays, when the sky was a perfect Southern Hemisphere blue, a few clouds drifting

231

in the sky. He was in the garden, wearing a pair of shorts and an old T-shirt, pulling weeds out of the lawn, when he heard the metallic sound of a pan hitting the ground, and then another. The dogs started barking, low slow barks that made him think an intruder had entered the house.

'Janette?' He threw a weed to the side and ran into the house.

She was throwing the lunch on the white-and-brown vinyl kitchen floor. She was tossing baked potatoes into the sink. Knives, forks and cooking utensils lay in an abandoned bundle on top of the open garbage can.

He recognised it immediately. He had seen it in his mates in the camp when they were in Angola, fighting the communists. She was 'going *bevok*.' When you released all the demons that possessed you. For some, the release only made space for more demons.

It took her a long time to release them. She pulled out the sofa cushions she had fluffed that morning. She emptied the drawers of his desk and littered the contents all over the house. When she took the crystal wine glasses from the wine cabinet, the ones they had gotten as a wedding present, he tried to hold her to stop her madness. She'd been stomping around the house, throwing and breaking things, all the while asking him questions he had no answer to.

When she had less vigour for her rampage, she turned her energy to interrogation. Asking him the same questions over and over. He was tired, and wanted the noise to end.

'Because it's what you wanted. Me cheating on you was exactly what you wanted. Now you have something to complain about for the rest of your life.' He sat in among the mess. Cushion covers, glass, receipts and magazines.

He loved Janette; she was beautiful when she smiled and he liked her two slightly crooked front teeth. The right overlapping the left. But she could get on his back — about his mother, his job, his hours, his friends. She was always worried about money when he told her not to be. Now, with the affair, she had one thing above it all to complain about. He'd given Janette focus.

* * *

Before the doorbell rang, Segert heard the clicking of high heels walking slowly up the cement path of his garden. When he opened the door, Carol stood solemnly, dressed in a white pencil skirt and a light pink blouse that was tucked in and fitted loosely, yet hugged her in all the right places. She looked like a witness who was about to speak in court. Except her lips were painted her usual impossible red. Behind her, he could just about make out the image of a driver in her gunmetal Audi. Only the back two windows were tinted.

Segert smiled a broad smile when he opened the door, although he didn't feel like it. He didn't really want Carol in his house, smelling of perfume when the house smelled of damp. She leaned in to kiss him on the cheek. He rubbed the red stain from his cheek.

'Segert.' She walked in, rubbing her hands together.

'You look lovely as always, but I don't think this house is fit for your white skirt.'

She surveyed the front room slowly as he spoke, and smiled at him before sitting down. 'Can I have a drink?'

He didn't have time for niceties now. Carol paid with sex, and he didn't want to have a go after that fat old Frenchman he met last week. But then again, he *had* changed the sheets and pillowcases just in case. Somewhere, there was a murmur of desire.

'My father did some business with Martin Diamond and his wife, Kimberly. Martin designed the hotel in Mauritius.'

Ja, he's an engineer or something.' Segert sat down opposite her.

'He was one of the architects.'

'I've got most of this already, how they met, but I want to know what Martin was like.'

'My dad said he's a solid guy, talented and hardworking. He was, like, twenty-five when he was working on that hotel.'

'And? Come on, I don't want his CV,' Segert said.

'He's just in a tough spot. He's a smart guy, but I mean, in our circles, you need something else beyond connections. A bit of sophistication. I can't explain it.'

'Money. A lot of it.'

'You can't just buy your way in. It's not that simple.'

'I bet.' Segert chewed the inside of his cheek with sarcasm.

'I mean, he leaned on Kimberly. And she was entrenched.'

'I called his office. He's outstation, just across the border for a few days. No one will tell me specifics.'

Ja, well. Think he's building another hotel with his wife's money. Most of us grew up together, and if you're new you better be exotic. You can't just be from Boksburg or wherever. Nobody cares about that.'

'Did you come all this way to tell me this? You could've just told me on the phone.'

'I wanted to see where you live.'

'Exotic enough for you?'

She looked at him sharply, took a sip from the beer he'd poured for her. Although it was almost impossible for him to believe that she was sipping a Castle. He looked at the bright red stain on the glass.

'I'm sorry about what happened, that's all.' She averted her eyes, looking intently at old photos on the wall of Segert and his brother when they were children.

Segert laughed quietly. 'Well, we weren't sorry when we were doing it.'

'And I wasn't the only one, was I?' Carol's eyes flashed for a moment, before she seemed to remember she wasn't supposed to care.

'Is that why you're here? To minimise your guilt?'

'You didn't answer me, Segert.'

He sighed. 'Was I the only one? I don't think so, and it doesn't matter.' He shifted in his seat, then stood up.

He had flashbacks sometimes of them together, and those afternoons could have been the only carefree part of his life.

'How's business? I mean, are you still bridging people?'

'I've got some competition, like I said last week. Nothing I can't handle.'

'So tell me about it. Do you want some more beer?' he said, deadpan.

'There's someone else around. From what I can gather, local.'

'Local?' He shrugged. 'Drugs? Arms? Girls? What they into?'

'Not drugs, as far as I know. Too sophisticated for that, probably. Who wants to get their hands dirty with high-volume goods?'

Segert was impressed and perturbed by her business-savvy. 'So what is it, then?'

My least favourite thing. These guys are also bringing in girls. I don't know how they're doing it; I don't really care about that stuff. But maybe your girl is a working girl now.' She reached into her bag and gave him a small, folded piece of paper. 'Martin Diamond has a sister; she has a birthmark or something on her face. She stays out of the picture. Bessy says no to the spotlight.'

She stood up, brushing her skirt for wrinkles and dust with her palms. She walked over to him and kissed him on the cheek, leaning into him, and grazed him lightly with her small breasts.

'That beer really suits you,' he joked.

'Shut up, Segert.' She laughed. 'That's her last address. I don't know how it helps you with finding a girl from the townships, but life is full of surprises.' For a second, there was a flash of sadness in her face, and then just as quickly it was gone. 'Invite me to your next wedding, will you,' she said, halfway to her car.

'You're a joker, Carol, a real joker.'

* * *

235

The address she'd given him was in Pretoria, a suburb called Hatfield. His map was in the BMW's interior door panel. He wound the window all the way down to let the breeze in. His finger traced the street name across a small crack on the map. The road seemed to lie in the shadow of the Versfeld stadium and the University of Pretoria. It was a good place to stash Augustine and Justice. He studied the map further. The university had several campuses spread around three and a half square kilometres. It would be full of young people. If he left now, he'd be there in just over an hour.

CHAPTER 29

A bank of clouds rolled in after lunch time, darkening the sky. The Transkei sun, strong enough to burn the clouds to vapour, only shone through in smaller and smaller patches. Maggie sat watching the TV and sniffed. The air was heavy with the smell of seaweed. A plastic cup bounced outside, past her open door. A red ball rolled quickly afterwards, children playfully screaming after it.

The first big drops fell like ripe bananas. Maggie stood up and saw a bright rod of lightning in the distance. The small group of children were still chasing the precious ball. *Winner has the next go!* But the loud rolling thunder ended the laughter. Thandie, one of Bam's grandchildren, picked up the ball, looking up at the sky.

'Go home now,' Maggie instructed. 'All of you.'

The clouds approached from the sea like a dark smoke. It didn't seem like clouds at all. Maggie hadn't ever seen clouds move so quickly. They pulsated like a school of dark jellyfish migrating quickly across the sky. The wind whipped up washing lines and women ran outside, squinting their eyes from the rain to get their clothes safely inside. Maggie's brother Cebo rushed in through the door, his vest and trousers clinging to his body. He struggled to catch his breath.

'A towel. Maggie, a towel, please.'

She got the towels from the small cupboard and nudged him away from the door.

'Stay there and dry yourself; you'll just make a mess if you move now,' she said, and went to start the fire.

The TV station lost its signal, and the fuzzy sound of white noise irritated Maggie. She switched it off. Outside, the sound of shouting for loved ones was warped by the wind pulling their voices high into the sky. Maggie and Cebo stood at the two windows of her rondavel, staring at the thick grey-brown clouds racing across the sky.

Tidal waves were surging far in the distance. Maggie could see one of the cows unable to get a foothold up the beach. The trampled bank was washed away. The other cows had already escaped to higher ground and were running across a field in Bam's direction. The rain sounded like bullets against the small hut. The wind bent the bristles of her roof as it was coming from all directions.

Cebo did what he always did in a crisis. He ate. But the storm didn't pass over quickly. He left his tin plate in the kitchen and wrapped himself in a blanket.

'This house is strong, Maggie. Don't worry.' He looked up at the roof, then tried to doze in the upright chair.

The tall grass and ripples of a storm surge in the nearby fields were white with lightning. Tiny streams of water trickled down from the roof along the edge of the wall. There was no way to catch the water into a pot, and so she sacrificed one of her blankets, hoping to soak some of the flood. Snapped branches hit the window and rain poured in quickly.

They took turns wringing the water from the blankets outside the window, but it was pointless. After midnight, water started coming in under the front door. She looked out the window into the darkness, trying to make out the buildings of neighbours. She looked downhill and, in a flash of lightning, saw the shopkeeper sitting hunched on the roof of his shop. The building half-submerged in the flood waters.

Her throat went dry. 'Cebo, do we have a torch?'

'You've spent too much time in the city. We have candles.'

Candles weren't any use in the wind, but it was pointless to argue with Cebo. Maggie watched the sky turn brighter. The sky was hazy. A patchwork. She didn't know where the sky, the muddy banks, storm waters and ocean started and ended. It was all blended into one horrible, dirty brown mess.

Her house was flooded, but it would stand. All her belongings were ruined. She and Cebo pushed through the waters, feeling sand and muck against their feet. Loose planks and clothes were tangled against branches.

They joined the groups of people walking the tarred roads to the closest city. She'd heard that Bam's family had walked ahead hours ago, in the dark. The rain started again, and a baby started crying. Maggie took a scarf off her head and gave it to the mother. Where they could find sturdy ground, they sat. Under a bus stop or underpass. Waiting for help to come.

***

The secretary beeped Martin's line. He'd told the Windhoek team he wasn't taking calls today. She sounded somewhat bemused when he answered.

'Mr Diamond, I have a collect call for you.'

'Collect?'

'It's from Transkei. I believe it's an emergency. The lady said she was family.'

'I said I don't want to be disturbed, but I'll take it. Thank you, Sharon.'

The phone clicked over to the collect call.

'Mr Diamond.'

'Maggie?'

'It was hard to find you, sir. I'm coming back.' She spoke without hesitation.

'What makes you think you can just demand a place?'

She realised he didn't understand her short-hand English. The directness when you switch from your mother-tongue to your third or fourth language, mixed with her urgent need to get away from the heat and wetness of a cyclone. But she pressed on, becoming more and more sure of her case. 'Mr Diamond, I believe Augustine has left. You must need my help.'

'How do you know that?'

'I've been contacted by Mr Berger. He was looking for her. Unless she is back . . .' No one had answered the phone, when she tried the old house. It was empty.

'How did he find you?'

'I don't know, that's his job. My job is to protect Belgravia Road, home. There is a disaster in Transkei, I can come.' She meant she could go to Johannesburg. 'Where is Nicholas?'

Martin felt that his life was realigning. 'He's here with me in Windhoek. Bessy keeps an eye on him. What happened where you are?'

'There was a big flood, sir.'

Martin understood that she had limited options and she preferred to go back to the relative comfort of her old job and routine. 'When will you be back, you think?'

'When the roads are clear, in a few days.'

'The house is locked up. Go to the Hallmark hotel in Johannesburg. Can you make it?'

'Yes, sir.'

'Tell them to call me. I will arrange everything from there.'

Her old travelling pass was tucked safely in a white handkerchief in her bra, with her post office savings book and a small bundle of cash she always had for emergencies. Cebo didn't have a pass at all, and wouldn't be able to follow her to the city. He would have to make his own way, after she gave him some money, and if she had her job back he could return to Transkei to fix their house. He didn't like the city life.

'I only have an old pass, sir.'

'Don't worry, no one's going to turn you in. If you have any trouble with the police, just tell them to call me.'

Martin could hear the smile in her voice when she said, 'Thank you, sir.'

'You will stay at the hotel until I collect you.'

'That's too much, sir. I'm not supposed to stay outside the house. I can get into trouble.'

'I have the keys. You can stay there, and, please, anything you want to eat or drink is fine.'

It was luxury she had never experienced, something she would always remember. What Martin knew of Maggie's nature was that she didn't fraternise with other domestics. Most were younger than her, and less professional. She wouldn't boast about this to anyone; that was good for him. And she would feel both like she was in the family fold and indebted to him. 'There's lots for you do, but I'll need help with one thing in particular.'

'Whatever you need, Mr Diamond.'

Martin had a price for her to pay to come back home, and Maggie was willing to pay it. Anything to get back to Belgravia Road, where she belonged.

CHAPTER 30

Segert blasted down Pretoria Road. The three-lane highway was deserted. He could make good time and get back to feed the dogs. The road to Pretoria had few man-made landmarks. If you didn't know any better, you'd think you were driving from one small country town to another. On either side were mostly truck dealerships, warehouses and petrol stations. Ahead was a bowl of open blue sky and bridges. Grass and shrubs held the soil together on the banks of the highway. He passed speeding white trucks carrying goods from the commercial centre of the Transvaal to the administrative capital of the Republic. He flipped through questions for Bessy and her family. He watched the speedometer; he was making good time. At the traffic light at Park Street he turned left, away from Loftus Stadium towards Sunnyside.

Mellville Street was a short residential road that ended in a dead end. The houses were a hodge-podge of bungalows of different shapes and sizes. 133 was constructed on a raised foundation of bricks, and the house was set back a reasonable distance from the street. The short brick fence surrounded the entire property and matched the reddish brickwork of the raised foundation. A well-maintained black BMW was parked in the driveway on the left, no discernible garage. On the right, a full-size metal gate was outside the raised foundation that entered the property on the side. No front door visible from the road. Segert guessed the front door was on the side leading from the full gate.

He drove just two houses down and parked on the street. Three hadeda birds were foraging for insects on a good-looking strip of government grass. They sank their long pointy beaks deep into the soil, extracting earthworms and larvae. It was the afternoon and they weren't bothering anybody. In the mornings and twilight hours, they screeched a bloodcurdling sound as they took flight, creating murderous storylines in peaceful dreams and disturbing nap times. Folklore had it they were afraid of flying. He slammed the car door to spook them, but they simply moved a few centimetres away and then returned to their invisible meal. He walked up the street to Bessy Diamond's house, holding a notebook with Augustine and Justice's pictures inside.

Segert jumped the short gate at the driveway and walked around to the front door. The net curtains on the front room windows were drawn but the heavy curtains were open. There weren't any dogs. He knocked on the door twice. The sun was behind him, so anyone looking through the peep hole would only make out a shadow. Inside the house, he heard someone walking towards the door.

The man who opened the door was young and wiry. His black hair was oily; he was the type of man who always looked like he needed a shower. He wore neat, shiny black slacks and an ironed white vest. His gold chain and rings glittered as he opened the door. In his hand was a golden delicious apple.

'Hello, can I help you?'

'I'm looking for Bessy Diamond. This is the address I have for her.'

'There's no Bessy Diamond here. What is this about? I rent this place.'

'How long have you been living here?'

'Over a year.' He took a bite of his apple and appraised Segert.

For a moment, the only sound was the man chewing. Segert didn't say anything. He figured the silence would make the man want to fill the vacuum of conversation with chit-chat and information. Polite people were unable to bear the stillness.

'Hope this isn't about property tax or something. I don't want my electricity cut off, or worse,' the man said.

'No, nothing like that. Do you live by yourself, or with any family that can help me? Maybe your wife has some information on Miss Diamond. Maybe she's spoken to the neighbours.'

The man looked down the street for any mode of transportation or Segert's companion, before taking a step towards him. 'What's this about?'

'Like I said, I'm looking for Bessy Diamond. She owns this house. She's probably your landlord.'

'I'm renting through Seeff, and they handle everything. You can go speak to them in the office in the main road.' He nodded to his left. 'Now, if you don't mind, I have to get ready for work.'

'What kind of work are you doing, Mr . . .' Segert fished for a name.

'I like your car. I'm a BMW fan, too. Mine's not a classic like yours, though,' the man said. 'Really nice neighbourhood. Try Seeff; they can help you find a place around here. Sorry I can't help you.'

'Actually, I was wondering if you've seen the woman, or her son. I have some pictures here.' Segert opened his notebook and showed the man two pictures. One of Augustine and one of Justice.

Nee, I haven't seen them. But if you want to find my landlord, contact the agency. Sorry I can't help you, or them.' He pointed at the pictures with his apple, and then moved to close the door.

'Thank you,' Segert said. 'I'll ask the neighbours if they've seen this missing family.'

'Won't hurt to ask,' the man said, as he shut the door, 'but if you're looking for them, maybe you should try the Cape Location. It's about fifteen minutes' drive from here. Next to the Asiatic Bazaar.'

He knew a decoy when he heard it. 'Thanks for your help. Sorry to have bothered you.'

The man watched Segert walk down the steps to the gate from the edge of the closing door.

Segert got in his car, and drove to a spot where he had a good view down Melville Street. He stayed in his car, expecting the man to get in his BMW and drive off to work. He was there ten minutes before the BMW backed out the inclined driveway and drove down Melville Street in the opposite direction.

There was no reason for a single man to rent such a large place by himself. This was a family home. All that was missing was a pool and some swings, maybe a dog too, Segert thought.

He parked his car just far enough away from the nearby stop street to avoid a traffic fine, then started to canvass the street. Only a handful of neighbours were home, and none of them were interested in Augustine and Justice's pictures. He walked past Number 133 again. The three hadedas had moved onto the grass, pecking for insects in the dark corners of the fence.

A scraping sound of a circular saw cut the birds' concentration. Segert turned to look at the house on the opposite side of the street. The garage door was closed and no debris for a renovation or remodel was lying on the driveway. The hadedas flew up over his head as he crossed the street, screeching into the afternoon light.

Berger knocked on the panelled garage door and stood back, waiting for someone to push it open from the inside. He held the notebook in his hand and put a smile on his face.

The man who pushed open the garage was middle-aged with a hard round belly. He wore dark blue jeans and a check shirt, and his safety goggles hung around his neck on a dirty elastic band. 'Can I help you?'

'Hello, sir, I'm looking for a missing girl and her son. Do you mind looking at some pictures?'

'Come inside, so I can get my glasses,' he said, and walked to the back of the garage, through to the kitchen. 'Don't just stand there, come inside,' he said and carried on walking.

The kitchen was large, but old-fashioned. The white walls had a sheen of yellow to them. Family pictures were taped to the old refrigerator among contractor cards and a monthly calendar. The window over the sink looked out to a large garden and a neglected swimming pool. The water had turned green.

The man grabbed his spectacles from the counter, then asked Segert for the pictures. 'What's this about?'

'I'm looking for a missing family. Maybe you've seen them around here?'

The man introduced himself as Gerhard, and called for his wife immediately.

But she didn't recognise the pair in the photos either, although her eyes lingered on Justice's face. Then she handed them back. 'Sorry, I haven't seen either of them. Why are you looking for them over here?'

'I've had a tip that she was in the area. Both of them.'

'Is she in trouble?' the wife asked.

'No, Missus . . .'

'Just call me Hilda.'

Segert fished in his shirt pocket for a business card. 'Here's my details, if you see her. It's just a missing persons case. Her family want to find her. Nothing more than that, don't worry. Can you tell me about your neighbour across the road, by number 133? He seems out of place in this neighbourhood.'

'We've been renovating for about three months. But that guy works nights, so he gave us a warning about our drilling. I mean, we are across the road, so it's not that loud, but he came over,' Gerhard said.

246

'And what?'

'He told me we can't drill before 9 a.m.'

'So, he was angry?'

'He met me at the garage door with a switchblade.'

'Tell the story properly, Gerhard. He had a peach with him,' Hilda said.

'A woman?' Segert asked.

'No, a Cape peach.' Hilda looked curiously at Segert, then cleared her throat.

'And he started cutting it at the door. While telling us he works nights, and he really needs his rest.' Gerhard said.

'Tell the whole story, Gerhard. He told you his name's Cutman, and he lives across the road. Then he cut the top of the peach and said he needs his rest. He works nights. We should start drilling after ten.'

'How long's he been living there?'

'I don't know. The owner moved away, but never rented it out or anything. She moved to South-West to get married. Now he's there, but we never saw him move in. One day, like, he was always there. But I think she still comes. Like, she stays overnight sometimes, or for the weekend,' Gerhard said.

'Whenever she comes, he is the one driving her,' Hilda said.

'Is that her car?' Segert asked.

'Don't know whose car it is. He and the car came together. She sometimes stays in the week,' Hilda said.

'How do you know all of this?'

'Because I see him at the shop. At the Spar. He buys Portuguese food. A big roll and some chips. Maybe some mince.'

'That's not Portuguese food,' Segert said.

'But sometimes, he has a trolley of food. Fruit, vegetables and everything. Then the next day, she is there. Maybe she's his sister, you know, I never really thought about it,' Hilda said.

'How old is she?'

247

Gerhard wiped his glasses with his shirt and let his wife answer. 'Late thirties, forty,' Hilda said.

'Thanks for your help,' Segert said, as Gerhard walked him out.

'Good luck,' Hilda shouted from the kitchen. Then told Gerhard to come back and get his spectacles, if he was going to use the circular saw. 'Otherwise, your eyes will end up like that peach.'

Segert crossed the road quickly and hopped over the driveway gate at Number 133. The kitchen door opened onto the driveway, but was locked. The kitchen windows were all closed. He scanned the contents of the sink. Dirty frying pan and a coffee mug. Then walked down the driveway scanning the windows. The bathroom windows were closed, a square bedroom window was locked, and the curtains drawn. He walked around the back of the house, which had a small grassy patch over which ran a heavy-duty washing line that attached to a high concrete fence. The bedroom curtains had been taken down. The single bed had been pushed against the far wall. An old boxing speed ball was held on the short wall by a reinforced steel arm. The bookshelf above the bed was empty but for neatly arranged black boxing gloves, rows of rolled gauze, what looked like medical tape, and a cluster of ornate switchknives on top of a pile of magazines.

Segert checked the windowsill for security alarm wires, didn't see any. He searched the grass for a rock, but couldn't find any big enough. He took off his boot and broke the window with it. He climbed through, grabbed all the knives and a leather case of syringes, then went through the house to the master bedroom.

The telephone began ringing in the front room. He scanned the corners of the hall for cameras, didn't see any, but still didn't think the phone ringing was a coincidence. He turned back the way he came, then jumped out the window, leaving it open. Quickly walked up the driveway and disappeared up the road to his car. He stuffed the knives in the cubbyhole, did a U-turn at speed, and burned rubber driving down Park Street. He took the turn-off to the Cape Location.

He parked his car in the open car park across the road from the mall, close to the train station and taxi rank. Then tried to stop and talk to some young people he judged to be around Augustine's age. Everyone sped up when they saw him, as if he was unclean, and his questions were left unanswered. No one was going to talk to him. He noticed his shirt was torn from climbing through the broken window in a hurry. His stomach growled. Before driving the knives down to Willem for examination, he jogged into Pick-n-Pay for a sausage roll and Coke.

At the far side exit, he saw a woman striding out the large double doors. She looked familiar; there was something about her. He started running through the mall, trying to reach her. When he got to the doors, she was crossing the street. It looked like she was walking a quieter but longer route to the taxi rank. He took off after her.

'What are you doing here? Segert asked her.

'This is becoming a habit, now,' Brown Sugar said. She carried on walking. 'Not you and that girl again.'

'Do you live around here?'

'No, and I didn't see your missing girl here or anywhere else.'

'Why are you dressed like that?'

'I'm coming from a funeral. I changed my shoes already. You look like something halfway between a Bible basher and an undercover cop. What happened?'

'Long story. Whose funeral was it?'

'Don't walk too close. Over a metre apart is OK. One of my primary school teachers.'

Segert stepped away and walked with her, but an arm's length apart. He wanted to talk to her about the Mine Dump serial killer, but decided against it.

'She was an old lady. Even taught my father,' Brown Sugar continued.

'Condolences. Were you close?'

'No, I didn't have a special relationship with her or anything. But she was the closest thing to just a normal human being that we get around here. She had a job for life, three kids, a house she owned. A husband that didn't drink too much. She had a little spice, but not too much.' She looked away when she said that, then started walking again to the train station. 'She had a nice send-off.'

'It seems she had a good life, then.'

'Not like your girl,' Brown Sugar said. 'Looks like she had *some* spice. Masala and all.'

'I'm beginning to think so, but you know everyone around here. In every square metre?'

'No, but the old ladies are the news reporters. Funerals are crying and food, and then gossip. Are you going back to Jo'burg? I could use a lift.'

'Nice segue.'

She gave him a look he'd recognised since he was a teenager. A look that was the equivalent of pushing him away.

'That means, nice transition in our chat to ask me for a lift.'

'If you don't ask, you don't get.'

'Actually, I could do with your help.'

'Talk and drive?' She smiled.

'I could do with the company,' he said, laughing, then straightened himself out. 'Talk and drive.'

They joined Pretoria Road south. The sun was sinking quickly as they raced towards the Johannesburg skyline. The last burning orange of the sun slipped behind the Hillbrow Tower. The basin of the city was cooling with darkness and the heat of the day would disappear into the sky.

Brown Sugar was sitting in the backseat at the passenger's side, looking out the window. Her grey cardigan pulled closed and her arms across her chest.

'I need to go to Eldorado Park. I'll need your help,' Segert said.

'I got the day off to come to the funeral. I don't want to cause roc'tions, asking for another.'

'Only be a few hours. It's for a good cause.'

'I understand you, but my boss isn't running a charity,' Brown Sugar said.

'I've told you about the other missing girls. The ones I found at the morgue. If we can find my missing girl, I might be able to stop the man who's killing girls. Have you heard about the Mine Dump Murders?'

'Mister—'

'You can call me Segert.'

'I just came from a funeral. I'm full up from sad stories. Just tell me what you need. I can see if I can make it happen. Take me to the Outlier Bar. I'm going to rest my eyes now.'

'I need you to meet one of my sources. She lives in Eldo's.'

'I'll speak to my boss. That's all I can promise.'

'I have to go drop something off at the South Rand morgue first,' Segert said.

'As long as it's not me,' she said. Then closed her eyes and drifted to sleep.

CHAPTER 31

Bessy always helped her brother. When they were growing up by the Copper Mountains, she always knew what to do. He was magic with a bat, lean like a policeman. He was their mother's child, and naturally everyone's favourite. She favoured their father, who had a big workman's back and legs thick as an ox. His only hobby was shooting beer bottles on payday. She was thirteen when she looked at the washing dancing in the wind and saw her mother picking at a bowl of grapes in the afternoon shade of the stoep and thought, *I'm going to get me and Martin out of here.* Mama loved their papa too much. And Martin was going to eclipse Papa, sure as the sun beat down and turned everything to prickles.

Martin was with her in Windhoek, but she knew it was a short visit. He couldn't be held back by anyone, least of all her. The three of them enjoyed the small charms of Windhoek together. It was her job as always, to tie up the loose strings. She'd taken Augustine's contact list and called her parents' house. On the third try an angry woman answered, then heckled her when she asked after Augustine. She struck Augustine's parents off the list of concerned affiliates. The only contact left was a pastor in Soweto, and for this she would need the help of

Maggie and then Cutman was available to finalise any matters that were past diplomacy.

* * *

When Brown Sugar knocked on the front door, Mrs Matthews was sitting in the empty kitchen. It was a Wednesday night; she was still used to having someone at home. Rosalind or Carl watching TV or listening to their music. Now they were growing up, it was just her and the dog. The old mastiff-terrier standing on his red mat, looking from the door to his owner anxiously.

'Hello, Mrs Matthews. I'm Brown Sugar. Sorry to disturb you. I'm looking for Rosalind.'

'Rosalind is working.' Mrs Matthews eyed her suspiciously. 'What kind of name is that?'

'A nickname.' Brown Sugar shrugged off the question.

Brown Sugar was wearing tight jeans stuffed into chunky ankle boots, and had foregone all makeup besides mascara.

'She's never mentioned you.'

'I'm looking for her school friend Augustine.'

'Augustine. That one!' Mrs Matthews purred at a private joke. 'Haven't seen her for a long time.' She looked for a car outside, noticed Segert sitting in his white van, then became more serious. 'What is this about? Do you want to come inside?'

Brown Sugar was overwhelmed slightly by the tall brown terrier at her legs. She didn't like dogs.

'Captain Morgan!' Mrs Matthews shouted at the dog. 'Please, please come inside.' Both of them knew how suspicious it looked, the white man alone in his van, parked by the stop sign. The neighbours would talk.

Captain Morgan whined at her feet, sniffing Brown Sugar's perfume furiously.

'Sit down,' Mrs Matthews commanded, and Brown Sugar hurried inside the short hall. 'Not you, never mind.'

The dog was just the right size to make Brown Sugar completely anxious. He followed her and whined at her feet, his big brown eyes excited, nails scraping on the floor. His head and snout pointed up. She was too afraid to sit.

'Have a seat.' Mrs Matthews gestured at the grey sofa. The room was chilly, and had a deserted feeling about it. The walls were painted in odd colours. A deep orange-brown of the African savannah on one wall, and industrial grey on the other. As if she ran out of paint halfway through, or changed her mind. The fern at the window looked tired. The pot had cracks in it, and the fern was overwatered. Copper coins and cigarette butts lay pushed into the dark soil. The room smelled slightly of damp.

Brown Sugar started tentatively, 'Mrs Matthews, we can't find Augustine. You know she had a boyfriend . . .'

'Yes, her teacher. Is that him outside? I thought he was younger than that. Augustine's boyfriend.' She tutted. 'What is going on these days? I can't believe her parents let them see each other. Although, I wasn't really surprised, because they used to let her run around buckwild when she was at high school.'

It was clear to Brown Sugar that Mrs Matthews was going to talk, not just answer any questions. And she was fine with it, as long as Rosalind's mother didn't start asking questions about her.

'Once I had to ban the two of them, Rosalind and Augustine, from seeing each other. But Augustine just came straight over here, her bags packed for the weekend, and acted like nothing was wrong.'

'Young people have a mind of their own. I know I did.'

'Mmm,' Mrs Matthews said. 'Would you like some tea or coffee, Miss . . .'

'Sure. I can't stay long though.'

'Is that him outside?' Mrs Matthews asked again.

'No. His name is Berger; I'm helping him find Augustine. He hasn't been able to get hold of Rosalind for a while. The phone . . .'

'Rosalind isn't around in the evenings. She works at the Spur down by the railway station. They give her a lift home at night. Must wait for kitchen staff to clean up before they can go. I'm grateful. Have you heard about all the coloured girls getting snatched up and killed?'

'No, where?' Brown Sugar didn't want to know about it.

'On the radio. Guess your age only care about that doof-doof music.'

They moved to the kitchen to switch on the kettle. The dog had followed them, but stood at the side of Mrs Matthews.

'It's dangerous him sitting here like that. I don't want the police or worse on my doorstep.'

Brown Sugar noticed Mrs Matthews dance around the question of who Berger was. She scanned Mrs Matthews intently. Her face was unlined and her cheeks full, but there was no ring on her wedding finger and the smell of a grown man was absent from the house. 'Is there another number I can reach you or Rosalind at? I can call her in the afternoon. Before she leaves for work. What time do you think?' Perhaps Rosalind spent some time at her father's place, Brown Sugar was picking at straws.

'These children used to sit on the phone all day. I've stopped paying it. Still takes incoming calls. If no one's here, you have to keep trying.

'So, no answering machine.' Brown Sugar sniggered.

'If you can't leave a message, it's probably full. I'm not a secretary,' Mrs Matthews said sternly.

Brown Sugar seemed to sober from her own joke. 'So how do you call people?'

'From work, like normal people.'

'Oh, OK,' Brown Sugar said.

'You know,' Mrs Matthews confided, 'Augustine left a message a while ago. A few months. She was calling from a payphone saying she'd send Rosalind something. I deleted the message. Rosa's at university. We need her to do well. She can't be pulled into a drama now.'

'You know Augustine hasn't been heard of since?'

'I'm sorry. I really regret it, but at the time it felt like the right thing to do.'

Brown Sugar had the feeling that Mrs Matthews had always been biding her time, trying to get everyone out of Rosalind's life. 'What was in the letter? Money?'

'It never arrived. You know the post office is unreliable.' Mrs Matthews was matter of fact, then added. 'She needs to make some money. I'm happy she has lofty dreams but we need to be practical too.'

Brown Sugar drank two sips of her milky tea and complimented Mrs Matthews on her home before she was able to push through the front door and step outside onto the *stoep*. The smell of dog, Mrs Matthews' nonstop chatter and Segert brooding in the dark in the wrong neighbourhood made her almost stumble as she ran to the van.

'Anything?' Segert asked her. 'You were in there a long time. Good news?'

Mrs Matthews smiled at them from the front door and waved them off as they receded down the road.

'Well?' Segert asked.

'She's working night shift at the Spur down by the railway station.'

'Then we should go chat to Rosalind at the Spur. Maybe get a burger, or a steak and chips.'

Brown Sugar laughed. 'I'm not eating there; I'm on a diet. The mother deleted a message that Augustine left on the phone. She said Augustine was bad news.'

* * *

The mall by the railway station was mostly empty. The small knock-off handbag shops were all closed. The only shop open on the ground floor, predictably, was a small bottle store that sold liquor through a hole in a bulletproof glass window. The Pick-n-Pay grocery store was closed. Their delivery truck was in the loading bay. The driver looked Brown Sugar and Segert up and down as they crossed the road, shaking his head to himself.

The Spur restaurant was at the top of the mall. It was a family-run chain found in most towns, known for its reliable prices and pretentions of Native American heritage. It was quiet tonight. Most of the tables were empty. They took a table alongside the window, but in the corner. Segert ordered two coffees, and Brown Sugar ordered an apple crumble with cream.

'I thought you're on a diet.'

'Maybe, I don't know. Let's see what happens.'

They scanned the waitresses looking for Rosalind's face. It didn't take long before they both realised she wasn't there.

Brown Sugar polished off the apple crumble, then called the waitress over. 'Excuse me. I was here a few weeks ago and a nice girl served me. Her name is Rose or Rosemary or something like that . . .'

'Rosalind, she stopped working here a while back. She was very good, yes. Can I help you with something? Some more coffee or an Irish coffee, maybe—'

'Just coffee. And the bill, thanks. Rose must be concentrating on her studies.' Brown Sugar sat back in her booth.

The waitress pursed her lips. 'Sure. She's studying law — everybody *had* to know. But she's probably still working somewhere.'

'Oh really? Around here somewhere?'

'I don't really know, Ma'am. Not a lot of places around here, but somewhere close, maybe.'

'I know what you mean.' Brown Sugar looked at the waitress' name tag. 'Chantal, thank you.'

* * *

Rosalind had been evading Segert ever since the fight in the field. He'd called and left messages but they'd been left unreturned.

He'd felt close to finding Augustine. Martin Diamond led to Cutman and her disappearance was tangled in that. Martin had somehow uncovered that she must've left some clue with Rosalind and that, even if she didn't know it, she'd have the key to where Augustine was or what happened to her. Or that Rosalind had Augustine's Freedom Papers. The dirty pictures that Teddy wanted recovered so badly. Lately, he didn't understand his own impulses. He knew Augustine needed the money. He sympathised. There was only one way to get it out of Teddy, against his will. And cutting that off made him feel he was pushing Augustine into a life closer to Brown Sugar's.

Segert and Brown Sugar were sitting in his car, about sixty metres down the road from Rosalind's house. The night was warm and still. A portable radio was playing American country music.

'Nicely done with that waitress,' Segert said.

'She was a talker; you could tell.'

'You didn't make it obvious we were looking for Rosalind.'

'She's a cash-poor student. We just need to know where to find her. The waitress didn't really know. The apple crumble was nice.'

She had a way of jumping from topic to topic. Segert wondered if it was Brown Sugar's way of scrambling his mind, keeping him off kilter. Or if it was something else. 'You made an effort to fit in there, so I appreciate it. It's not your scene.'

They'd been parked down the road from Rosalind's house, in the public swimming pool's car park, for over three hours. The Spur was the only restaurant open in the mall after six. They'd driven along the streets close to the railway station but couldn't find any restaurants open this time of the night. They came back to where the night started.

'Thanks for coming out tonight. I really needed, and don't take this the wrong way, a woman's touch. I couldn't just go to Rosalind's house, just me.'

'Not the first time someone spoke about my touch.' She chuckled.

He always regretted his big mouth.

'What do you want from this girl anyway?'

'I just need some information about her missing friend.'

She looked at him intently. 'This is like a holiday from my other job.' She smiled.

He sensed she had retreated for a second, or her mind had jumped to something else.

* * *

A white combi-van stopped outside Rosalind's house. And out climbed Rosalind in blue jeans and featherlight bomber jacket, carrying a backpack. She opened the short iron gate and waved the van goodbye. Segert took pictures of the van as it passed.

'What now, are we going to follow the van?' Brown Sugar asked.

'What for? We know where Rosalind is now. Just knock on her window and ask her for the pictures Augustine sent her.'

'Aaah.' She was disappointed.

Brown Sugar jumped out of the van. She was about to walk down the road to Rosalind's bedroom window when a man climbed over the short concrete fence, and ducked low in the front garden. Then moved over slowly to Rosalind's window.

Brown Sugar looked at Segert, with a what-now face.

'Come back,' he hissed.

She ignored him, ducked low and moved over to the hedge across the road.

She watched Rosalind open her window and whisper, then let him through the window.

Brown Sugar edged away from the shrubs, back to the van.

'Who was that?' Segert asked.

'That's her brother, I think. She was talking about "Mummy".'

'A bit late.'

'Do you still want me to go knock on her window?'

259

'Not with a possible gangster in the house.'

'Gangster? A naughty boy, maybe, not a gangster.'

'At that size, he's a gangster. Too tall to be considered a naughty boy. I have the number plate. I can get someone to run it. I'm taking you back to Outlier.' The brother fitted the description of the boy Teddy was talking about. Things were starting to fall into place.

'Praise the Lord, I need a drink.'

Segert started his van, did a three-point turn and drove past Rosalind's house. The light went out as they joined the main street.

This morning, Segert had offered to pay her pimp for her help. But he'd waved away the offer magnanimously after looking at the picture of Augustine. 'Number One, I'm always happy to help someone of my community. Number Two, if this leads to the Mine Dump Murderer, good for me. You have to stop that nutcase. Number Three, what's a favour between friends?'

Segert was grateful for the help, but it was a future headache, being indebted to a pimp. He aimed for the nearest garage to relieve himself, then up to the Outlier Bar to deposit this livewire into her usual life.

The roads were sleek with dew. The van cruised down the long main road. Suburbs have one thing in common, all over the world. They're even less interesting at night. The pavements were empty. Houses darkened. Segert used to jack cars from middle-class neighbourhoods with Rousseau when he was a teenager. Out of spite and boredom.

He wanted to ask Brown Sugar if she was all right going back to the Outlier. But he knew she wouldn't go for that, and it would be back to the antagonism that hung like a cobweb between them. So, he said something stupid as she was pretending to fall asleep.

'You look nice like this. Boots and trousers.'

'Back off, Segert, not tonight.' Her voice as sharp as a whip.

He hadn't laughed like that in months.

CHAPTER 32

Segert woke up late, and clenched the spare pillow on the empty side of the bed to his face. His clothes were lying in a heap on the floor and he felt too groggy to get up and make a pot of coffee. He could hear the light traffic of Louis Botha Avenue, and he lay there for a minute, staring at the dusty wooden elephant sculpture he'd bought at a market somewhere that was standing on his chest of drawers. He had a Brown Sugar hangover. He'd been stupid enough to not just drop her outside the bar, but go inside for one. She'd walked ahead of him, and he'd turned to see the barrel-flames in the distance, warming the homeless under the highway.

The bartender was happy to see him, and the last thing Segert remembered saying before everything became a blur was, 'One more drink and then I'm staying.'

The phone started ringing, and he jumped up and ran to his office.

'Segert Berger.'

The voice on the other side was hesitant. It took Segert a few seconds to recognise who was talking to him. 'Have you found Augustine yet, Mr Berger?' Pastor Moloi asked.

'Pastor Moloi? No, I haven't found her. Do you have anything for me?'

A woman befriended my wife and came to our house. We thought nothing of that, really. But she asked if we know any Indians. And we thought, for what? Why would we know Indians? We didn't question it, but this lady, something didn't seem right.'

Segert let him speak, an uninterrupted flow of information. He could make sense of it later. He started with the last point.

'The woman, what was off about her?'

'Nothing at the time. She's an elder. She wouldn't really befriend my wife. If anything, she would be my mother's friend or acquaintance. But because she's a pastor's wife, many people of all ages respect and befriend her. But it was the questions, and then disappearing.'

'What's her name?'

'She called herself Mama Funeka.'

'Do you have a first name?'

'She was from Tsitsiki in the Transkei.'

'Did she have a Christian name?'

'We don't use white names among ourselves. I guess I recalled you saying Augustine had an Indian surname. She didn't look Indian.'

'Yes, her father is Indian,' Segert said matter-of-factly. 'When was she last there? The elder.'

'About two weeks ago, but something made me think about you.'

'Did you tell me absolutely everything about Augustine? Did you leave anything out?'

'Like what?'

'Are you sure you told me everything about Augustine, Pastor?' Segert said again. 'Does your mother know anything?'

'If she did, she'd tell you. Now she's telling me all this is my fault. As if I brought her and Justice here.'

'Where are you now, Pastor?' Segert asked.

'I'm at home.'

'Was Augustine at your house?'

Segert could hear the pastor swallowing hard. 'Yes, she and the baby stayed here on the night we met. Didn't we tell you?'

'Was that the only time she was at your house?'

'Yes.'

So, Segert thought, *she hid Teddy's pictures at his house.* Segert could have laughed. Augustine had to have left something at the pastor's house.

'Did she already have a job, do you know?'

'She was starting the next day. She was only here overnight.'

'It's probably nothing, but if you feel like something is really wrong, go on a visit to your family or your wife's family. Pastor, look after yourself. I'll check up on you. Call me before you go.'

Segert thought. All the houses in the locations were small. Moses's family house was large in comparison to most, but still only half the size of his own bungalow. If Segert wanted to get to the photos, they would be easy to find. Probably under a sink or beneath a sofa. He could charge Teddy a retrieval fee. Going into Soweto, that wasn't going to be free, as far as Teddy was concerned. His mind ticked over. But he didn't understand why Maggie would be asking about Augustine unless she was blackmailing Martin, too, or he was trying to track her down.

Then he checked his machine and Rousseau's most conspiratorial voice crackled through. Segert chuckled to himself.

'I have your van spotted at an address in Parkview. A few times during the day. Six-pack *braai* when you solve the case?'

Segert had to hand it to him, Rousseau could be resourceful. He called him back to get an address.

* * *

Segert needed to call Teddy, but he peered through the small side-window into the backyard. Simba looked restless. It was a cool morning. And when he needed to clear his head, the best company was his dogs. He put on his shorts and cleaned the dog bowls. Trigger and Simba could tell there was something on his mind, and rubbed their bodies along his legs when he put down their breakfast of two-day-old spaghetti Bolognese. He sat down on the stairs by the back door and had a bowl of cereal and cold milk, but couldn't stomach it. He put his spoon down and watched his boys clean up their bowls.

'You ready for a walk?' he asked them as he put their leashes on.

They moaned in unison.

'We're just walking today, OK?' He looked deeply into Simba's eyes. 'Take it easy on me this morning.'

Trigger grunted like he had other plans.

Segert walked them down 16th Avenue into the suburbs. They stopped to smell trees, relieve themselves and bark at every single dog in the neighbourhood. And that was a lot. It wasn't like them. Segert redirected them to a park and let them out for a run. They ran towards a fallen tree, sniffing the long grass around it. Segert thought about what to say to Teddy, and why he even cared enough to be thinking so hard.

He waited till after lunch and called Teddy at school.

'Hey, I have some news.'

'Do you have them?'

'No, my remit is not retrieval,' Segert answered.

'OK. So glad you called me about the new Cambridge books. I will come and pick them up on my way home. Thank you kindly.' Teddy clicked the phone and returned to the staff room.

* * *

When Teddy turned up at Segert's house, the sun was starting to set. A group of boys and girls were playing a game of rover in the street and turned to look when Teddy parked his

Toyota too close to their action. He nodded towards them, and they moved further down the road.

The Teddy walking here wasn't exactly the same Teddy that came stumbling up the garden path the first time. And it wasn't just about the money.

'Nice to see you again,' Segert said without getting up. 'Have a seat.'

'Why are you talking about a retrieval, as if it's a kidnapping or something?'

'It got you here, didn't it?'

'What news do you have for me?'

'First the bad news: I don't know where they are right now.'

'What's the good news?'

'I don't have any good news.'

'Why am I here then?'

'I didn't invite you.'

'You said you had news.'

'You're right,' Segert conceded. 'But first, I want to know, have you told me everything?'

'I think so. I've told you everything you need to know.'

'Is anybody after her for anything else? If I'm involved in something deeper, you have a responsibility to tell me.'

Teddy looked shocked. 'What are you talking about?'

'Have you had her followed for some reason?'

'I've left the entire responsibility for finding them to you. Now you're making me regret it, Berger. What are you not telling me?'

'If it's not you, then someone else is looking for her, for both of them. Does she have anything else valuable that you know about?'

'She was never involved in anything. She worked as a cashier, we got together, had a baby, the end.' Teddy was liberal with the truth. He wasn't going to give his game away.

'Did she steal any cash from the tills?'

'I don't know, do I? Maybe when she was planning on leaving me, she stole some money to get away. What's going on? Did someone contact you?'

Segert felt the tug for information, but didn't say anything.

'I'm paying you. I'm your client, remember?'

'The last people to see her say that they're being followed and they're scared.'

'Who's following them?'

'Hell if I know.'

'I was having a nice day until you called.'

'I'll get us a drink. Coffee?'

'Something a little stronger.'

'Part of the service.' Segert disappeared into the house.

Teddy kicked the tree stump that served as the outdoor coffee table. If anybody got their hands on those pictures, he was done for. He didn't care who else was after her; he needed to make sure those pictures were buried, and he didn't mind if she was buried right along with them.

Segert re-emerged and handed him a beer. 'We have to assume that whoever is looking for her is dangerous. For argument's sake. If it's nothing, then you were paranoid but prepared.'

'I'm sure it's nothing. There's security forces everywhere. Who saw her last?'

'You're right.' Segert took a sip from his beer. 'It could be nothing.' He thought there was nothing wrong with saying she'd been to a church. 'She went to a church, a Zionist church, and the congregation helped her out. Nothing to get suspicious about.'

'Maybe the pastor is being followed for something else. Churches are safe routes, smuggling out wanted elements and revolutionaries. It's got nothing to do with Justice and Augustine. What's the name of the church?'

'I don't think it even has a name. They held it in a derelict building in town.'

'A Black church?' Teddy's eyes went big.

'Yes.'

'It's got nothing to do with Augustine, I can tell you that. They're just looking for money, and to hell if I'm going to pay for it. They're probably mixed up in something else.'

'I'm sure you're right. I thought I'd let you know.' Segert didn't mention the woman who was looking for Augustine. He guessed it was Maggie. But then Augustine could be pissing off all kinds of people and any one of them could've been an old black woman. But one thing for sure, Teddy didn't care about her or the child either.

CHAPTER 33

It was 11.30 a.m. the next day, and Solomon's kitchen had just opened for lunch. Segert was reading the paper in the back corner, drinking a bottomless black coffee that the waitress kept fresh. His friendship with Solomon was still touch and go after the Health Department closed it for two weeks. The bar was empty mostly, except for a few middle-aged men who sat alone at tables or wordlessly next to each other at the bar drinking beer and eating burgers. An old cricket match on the TV was holding most of their attention. They weren't usually a quiet bunch; most of them knew each other. Some of them were even in here together last night. The reverential silence was the result of hangovers. They'd warm up to each other again before lunch time was over.

The leading story in the paper was the police shootout with the Stander gang, bank robbers led by an ex-policeman. Apparently only one of them had been killed. Stander, the ex-policeman, and the other bank robber were nowhere to be found.

Segert was interested to see how it would play out. He thought of how Carol was reading the same headline as a potential loss of earnings. He could imagine her laundering some of their money. She just craved that type of excitement. A pen traced his thoughts on a serviette.

'Interesting story. You think you can bring in Stander?' the waitress asked. She was a friendly woman in her thirties. Her fat spilled out over her black apron and Segert suspected she was flat-footed.

'Too audacious for my blood. I don't think anyone wants him to get caught. Stander, I mean.'

'I know your meaning. He's making a joke of the prison service. But it's exciting to see him get away with it. You want anything to eat?' She told him about the minute steak special, and he asked for one in a Portuguese roll.

He watched her waddle off to the back, turning over in his mind the expectations of his meet with Willem. He tapped his foot against the table leg.

Willem sauntered into the bar, more relaxed than Segert expected. He came to sit opposite him.

'What have you got? Why didn't you want me to come to your office?' Segert asked.

Willem turned to check if anyone was walking close to him before speaking. 'It's my day off, and I don't think you wanted to wait. Where you get the knives and drugs?'

'Took it from a guy calls himself Cutman.'

'Hectic.' Willem's eyes went big for a second.

'Very.'

'Is he in custody? How'd you get the bag?'

'I broke into his house.'

Willem put his hands up. 'OK, I never asked you to break the law.'

'Tell me.' Segert went serious.

'All negative for blood. But absolutely thoroughly cleaned. If I didn't check the blade, I'd think they were new. One of them has a depth that's similar to one of the murders. Could be a possible match. What you know about him, the guy I mean?'

'Not much. He likes boxing, looks dodgy.'

'Ah, of course. "Cutman" is a job. The person who cleans the boxer's face, ringside.'

'He doesn't seem like the medical type.'

'No, it's not licenced. They work with the boxers and promoters. Nobody's going to pay for real medical doctors unless it's insured. Go to the sports pages, see if there's any boxing matches coming up soon.'

The waitress came over and asked Willem if he wanted something to eat.

'I'll have what he's having, if it's just a coffee.'

Segert leafed through the paper and only saw ads for boxing matches in Sun City. 'Where do we find the amateur boxing circuit?'

The waitress came back and brought Willem a cup of coffee.

'That's going to be like finding a needle in a haystack. Every boxing gym will be on that circuit.'

'What are you going to do, give this to the cops? Zero interest.' Willem kept his voice low. 'Go to the gyms close to where the girls were found.' He pulled out a Bic pen that had teeth marks on the lid. 'I'll write you a list.'

Segert's steak arrived, but he'd lost his appetite.

* * *

The Blue Ribbon Bout on Saturday was a good way to repay Rousseau. It was being held in a small hotel in Kempton Park, close to the airport and the abandoned Village Farms mines where three bodies had been found.

'It's business and a pleasure having you with me,' he'd said when he called Rousseau.

Wes would be off the hook from a meet-up, and Segert could continue to avoid his brother. The downside was he'd have to stay sober.

The mercury was already dropping quickly when Segert and Rousseau arrived, just after 7 p.m. The Citi Lodge was in the flightpath, and an aeroplane screeched overhead as they followed the crowd to the convention centre.

The boxing ring was set up on the floor in a large conference room, and the spectator chairs were arranged around the ring on three sides. The room was humid with human breath and the heaviness of throbbing music. A pair of young fighters were warming up in the ring. It felt like a boxing gym with everyone on the same level and the crowd close to the action. A small group of press had gathered in a cordoned-off area in the back left, drinking free booze.

'Let's go get something to drink,' Segert said, and walked to the bar on the opposite side of the room.

He looked across the room for Cutman. Some staff came in and out of the door close to the press bar. He handed Rousseau a R5 note and told him to get himself something, and strode across the room. The lights started to dim slightly as the music was turned up. He went around the chairs and down the aisle to front row to get to the door. A group of young men in suits started shouting to each other in another language, and one of them spilled his beer on Segert's black sports jacket.

'Ssorry,' he slurred, trying to stuff money in Segert's pockets. He took it and walked off in a huff, but he had a good excuse to look for a restroom.

The wide corridor was filled with people. An announcer was warming up his voice, a quartet of ring girls were practising their poses, but stepped aside to let him through.

Segert walked to the back, towards what he hoped would be the boxers' areas. He scanned the room, then cut across the corridor to another, but was stopped by a bouncer.

'I'm looking for a bathroom, sorry.' He walked out, then pushed the green bar on the exit door, and found himself on the other side of the car park. He was walking back to the front of the convention centre when a white people-carrier pulled up into the light by the back door. The driver jumped out, knocked on the exit door twice, then went round to the sliding door and started unpacking boxes of alcohol that were laid on the floor in between the seats.

Segert jogged over. 'Do you need some help? Seems like a lot for one guy.'

'It's fine, boss, no problem for me,' the driver said.

Segert ignored him. 'It's no problem. What's a spare pair of hands if you can't use them?'

They packed the boxes on top of each other, until someone left the door open with a doorstop.

'Sir, you can't help me carry this in. If my boss finds out, he will get angry.'

'No problem. How about I guard while you take it in?'

The driver was confused, but carried the boxes down the corridor.

'You know,' said Segert casually, as the man took the box of plastic cups from the front seat, 'I'm sure I've seen you around somewhere before. You deliver people late at night. Can't remember now.'

'I go wherever the job takes me.' Fear was creeping into the driver's voice. 'Mostly office clean-ups.'

'Do you have a schedule or is every night different?'

Rousseau came walking through the doors, carrying an extra Coke. 'I was looking for you. What happened?'

'Just had to help this man with some boxes. I need a leak.' He nodded at the driver, then walked around the corner, Rousseau trailing behind him.

'You recognise the plates?' Segert asked over his shoulder.

'That's the one you gave me last week.' Segert smiled. He now had a link between the van and the random block of flats on the neglected side of Parkview.

Segert wondered where it would lead. There was no way Rosalind was giving up her tips at Spur to be an office cleaner. But he'd already spooked the driver. He wasn't going to get anything else out of him.

Rousseau's nostrils dilated as he inhaled the prospect of the opening bout and motioned for him to come inside. 'Let's get in there and get a few. I need something stronger than this.'

The first two bouts were over within an hour. The promoter announced a twenty-minute break and Rousseau took the chance to go to the men's room. He was tipsy and stumbled over a chair that had been pulled away from the stage. He fell down, staring at the faces looking down at him. The crowd parted like curtains at the beginning of a show. Between him and Segert was Cutman, who had been walking to the back of the ring.

It was the surprise of seeing Rousseau lying on the floor and Cutman cutting across to the back of the ring that made Segert shout, 'Hey!'

Rousseau got up and took chase, but was intercepted by a security guard. He was hit so hard that blood flew from his mouth onto a woman who was walking back to her seat. Segert landed a blow on the security guard, and, in the rush of people who protected the woman and the security guards, a brawl started.

Cutman ran towards the corridor and then out the back door. It would be impossible to reach, and Segert ducked to escape through main entrance. A small car screeched out of the parking lot. He could follow the car up the highway or save Rousseau, returning him in one piece to his wife like he'd promised.

* * *

Through the rain and the beating of windshield wipers, Segert kept track of Cutman driving south on the M2 towards central Johannesburg. He stayed well back, only accelerating when they were close to an exit ramp. On the opposite side of the highway, a group of police vans were advancing, sirens blazing.

Cutman slowed at the curved exit off M27 exit that joined Jan Smuts Avenue, then barrelled across an amber traffic light.

The road was notorious. You caught one red light, you caught them all. He watched Cutman's taillights cruising through three green lights before he turned left, out of view.

Segert parked behind a giant yellowwood on Jet Park Road and walked across the park. The streets were deserted. The unseasonal rain gave the semi-industrial area an eerie feeling.

The ground floor looked like regular grocery shops that had already closed for the day. The first floor of the apartment block was in complete darkness, but on the top floor in the furthest right corner he could make out fluorescent tube lights.

Segert took a closer look at the car park. It was half full with new model BMWs and Benzes. This was Honda and Toyota territory. He walked to his car, drove to the other side of the park.

At 11 p.m., Segert climbed the stairs by the management office and buzzed on the security gate that cut off the flats from the ground floor. He heard light music coming from somewhere inside. Whoever was inside would answer.

A tall, olive-skinned man opened the back door of his flat, looked Segert up and down quickly. He was wearing a black suit and had slicked-back hair. 'Cash or credit card? On the statement it'll say G.C. Pty.'

'How much?'

'Two hundred.'

Segert could just expense it to Teddy's account. 'Card is fine.'

The man said, 'Come this way,' and stood aside.

Inside, a girl was dancing on a stage wearing chaps and a cowboy hat. A disco ball hung in the middle of the narrow club. An ABBA song, 'Fernando', was playing at an even volume and wasn't congruent with her teenage gyrations.

'Beukes's kind of place,' he said to himself, then ordered a scotch from a bikini-clad waitress as he sat down in a booth. He drained another scotch, then walked around looking for someone to talk to. He passed the bathroom and pushed open a black door. The first room was dark, a light crystal ball beat dimly against a red and black background of a stage area. There was a red chaise longue perched on the top of the stage and two young Eastern European women were casually sitting on it. One of them was picking her nails. In the corner, two women sat in a booth counting colourful chips.

He pushed the door to the second room that was packed with crap tables, poker, blackjack and roulette. In the short time he walked the floor he counted two dozen people. None of them were smiling. Segert stopped for a second. He recognised one man on the crap table: it was Carol's father, beside him a distinguished-looking older man who looked even more monied.

This is what Carol was talking about. Gambling had been banned for almost twenty years, but small casinos kept popping up, usually close to the border. It was an opportunity she was missing out on. He walked briskly to the door at the opposite end of the room.

Through the white chipboard door, he found the remnants of badly furnished living quarters. An old green sofa with cigarette burns, parquet tiles coming apart. Plates stacked to dry on the side of a sink. This was where the fluorescent lighting was coming from. One of the girls he'd just seen onstage walked through the door.

'What you doing in here?' she whispered when she saw him. 'Get out.'

'Do you know Rosalind?' Segert asked. 'I'm looking for someone called Rosalind. Someone downstairs is looking for her.' Better not mention Augustine now. Too risky.

'You'll get her in trouble. Come back this way.' She grabbed his arm and led him towards the door.

A big man with a wide jaw and fat trapeziums opened the door before she got to it. Segert hadn't clocked him earlier. The doorman he'd sized up, him he could take, but this one . . .

'You can't be here.' The big man hit his right hand into his left fist.

'No, no, it's OK. He's lost,' the girl said. Her breasts were still exposed. The fluorescent light made Segert want her to cover up. 'He's looking for the bathroom.'

'Get out,' the big man said, his voice thick.

'Your girls don't have to worry about me.' He turned back to the girl. 'Where's Rosalind? Is she here?'

The stripper ran out, throwing the door open, and Segert tried to follow her. Two men came in as she left, one of them the bouncer.

His shoulder was twisted back as they punched him in the ribs. They only hit him in the face once. Then they dragged him through the kitchen to a hole in the wall that opened into a darkened room. Segert felt the linoleum on his shoes even though he was only half-conscious. He was thrown onto a chair, his hands were tied behind his back and his legs duct taped together.

One man left, closing the door behind him and the other switched on a dim floor lamp. Segert could make out that there were bottles of drinks, clean glasses and dry food in the far corner. This was a storeroom. To his right was a kitchen window with the curtains drawn and a black horizontal blind pulled across, about two inches below the top of the window. The sink and plumbing had been gutted below it. He struggled with the ropes, twisting his hands and reaching for the outside of the rope to find some slack.

In the corner of the room, Cutman was taking off his jumper. 'This is my work jumper. Only boxers' blood is allowed.' He grinned. He walked closer, then punched Segert in the face. 'That's for breaking into my house.'

Segert threw himself and the chair onto the floor, then kicked Cutman in the shins.

'You son of a—' Cutman shouted.

Segert loosened the rope enough to stand, kicked the chair towards Cutman and wriggled towards the shelves of bottles.

Cutman grabbed the mop and hit Segert in the face. Berger spat the strands of the mop out, as he loosened the last knot on the rope binding his hands, brought his arms forward and used the rope to cut the duct tape. Cutman kicked him in the back. But Segert grabbed his ankle and Cutman fell to the ground.

'Where is she, and what did you do with the baby? Did you kill her like the other girls?' Segert punched Cutman and held his arm in a fist.

Cutman laughed. 'You'll never get out of here to find out.'

Segert tied him up and put duct tape over his face. 'Ssh, be quiet.' He thought about climbing through the window, then fished in Cutman's pocket for a lighter, reached for a bottle of vodka, poured it onto the mop head and set it ablaze. He climbed through the window and ran across the front passage on the first floor to the back stairs.

* * *

The fire alarm woke Carol, who was dozing in the back of her Audi.

'Oh my word.' She jumped out of the car when she saw Segert's bloodied face. 'What's going on?'

'I got the—'

'OK, don't speak. Just catch your breath, rather.' The fire alarm had been switched off and no one left the building.

'What are you . . . ?' Segert tried to talk. Carol's driver helped pull him up and together they supported him through an alley to his car.

'Did you follow me?' he slurred.

'I'm a little more sophisticated than that. Give me some credit.' Carol took his car keys and opened the door. 'Catch your breath,' she said as she wiped her hands.

Her driver stood guard at the back of Segert's car.

'I'm not ungrateful to see you, but what are you doing here?'

'If anyone was going to find out who the new trade in town is, it was always going to be you. Look at this car park. It's full. Residential area. Low-income white neighbourhood, no police patrols. I mean, this is brilliant. Bet you the fire department doesn't even come.' Carol was excited by the prospect.

'I need to call the police. This is my missing girl case,' Segert said.

'Who is it?' She nodded towards the apartment block.

'I'm looking for Augustine Pillay.'

'I mean, who's running the show?'

Segert got ready to start his car. 'I need to get out of here. I'm reporting this place to the police, but there's a girl in there you need to get out for me.'

Carol's driver knocked on the boot.

'Her name is Rosalind. Get her home.'

CHAPTER 34

The next day it was in the papers. Carol brought him the newspaper, a jar of arnica cream and a six-pack of Windhoek lager.

> *Gambling den foiled. Directors of company are listed as OAP close to border with South-West Africa.*

Segert was on the phone with Willem. 'I think we got our guy, but not for what I thought.'

'There was another murder last night. So unless he could be at two places at the same time, I don't think so.'

He dismissed Carol's concern and told her had to head out. Before he left, he called Wes for a favour.

'I'm going over to the Diamond house now. I have a favour to ask. A big one.'

'My favours are running low at the municipal court, so I can't promise . . .' Wes sounded tired even though the clock hadn't hit eleven.

'I don't think it'll involve the court,' Segert said. 'I need you to give someone a job. A law student.'

'How am I going to afford that?' Wes was confused.

'Perhaps replace Helen?'

'Why?'

'This girl needs a job to finance her law degree at Wits.'

'Can't she get a job somewhere else? And before you answer, does she have something on you? Do you owe her anything?'

'No, nothing like that. I just think this is the best thing I can do considering the situation she's in. She's from Eldorado Park.'

'Oh.'

Segert could hear the wheels spinning in Wes's head.

'I'll get back to you on that,' Wes said. 'But there's one thing I need from you.'

'Not now, Wes,' Segert said.

'I think you should talk to Janette.'

'We all have regrets, Wes, but I'm not doing it.'

* * *

It was late morning when Segert took the road to Greenside, to Martin Diamond's house. He put the radio on, but it already felt like fifty people were milling about in his head. His body was aching, and he had a call sheet a mile long. The best thing to do was just attack the problem head on. Segert was in a combative mood, and he directed his anger into the intercom at the Diamond house. A softly spoken woman answered.

'Mr Diamond isn't here, I'm afraid. He's away for business.'

'I just have a few follow-up questions. I'm a private investigator.'

'Private investigator? What's this about? Come in.'

Segert drove up the allée and parked at the front door. The woman who'd answered the intercom was waiting outside. She was dark-haired with blue eyes. Heavy set with narrow shoulders and wide hips. What women call pear-shaped. She had a friendly smile that creased the plum-coloured birthmark at her left eye. Her clothes and shoes were simple, a layered hand-knitted cardigan and blouse. It was clear that she didn't belong in this mansion, but the way she occupied space made it known she had become comfortable at Belgravia Road.

'Hello, I'm Bessy. Martin's sister. Come in. I'll get you some coffee and milk tart. We can chat.'

'I'm surprised to see you here. I thought you'd be down at the courthouse with Cutman.'

'He's my tenant, yes. But I can't vouch for what he does in his spare time.'

'I called once before, but it wasn't you; it was Ms Santos.'

'That's me. I'm widowed. I moved to South-West Africa for my husband. He was an engineer. God bless his soul.'

'I've been to your house in Pretoria, looking for the girl who used to work here.' Segert wanted to see any recognition on her face.

'Oh, you're in luck.' Bessy smiled.

'Really?'

'She's in the back, with the baby. You can go chat while I get the coffee ready.' Bessy nodded in the direction of the kitchen.

He knew immediately when he looked at them through the sliding doors that it wasn't Augustine. Was it Maggie?

'Go through. I don't mind, really,' Bessy said. Her frumpy and dumpy persona always put her above suspicion.

* * *

Maggie was sitting on a green-and-black tartan waterproof, dressed in white overalls and flip-flops. Her legs crossed in front of her. The baby was a happy toddler, Martin's boy, and he smiled at Segert, showing his front teeth. Maggie turned to look at the newcomer quickly.

'Maggie, it's Segert Berger. We spoke on the phone, a while back.'

'Oh, it's you.' She was surprised to see him, but kept her composure. She held up Nicholas and bobbed him up and down.

'Nice to meet you.'

She didn't answer. Her attention was on the boy, who had come loose from her grip and started walking quickly towards the pepper tree at the edge of the garden. She didn't get up, but watched him carefully.

'I'm still looking for Augustine. Do you know where she and her baby, Justice, went? The baby's father wants to know. You can imagine.'

Bessy called for Segert and asked if he wanted his coffee indoors or outside. 'It's no bother either way,' she added.

'I'll drink coffee with you, if that's OK.'

She looked overjoyed for the male company.

'You can tell me, and I won't bother you or your boss again,' Segert said to Maggie.

'They were never here, Mr Berger. Isn't that what boss Diamond told you, all that time ago? That should be enough.'

'Then why were you at Pastor Moloi's? I don't believe it was a coincidence.'

'Mr Berger, she was never here.' She tutted with agitation. Then she remembered herself: that even though this was her home, and she was assured a place, that Segert held a power she could never have. And he was using his power to push down.

Segert laughed. 'Paulus told me you had a way. You're saying I told you about her, and you found out where she had been on your own? For no reason.'

'I'm an old woman, Mr Berger, but I still have my uses here at the Diamond house. I don't know what Paulus told you. I don't know what goes on in the minds of old drunk men,' she said matter-of-factly.

He went down onto his haunches. 'Do you think what happened to them won't happen to you? Why did you go to Pastor Moloi's? Did she leave something there?'

She laughed again and looked away to Nicholas.

A black cat slinked on the vibracrete fence, recoiled, then jumped into the pepper tree.

'I don't know where they went to after that. She didn't leave a trace.'

'So, I can take it she is never coming back here?'

'I lost track of her after that. If anything happened to her, it was Pastor Moloi.'

Segert laughed, 'What about Cutman? Do you know him?'

She remained silent.

Augustine had gotten in over her head. That much Segert knew.

'Why would you help any of these men? One of them, at least, did terrible things. You have a choice.'

She thought for a second before replying. 'Choice? Between what and what? Nothing changed here except Miss Kimberly died. I only do my job.'

Ja, nothing changes, huh? When is Paulus coming back?'

Maggie shot him a baleful glance, then retreated to her benign domestic persona. 'I don't make the decisions here, Mr Berger.'

Segert walked away. He recognised the act. Sometimes playing stupid was a survival tactic, meant to skirt responsibility.

'I'll be keeping an eye on the pastor,' he lied. 'So maybe leave him alone.'

* * *

Segert drank black coffee and ate oven-warmed milk tart in the front room with Bessy. He wanted to sit in his discomfort. The pastry was buttery and crumbly, the way his mother used to make it. Maggie's words echoed in his mind. There had been so many surprises in this little case. No matter where he looked, Martin Diamond was protected at every turn.

What's it like to be so special? he wondered.

The more he dug into this case, the more he lost all sense of reality. Who was anyone, and what was everyone doing? Everything was held together with the lightest piece of string, and if you tugged at it, the whole thing came undone.

Bessy was talking at him. 'It's just a joy to have him around. Look at him. Do you have any children, Mr Berger?'

'No, it's not for me, I don't think.'

'A handsome man like you, not having any children. That's a sin.' She laughed.

'I have trouble keeping the right lady. It's the job. Late nights, unsavoury characters.'

'Women, we overlook almost everything.'

'It always starts out that way.'

'Yes, well, in my case, I already have to overlook that you're probably responsible for breaking the window in my house.'

'Your neighbours say Cutman had been intimidating them with knives and threats. Perhaps it was one of them.' Segert felt his spine unfurl.

She took a sip of coffee. 'I don't know, perhaps you'd like to call the number and check if he's back at home.'

'He's been released on bail, then?'

'I don't know, but he will probably be out soon.'

'I heard he drives you around. Perhaps I should come by later.' Segert smiled. 'Refresh his memory.'

'If you ever see him again, it won't be here. He's not the forgiving type, and you did break his bedroom window.' Then she changed the subject back to his love life. 'Women like looking after people. I'll give you a small jar of arnica cream for your cheek.' Her voice was calm and regulated. She walked to the medicine cabinet in the kitchen.

'Thank you, but it's not necessary. Do you know anything about Augustine Pillay, who used to work here?'

'It was always Maggie and the gardener. No one else.'

Segert didn't look back as he walked to his car, his keys jingling in his hand, but shouted a singular word usually directed at a small scruffy dog lifting a leg against your rear tyre; baboons intruding on a Sunday family *braai* on your beloved annual seaside holiday; or a bed of scorpions you've discovered in the hollow corner of the veranda. It was not just his breath leaving his body.

* * *

He found himself driving the M1 down to Eldorado Park instead of returning to Orange Grove. By now the afternoon sun was hot, and the roads light with traffic. When he took the right turn off the Golden Highway and saw the yellow Casspir, he exhaled slightly. It was safer to be in the townships. The rifleman was stationed on top, pointing his weapon twenty-four hours a day. Segert was safer here than anywhere else in Jozi. No wonder Teddy liked working in the schools in the townships. He had twenty-four-hour protection.

Carl was sitting in the backyard when Segert knocked on the door. He came round the back, and slowed when he saw Segert.

'Can I help you, sir?' he asked.

'Is Rosalind here?'

'Not yet. What's this about?'

'Don't worry, she knows me. I was supposed to come round earlier,' Segert lied.

'She didn't mention it.'

'You look like you need a smoke.'

Carl hesitated before he accepted the smoke, but reckoned if the man knew Rosalind it must be OK. 'I can't smoke here. My mother. I'll tell Rosalind you were here.'

'Let's go for a short walk, by the pool.' Segert offered him a cigarette from a pack and led the way.

Carl was surprised how well this man knew the area. 'Cool.' After a few drags, he asked, 'How you know Rosalind?'

'We have a friend in common.'

'Someone from university?' Carl guessed.

'Actually, we have two friends in common. I think you know both of them.' Segert let that sit with Carl as he exhaled smoke in his face.

'Maybe.'

'It's more than a maybe. I'd say you've been blackmailing Theodore Beukes.'

Carl threw the cigarette to the ground and started running. He ran away from the main road, into the neighbourhood. Children playing in the park and groups of errant teenagers started scattering as soon as they saw Carl's commitment to getting away. Ice lollies were dumped on the road, girls hid behind bushes or in shops, little children abandoned jump rope or marbles and ran home, disturbing their grandmothers' soap operas. The children were gathered in hugs and then ushered into the rooms furthest from the front door and the possibility of stray bullets or tear gas. Everyone was offered sugar water to calm down.

Carl was smart. He was running away from the Casspir and any support for Segert. He was fast, too. Carl had been on the Eldorado Park athletics team since he was six. Competing regionally for small accolades for long jump and sprints. He'd just quit last year, because they wanted too much from him. Friday nights and weekend mornings on the track was too much to ask. But he enjoyed running now; after the first two hundred metres he relaxed into his pace. He took a left at the end of the street and ran down towards Pimville. He could get lost in the estates.

Carl flew across the two-way. Cars braked hard left and right. A minibus jumped the pavement to avoid ramming a car. Carl hopped a fence and ran through a line of flapping washing.

And went down like a sack of spuds.

By the time Segert climbed the concrete fence, Carl was lying in the grass, his head bleeding. An old man in a wheelchair was smoking a cigarette on the *stoep* by the back door, a pile of rocks on a table next to him. Another rock, with blood on it, lay by the fallen Carl.

'I'm tired of people stealing our washing,' he explained as Segert approached.

Segert pulled Carl up by the arm.

'I need to get those photos back. Give them to me.'

'I don't have them anymore.'

'You better get them and give them to me.'

'You better give the man what he wants,' the old man chimed in.

Segert kicked the bloodied rock out of the way, and nodded at the old man out of respect. He had a good aim.

* * *

Segert held Carl by the arm all the way back to his house.

'You're getting money off Beukes, so where's the pictures?'

'I'm not getting a cent off Beukes.'

'Stop lying.'

'Look, I used to. I went there; I went to the school. I got money. I was happy. Too happy.'

'What happened?'

'Some other boys found out, and they took it over.'

'Bigger boys or gangsters?'

'Same difference. It's easy money, and I can't stop them.'

'Where's the pictures?'

'I burned them.'

'If you are talking *kak* to me, I swear—'

'They beat me up and took it.'

'If Beukes stops paying them, then what?'

'They slash his tires, hurt him maybe. Why don't you just turn up at the school and scare them?'

'That's not my job. Do they know anything about him besides where he works?'

'Don't think so. It's overkill to find out where he lives for a few hundred rand. It's drinking money, is all.'

Carl suggested that if it was such a big problem Beukes should just change schools. 'He can get another job and leave us alone.'

'You were blackmailing him, remember?'

'No one told him to come here. You want to be separate, stay separate. Why do you people like popping in with us? Let us go.'

'When is your sister coming home?'

'She comes about three or four.'

'What was on the pictures?'

'The man, naked. And girls. Young girls. It's disgusting.' Carl pulled a face. 'Do you have another cigarette?'

'I thought you don't like to smoke at home.'

'It's been a tough day.'

Grannies were coming out again to sit on the *stoeps* overlooking the roads and letting children back out to play.

A small group of youngsters walked down the road past Carl's house to sniff the air and whisper among each other. 'Afternoon, Carl,' a brave girl called.

He waved his cigarette at her.

'I need to use your phone. Will it be OK?' Segert asked.

'Phone is blocked. You'll have to use a public phone. There's one down the road there by Al-Rahman's. They walking that way, don't walk too close. You make everyone nervous. I need to go wash my face. Do you really know Rosalind?'

Segert remembered that Brown Sugar also wanted him to walk a short distance away from her. 'I have some arnica cream for your head.'

'Can you get me a packet of Niknaks from the shop, also?' Carl asked.

Little brothers, Segert thought and walked towards his car to get the arnica cream and loose change for the phone.

* * *

Segert called Rousseau at work, but he was busy on a vehicle inspection and couldn't be interrupted. He walked back up the road to Rosalind's house, thinking how he would repay Rousseau for last night. The sun was in his eyes and his head was slightly bowed. The late afternoon rain was approaching and he zipped his tracksuit top up his neck to his Adam's apple. Three children were playing on a swing-set in their front yard, and yelled at him.

'Mister, give us some Niknaks,' they chorused together playfully.

He laughed at the hustle and walked to the fence, emptying his pockets of change.

When he got back, Carl had smeared the whole jar of arnica cream on his forehead. He stood leaning on the *stoep*, resembling a young man ready for his initiation rites to manhood.

'Going to the mountain?' Segert asked.

'What?'

'Forget it. Here's your snacks.'

'Rosalind called to say she was studying late at the library.'

'Tell her to call me tomorrow.' He almost told Carl that Rosalind had a new job if she wanted it. But Carl was a younger brother and a terrible messenger. 'It's important.'

* * *

Segert heated canned tomato soup and poured it into two coffee mugs. Willem was in the spare room leafing through his book of murder dockets. Segert was excited to spend the night talking shop. Part of him wanted this whole thing with Augustine over, and part of him wanted it to never end. Wes was right, going corporate was going to save him financially. But finding Augustine and this murderer was bigger. He'd just sat down and taken a sip from his cup when his dogs barked. He reached for the pistol on his desk and checked through the curtains. Carol's Audi.

The white streetlight made her look transparent, like a jellyfish. She was back to wearing a black pencil skirt, white silk blouse and a black suit jacket. High heels and red lipstick. So, this was another business meeting. He took a big gulp of his soup as he opened the front door.

'Was checking if you're all right. You haven't been in touch,' Carol said.

'I'm a bit busy cleaning myself up. Twice in one day Carol, aren't I lucky?' Segert said.

'I can't stay long, just wanted to . . .' Carol moved to the sofa and sat on the armrest.

'Share some info about last night?' Segert asked. 'You got Rosalind out of there, I forgot to thank you.'

'I did. I'm not going to ask what's going on between the two of you. She was tight-lipped all the way home.'

'She was helping me on a case.'

'Did you talk to Martin Diamond?'

'Clean as a whistle.'

'That's not good.'

'It's beyond me.' Segert realised she was here on a fishing expedition.

'If anyone could've sussed it out, it would be you.'

'That's exactly my thought, but about you.' He stared at her.

'I've got a nine o'clock. Take some rest, you look tired.' She propelled herself back into the navy-blue dark night. He was mad at her, and she didn't know why.

Segert put the pistol in the back of his old jeans and went back into his dark room.

'Who was that?' asked Willem Du Plessis.

'She helps me with work from time to time. Tell me about these girls.' Segert pointed to the dockets in Willem's hand.

'You sure you don't mind this? You seem busy,' Willem said.

'I can finish cleaning up in the morning.' Segert sat down. 'I have a theory. I could be wrong.'

'OK.'

'From what you told me, about these killings. It has to be a madman. A crazy guy. In any case, you checked the axe.'

Willem tried to follow what Segert was saying. 'Yes. It was negative for human blood.'

'The guy it belongs to is one hundred per cent crazy, and he's been convicted of rape.'

'There's a lot of crazy people in the world,' Willem said, 'but few capable of this.'

Segert started pacing the small dark room. The pendant light bulb grazing his head. 'He's homeless, but lives in a field across the road from his parents, so they can see him. He's off; he's just . . . off. Apparently, he went crazy one Christmas Day and, the father said, he moved there out of spite. Which, if you meet him a few times, you get. He just has that streak in him.'

Willem looked down at the Musgrave pistol on the table next to the solution tank.

'I just had a moment when I was looking at someone today, and I realised, I could be looking at the wrong person, but for this. I need to find out how strong or tall this guy is, who's killing these women. Something, if you want my help. Do you?'

'I'm not qualified to build a profile, but someone's got to do it.'

'I'm surprised someone hasn't already.'

CHAPTER 35

Martin climbed into the old wooden frame bed. It creaked. He was wearing light blue brushed cotton pyjama pants. Above the bed was a large rectangular window that let in bright sunshine in the morning. At night, you could see out into the clear heavens. Thousands of bright stars, and tonight a crescent moon was peeking over the *kopjes* in the distance. The wind was the only thing you could hear, and the rustling of the monkey tree against the outside wall. He'd bought this house just outside the holiday town of Hartebees before he was married. Here he could be himself. The air was clear and there were no neighbours for miles. If someone screamed, no one could hear them. It reminded him of his childhood home in in the Copper Mountains in Namaqualand.

He planned to take a sailing trip on Hartbeespoort Dam the following afternoon, a Saturday. He'd catch up with the CEO of Sovereign Hotels. His company was competition, but they kept each other in the loop with industry news. Old guy, he liked to drink Chardonnay and eat creamy shellfish pasta on his sailboat like a middle-aged woman. In large amounts. They'd end up *braaiing* at his house with the family. Martin didn't mind. The stars out here were beautiful, and he had

nothing against drinking wine all day on a sailboat. He needed some time to unwind and relax. Bessy and Maggie were more than capable of looking after Nicholas. And the office could manage without him for a few days. They had engineers who could handle any eventuality.

On the side table, which was just two old vinyl suitcases, stacked one on top of the other, were his reading glasses and crossword puzzle book. He started a new puzzle on a random page. His pencil was dull. He'd emptied Augustine's old suitcases in an industrial skip on the Brits highway and deposited them here after that PI came to his house. He liked the suitcases; they had a certain worn-out chic that suited this old house. He hardly thought of Augustine. She'd been sweet, one hundred per cent, and easy to control, but she'd been all wrong. She wasn't worth the effort to conceal, and nobody cared about her. Besides her son. Martin did them both a favour. Then this character from the sticks came looking for them.

He knew he would be tired in five minutes, but the crossword was a ritual that had kept him company ever since Kimberly had died last year.

* * *

The note was placed carefully under the front door. When Segert opened the small white envelope, the bleached paper had a printed address he didn't recognise, but it was dated 4 p.m. Saturday 12 June 1984, and was signed, *A*. No other details.

Segert had never turned down an invitation to danger. It would be rude. He called Rousseau at home.

'Iceberg, what's happening?' Rousseau asked.

'I need your help,' Segert said matter-of-factly.

'OK, but this is the last time.' Rousseau was sore about the drinks.

'I need you to come with me up to Hartbeespoort. On Saturday.'

'Oh. Road trip. *Padkos!* I thought you wanted . . .'

'I need an extra body, and you're the only person I can trust, and you're the best driver I know.'

'You don't have to butter me up. I'll drive.'

* * *

Rousseau and Berger backed the van out of the driveway on Saturday at 11 a.m. The dogs sat on brown blankets in the back, on their haunches, tails curled behind their backs like two elegant sphinxes. Rousseau's wife packed *padkos* of cheese and avocado sandwiches, boerewors rolls, spinach and feta pies and a flask of strong black coffee. When they filled the tank, they bought a six-pack of Castles at the petrol station.

About halfway to Hartbeespoort Segert noticed Carol's car following them. He told Rousseau to pull over on the hard shoulder and waited for her to step out before he cut the engine.

'What are you—?' Rousseau asked.

Segert got out of the van and strode down the layby. 'Why are you following me?' he asked Carol.

'Because you don't tell me what you're up to and where you're going. I'm worried about you. And you and I both know that you could care less about the little coloured girl and her child. The cars led you to G.C.'

'G.C.?'

'Grand Canyons, the club. The cars led you to that establishment. You got thrown down the stairs, remember?'

'So, you're not worried about me that much, it turns out.' Segert walked back to his van.

'Iceberg strikes again.' Rousseau chuckled. He could never figure out how come Berger always had women to push away. The dogs groaned in agreement.

At lunch time, they stopped at the Cradle of Humankind site and took the dogs out for a walk. Rousseau went to browse the market for some knick-knacks for his wife, sandwich in hand, crumbs down his shirt. Segert took the bowls out from the back and filled them with bottled water. The dogs were eager to drink and sniffed the air. Petrol, diesel, red sand, open air and cat's tail grass. Trigger stretched as Segert put on his leash. Simba licked his lips as Segert finished the boerewors roll and crumpled the oily sheet paper. From the corner of his eye, he could see Carol walking towards him.

'So, you came all this way to take your dogs for a walk?' His eyes were black and his face expressionless.

'I'll come along for a walk, if you like.'

Segert looked at her high heels and raised his eyebrow.

'Let me change my shoes quickly and get some water.'

They didn't walk long before he started talking.

'I should've known, with that whole block of flats, that you wouldn't be able to resist.'

'That's deep pockets. I'm not leaving it. I have questions.'

'But that's not really affecting your business. You're not into the skin trade. I always admired you for that.'

'I guess that's a compliment. But don't admire me for that. Neither of us knows my limits yet.'

'OK, Carol, calm down. Can't you just ask your father?'

'My father? Are you joking? You still haven't told me what we're doing out here.'

'We're going to meet the girl and the baby,' he said. He knew it was some sort of trap. But who lays a trap for 4 p.m. in the afternoon? Martin was playing a little game, and Segert obliged. He'd always liked games. He was always popular at school and had lots of playmates.

'Really, where?'

'She's staying around here, being taken care of. Away from prying eyes.'

'She's not going to leave with you.'

* * *

Later that day, they drove up the small dirt road in a reluctant convoy and waited at the house where they were set to meet

295

'A'. Segert sat on the exposed brick *stoep* at the front. He'd peeked through the windows and seen dishes in the kitchen, and a magazine lying on the floor. She'd been here.

He looked over to where Rousseau sat in the van under a cabbage tree about ten metres away. The back doors of the van were open, letting in air for the dogs, who were dozing. Maybe he could spend the night at the lodge they'd passed, with the dogs, Segert mused. He could ask Carol to take Rousseau back.

They'd waited over an hour when Segert walked back to Rousseau. Carol was parked further down the dirt road, beside a large aloe blooming red cone-shaped flowers. She got out the backseat and walked up to the van. Her driver stayed in the car.

'I'll give it another half hour, then I'll call it a day. Come back tomorrow. This happens. I'll stay at the Lanseria Lodge, the one we passed a few kilometres back. Carol, can you take Rousseau back?'

'I'll follow you guys to the lodge, then pick Rousseau up,' she said as she walked to her car.

'OK. Give me a minute. I need a leak.' Segert would've ordinarily relieved himself behind the van or the bushes close by, but Carol was there, so he walked to the back of the house.

The rifle shot hit the gutter pipe next to Segert, and another hit the red-brick wall next to him. He ran around to the front of the house. Rousseau was already driving towards him, the back doors swinging as he hit rocky terrain. Trigger and Simba jumped out the back and went tearing towards the direction of gunfire. There was a soft thud, a yelp. Trigger went down. Segert ran to him. Rousseau drove round in front of them, protecting Segert from the sniper's aim. Rousseau scrambled out of the front seat, out of danger. Fear and excitement on his face.

'Is he dead?'

'No. They got him in the front leg.'

'Where's your gun?' Rousseau asked.

'That's a long-range rifle,' Segert said. 'My gun won't do anything.'

'What about Simba?'

'I'm going after him.' Segert disappeared into the brush, hollering to Simba to come back.

Carol's car had stayed back until the firing stopped, but now drove up quickly to Rousseau. Her driver, a short man with thick, dark hair, got out, took a rifle from the boot and ran in Segert's direction. He found Segert in a bank with Simba, who was still sniffing the air in excitement.

'He wasn't that far. We can go in her car,' the driver said.

They ran back, Simba in the lead.

'Rousseau, take Trigger to a vet. Must be one in town. Carol, go with, we need your car.' Segert whistled at Simba twice and he jumped into the van, where Trigger was limping, trying to get up and stand.

Segert and the driver raced in the direction of the *kopje* the shots had come from. In the distance, a few taillights blinked on the National Road. A cloud of dust was settling behind a navy pickup joining the road.

Carol's driver stopped the car and squinted through his scope. 'Dirty plates, single driver, can't tell if it's our guy. Toyota *bakkie*.' He squatted down to look at the tyre marks left in the sand. 'They were here a long time.'

Segert looked at the footprints leading to and from the car. One set. Small feet. Maybe a size seven. Small for a man. He remembered Martin's skinny feet in those silky argyle socks. 'That sonofabitch was really serious about this. My dog could've gotten his head blown off!'

They went back to the car and headed towards the nearest town. The sun was setting, the clouds reflecting the purples of the wildflower fields. In the distance, Segert could see the Hartbees cable car descending the Magaliesberg Mountain. It had been a warm day and the cable cars had probably been packed with tourists looking out over the dam, and the dry savannah. This was the place where Africa started. The

Magaliesberg were the oldest mountains in the world; they'd overseen everything. Dinosaurs, the first family of humans, the movements of Africans to the north then back again, skirmishes with invaders looking for gold and diamonds. It was the most silent place Segert had ever been. All he could hear was the sound of his heart pounding.

They found Rousseau and Carol in the nearest town.

'Thank God, you're OK. What happened?' Carol asked.

'Nothing happened. How's Trigger?'

Rousseau answered, 'He's OK. They have to operate. I'm guessing you're staying overnight, anyway.'

'Somebody could've gotten hurt, Segert. It's not worth it,' Carol said.

'Somebody was hurt: Trigger.'

'What now?' she asked.

'This is too deep for me. You rich guys can play this game. The case fees won't even cover the vet. And for what, Carol?'

Carol knew better than to offer him cash or offer to pay for the vet. So she didn't. 'What about Augustine? She wasn't ever here. And Rosalind? She's still mixed up in this,' she said.

'She'll be fine,' was all he said.

'Really? How do you know?' Carol asked.

'She's OK for now. I'm not going to ask if you're going to keep pursuing this. Just leave me out of it. It's all yours. But if you find that missing girl, you let me know.'

* * *

Bessy took the first turn off Brits, slowed at an empty four-way stop street and put her rifle and the blanket it was wrapped in under the passenger seat. Then she laughed, thinking of Segert's shoulders shaking quickly with the first shot, and him running and zipping his trousers as he ran to his dog after the second. She hit the steering wheel as she laughed. The horn gave two youngsters on bicycles a fright, their eyes wide and bright in her headlights.

And she started laughing all over again.

She parked her old beat-up *bakkie* in the garage of her condominium overlooking the dam. She'd stay the night, then get back to Belgravia Road in the morning. Martin would be none the wiser. About any of it. He always was full of himself, but he didn't know anything. He'd yet to learn about women. He didn't even know about Grand Canyons, or this condo; he didn't know she had this much money. As dumb as a baboon. Hidden in the cocoon she constructed for him.

* * *

Segert wasn't going to leave it like that. He didn't have any proof. Everybody had given up on Augustine. Part of him kept looking out for her on the streets behind the railway stations. Carol always had a lead for some work that was too small fry for anything she wanted to be involved in, but appealed to his fighting side. It took him south sometimes. He'd drift past Wes's office and offer Rosalind a lift home. She always insisted he drop her at the library. She was keeping her dream of being a lawyer alive by keeping it a secret from her mother.

Segert began dropping three Castles with Johnny and asking for any news. Johnny used to get upset, at first. Now Segert was like any other visitor on the street. He had feelings about it but, he also had three free beers.

'Same same,' he'd say.

Each time Segert was there, which wasn't often, it looked like Augustine's old house was falling further into disrepair. The small lawn was mostly sand. The iron gate had a broken hinge.

He went by Angelo's hut to check for carvings and taunt Angelo about the axe he was withholding. He stayed in his car when he rolled up for *braai* wood. But Angelo had been converted by a library book and declared he was going back to school to become a psychologist. Segert headed straight for Solomon's that day.

Now and then the phone rang, and Willem's message was like a thunderclap.

'I have another one. Call me.'

EPILOGUE

29 years later

It'd been three weeks since the Botes murder–suicide that had gotten Diamond Suites bad press. It was the New Year now, and people had their New Year resolutions and distractions to consider. The ANC basked in its centenary with a giant party in the blazing heat in Bloemfontein, a family gathering that refused to revive the talk of corruption and cronyism. It was business as usual for 2012.

Nicholas didn't really want to pick up his dad's new girl-friend. But his father wanted them to get to know each other on the long drive up to the dam. Bessy had extended and ren-ovated her old place and they were having a company party to celebrate branching out to Antananarivo and Maputo.

Nicholas parked at the stairs of the two-storey apartment block. In the twilight, it looked halfway decent. It was an old building, maybe thirty or forty years old. Painted a light brown, the windows white with spots of mould here and there. Young children were playing a game in the parking lot, probably *kennetjie* or some game without balls. They stopped to look at the Land Rover driving slowly over the speed bump towards them. When he stepped out of his car, they gave him a once-over, then continued shouting and running towards a miniature cricket post made from two cement bricks.

He rang the doorbell and waited to hear the sound of high heels on a wooden floor. He didn't. When the light went on inside, he assumed she must have carpet.

'Hi, Nicholas.' Liesl smiled. 'So nice of you to pick me up.' She stood to the side to let him in.

She was wearing tight blue jeans and a black silk blouse that was loose but tucked in. She wasn't quite his type, even if she could pass as Spanish or Portuguese. But if Martin had come to pick her up for himself, he would've approved her outfit. She was practical.

'At your service,' he said, keeping a smile in his voice.

'Can I offer you something to drink? I just need to finish my makeup. Coffee?'

He sat down on her grey sofa. His legs wide. 'Nah, I'm OK. Go ahead.' He was appraising the art and photographs on the wall. She'd travelled a lot. There were photos of her at the pyramids of Giza, cathedrals in Barcelona and water-skiing somewhere in the Med, he guessed.

'Just a minute!' she shouted from the back. 'I'm just zipping up my bags.' The small flat smelled of Elizabeth Arden Red Door and burnt toast.

When she came back, five minutes later, she wore red lipstick, and had a small suitcase by her side.

'You look lovely. I'm impressed.'

She smiled. 'The Diamond seal of approval.' She gestured towards the door, black heels in her hand, a red crocodile clutch in the other.

There was always traffic on a Friday night. In the ten or fifteen minutes that he'd been at hers, cars had started to slow down, bumper to bumper on the main road. He hadn't noticed the silver BMW following him from home. It'd been following him for weeks watching his movements, getting acquainted with his rhythms. Tonight was out of the ordinary, but the driver kept a full tank. She would follow him wherever he went.

'How was your day? Anything exciting happen?' Liesl asked, as they turned out of the parking lot.

'Not really. Working on contracts, meetings with finance. You know.'

'Not really, but I get it, I guess. Operational stuff, right?'

'Ja. I'm more involved in the day-to-day operations of the hotel group than my father.' Nicholas didn't know what Martin'd said to her about it. He was sure his father wouldn't want to say, *I'm retired and I spend most of my time playing golf with my buddies, who fantasise about cultivating affairs with someone half their age.* In other words, her age. 'My dad left this afternoon to go to the dam. One of us has to be there to organise everything.'

They drove out of Johannesburg, up north on the big highway to Pretoria. The blood orange sun was setting to their left, over housing estates and security-gated communities, until there were only a few small houses with patchwork grass and old *bakkies* parked in the driveways. The traffic was making it a long quiet drive, and Liesl went to the back to nap, allowing Nicholas his traffic jam frustrations and mumblings through Lonehill.

* * *

Janette Berger had maxed out her credit card hiring the sportscar. After a quick explanation on mileage allowance, the saleswoman at the Hertz counter smiled and asked, 'Going somewhere nice?'

'Oh, a few places. I've relatives down from the UK this Christmas,' Janette lied. 'I'm taking them to see the sights.'

Wes and Doreen Petersen had tried consoling her. They'd been good to her, keeping the secret of her and Segert's child all the years. He wasn't father material. And, for sure, not to a girl. Still, she named the beautiful baby girl Sunette. And as she got older, Janette told her a little bit about Segert. But Wes, being Wes, leaked when he grieved and asked her if she knew anything about the Diamonds and Segert. Doreen had given him a cold hard stare. But it was too late, and it was enough. As usual, Segert's decisions had come to roost in her life. Martin Diamond had found out that Jacques was related to Segert and fired him before Christmas. And Jacques had had enough of failure.

She should never had let Sunette marry a recovering drug addict.

Janette would succeed where Segert failed. She didn't have a plan at the start, but when she saw Nicholas, posturing in his youth and condescending pride, she'd decided on a target for her revenge. She'd lost her husband to a whore, her child and blessed grandchildren in shameful horror. Whatever happened next, she was going to be the architect of pain for once. For once.

The road opened up. The clouds were turning a pink hue as the sun set. The Brits highway was a straight four-lane highway that went past Johannesburg's second airport, Lanseria. The road was flat for twenty or so kilometres and on either side the veld was a patchwork of thorn trees, short round shrubs and spiny ferns. Crane flowers grew wild further from the highway, the orange and purple flowers looking out inquisitively among the short light green grass and burnt orange soil. The air was dry and crisp, the type of night anyone with a good car likes to drive into. As the sun set behind the Magaliesberg Mountain, Nicholas switched on his brights and the Land Rover seemed to eat up the black asphalt.

The road slimmed to a two-way stretch. Janette turned her lights down. Nicholas was the only car ahead of her, and she could navigate the slight curling of the road by his headlights. They passed through a cut in a small hill, then over a dried-up riverbed, when Janette put her right foot down on the accelerator, left foot on the clutch as she slid into sixth and drove hard into the right side of Nicholas's bumper. She was aiming to make him lose balance and spin. The Land Rover veered left and right quickly.

He slowed down. A shadow moved up from the backseat, lurching forward at Nicholas and back at Janette. She swerved quickly and hit the Land Rover on the left side of the bumper. Still, the sonofagun stayed on the road. Janette sped up beside him and hit the side of the Land Rover, matched his speed for a few seconds, and then drove to the right, pushing him off road. It didn't work. She let him go ahead and drove behind him. He might punch the brakes, so she stayed a safe distance behind, revving her engine loudly as she came up close, then backed up. He tried to dodge her, jumping across lanes, she turned her brights up. The road took a steep gradient and he gained some space ahead of her. He moved back to the left lane as he approached the top of the hill. The landscape below was pitch black. An extra-terrestrial territory of thorn trees, shrubs and the odd dark shadows of ancient rock spires. The horizon filling with stars. The moon was on the right, following them through the ride.

Janette drove up beside them tussling her mangled car against his. The scraping sound was familiar and jarring and comfortable. This is what it felt like to fulfil your dreams. She gritted her teeth. Nicholas bumped her car, but she drove hard down the hill beside them. She was sorry for the girl who'd gotten caught up in this. She bumped the Land Rover hard, the metal squealing as Nicholas braked. The downward momentum of the hill coupled with the sportscar's speed shoved the Land Rover into a sharp roadcut on the shoulder of the highway. The bonnet crushed against the rock, debris tumbled from the rockface onto the roof. The vehicle made the mechanical crushing sound of a scrapyard compactor when it stopped. As if a soul was leaving its body. Janette slowed her car to check if Nicholas was moving. He was slumped over the steering wheel, blood dripping from his head. The girl was lying between the seats, not moving. In the white headlights of an oncoming meat transportation van, Janette's last fears were washed away.

***

There'd been a thunderstorm the previous night. The ferns and flowers in the garden looked sprightly and nourished and swayed gently in the dry morning breeze. When Nicholas opened his eyes, the sky was the colour of blue clay. His head felt tight, and he put his hand up to feel a thick bandage. The only sounds in his room were the ticking of the heart machines. Outside he heard voices, but they were indistinct, sounding more like the whirring of ceiling fans. His neck and shoulders hurt, and he grimaced in pain as he put his arm down. He pushed the red call button for the nurse.

'We were worried about you for a while.' She smiled.

'A while? Where am I?' Nicholas asked.

'You're at Harties Medical Centre. I'll get the doctor for you, Mr Diamond.'

The quietness made him nervous. Instinctively he wanted to reach for his mobile phone. A few minutes later a doctor opened the door. He had salt-and-pepper hair, freckles on his nose and a large round head. His eyes were cool and distant.

'Mr Diamond. So glad to see you're awake. Do you mind if I have a look at you?' He pointed a penlight in Nicholas's eyes.

'Can you sit up? Any pain?'

Nicholas shook his head no, but his slow movements betrayed him.

He put a stethoscope on Nicholas's back to check his lungs.

'What happened? All I remember is someone trying to run me off the road . . . What about Liesl? How's she?'

The doctor's face fell a millimetre. He put the stethoscope around his neck and inhaled. 'I'm sorry. They tried reviving her at the scene. I believe she was your father's girlfriend. He was of course notified. And her family.'

Nicholas lay down. 'Where's my father?'

'There are a few other people who would like to speak to you first. But we'll only call them when you're feeling ready.'

'Who do you mean? Work?'

'No, the police and a few other people.'

'Oh ja. Of course, but I still want to see him today. I don't like hospitals.'

The doctor smiled at him. 'Rest. You took quite a hit to the head. Your vitals look good, the neurologist will check up on your progress.'

* * *

Segert was sitting outside the hospital room. Segert, now in his seventies, was still strong in his legs and shoulders. He wore a pair of moss green shorts, black T-shirt and a pair of sandals that had a thick band across the front and a strap round the back. His legs were tanned, the skin papery and thick with blue veins.

'You look like you work in an orchard.' Rosalind walked over to him. She still had that nasal flatness in her voice.

He smiled, stood up and put his arms around her. 'Women still love these legs, Your Highness.'

'I bet.' She looked them up and down. 'But seriously, Your Honour will do.' It was their joke.

'How are the kids?'

'They miss you,' she lied. 'They're getting big and I'm getting old. Fifteen, twelve and nine.'

'Quite a countdown you got going,' he joked.

'Your arses, Segert.'

They laughed together but it turned nervous. Rosalind still didn't know what to say about Sunette, Segert's daughter, who had been murdered by her husband last month. She cleared her throat and looked down the corridor. 'Fancy a coffee?'

Nee, I'm all right. Can you believe . . .' Segert nodded to the hospital room.

She shook her head, wishing she had a Styrofoam coffee cup to stare into. 'Sorry about Janette, and you know . . .'

'Thanks for getting the blood test approved. It must've cost you a few favours,' Segert said, avoiding her condolences.

'I'm not going to be the one to tell him his dad's a convicted paedophile, that's all.'

'Funny though how he got caught.'

'There's nothing funny about any of it.'

'Guilt by gentrification. Come on. What a headline. Those perfectly preserved Polaroids found behind a cistern. The picture of the digger bucket with the toilet in the decimated printing works. It was gold.'

She laughed. 'You can be the one to tell him, your papa is *that guy*.'

'I never met her, but she had a style, your friend. A style.'

Then Rosalind's face became soft, and she looked away as a tear welled in her eyes. 'Yes, she definitely would've enjoyed that.'

* * *

When the time came, they went in to see Nicholas accompanied by two detectives.

'Mr Diamond, how are you?' One of the detectives sat down at the edge of the bed. He was a short black man with a bubbly personality, who didn't have the ceremony for serious situations. Rosalind cleared her throat and he stood up. 'Sorry about that, sir. How are you feeling?' he continued.

'Could be better, my head . . . Are you here about the accident?'

'Yes, yes. Tell us what you can remember. Do you mind if I tape it, just to make sure I have everything.'

Nicholas recounted as much as he could. The cops shook their heads in the appropriate places.

'I think we have everything. There's something else we have to talk about.'

'OK. Go ahead.'

'Your doctors had to check your medical history. They found a few issues.'

'Like what.'

'Well, it seems your blood type for a start.'

The second detective said, 'You can't change your blood type. It seems you are not Nicholas Diamond.'

Nicholas's vision narrowed. He could only concentrate on one person at a time, and what he was hearing didn't make sense.

'You'll have to speak slower because what I heard doesn't make any sense.'

'They checked your blood in the system and you came out as a hit with someone else.'

'What?'

'There's some people here to see you.'

'What do you mean? I am not Nicholas Diamond. This is ridiculous. Just ask my father.'

'Your father is in police custody.'

The detectives introduced Segert and Rosalind. Telling him about his father, and the DNA test. The heart machine ticked over faster.

'Your real father is a man called Theodore Beukes, he's in jail for a series of offences. Your mother went to school with this woman. They were also distantly related.'

'She is a judge, but she's not here in an official capacity.' The cops pointed to Rosalind.

Nicholas looked at her. A smartly dressed woman, older, from the old Apartheid days of segregated schools. A coloured woman. Her skin tone was what Jo'burgers called cappuccino, a mixture that told the story of South Africa.

She smiled at him, a jacket over her folded forearms.

'Your mother was her distant cousin, but they were very close.'

Nicholas wasn't computing. 'But Kimberly . . . ?'

'The real Nicholas Diamond probably died of what we now understand as AIDS-related complications when he was a baby. We've been told. Like his mother. Kimberly Diamond had left the estate and business in the name of her son, and if he died then there were provisions for the sale of property and transfer of title to numerous charities in the name of her brother, Ryan. Martin Diamond had to have a son alive, so he could have control of the estate.'

'That's where you come in,' Segert said.

Nicholas looked confused. The computer in his brain working and resetting and trying to get all the information straight. It wasn't a revelation that his father was a schemer. Nicholas had the same level of tenacity and manipulation. But Martin had taken a child from someone else to keep his hands on the business.

The room was silent. The blood pressure machine automatically puffed up to take his hourly pressure.

'You mean . . .' Nicholas's voice was thin and dry with bewilderment. He looked at all of them in turn. They nodded at him slowly, to help him deduce the facts. 'You mean, I'm not white?'

* * *

Martin was dressed in standard issue grey overalls. He'd been denied bail. A flight risk. Limitless resources the prosecution's office petitioned.

His back was strong. He sat upright. His eyes were alert. He'd enjoyed the trappings of a successful and prosperous life. His sister was waiting outside. Looking dumpy and brittle as ever.

'He had nothing to do with this.'

It was visiting hours and he waited for Segert at a large round table. It was a Sunday afternoon and the room was full of noise and chatter.

'Finally, here we are,' Martin said.

'Here you are.'

'You always knew where to find me.'

'That was never the problem. It was Augustine we were trying to find.'

'Really. You had half the traffic cops on me . . .'

Segert held his hands up as it had nothing to do with him.

'What's going to happen to Nicholas?'

'Justice?'

Martin recoiled at the name.

'I don't have a legal brain. I don't know if he's still going to get what Kimberly left for her son. Bessy can sort you out.'

'Bessy is also another *kwaal*.'

They chuckled together unexpectedly. Neither could make eye contact and remained silent for a minute.

'You could've just left it. Everyone had moved on,' Segert said.

'But I like to win.'

'You would've won. There wasn't a trace of Augustine. And I let it go.' Deep down Segert had never wanted to break Rosalind's heart with what he thought probably happened.

'There wasn't a trace of your child and I still found her. I expected something, but your son-in-law was very reactive. I could say nobody expected that, but I did make predictions.'

Segert struggled to maintain his composure. 'They're pulling up your floorboards in Greenside and Hartebees.'

'I'll send them an invoice. You think they're going to find anything?'

'You've dragged at least two families through the mud, they'll find something. Just confess, put all the ghosts to rest. He'll never look at you the same way again.'

'If they want to keep me here, they're going to have to work. Nothing is easy. How is Nicholas?'

'He'll survive.' Segert got up and left.

He was free to leave and Martin was sitting alone at a prison table. But there was little satisfaction. His fear was that, somehow, he was just as guilty. He'd thrown away a life. His daughter. He was responsible for Janette's death too. She was never out of harm's way since she'd met him. The parking lot was full and a young boy in torn clothes came to his car window to beg for change.

'Get yourself something to eat,' Segert said. He headed out the prison gates to his home in Orange Grove.

THE END

GLOSSARY

brah: young man, friend
braai: a barbecue or cookout
blerrie: informal, bloody, as in annoying, perverse
skrik: fright
bakkie: pickup truck
boere: farmer, Afrikaner
boerewors: beef sausage
stoep: veranda
naartjie: satsuma
Vellies: short for veldskoene: a type of leather walking shoe adapted from traditional Khoisan/Indigenous peoples
asseblief: please
Boet: brother
dronk verdriet: drunken melodrama, depression
bevok: crazy
padkos: food for a road trip
kennetjie: a children's outdoor game involving tipping a peg resembling the bails resting on stumps in cricket
kopje: Small hill or bluff
kwaal: a problem or nonserious ailment

THE JOFFE BOOKS STORY

We began in 2014 when Jasper agreed to publish his mum's much-rejected romance novel and it became a bestseller.

Since then we've grown into the largest independent publisher in the UK. We're extremely proud to publish some of the very best writers in the world, including Joy Ellis, Faith Martin, Caro Ramsay, Helen Forrester, Simon Brett and Robert Goddard. Everyone at Joffe Books loves reading and we never forget that it all begins with the magic of an author telling a story.

We are proud to publish talented first-time authors, as well as established writers whose books we love introducing to a new generation of readers.

We won Trade Publisher of the Year at the Independent Publishing Awards in 2023 and Best Publisher Award in 2024 at the People's Book Prize. We have been shortlisted for Independent Publisher of the Year at the British Book Awards for the last five years, and were shortlisted for the Diversity and Inclusivity Award at the 2022 Independent Publishing Awards. In 2023 we were shortlisted for Publisher of the Year at the RNA Industry Awards, and in 2024 we were shortlisted at the CWA Daggers for the Best Crime and Mystery Publisher.

We built this company with your help, and we love to hear from you, so please email us about absolutely anything bookish at feedback@joffebooks.com.

If you want to receive free books every Friday and hear about all our new releases, join our mailing list here: www.joffebooks.com/freebooks.

And when you tell your friends about us, just remember: it's pronounced Joffe as in coffee or toffee!